BOOKS BY MEARA PLATT

THE FARTHINGALE SERIES

My Fair Lily
The Duke I'm Going to Marry
Rules for Reforming a Rake
A Midsummer's Kiss
The Viscount's Rose

KINDLE WORLDS: REGENCY NOVELLAS

Nobody's Angel
Kiss an Angel

The Duke I'm Going to *Marry*

Cover Design by Greg Simanson

Edited by Laurel Busch

This is a work of fiction. Names, characters, places, brands, media, and incidents are either the product of the author's imagination or are used fictitiously. Any resemblance to similarly named places or to persons living or deceased is unintentional.

ISBN: 978-1-945767-04-3

A FREE NOVELLA

Sign up for Meara Platt's newsletter at bit.ly/ifyoukissedme
and you'll receive a free, exclusive copy
of her Farthingale novella,
If You Kissed Me.

For Roger, always in our hearts

CHAPTER 1

Mayfair District, London
November 1818

WHEN DILLIE FARTHINGALE crossed to her bedroom window to draw the draperies before retiring to bed, she never expected to wind up in front of the Farthingale townhouse, elephant gun in hand, worried that she'd just shot the Duke of Edgeware. Not that this season's most eligible bachelor and dangerously handsome rakehell didn't deserve shooting. He most certainly did, but not by her.

"Crumpets!" She fell backward after getting off a shot that merely startled the duke's assailants. She aimed lower, getting off a second shot that almost ripped her shoulder out of its socket with its recoil. Scrambling to her feet, she reloaded and hurried out of the townhouse, shoving open the front gate that led onto Chipping Way, eager to inspect the damage and dreading what she might find.

Her street was one of those charming, quiet streets, a most desired location in London. Eligible dukes did not die on such streets. "Ian, you idiot! Are you hurt? Who were those awful men, and why were they attacking you?"

She knelt beside him, her heart firmly lodged in her throat. Her nightgown and thin wool shawl offered little protection from the midnight chill. Had Ian's eyes been open, he would have been ogling her, for that's what rakehells did best. Ian Markham, as the duke was known, was as rakish as they came, but he would never dare more with her. She was related to his best friend, and as disreputable as Ian was, he did have a code of honor. Of a sort.

She had never considered Ian more than a mere nuisance deserving of a frown or indignant tip of her chin. Certainly not worth shooting, except for that one instance when he'd thoroughly surprised her by kissing her with enough passion to curl her toes. It had been their first and only kiss, a case of mistaken identity in a moonlit garden, for he'd expected another lady to be standing beside the lilac tree where Dillie happened to be hiding while she innocently spied on her neighbor's dinner party.

Dillie had been trying to forget that kiss for the past two years. No doubt the duke had put it out of his mind immediately.

"Ian?" He appeared to be unconscious, his large, muscled body sprawled beneath the tree she'd practically splintered in half with the force of the elephant shot.

She set down the gun and shook him lightly when he failed to respond. "Oh, please wake up."

He opened his eyes with noticeable difficulty, his gaze decidedly fuzzy as he cast her a pained grin. "Bloody blazes, it's you. What are you doing here?"

"I live here. You're the one who's out of place."

His eyes were still unfocused. He blinked them slowly in an attempt to regain his vision. "Oh. Right. Then I ought to be going." But he made no attempt to rise. "I'll be off now. Good evening, Daffy."

Dillie ground her teeth in irritation. "Don't call me that." In a moment of madness, her parents had named her Daffodil, but she'd managed to sail through most of her nineteen years avoiding that hideous appellation. Everyone called her Dillie. Everyone but Ian Markham, the arrogant, infuriating Duke of Edgeware, who took every opportunity to torture her with the use of her given name and every ridiculous variation of it that came to his fiendish mind. "The name is 'Miss Farthingale' to you."

"And I'm a duke. That's *Your Grace* to you."

She fisted her hands, wanting to pound the feathers out of him, but those two blackguards who'd attacked him seemed to have done a wickedly good job of it already. They were hired ruffians, certainly paid by someone angry enough to want him dead. "Very well. *Your Grace*, you idiot! Whose wife did you seduce this time?"

"That's better. About time you showed proper respect for my title." He tried to sit up, but he couldn't and fell back with a gasped oath, struggling for breath as he clutched his side.

Dillie shivered, not only from the wintery chill in the midnight air, but also from her concern that she truly might have shot him. She had been aiming for those awful men. To be precise, aiming a warning blast above their heads to frighten them off. She was sure she'd hit one of the larger branches of the sturdy oak tree standing by the front gate. It now lay splintered on the ground near Ian.

She glanced around. His attackers had run off, frightened but unharmed. So why was Ian still on the ground, fumbling to rise and determined to hide his obvious agony? "Let me help you up."

He brushed her hand away when she reached out to steady him. "No, I can manage."

"Are you sure? Because you seem to be doing a spectacularly dismal job of it." She couldn't see him very well. The only light available was from the moon's glow, a full, silver moon that shone brightly against the crisp, starry sky.

"Are you still here, Daffy? Why don't you go away and leave me to my misery?" He sank onto the cool grass with another pained gasp, his head thumping against the hard trunk of the oak tree as he fell back.

"I'm having far too much fun watching you struggle," she said, though her heart was still in her throat and she was now seriously worried about him. Another shattered tree branch dangled precariously overhead, held up only by a small scrap of bark. It was in danger of falling atop him.

She reached out again, determined to move him out of its path, but as she touched his jacket she felt something warm and liquid seep through her fingers. "Ian, you clunch! You're bleeding. Oh, my goodness! Did I hit you?"

She let out a sob, now worried that she truly had done him

damage. The air released from her lips cooled and formed a vapor that swirled about her face. It was too cold for Ian to be left out here for very long, and he wasn't in any condition to get up and walk on his own. "I didn't mean to shoot you."

He took hold of her hand, gently stroking his thumb along her palm to calm her down. "You didn't. I've been stabbed."

Dillie gasped. Was that supposed to calm her? "I'll get help. Don't move." Even in the dim light, she could see the crimson stain now oozing through his fancy silk vest. As she scrambled to her feet, the Farthingale butler came running through the gate. "Oh, Pruitt! Thank goodness! Fetch Uncle George. He must come right away, and tell him to bring his medical bag."

Pruitt's eyes rounded as wide as saucers the moment his gaze fell on Ian. "At once, Miss Dillie." He hurried back into the house as fast as his old legs would carry him. She heard him shouting up the stairs for her uncle, something the staid butler had never, ever done before, even when faced with an army of boisterous Farthingale relatives and their unruly children. Pruitt never lost his composure. His voice never rose above an ordinary, conversational tone. *Never.*

Until tonight.

Dillie sank back to her knees beside Ian. His hands were now pressed against a spot just above the left side of his waist. "That's it. Use your palms to press down hard on the wound," she instructed while quickly removing her shawl. The clunch was bleeding everywhere, and that meant he'd been stabbed more than once. She folded her shawl and then, nudging his hands aside, firmly pressed it to his waist and secured it by tightly tying the ends about his body. Big body. More solid strength than she'd realized. "Where else hurts?"

"Right thigh, just above my knee."

She ran her hand along his thigh, careful to avoid the hole in the fabric where he'd obviously been stabbed. He tensed and let out a laughing groan. "Better not touch me there."

No doubt to hide his extreme pain. She grabbed the velvet ribbon from her hair, ignoring the sudden cascade of long, dark strands about her shoulders and down her back. She used the ribbon to form a makeshift tourniquet around his thigh, hoping it was tight enough to stem the flow of blood from his leg until her uncle arrived to properly treat him.

Her hands were beginning to numb. It was freezing outside, the grass hard and crunching beneath her knees. A cloud of vapor formed with her every breath. She'd given up her shawl and was definitely underdressed. "Where else?"

"My forearms are sliced up, but not too badly. My jacket sleeves absorbed most of the damage." He studied her, as though noticing her for the first time. Really noticing her, a sign that he'd finally regained his full vision. He cast her a wickedly seductive grin. "There's a hard ache between my legs."

More injuries? All her fault. "Oh, dear! How bad? Show me."

"Did I say that aloud?" He let out a deep, rumbling laugh. "Gad, you're innocent. Don't look so stricken. The ache will disappear once you put on some clothes. Maybe."

"What?" She was in a panic, her heart pounding through her ears, and he was tossing jests?

"Your nightgown hides very little," he continued, as though needing to explain the meaning of his jest. "If you lean any closer, I'll have a clear view down your—"

She smacked him. Then smacked him again for good measure.

"Bloody hell! Wounded duke here. Show a little mercy."

She wanted to smack him again, but as he said, he was seriously injured. The folded shawl she'd applied to his waist was already stained through with his blood. He took hold of her hand, no longer smiling. She stilled, unable to draw a breath, for the first time realizing that he might not survive into the morning. "I'm so sorry, Ian. Just keep your mouth shut and I'll stop hitting you. Much as I hate to admit it, I don't wish you to die."

He gave her hand a light squeeze. "Much as I hate to admit it, I'm glad it's you by my side if I am to die." He paused, the effort of speaking too much to manage. "I thought you'd returned... to Coniston with the rest of your family... all five thousand of them." Those last words were spoken through shuddering pain.

Oh, God! Not you, Ian. You're invincible. She shook her head and tried to keep her voice steady. "They went on ahead." But her voice faltered as she tried to hold back tears. "All five thousand of them, traveling north like a great horde of locusts, eating everything in their path. I stayed behind with Uncle George to help him close up the house and enjoy the blessed quiet."

"Guess I've foiled your plans." He sounded weak, his words even more strained.

She melted at his soft gaze. Ian, with his gorgeous gray-green eyes, had a way of melting female hearts. Good thing it was dark and she couldn't clearly see the beautiful green of his eyes. That soft glance was devastating enough. "We were supposed to leave yesterday, but my uncle was called to a medical emergency. We had to delay our departure."

"Must thank the poor, sick blighter." His voice was weaker still. "I mean it, Dillie. If I'm to die tonight, I can't think of anyone I'd rather have beside me than you."

There were times when Ian rankled her.

In truth, he always rankled her.

But not tonight.

"Keep breathing, you clunch," she said in a ragged whisper, keeping tight hold of his big, cold hand.

IAN AWOKE IN an unfamiliar room, uncertain how much time had elapsed since he'd been attacked. At least eight hours he guessed, for the morning sun was streaming in through the unshuttered window, glistening against the peach silk counterpane that covered the bed in which he lay. He recalled Dillie asking him about his assailants, but he didn't know who had sent them, only that they'd done a good job of carving him up with their knives.

Where was he? Somewhere safe, of that he was certain.

He had to get word to the Prince Regent. He suspected those men were disgruntled agents of the now exiled Napoleon, seeking retribution for his dismantling of the French spy network that had flourished in England until recently. Ian and his friends, both of whom now happened to be married to Dillie's sisters, had crushed the web of spies and exposed its leaders, some of whom had held prominent positions in the English government. Was this attack an act of revenge?

Or part of a more sinister scheme?

He tried to move his hand and realized someone was holding it. Someone with a soft, gentle touch. He glanced down and groaned. Dillie, primly dressed in a morning gown that hid all her good parts from view, was perched on a chair beside his bed, her slender body slumped over so that her head and shoulders rested on the mattress beside his thigh. Her dark hair was loosely bound, flowing down her back in a waterfall of waves. Her lips were partly open and she snored lightly.

Hell. She looked adorable.

What was she doing here? He glanced around and realized he must be in her bedchamber, the one she'd shared with her twin until last month. There were two beds, two bureaus. Matching sets of everything. *Bloody hell.* He had to get out of here fast. But how? His arms and legs felt as though they were weighed down by blocks of granite. He'd lost a lot of blood and knew he was as weak as a damn kitten.

"Dillie," he said in a whisper.

She responded with a snore.

"How long have I been here?"

Not wishing to wake Dillie when she failed to answer, he tried to move his free arm. A mistake, he realized at once, suppressing a yelp as a lightning bolt of pain shot from his waist, straight up his arm, and into his head. His temples began to throb and his heart began to thunderously pound against his chest.

It wasn't only pain making his heart pound. Dillie was temptingly close. He had only to reach out and... *better not.*

Why had he been settled in Dillie's quarters? He recalled being carried into the Farthingale townhouse and up the stairs by a team of footmen. What had Dillie said shortly before he'd blacked out? "Put him in my room, Uncle George," she'd insisted, explaining that the rest of the house had been closed up for the winter, the beds stripped of their linens and the mattresses put out to air.

Her uncle would never have agreed to the arrangement otherwise.

Ian let out a breath as the pain to his temples began to fade and then looked around the room again. The feminine, peach silk bedcovers and peach and white drapery suited Dillie. Sweet summer peaches was her scent, refreshingly light and fragrant.

The furniture seemed a little young for a girl her age. Dillie was nineteen or twenty years old by now, and of marriageable age. He frowned. No doubt the family expected her to marry soon and leave the household. The other four Farthingale daughters were already wed and several had children. Dillie's identical twin, Lily, had married only last month. Dillie wouldn't last another season. She was too beautiful to remain unattached for very long. And clever. She'd marry well.

Just not him.

That was for damn sure.

He wasn't the marrying sort, didn't want a woman in his life making demands on him. Cheating on him.

Dillie let out another soft snore, revealing she was still soundly asleep. How long had she been sitting by his side? Clinging sweetly to his hand? He liked the gentle warmth of her hand and the way her fingers protectively curled about his.

Felt nice. Too nice.

He carefully slid out from her grasp, but instead of drawing away from the dangerous innocent, he allowed his fingers to drift over the glistening waves of her dark hair. So soft. Unable to resist, he buried his hand in her silken curls, caressing the long, thick strands that fell over her shoulders and down her back. *Bloody hell*. She felt nice.

Too nice, he reminded himself again.

He stopped, desperate to climb out of bed before he did something spectacularly foolish, such as pulling her down atop him and kissing her rosy, lightly parted lips into tomorrow. No, not just into tomorrow. Into next week. Perhaps into next month. No woman had ever held his interest longer than that. He preferred it that way. Easier to remain unattached. Easier to remain free of messy obligations.

Perhaps that was why Dillie always referred to him as an idiot.

He was one, but not for the reasons Dillie imagined. He was an idiot because he couldn't seem to get *her* out of his thoughts. Going on two years now. No doubt because she, unlike all other women, found him completely unappealing. Where others would shamelessly proposition him, would flirt, swoon, scheme, or find any reason to gain his attention, Dillie usually cringed when she saw him coming.

She was a challenge, a beautiful, dark-haired, blue-eyed challenge. Where others succumbed, she resisted. But he knew better than to take up the gauntlet against Dillie. He wasn't certain he could win. She was different. She was dangerous. One look at the girl and all blood drained from his head to amass in a hot pool between his thighs.

He couldn't think straight when his loins were on fire. Could any man?

Unfortunately, Dillie managed to set him ablaze every time she looked at him. Didn't have to be much of a look, just a glimpse was enough. Sometimes the mere sound of her voice got him hot. He even knew her scent, that refreshingly sweet trace of peach blossoms wafting in the air.

When it came to Dillie, he was like a damn bloodhound, able to recognize her presence even amid the heavily perfumed odors that permeated a room. He didn't know why the girl had that effect on him, for she wasn't the sort of woman who usually gained his notice. He liked elegant, more worldly women. He usually sought out the married ones who were bored with their husbands, for such women were interested in mere dalliances and expected no promises.

Dillie required faithfulness and heartfelt promises.

Dillie demanded everlasting love.

She disapproved of his scoundrel ways and never hesitated to tell him so. She didn't give a fig that he was a rich-as-Croesus duke. She wasn't impressed by his wealth or title.

She wasn't impressed by him.

Ian moaned.

Dillie must have heard him, for her eyes fluttered open. Those big, soft blue eyes that stole his breath away every time she looked at him.

"Ian, you're awake. Thank goodness." She cast him a beautiful, openhearted smile.

He closed his eyes and sank back against his pillow, drawing his hand away before she noticed that it had been buried in her luscious hair. "I feel like hell."

She laughed lightly. "You look like it, too."

"Ah, I knew I could count on you for compliments." He opened one eye.

Her smile faded and she began to nibble her lip. "You've been unconscious for three days." As though to prove her point, she leaned forward and ran her knuckles along his chin, gently scraping them against his three-day growth of beard. "If it's any consolation, you look wonderful for a man who's spent that much time fighting at death's door."

"Was I that bad?"

She nodded. "Let me feel your forehead. You were running a very high fever." She placed that same hand across his brow. "Oh, thank goodness. No longer hot."

He was hot. She wasn't looking low enough.

"Have you been by my side all this time?" Both his eyes were now open and trained on Dillie. Her morning gown was a simple gown of gray wool, its only adornment a velvet ribbon of a slightly darker gray trim at the sleeves. Her hair was long and loose—as he well knew, since he'd just run his feverish fingers through it. She had a sleepy look in her eyes, slightly tousled hair, and a smile as beautiful as a moonbeam.

She was the most beautiful girl he'd ever set eyes upon.

He wanted her badly... naked and in his bed.

It was one thing to have those desires, but another thing altogether to act on them.

"Yes, I've been beside you most of the time," she replied, unaware of the depraved path of his thoughts. "Uncle George had to tend to that important patient of his, so he hasn't been around much. He left me in charge of you. Fortunately, the stab wound to your side was the worst of it. And it was bad, if you wish to know the truth. The blade missed your vital organs by a hair's breadth. You wouldn't have pulled through otherwise."

The notion seemed to distress her. It felt odd that she should care whether he lived or died. No one in his family did.

In truth, he didn't either.

"I never lost faith that you would survive. You're strong. And Uncle George is the best doctor in all of England," she said with noticeable pride. "He cleansed your wounds thoroughly and stitched you up. Your arms weren't slashed as badly as we'd feared, and the stab wound to your leg wasn't very deep."

She sounded efficient, as though she were taking inventory. Suddenly, she paused and there were tears glistening in her eyes.

Surprised, he reached out to run his thumb along the thin trail of water now sliding down her cheek. He winced as a painful jolt shot from his fingers to his brow. He'd braced himself against the expected pain, but it hurt like blazes anyway. One of those assailants must have sliced through muscle. Perhaps cracked one of his ribs. The mere raising of his arm would not have caused him agony otherwise.

No matter. Dillie was worth it.

"How silly of me." She shook her head and let out a delicate laugh. "I don't know why I'm crying now that you're better."

He arched an eyebrow. "Disappointment?"

Her smile faded. "How could you even think such a horrid thought? Of course I'm not disappointed. I would have been shattered if you'd died. In my bed, no less!"

"Right. Nobody likes a dead duke in their bed."

She was frowning now, but made no move to remove his hand, which was once more caressing her cheek. Her blue eyes still shimmered with tears. "It would be especially difficult to explain away to the authorities."

He nodded. "Or to the patronesses at Almack's. My death would have been quite the scandal, and certainly the ruination of you."

She tipped her head, turning into his hand so that he now cupped her chin. She didn't notice, obviously distressed by his words. "Surely not my ruination."

"Dillie, nobody would have cared that you'd worked tirelessly to save my sorry life. All they would have noticed is that I'd departed this world in Dillie Farthingale's bed."

"You're simply being your cynical self, thinking the worst of your fellow man."

"And you're thinking like a wide-eyed innocent. People will

always disappoint you. The sooner you realize it, the better."

Her gaze turned tender. "Ian, who hurt you so badly to make you feel that way?"

He laughed, and then winced as the effort sent more shooting pains up and down his body. "No one." *Everyone.* "I was born this way."

"No you weren't. Children aren't born cynical."

"I'm a man now. I'm as manly as they come."

She rolled her eyes. "I suppose all the women you seduce tell you that."

"Breathlessly and often." Damn, she had beautiful eyes. A soft, sky blue.

"You aren't as manly as you think." She slipped away from him and rose to grab a clean cloth from a stack beside the basin of water on her nightstand. Grinning mischievously, she dipped it in the water and wrung it out. "I had to hold you down while Uncle George treated your wounds. You cried like an infant the entire time. *Waah, waah,* just like a baby," she teased, making a pretense of rubbing her eyes and sniffling like a child who'd fallen and scraped a knee. "Amos, our strongest footman, had to help me hold you down."

He laughed again, then winced again. "Good try, but not possible."

"How do you know?" She arched a delicate eyebrow. "You were barely conscious most of the time."

His merriment faded. "Dillie, you saw my body. These aren't my first scars, and they're not likely to be my last."

She returned to his side and set the cool, damp cloth over his forehead. She didn't sit down, but remained standing and slightly turned away, as though suddenly troubled. "Very well. You didn't cry out. Not even once," she said in a whisper.

"I know." He'd shed his last tears at the age of four, spent every last one of them wishing... no matter, his life had been changed forever that day and he'd learned to endure.

Were her eyes watering again? He didn't want her to cry over him or feel anything for him beyond her usual disdain. "Where are my clothes? I have to get out of here."

She whirled to face him, her eyes wide in surprise. "The ones you wore are ruined. Your valet brought over several outfits. Choose whichever you like, but you're not leaving here until Uncle George gives his approval."

"Nonsense. I'm fine." He sat up and swallowed a howl as he tossed off his covers, swung around to the other side of the bed, and rose to his wobbly feet. Damn! That hurt!

Dillie let out a gasp and clamped her hands over her eyes. "Ian, you idiot! Get back in bed. You're naked!" Her cheeks were a hot, bright pink.

"What?" He glanced down. No wonder he'd felt a sudden rush of cold air against his chest... and other parts. He was too unsteady to walk and too angry at his infirmity to get back into bed. He wasn't a doddering old fool who needed porridge and bed rest. He was young, strong. He refused to think of himself as dazed and stupid, but that's precisely what he was. He hadn't meant to shock Dillie. She was a decent girl.

Luscious and decent.

Now that she'd seen his naked backside, for one crazed moment he considered turning around and—

No, that would be an incredibly stupid move.

Finding a pebble of sense, which happened to be the only thing rattling around in his foggy brain at the moment, he wrapped the peach coverlet securely around his waist and turned to face her.

As he did so, he saw her fashion a peephole between her fingers. So the girl wasn't a paragon of virtue after all. She wanted to see him naked. He grinned. "Like what you see?"

She gasped and looked away. "I wasn't staring at you. Not in that way. My only concern is to keep you from falling and slashing open your healing wounds. You're an idiot. I hate you. Why can't you behave?"

Good question. One for which he had no answer. Well, he did have an answer, just not one she wanted to hear.

"Find me my clothes." He sank back onto the bed, ever careful to keep the covers about his waist. He was loath to admit he was dizzy and had almost fallen, just as she'd feared. He resolved to eat as hearty a meal as he could manage and then get dressed. Once he had regained his balance, he'd walk out on his own. No, not just walk. Run. His damn blood was pooling around his loins again. In another moment he'd be conspicuously hard and throbbing. "Why aren't you married yet?"

She let out a choking laugh. "I'd hit you if you weren't already bruised over your entire body. None of your business. Why aren't *you* married?"

"Bachelorhood suits me fine."

"Good, because I have no intention of marrying you."

"I don't recall asking you."

"You raised it. What made you think of marriage?" Suddenly, she gasped. "It's that Chipping Way bachelor curse. No, no, no. It can't be true!" She sounded pained. And scared.

Not as scared as he suddenly was. What if the curse did prove true? "I don't believe in it either."

"But you ran down my street. And now you're worried that you inadvertently fell into the Chipping Way trap." She sounded horrified. "For pity's sake, why did you do it? There are a thousand streets in London. You could have chosen any of them. Why mine?"

"It wasn't intentional. I was running for my life, and you should have been back in Coniston. Don't tell me you're the superstitious sort. You can't believe in that silly curse. Your sisters would have met and married their husbands no matter what. They fell in love. I'm not loveable. I'm a dissolute who intends to stay that way."

She paused to study him, her expression a little too thoughtful for his liking. "Why did you just say that?"

"Say what? That your sisters would have met and married—"

"No, about your not being loveable."

He laughed and shook his head. "No one on this earth cares about me. No one ever did. Not even me."

DILLIE CAME AROUND the bed to face Ian, wanting to be angry with him and at the same time wanting to throw her arms around him to assure him that someone cared. Someone must have loved Ian at some point in his life. His parents. His siblings. A sweetheart?

She felt a pang in her heart. It wasn't jealousy. She'd have to care for Ian in that way to feel such a thing. She didn't care for him and never would. Absolutely not. "I'll fetch your clothes." It was of no moment that looking at his broad, lightly tanned chest and the soft gold hairs that lined its rippling planes was making her lightheaded. She glanced away from his dangerously gleaming, gray-green eyes.

Ian knew how to make women swoon.

Fortunately, she never swooned. She was too practical for such nonsense.

Nor did his muscled arms make her body tingle. She was merely responding to the ugly, red gashes crisscrossed on them.

He wasn't in the least attractive. Not after three days of sweating out a high fever. Besides his ragged growth of beard, he had a large cowlick sticking up from his matted honey-gold hair. It didn't matter that some of those gold curls had looped about his neck and ears in a manner that made her fingers itch to brush them back. The cowlick made him look ridiculous.

Ridiculously handsome.

No! She refused to find him attractive. Absolutely not. Not in the least. Yet, the casual way he dismissed his wounds tugged at her heart. He was used to pain, used to hiding deep, ugly scars. The horrible sort, the unseen ones capable of destroying one's spirit.

Who had done such a thing to Ian? The elephant gun was still loaded. She wanted to hunt down those wicked people and shoot them with both barrels.

CHAPTER 2

AFTER BREAKFAST THE next morning, Dillie decided to sit down and play the piano. She needed to clear her mind, and anyway, she hadn't practiced in months. There had been too much to do to help her twin sister plan her wedding. In truth, she and their mother had done most of the planning while Lily was, as usual, absorbed in her baboon research. Then all those Farthingale relatives had descended on their townhouse from all over the British Isles to celebrate Lily's big day and Dillie had been enlisted to help her mother entertain them all.

Dillie entered the music room, looking forward to the solitude. It was a cold, rainy day, the sort of day to sleep late or cozy up in a chair by the fire to read a good book. She'd looked in on Ian earlier. He was sleeping comfortably, his forehead cool. His valet had delivered a leather pouch full of important papers that Ian would review when he awoke. Her uncle had allowed it now that Ian was no longer delirious. However, he hadn't allowed Ian to leave their home, for he wasn't completely out of danger yet.

Ian's fever had returned last night.

Fortunately, he was cool by this morning and looked stronger. Dillie could tell he was on the mend because he was frustrated, impatient, and eager to climb out of bed.

Mercy! The sight of him as he'd lunged out of bed yesterday, not a stitch of clothing on his muscled torso, still had her heart in palpitations.

With Ian's health improving, Dillie realized she was no longer needed to tend him. Ashcroft, his valet, would now take over nursemaid duties. She was glad for the change, and glad that he would be gone by the end of the week, for the sight of London's most eligible bachelor occupying her bed, his big, hard body taking up most of its width, had left her moon-eyed, witless, and vulnerable.

However, she would miss him.

Would he miss her? Of course not. Ian had a beautiful mistress and a circle of dissolute friends who would quickly occupy his time.

She sat on the piano bench, took a deep breath, and struck the first chord of a concerto she particularly liked. Her fingers flew over the ivory keys, for she knew the piece by heart and didn't need to concentrate to play it perfectly. In any event, how could she concentrate with Ian upstairs? In her bed. Still naked.

She finished the concerto and began to play one of her favorite madrigals, singing along as she played the sweetly melodic, but wistful, tune about a young woman's true love lost at war. Then she played another, and in this one the fair maiden died in her lover's arms.

"Do you know any songs that don't involve death?" Ian asked, limping into the music room and surprising her while she searched through her folios for some merrier tunes.

She turned to face him, relieved to see that he was clean shaven and properly dressed. Fully clothed. Incredibly handsome. He had on a white lawn shirt and dark gray breeches molded to his long, muscled legs, and he wore knee-length polished black boots. His cravat was a deep green silk that matched the forest-mist color of his eyes, and his gray silk vest brought out the silvery glint in them. No jacket, though she wasn't surprised, for the worst of his wounds, the one at his waist, had not yet healed and the weight of the jacket would only be an irritant.

He looked almost as good as he had yesterday while naked and rising from her bed, his broad shoulders and muscled arms flexing as he strained to stand.

Stop thinking of him naked.

Of course, she couldn't. The mere thought of Ian without a stitch of clothing turned her legs to pudding and left her heart pounding so hard its rampant beat could be heard across London. No doubt

Ian heard its rapid *thump, thump, thump.*

She let out a light laugh, feeling a little shabby, for she had on a simple day gown of dark blue wool, albeit a fine merino wool, and her hair was simply drawn back in a dark blue velvet ribbon. "I never realized quite how morbid some of these songs are."

"Will you play another for me? A merrier one this time." He surprised her by sinking onto the piano bench beside her, his broad shoulders grazing her slight shoulders as he settled awkwardly, obviously feeling pain with his every movement. He made no attempt to draw away. Did he realize that their bodies were still touching?

Dillie felt a rush of heat to her cheeks, not to mention her heart was still thumping so violently it threatened to explode. "Of course. I'll look through these."

He leaned closer to peruse the folios propped on the piano's music stand. She caught the scent of lather on his now beardless jaw, and the subtle scent of sandalwood soap along his throat. She ached to tilt her head and nuzzle his throat, shamelessly inhale great gulps of Ian air.

The folios fell from her hands and clattered to the floor. The smaller, unbound music sheets simply wafted across the room. "I'll get them!" Her twin often *eeped* when she felt uncomfortable. No one had ever made Dillie feel uncomfortable until now. Her cheeks were on fire as she jumped to her feet and began to gather the scattered papers.

She sensed Ian's amused gaze on her as she bent and twisted her body under various pieces of furniture to gather every last one of them. Her face was flushed, something she could blame on her exertion and not on her heated response to Ian's stare.

He grinned at her when she sank onto the piano bench, folios in hand, and attempted to prop them against the music stand. "Here, let me help you," Ian said, no doubt taking pity when she failed miserably to right them. He reached out to catch a few of the music sheets that were once again slipping away, and accidentally caught her hands, which were all over those folios.

"Eep."

His big, warm hands remained on hers.

"Eep. Eep."

He grinned, that sensual Ian grin all mothers warned their daughters about.

"Ian, I can't play while you're holding my hands. *Eep. Eep.*"

He appeared reluctant to release them, but it couldn't be so. "What's wrong with you? Do you have the hiccups?"

She nodded. "I often get them when I play the piano. *Eep.*" She turned away and rolled her eyes. He wasn't the idiot. She was. She shot off the bench and rang for Pruitt, ordering tea and lemon cake for Ian and herself. To keep herself busy until the tea arrived, she made a show of clearing her throat, as though attempting to rid herself of the hiccups she never had. Satisfied with her turn at theatrics, she returned to her seat at the piano, careful not to touch any part of Ian's big body. Even the slightest contact would cause her heart to burst.

She imagined what the gossip rags would report. *Remains of one Daffodil Farthingale were found exploded all over well-used piano in the family's music room. Notorious rakehell Duke of Edgeware last to see her alive. Cause of death was determined to be excessive rapture.* "You'll be more comfortable over there," she said, pointing to a pair of cushioned chairs by the hearth.

"Are you that eager to be rid of me?"

She nodded, though it wasn't for the reason he believed. A delicious heat radiated off his body. That heat, mingled with his divine scent and glorious, sinewy strength, was devastating to her resistance. In another moment, she'd be cupping his face in her hands and drawing him down so that his mouth met hers. All that stopped her was that she didn't know how to kiss. Indeed, she was ridiculously incompetent at it. She'd only been kissed the one time, two years ago, and Ian had been the one doing the kissing. "I don't wish to accidentally hurt you. I play with my elbows out and I might jab you."

Ian shook his head and sighed. "I'm not delicate, Dillie. Ah, tea is here. Set the tray down on the table beside the hearth, Pruitt."

"Of course, Your Grace."

Ian winked at Dillie. "See, he doesn't call me an idiot." He held out his hand to her. "Join me. You can play that merry tune afterward."

She ignored his hand, but agreed to move from the piano. She was eager to put some distance between them, though the chairs beside the fireside were only slightly separated by the small table upon which Pruitt had set the tray. She and Ian would still be too close for her liking, but not practically atop each other as they were on the piano bench.

He surprised her by taking her hand and placing it on his forearm. "I'm not delicate," he repeated when she hesitated putting any weight on his forearm. "My injuries are healing nicely."

"But they were serious. Half your body is still bound in bandages."

He shrugged. "They'll come off soon." Then he shook his head and laughed. "I'll give you fair warning before anything else comes off."

She tried not to grin, but couldn't hold back. "The sight of your naked backside as you rose from my bed is seared into my eyeballs. I'll never forget it." Her grin broadened. "Now I'm doomed to think of you whenever I look at a plate of firm and golden hot cross buns."

He arched an eyebrow. "Firm and golden? I'll accept that. Beats pale, wrinkled, and scrawny."

He continued to gaze at her in a gentle, I'm-enjoying-your-company manner that made Dillie's heart beat erratically fast again. She didn't want Ian to like her. Nor did she wish to like him. She was used to his condescending arrogance, and found him easy to resist when he was his usual, irritating self. But a charming, attentive Ian was devastating to her composure. She wanted to climb onto his lap, put her arms around his neck, and kiss him senseless.

She cleared her throat as she reached for the pot of tea, struggling to concentrate on pouring the hot liquid into the delicate teacups and not all over her shaking hands. "I've given some thought to the Chipping Way curse. Quite a bit of thought to it actually," she said, hoping to strike a casual tone.

"Have you now?" He eased into the chair beside hers and took the offered cup of tea, but he paid little attention to it as he waited for her to continue. What was he thinking? No matter, she preferred to do the talking.

"I have. And I've realized that you can't possibly be the man I'm going to marry." There, she'd said it. But his lingering silence began to put her on edge. "I'm sure you're every bit as relieved as I am. Not that you believed in the superstition. Nor did I, not really. But one can never be too careful about such things."

Still silent. Why wasn't he pleased? Smiling in gratitude? She began to fuss over the refreshments, suddenly afraid to look him in the eye. Not that he was looking at her. He wasn't. His gaze was now fixed on the fire blazing in the hearth.

"I see," he said finally. "How did you come to that momentous conclusion?" He seemed tense as he spoke, but he couldn't be. He'd made no secret of his thoughts on marriage. He didn't wish to be tied to her any more than she wished to be tied to him.

"When my sisters met their husbands on Chipping Way... or rather, ran headlong into them on Chipping Way, it was their first meeting. It happened all four times. First Rose's kiln exploded and Julian ran to her rescue. Then Laurel almost killed Graelem by running him down with her horse. Gabriel responded to Daisy's cries for help and rescued our young cousin from a fast-moving carriage, and Lily met Ewan when his dog ran her over. These were all first meetings—love-at-first-sight sort of blinding bursts of attraction."

"Like a brilliant show of fireworks."

"Yes," she said with a satisfied nod.

"And each first meeting was on Chipping Way." Ian now turned to study her. "So that's how you concluded that we're not destined for each other. Because you and I have known each other for about two years now, so our encounter of a few days ago couldn't possibly be a love-at-first-sight sort of thing. But what of our first encounter? Two years ago."

She tipped her head, confused. "It was an unusual first meeting, I will admit." They hadn't been properly introduced. In truth, they'd never met before. He'd swept her into his arms that night in her neighbor's garden, wrapped his strong arms about her waist and drawn her so close their bodies had melted into one. She remembered it as though it had happened only yesterday. The memory of his hard, sinewy body in direct contact with her softer curves was still vivid.

Her body warmed each time she thought of it, but not because Ian had been holding her. Or kissing her. *Holy crumpets! What a kiss!*

No, it was simply because she had been so surprised.

Yet, she would never forget the way he'd lowered his head and... oh, the feel of his firm, possessive mouth on hers. Exquisite. Nor could she forget that all his heat and passion were meant for another. He'd simply come upon the wrong girl. "We both know I wasn't the lady you expected to find."

"But we did *first* meet on Chipping Way. Right next door in Lady Dayne's moonlit garden, to be precise. You were hiding behind the lilac trees, spying on her guests."

She set down the slice of lemon cake she was about to pop into her mouth, and felt the warmth of a blush begin to spread across her cheeks. Even the tips of her ears were hot. So was her neck. "But I was in her garden. Not on the street." Though Rose and Julian hadn't met on the street either. Their first meeting was right here, in the garden attached to the Farthingale townhouse. "And I wasn't doing anything wrong. Well, not very wrong. I was merely curious about the party. You make it sound as though I were up to no good."

"You were lurking in the shadows."

She added two lumps of sugar to her tea, and then took a long sip in order to temper her hot retort. He was goading her again. But why? She was trying to put him at ease, assure him that there could never be anything more than friendship between the two of them. "I was innocently peering, not lurking. Since when is curiosity a crime? And speaking of innocent, your kiss was anything but that."

He frowned lightly. "Don't remind me. It isn't my practice to frighten genteel young ladies."

"We've gotten off the point." She took another sip of her tea. "All I wished to say is that you're not destined to be my husband. So we can both breathe a sigh of relief. I won't be burdened with a husband who doesn't love me, and you won't be burdened with a wife you don't want."

He didn't appear convinced. "If anything, you seem to have proved quite the opposite point. If there is such a thing as the Chipping Way curse, then you and I are doomed to wed."

She shot out of her chair, her hands curled into fists at her side. "Are you purposely trying to distress me?"

He calmly set his cup down on the tray and rose to his impressive full height. "It's you who has distressed me, Daffy."

Ugh! He was riled. She hated when he called her Daffy.

"I hadn't thought of our first meeting," he continued, "until you made a point of raising it just now. As for sparks flying and love at first sight... well, it might not have been love, but that first kiss between us was anything but tame. Don't even think to deny it."

About to protest, she clamped her mouth shut instead.

He was still staring at her as he spoke. More like glowering at her. "I kissed. You responded. Ardently."

She glanced toward the door to make certain no one was nearby. "How dare you!" she whispered harshly and came around the small table to stand directly in front of him. "I wasn't ardent. I was struggling for breath. You had your tongue stuck halfway down my throat. And if you call me Daffy again, I'll pour hot tea over your swelled head!"

"Are you seriously going to deny enjoying our first kiss?"

"Our *only* kiss. I hated it."

There was a dangerous gleam in his eyes. Perhaps *hate* was too strong a word.

"You melted at my touch. Must I prove it to you again?"

"Go ahead. I dare you." She tipped her chin upward in indignation. A bad move, because his arms clamped about her waist and the next thing she knew, she was up against him. Oh, he felt so good! *Say no! Tell him to stop.*

But she didn't. She wanted that second kiss.

Ian, the bounder, must have seen the yearning in her eyes. He let out a wrenching groan as he closed his lips on hers. All rational thought fled her brain. She was left with nothing but a hot coil of sensation that wound tightly in her stomach and then burst throughout her body in a shower of flames.

She was so shaken she couldn't remember her own name. Not even if her life depended on it. What was it again? Phlox? Peony? Bugloss?

He let out a husky, animal growl that cut the legs out from under her. In a good way. In the best way. Fortunately, she was still swallowed in his arms and he didn't seem ready to let her go. She would have fallen otherwise. Her legs were softer than pudding. "Ian," she whispered, her voice laced with exquisite agony.

He dipped his tongue between her lips, gently parting them. Gently probing. Not so gently invading her mouth as he deepened the kiss and urgently plundered. She was already hot, practically on fire, but it felt as though he'd turned up her furnace to as high as it could go. To infernal-fires-of-hell hot. And even hotter than that.

She felt so good wrapped in his arms, loved his strength and the heat radiating off his big body. Loved the warmth of his lips on hers, the subtle scent of sandalwood on his neck. Her hands moved higher, her fingers curling in his clean, thick hair to draw him even closer and keep his lips planted on hers.

Oh, no! This can't be happening. We don't like each other.

Or do we?

No! We can't!

She was on the verge of tears by the time he ended the kiss. She didn't want exquisite bursts of fireworks. She didn't want starlight or intoxicating kisses in the moonlight with Ian. He was a hound and a dissolute. She refused to be another of his conquests, another notch on his bedpost.

"See," she said, struggling to hold back sniffles. She was still in his arms and not quite ready to pull away. "Nothing. There's nothing between us at all."

"Right. I can see that." He traced his thumb along the curve of her cheek. "Dillie, I'm sorry. I wasn't trying to hurt you. I don't know what the hell I was doing just now. I'm an idiot, as you well know. I know you don't love me. What I made you feel was passion. Desire. I manipulated you into feeling these sensations. It isn't the same as love. Don't be afraid that it might be."

"Are you certain?" she asked against his chest. She wasn't crying. Not crying, though his shirt and vest were now moist. "Because if the Chipping Way curse applies to us, then I think I might jump in the Thames right now and let myself sink into that dirty water. I want a husband who loves me, who thinks I'm special. I'll never have that with you. You don't even like yourself."

He sighed. "I think I had better go."

She nodded, but remained leaning against him, loving the gentleness of his arms around her. "Yes, please do. You have a full pouch of work upstairs. I won't detain you. I'll close these doors once you leave so my piano exercises won't disturb you."

"No. I mean I had better go. Leave this house. I've overstayed my welcome." He eased her out of his arms. "Will you be all right?"

She nodded. "Most certainly."

"Very well, I'll... in a moment." He sighed. "Hell, I can't leave you like this."

She let out a shaky laugh. "How? Knowing that you have the power to melt my bones with your kisses? I should have known better than to challenge a rakehell at a sport in which he excels. You wouldn't be much of a rakehell if you couldn't kiss the slippers off a girl. It doesn't change anything between us. You don't wish to marry. And I don't wish to marry *you*. Nobody's hurt."

He cast her an almost imperceptible nod. "I'll have my valet pack my things, what little was brought here. I'll be gone within the hour."

She breathed a sigh of relief. "A wise plan. Oh, and Happy Christmas, Ian."

He arched an eyebrow. "It's a little early yet."

"But Uncle George and I will be leaving for Coniston in a few days, as soon as his other important patient is on the mend. I doubt you and I will see each other until next year, so I thought to wish you happy holidays, even if it is a little early."

He cast her an appealing, but guarded, smile. "Happy Christmas to you, Daffy." He tweaked her nose, and then leaned in and kissed her on the cheek, a soft, lingering touch of his lips that was so poignantly tender it brought an ache to her heart. She realized this might be the last time they'd ever touch. Apparently, he realized it as well and wanted her last memories of him to be gentle. "I wish you every happiness," he whispered.

IAN DIDN'T LET out the breath he'd been holding until he reached the safety of Dillie's room. His valet looked up in surprise as Ian shut the door and then fell heavily against it with a groan. "Pack up my belongings at once, Ashcroft. We're leaving right away."

"Your Grace, you don't look at all well." The poor man appeared quite alarmed.

"Didn't say I was, but I have Miss Farthingale's reputation to consider. I've been here almost a week and word is bound to get out if I remain in her care any longer." Of course, the real problem was his raging desire for the girl. He'd kept it under control for two damn years, and then lost all reason and kissed her again in the music room.

He was an experienced scoundrel and ought to have been wiser, but no. He was still an idiot when it came to Dillie. Nothing had changed. She still turned his blood molten. His heart still slammed against his chest whenever she smiled. Her lips were still as soft and sweet as summer peaches.

Lord, he loved peaches.

Damn the girl. Damn her pure and innocent heart.

"Send a messenger to Miss Giraud. Let her know I'll be visiting her this evening."

Ashcroft's eyes narrowed and his lips became pinched. "Is that wise, Your Grace? Your wounds aren't fully healed."

"No, it isn't wise. I don't care." He needed the scent of a heavy French perfume and the naked warmth of an experienced lover to clear Dillie from his thoughts. Dillie's first kiss had been spectacular, slamming him to the ground with its innocent power. But this second kiss had sent him soaring into the heavens, lifting him into the clouds higher than he'd ever been before, and then slammed him even harder to the ground.

Every muscle in his body was still taut and twitching with desire. Every damn one. Especially the one between his legs. It was granite hard and painfully throbbing.

Someone had to ease that pain. Chantal Giraud was paid to do just that.

CHAPTER 3

London, England
March 1819

"DAISY, SHE'S SO precious," Dillie said, laughing as she wrapped her ten-month-old niece in her arms and inhaled her sweet baby scent. "I missed you, Ivy. You've grown so big." She hadn't seen her sister Daisy or her little niece in months, not since Christmas at Coniston Hall, the Farthingales' country residence.

Now that Dillie and her parents had returned to London, she was eager to catch up with all her sisters. Daisy and her husband, the first to arrive back in town, had invited her to tea, and Dillie looked forward to passing a most pleasant afternoon with both of them. "Where's Gabriel?"

"He'll be along soon," Daisy said with a shrug. "He had to report to the Prince Regent, something about an incident that occurred a few months ago. He won't tell me what it's about because he's afraid I'll meddle."

Dillie shook her head and grinned. "Imagine that, accusing a Farthingale of meddling."

Her sister laughed. "Perhaps we do stick our noses into other people's business on occasion, but we do it with the best of intentions. Speaking of other people's business, what have you been up to since I last saw you?"

"Ugh! Absolutely nothing. I've been bored to tears." Dillie twirled Ivy in her arms, and then nuzzled her pudgy cheek, once more inhaling her baby sweetness. Of course, she knew that the light scent of powder and lavender soap would soon give way to the less pleasant odors of burps, spit-ups, and other unmentionable products that routinely emanated from the lower parts of infants. She didn't care. Children were meant to be loved and fussed over, no matter what came out of them, whether from top or bottom.

She kissed the little angel's chubby, pink cheek and was rewarded with a heart-tugging smile. Ivy had the look of a Farthingale girl, dark hair and big, blue eyes. Well, right now her hair was more a dark cap of curly fuzz, but she was still young. "Your father's going to have his hands full chasing the boys away," she whispered in her niece's ear.

Ivy burped.

Daisy smiled as she poured a cup of tea for each of them and set a treacle scone on each of their plates. "I think Gabriel will have a few more years before he needs to worry. You've caught Ivy on a good day. Usually she's all squawks and howls at this hour. It's her nap time, but she seems quite fascinated by you and has forgotten that she's tired. Watch out for your earrings. She may be little, but she's fast. Before you know it, she'll have her fingers wrapped in the loops and tugging until *you* howl."

"She's already pulled out half the pins in my hair." Dillie nuzzled her niece's soft neck and got a giggle out of her. "Isn't that right, you little devil? And what will your Grandmama Sophie say when I return home utterly disheveled?"

Ivy responded with another burp.

Dillie laughed softly and nuzzled her again. Ivy let out a joyful squeal.

"She really likes you, Dillie. She's rarely content with anyone but me, Gabriel, or Nanny Grenville holding her."

"And I adore her." Dillie suddenly felt wistful. Though she loved her family, every last irritating and snoopy member of their boisterous Farthingale clan, she and her sisters had always been especially close. Now, all her sisters were married and starting families of their own. She was the one left behind. She hadn't really felt the changes until Lily had married Ewan Cameron and settled in Scotland, in the Highlands no less.

She knew Lily was enjoying her life with Ewan, for her happiness was apparent in all of her letters. Would she ever find that same happiness? Dillie wasn't surprised to be the last to leave the Farthingale roost, for she was the youngest daughter, even though only by a few minutes. She just hadn't expected Lily to leave so soon.

Now with her twin suddenly gone, she'd had no time to adapt to the inevitable changes and hadn't quite taken them all in yet. Feeling alone and adrift were new sensations, ones she did not particularly like.

She dismissed her wistful thoughts when Daisy's husband strode into the parlor. Gabriel headed straight for Daisy and planted a noisy kiss on her cheek. "Missed you, love," he said with a wicked grin and devilish arch of an eyebrow.

Dillie rolled her eyes, and then tickled Ivy's chin to gain her attention. "Your parents have been apart no more than a few hours, but one would think they'd been apart for months. Your father is shamelessly ogling your mother."

Daisy blushed. "I missed you, too. Behave yourself, Gabriel. We have company."

He turned to Dillie, walked to her side, and planted a chaste kiss on her cheek. Then he gazed down at Ivy, who was cooing in Dillie's arms, and his expression turned soft and doting. "How's my little potato doing?"

Dillie grinned. "I hope you're not referring to me."

He chuckled. "No, you look great. The winter months at Coniston obviously suited you. John," he said, referring to her father, "must be in full fret, wondering what surprises this London season will bring. None of your sisters managed a traditional courtship. You're his last hope."

"I'll do my best to get it right," she assured. "After all, I'm the sensible sister. Dutiful, polite. Perfect."

Gabriel nodded. "Ian seems to think so."

Dillie's heart skipped a beat. "The Duke of Edgeware? I hadn't realized he was back in town." She tried to sound casual, but knew she'd failed. Her cheeks were growing hot and so were the tips of her ears, tell-tale signs that Daisy would have noticed had Gabriel's broad shoulders not been blocking her view.

"Nor had I," Gabriel said with a shrug, obviously unaware of her turmoil, "but I ran into him at White's earlier today and invited him over." He gave Ivy a big, juicy kiss on the top of her head before returning to his wife's side. "Hope you don't mind, love."

"No, of course not." Daisy shot Dillie a speculative glance. "We look forward to seeing him, don't we, Dillie?"

She *eeped* in response. *Oh, crumpets!* Her winter at Coniston may have been too quiet for her liking, but she wasn't ready to see Ian yet. Why was he in town and not at Edgeware? It was only late March, and London was not yet at its best. The air was still too cold for satin gowns and bared shoulders. Soot still spewed from hearth fires lit to ward off the wintery chill, and a smoky coating of gray hung over London, blocking the sun and all trace of glorious blue sky.

A light odor of dead fish still wafted off the Thames. Of course, there were always odors emanating off the Thames, no matter what time of year.

"How is His Grace, by the way?" Although she thought of him as Ian, and at his urging would call him that whenever they were alone, he was a duke and his title had to be respected when in the company of others.

"Looking fit as ever." Gabriel eased onto the settee beside Daisy and lazily stretched his arm across its back. He looked so comfortable and happy. So did Daisy. "He had business in town and had to come down early."

"Will he be off before the season starts?" Daisy asked. She poured her husband a cup of tea, and then rose to take Ivy from Dillie's arms when Ivy began to fuss.

Dillie wasn't quite ready to let go of the little bundle in her arms, so she motioned for Daisy to sit down. "I have her. Go on, Gabriel. You were saying?"

Gabriel frowned lightly, as though worried about his friend. "He plans to remain in London, even though he knows it's dangerous for a bachelor to do so. He's raw meat and every predatory society mother will be after him for one of her daughters."

Dillie rocked her niece in her arms to keep her content. "Hear that, Ivy? England's most eligible bachelor is going to brave the London battlefield. Should make for an exciting few months."

Ivy let out a squawk. Then another. Then she let out a howl that filled the room despite her tiny lungs. Daisy sighed as she rose again. "Nap time for you. Nanny Grenville's waiting for you upstairs."

Dillie once more motioned for her to stay seated. "I'll take her up. I know the way." She patted Ivy's back gently as she continued to rock her. "You two lovebirds seem to need a moment alone anyway."

Gabriel laughed and nudged Daisy down beside him. "Excellent idea. Let me show you just how much I missed you."

Daisy lightly swatted him on the shoulder. "Come right back, Dillie. You haven't touched your tea yet. More important, we haven't exchanged the juiciest bits of gossip."

"First of all, I haven't got anywhere else to go, so you're well and truly stuck with me all afternoon. Sorry, Gabriel, you'll simply have to endure. And second, I love gossip." She made a silly face that evoked another giggle out of Ivy. "I hope you have something thoroughly scandalous to share, because I have no news whatsoever. Life at Coniston has been dull as dishwater."

She walked into the hallway, singing softly to the squirming bundle in her arms, but hadn't quite made it to the stairs when Ivy suddenly let out another squawk and decided to get playful. She grabbed Dillie's hair with one tiny hand, winding her fingers in what was left of Dillie's once stylish curls and efficiently pulling out several more pins.

At the same time, she raised the other tiny fist and wound her fingers in the loop of her earring. Then, with a demonic grin, she tugged with all her little might. Dillie let out a laughing yelp. "No, Ivy! Let go of Auntie Dillie. You need to—ow!"

Apparently, her niece took Dillie's pained laughter as a request to continue. She tugged again, taking out more hairpins with one pudgy hand while pulling on the earring with the other. "Ow. No, I—"

Ivy squealed and began a new game called Slap Dillie's Face. Thankfully, playing that game meant she had to release the earring she'd been holding in a death grip. While Ivy was busy slapping Dillie's nose, Dillie managed to extricate her little fingers from the strands of her hair, but not before significant damage was done to her fashionable chignon.

"Need assistance?" someone asked from behind her.

She whirled to face the new arrival. *Ian.*

"Like your new hairstyle." He gave her a long, lazy grin that warmed her blood and made her heart skip beats. "That crazed, maniacal look suits you, Daffy. Not every woman can pull it off as well as you do."

She hastily attempted to tuck the stray ends behind her throbbing ear, but she knew she was doing a dismal job of it. He, of course, looked stunning. Dressed to perfection, yet still too big and broad shouldered to carry off the foppish appearance of society elegance. His look was one of dangerous elegance.

His eyes were even more beautiful than she remembered, a misty, summer green flecked with hints of deep gray. They were a true representation of Ian, incredibly handsome and at the same time haunted. The gray was the shadowed part of Ian, the part he always kept hidden. The part that made her want to throw her arms around him and hug him tight. Instead, she shook her head and laughed softly. "Meet my stylist. Her name is Ivy. She's very much in demand. Do you have a smile for His Grace?"

Surprisingly, she did. A sweet, open-hearted, ear-to-ear smile that stole Dillie's breath away. And that's when she saw it, the look of indescribable pain in Ian's eyes. It was only there for an instant. Had she blinked, she would have missed it.

But it had been there.

She'd thought to toss off a cleverly cutting remark to continue their usual wry banter, but her heart was still struggling with that glimpse of his pain. She couldn't jest with him now. In truth, all she wanted to do was put her arms around him and draw him close. "You look wonderful. How do you feel?" She hugged her niece instead. It was safer. Ivy responded by letting out a gurgled *coo,* and then began to contentedly gnaw on Dillie's chin.

"I'm in the pink. Stab wounds have all healed. Are you going to let your niece chew the flesh off your chin?"

"She isn't a cannibal. Honestly, Ian." She rolled her eyes when he continued to stare in fascination, as though infants were unfamiliar creatures to him. They probably were. During their week together he'd never mentioned brothers or sisters, nieces or nephews. She suddenly realized that she knew nothing of his family. Or if he even had one.

Odd that no one had ever mentioned his relations, considering the constant gossip one heard about him. "She's only teething. The pressure against her gums helps soothe her ache. It doesn't hurt me."

"You're remarkably at ease with her." He was still studying her and Ivy, taking them in as though they were a portrait hanging in an elegant hall, his gaze following each line and curve to determine how child and woman flowed together.

"How can I not be? Besides growing up with all my Farthingale cousins, I now have a slew of nephews and nieces to adore. They're all perfect. I melt whenever they look at me with their big, innocent eyes." She paused a moment, realizing that Ian had never once called out for anyone dear to him, even when he had been delirious in those first days after the attack when his survival had been in doubt. She silently berated herself. Because of her thoughtlessness, he might have died alone in her bed, no loved ones beside him.

She resolved to find out about his family. What if he were attacked again? It wasn't a matter of snooping. She was simply being thoughtful. However, she couldn't ask him straight out. He would have spoken of relatives if he'd wanted to during those hours they'd spent together. No, she'd pry the information out of her elderly neighbor, Lady Eloise Dayne.

Eloise, who knew everything about everybody, was a kind and sensible woman, not the sort ever to lie or twist the truth. Indeed, Eloise would be the perfect source since she was practically a part of the Farthingale family. Her grandsons, Gabriel and Graelem, were married to Dillie's sisters.

Ian continued to watch her and Ivy, drinking them in with his gaze. Ivy was still suckling her chin and her little hand was no longer fisted, but open and resting on Dillie's cheek, stroking it lightly.

This felt nice, standing here with Ian, cradling Ivy in her arms.

Her heart skipped beats again, as it always did when Ian stood close. She could feel the subtle heat and power radiating off his body.

She shook out of the wayward thought, afraid to allow Ian too close, for he always overwhelmed her senses. He overwhelmed her heart. She couldn't allow it, for she was about to enter her second London season. She wanted to meet the man she was going to marry and start a family. Ian wasn't the marrying kind. He'd made no secret of his desire to remain a bachelor.

She cleared her throat. "Did you ever find out who was after you?"

He shrugged and propped his elbow casually on the staircase newel post. "No. It isn't important."

She knew him well enough to understand that Ian was never casual. "You're doing that thing again."

He arched an eyebrow. "Doing what thing?"

"Carrying around that I-deserve-to-be-miserable chip on your shoulder."

He ignored the comment, just as she expected he would. But she was a Farthingale, and Farthingales spoke their minds, whether or not anyone wished to hear their pearls of wisdom. "Did you miss me?" he asked instead, obviously wishing to change the topic.

"It so happens, I did. It isn't every day one finds a handsome duke in one's bed. Life after that can seem deadly dull."

"You think I'm handsome?"

She rolled her eyes again. "You know you are. Everyone knows you are." Ivy released her chin long enough to let out a squeal. Dillie laughed. "See, even my niece thinks so. You're devastating to all women, even those who can't walk or talk yet."

Their conversation was interrupted by Nanny Grenville's arrival. "There you are, my little princess!" said the amiable older woman. "Do you mind if I take her, Miss Dillie?"

"Not at all." She gave Ivy a kiss on the cheek—in fact, several kisses on her plump, pillow-soft cheek—and then handed her over. "Glad you're here to rescue me. I've been thoroughly mauled by this ten-month-old, as you can see."

Ivy's nanny shook her head and sighed. "You aren't the only one she's bested. She may be little, but she's quick with her fists." She gave her charge a quick hug. "Aren't you, my little princess?"

Dillie watched niece and nanny disappear up the stairs, and then turned to Ian. She blushed, realizing he'd continued to study her all the while she'd been watching Ivy. "There's spittle oozing down your chin," he said, his voice seductively tender.

She winced. "I know. Incredibly alluring, isn't it?"

He let out an unguarded laugh. "Absolutely. Thoroughly irresistible. I'm struggling to hold back my desire. Here, let me wipe it off you." He withdrew a handkerchief from his front pocket, tucked a finger under her chin, and tipped her face upward so that she met his gaze.

Holy crumpets! There was something wonderful in the way he smiled at her, in the way that smile seemed to dance in his eyes. Her cheeks and ears were heating up again. So was the rest of her body. Unbearably hot. Melt-one's-bones hot.

He gently dabbed her chin, and ever so gently wiped the corners of her lips.

His knuckles grazed her lips.

She *eeped. Crumpets!* He was having far too much fun drying her off. "My hair's a mess," she said, hurriedly drawing away. She removed the last of the hairpins, most of which were dangling amid the long strands, and gave her hair a quick twist in order to fashion a passable bun at the nape of her neck. She stuck the pins back in to hold the style in place and hoped it would last through the afternoon, but she wasn't sure. She hadn't done a very good job of it.

Ian was still studying her.

She whirled to face him. "What?"

He acted as though he didn't know what she was talking about. "Is there a question in that comment?"

"Why are you still looking at me?"

"Should I look away? You aren't that hideous. Indeed, at times you're quite nice to look at. Not right now, of course. I think Ivy gave you a shiner. And your earlobe is a bright, apple red." He touched a finger to her ear, and then trailed it lightly down the side of her neck. The pulse at its base began to throb and a deliciously hot tingle ran up her spine. *Mercy!*

"Stop it, you clunch. And why don't you care that you haven't found out who was after you? If I were you, I'd make it a priority to run those villains to ground."

"But you're not me."

He sounded quite smug. Had she felt sympathy for his plight? Well, no longer. She wanted to grab him by his exquisite lapels and shake him till his teeth rattled. "Fine, don't look for them. I won't save you the next time. No, I'll stay cozy in my room and pop grapes in my mouth while I stand by my window and watch you slowly bleed to death."

He let out a deep, unrestrained laugh. "Dillie, you're the farthest thing from a bloodthirsty wench I've ever met. Your instincts are to nurture and protect. You're far too generous, you love faithfully, and you'll protect even those you don't like very much. Such as myself."

"Are you mocking me?"

He took her hand and stuck it on his arm. "No, quite the opposite. I just gave you a compliment, you impertinent little baggage. You're soft-hearted and yet quite fearless when you need to be. I'm still in awe of the way you chased off my attackers. Who taught you how to shoot an elephant gun?"

"My Uncle George," she admitted with a wince. "He caught Lily and me one morning trying to break into the cabinet where he stored his collection of weapons. Rather than scold us, he thought it safer to teach us how to use them. We were twelve years old at the time and that gun was enormous, much bigger than we were. He taught us how to load it, but wouldn't allow us to fire it because he thought the force of the recoil would break our young bones."

He glanced at her shoulder and frowned suddenly. "I never thought to ask. You didn't appear to be hurt, but—"

"I wasn't." She shook her head and laughed lightly. "Although the force of the recoil did knock me onto my dainty derriere. Twice. The thick carpet in my bedchamber cushioned my fall. I'm surprised Uncle George didn't come tearing into my room at the roar of that first shot, but he'd been up for two days straight with that important patient of his and was exhausted. He fell asleep fully clothed—jacket, cravat, boots—and was snoring before his head hit the pillow. Nothing was going to wake him up."

"Except your butler."

Still smiling, Dillie nodded. "Poor Pruitt, he had to duck my uncle's fists as he shook him awake. But all turned out well, thank goodness. You're alive."

He covered her hand with his own when she began to tremble, for it was still resting on his arm where he'd placed it when preparing to escort her into Daisy's parlor. "Come along," he said with unexpected tenderness, "or Daisy and Gabriel will wonder what's become of us."

They managed only two steps before Dillie held him back. "I forgot to mention, Uncle George and I never said a word to anyone about... you know."

He arched an eyebrow. "About my week in your bed?"

"I wish you wouldn't put it quite like that. We thought it better to keep the incident to ourselves. No one knows but the three of us."

"And Pruitt. And Ashcroft," he pointed out. "And your footmen and my coachman."

Dillie pursed her lips in thought. "But they're all loyal. They wouldn't tattle, would they?"

He shrugged. "Let's hope not."

THE QUIET AFTERNOON Ian had hoped for turned out not to be so quiet after all. He had expected to meet Gabriel at his home to discuss business and other matters of national importance, including who had tried to kill him last November. He hadn't expected to find Dillie there visiting her sister.

The sight of Dillie standing in the entry hall, holding her niece in her arms, had sent his heart shooting into his throat. She had looked so happy. He couldn't remember when he'd ever felt such joy. He didn't think he ever had.

She was laughing and cooing over Ivy, the love she held for that baby shining through her glorious blue eyes, even as Ivy wreaked havoc on her hair and practically tore the earring off her earlobe. Dillie hadn't minded at all. She'd held the child so naturally, as though the squirming bundle in her arms were simply another appendage.

She would make a wonderful mother. Unlike his own.

Dillie had caught him staring at her. In truth, he hadn't been able to take his eyes off her. It wasn't simply that she was beautiful. There were many beautiful young women in London, though none came close to Dillie's spectacular allure. She had a magical, inner glow, a moon-and-stars sparkle that made him ache to take her into his arms and hold her close forever.

Of course, forever for him meant about a month, for that was the longest any sweet young thing had ever held his interest. Dillie was the exception, but only because she was forbidden fruit. Gabriel and Graelem would cut out his entrails and feed them to the carrion birds if he ever hurt Dillie.

Ian fidgeted in his chair. Gabriel and Daisy had taken over the settee, leaving him no choice but to claim the seat beside Dillie's. He spent the next half hour forced to pretend that her soft laughter and sweet blush did not affect him. Daisy, her own blue eyes sparkling with mirth, had taken over the conversation, relating the latest scandals making their way around London. Dillie had responded with the innocent awe of a child.

He couldn't remember ever being that innocent.

He shifted uncomfortably once more, tortured by Dillie's nearness and his inability to touch her. He couldn't conceive of a worse punishment... and then Daisy's other guests arrived. By the time Lady Eloise Dayne was announced, the servants had set out an elaborate display of sweets and other refreshments to accompany the afternoon tea.

He rose as Eloise entered and greeted her warmly. She was Gabriel's grandmother and neighbor to the Farthingales on Chipping Way. He truly liked the old dowager. She was helpful, perfectly agreeable, and a genuine delight.

Not so delightful was Eloise's tiny companion, Lady Phoebe Withnall, the *ton's* most notorious gossip. *Hell.* This could be bad. In truth, he liked Phoebe as well, and despite her ruthless reputation, she'd often gone easy on him. Often, but not always. The woman had ears planted in everyone's walls, or so it seemed, for she had a way of digging up secrets that were meant to be shrouded in darkness for eternity.

Had the old bloodhound picked up the scent of his injury? And his recovery in Dillie's bed? Dillie had assured him that she and George hadn't mentioned the incident to anyone. He hoped it was true.

Phoebe's beady-eyed gaze homed in on him, and her pointed nose began to twitch as she inspected him from head to elegantly booted toe. She was like a hound on the hunt, sniffing him out. "You've been quiet these past few months, Your Grace."

He'd spent years fighting Napoleon's ablest soldiers and spies, been captured a couple of times, and survived torture. He wasn't about to make a slip under the heat of Phoebe's questioning gaze.

Dillie would, though.

Fortunately, Phoebe's attention was still trained on him. Her nose twitched again, a sign she was contemplating her strategy. "Where did you spend your holidays?"

He shrugged. "Quietly at Edgeware."

"I heard you stayed in town longer than expected last season. Any reason?"

Dillie had been about to lift her teacup to her lips, but let out a soft gasp instead. "Too hot," she hastily muttered, easing her hand off the cup, no doubt afraid she'd draw further attention to herself by spilling her tea if the conversation suddenly turned alarming.

Ian was good at hiding his thoughts. Dillie hadn't any such talent. She'd be *eeping* like a demented bird the moment the old woman trained her gaze on her.

In truth, he liked those throaty little sounds Dillie made. Proof that he unsettled her. Not that he would ever act upon that proof. Still, it mattered to him that Dillie was not quite as resistant to him as she would like to believe.

Phoebe asked him several more questions, to which he purposely gave empty responses. Finding little gossip fodder from him, she turned her attention to Dillie. "Drink up, girl. Why aren't you touching your tea?"

"Daisy and I finished a pot before you arrived, Lady Withnall," she answered, smoothly managing her lie. "A lovely oriental blend with a hint of orange peel. Delicious."

"I see." She remained staring at Dillie. *Hell.* This was going to be bad. Dillie wasn't used to this sort of scrutiny. Having been raised in a large family, she'd probably had to fight for every scrap of attention. He wasn't certain how long she could maintain her unaffected manner. The *eep* was on the tip of her tongue. It would take nothing for her to blurt it out. "Heard you also remained in town after the season."

"Yes, with Uncle George. I stayed behind with him to close up the house. He's also been training me to assist him in his medical matters." She clasped her hands together, no doubt to keep them from shaking. She smiled and stopped talking. Good. She was a smart girl and knew to keep her responses short and sweet. She wouldn't offer conversation that could be turned against her.

Ian shot her a sympathetic glance, as though to say, "You can do this."

She swallowed hard. She wasn't a practiced liar.

Phoebe took a bite of her treacle scone and slowly chewed, her gaze still intently fixed on Dillie. "Have you done it yet?"

"It?" Her frantic gaze shot to him, saved by the fortunate fact that Eloise was now seated beside him and Phoebe might believe she'd turned to Eloise for guidance. He knew what was racing through Dillie's mind. She was thinking of their kiss. She was thinking of his naked body. "Forgive me, I didn't understand the question. What is it that I'm supposed to have done?"

"Tended to any of your uncle's patients, of course. What did you think I was talking about?"

Ian could see that Dillie's mind had frozen at the very moment she needed to think fast. Had Phoebe already spoken to George? What had he answered? "I'm sure whatever Miss Farthingale did was under her uncle's supervision. Of course, I can't imagine he'd ever leave her alone with any of his patients, or admit it to you if he had. She's merely in training. Not trained yet."

Dillie shot him a smile of gratitude. Obviously relieved, she raised her cup to her lips and drank.

However, Phoebe wasn't finished with her yet. "I see. Can't be trusted on your own."

Dillie swallowed hard, the hot liquid obviously searing her throat as it went down too fast. "Not in the least."

Hell. That came out very wrong.

"I mean, not medically." She began to fidget. "Otherwise, I can be trusted. Of course I can be trusted. Why would I not?"

"You tell me. You're the one who seems concerned about it." Though she and Phoebe were seated across from each other, separated by a tea table, Dillie must have felt as if the harridan were breathing down her neck.

She was in trouble here, but knew better than to glance at him again. She turned to Daisy instead, silently begging for help. The Farthingale sisters were close, always supported each other. Ian wondered how it felt. He'd experienced support on the battlefield, could always rely on Gabriel and Graelem to guard his back. There were other men he trusted as well. But that was during wartime, saving England and the Continent from Napoleon's army.

He'd never felt the soft, nurturing support of a woman.

Hell, he'd never felt any family support.

Daisy sprang into action. "Ah, I see you've finished your tea, Lady Withnall. How did you like it? Isn't the oriental blend delightful? It's a new one I discovered in a local tea shop. Oh, and I discovered the quaintest bake shop as well. Dillie, I have a special treat for you."

"You do?" Dillie smiled her thanks at the change in conversation.

Ian stifled a grin as he watched her. She was feeling more relaxed now that Daisy had come to her rescue. Dillie popped a bite of sardine and watercress sandwich in her mouth, obviously didn't like it, and then lifted the cup to her lips to wash down the hideous combination. "Mmm, good," she muttered unconvincingly.

She took another gulp of her tea just as her sister added, "This little bake shop makes the most delicious hot cross buns. I ordered them special just for you. Here, try one. Don't they look tempting? So firm and golden."

Dillie choked on her tea.

Ian jumped to his feet to help her, positioning himself to block her from Phoebe's view. *Bloody hell!* The girl wore her expression on her sleeve. She was thinking of *his* naked buns, and it took all his control to keep from bursting into laughter.

He grabbed the cup from her trembling hand before she spilled its remaining contents onto her lap.

Eloise came to his side to help. "Oh, Dillie! You know that sardines don't agree with you. Poor dear. You ought to have stayed with the sweets. I know just the shop Daisy mentioned. I'll invite you over next week." She stared sympathetically at Dillie. "Then you can taste *my* golden buns."

Dillie coughed again. Gagged actually, as the mix of tea and sardines that had lodged in her throat now threatened to heave upward. Thankfully, she managed to hold it all down. Almost. A droplet of tea had dribbled down her chin. Ian wiped it off with his thumb.

She was an adorable mess.

He still wanted to draw her into his arms and kiss her into forever.

Daisy and Gabriel were now standing over him, eager to help. Daisy squeezed between him and Dillie, and leaned in close to her sister. "Dillie, are you all right?"

Dillie responded with a sneeze into the handkerchief Ian had just withdrawn from his breast pocket and stuck in front of her face.

Daisy and Gabriel took a quick step back. "I'll fetch you a glass of apple cider," Daisy said.

"I'll go with you," Gabriel added, hastily following her out of the room as though the thought of being left alone with Dillie was as appealing as cleaning Ivy's soiled bottom.

Ian knelt beside Dillie as she sneezed into his handkerchief again. "I'm so sorry!" Her eyes were now tearing and her face was red hot.

"It's those dratted sardines," Eloise said sympathetically.

Dillie nodded furiously. "You know what they do to me. And I think there's too much pepper on them!"

Curious. He'd eaten one of those sandwiches and had encountered no such problem. He'd also seen Dillie pepper her food before and suffer no ill consequences. Was she truly suffering, or was the little actress faking? If so, she was doing a damn good job of it.

She sneezed again.

Maybe not faking. Her face was as red as a cranberry and her breaths were still shaky. Perhaps she was genuinely in distress. He frowned and moved closer.

She looked vulnerable and scared, seeming to plead for his help not only in distracting Phoebe but also in helping calm her down. Of course, he would do all in his power. Her breaths were erratic. From the pepper and sardines? His heart tightened. "Dillie, close your eyes and breathe slowly."

"I can't."

"Yes, you can." She'd found her voice, which meant she was getting air into her lungs. He kept his tone calm and even. "That's it. Here, take my hand. You see, I have you. I won't let you go until you're feeling better."

"Promise?"

He nodded. "I promise."

Phoebe was still intently eyeing the pair of them. Fortunately, Dillie was too distraught to notice. "The mention of hot cross buns seemed to set her off," Phoebe mused.

"No, it was the sardines," Dillie rasped back, but cast him a pained glance, for she knew that *he* knew perfectly well what those buns represented.

He cast Dillie a soft smile.

She groaned. "Must we spend the entire afternoon discussing what I do or do not like to eat? It seems some people have nothing better to do than spy on others and report their findings to everyone who will listen."

She'd spoken to him in a whisper, but since Phoebe had the ears of a vampire bat, she heard the remark as well. "You're a debutante now," she chided. "Everyone will scrutinize you."

Dillie looked as though she were about to burst into tears again.

When Daisy returned with the glass of apple cider and a damp cloth, Ian couldn't seem to let Dillie go. Instead of stepping aside and allowing Daisy to help her sister, he took the cloth from her hands and began to dab it across Dillie's lips.

Dillie groaned again as she felt his hand against her cheek. The others would mistake it for embarrassment, but he knew Dillie was responding to his touch. He wasn't surprised. He was also responding to her nearness, her softness.

This was bad.

He eased away and handed the cloth back to Daisy, silently

watching as she turned fuss and feathers over her sister.

Phoebe shook her head and sighed.

Ian straightened to his full height, worried that the meddlesome harridan was about to insult Dillie now that she appeared to be calming down. Even though he considered Phoebe a friend, he'd haul her out of the house and toss her to the sidewalk if she dared utter a cross word.

But Phoebe merely let out another sigh. "You poor, poor dear. I now understand why you're the last of the Farthingales to marry. I'm worried about you, gel. All those years of training haven't done you much good."

Eloise came to her defense. "Now see here, Phoebe. Dillie is delightful. She'll have a dozen eligible bachelors swooning at her feet within the fortnight. Mark my words. You haven't caught her at her best just now."

Phoebe turned to Ian. "What about you, Edgeware?"

He arched an eyebrow. "What about me?"

"You seem interested in the girl. You came to her rescue—"

"As we all did."

Her sharp nose wiggled. "But—"

"Lady Withnall, please," Dillie interceded. "Haven't I humiliated myself sufficiently? I'll readily admit that I'm a duckling among swans. I've never been anywhere without one or more of my sisters close at hand. I don't do well on my own, as you can see. I'm miserable enough about it. Please don't let the world know."

Ian had rarely seen any softness in Phoebe Withnall. The woman seemed to thrive on the fear and pain of others, so he was quite surprised when the old harridan actually smiled at Dillie. Not one of her gloating, triumphant smiles, but a tender, indulgent one. "My dear, your secret is quite safe with me."

Dillie let out a shaky breath. "Thank you."

The old harridan turned to Eloise. "I think we must be off. Lady Dowling is expecting us. She's eager for my news about her husband. That wine-soaked old sot. She's better off without him." She tipped her head at Ian. Said nothing. Just smiled. That worried him. "Daisy. Gabriel. Come see us off."

Which meant she'd purposely left Ian alone with Dillie.

Bad.

She knew Dillie liked him. Did she realize just how much he liked Dillie?

"CRUMPETS." DILLIE GAZED at Ian, her heart beating wildly and eyes still wide in panic. He, the bounder, looked magnificently composed and controlled. "No good will come of this. I made an utter fool of myself."

"You were fine. Even Lady Withnall likes you, and she doesn't like anybody."

She rolled her eyes. "How can you say that?"

"What would you like me to say? That you allowed an infant to get the better of you, then allowed a woman no bigger than that infant to scare you into a sneezing frenzy?"

She had hoped he would tell her that he admired the way she'd handled herself, that he'd ached watching her hold Ivy and was proud of the way she'd handled Lady Withnall. He wouldn't say any of it, for it wasn't true.

She had behaved like an idiot. She had a welt on her chin from Ivy's teething. Her hair was about to tumble about her shoulders once again. And she'd suffered a sneezing fit after accidentally biting down on those sardines, her reaction chasing host, hostess, and guests from Daisy's parlor. Had she not been so distracted, she would have seen what she was about to put into her mouth and never taken a bite out of it.

Only Ian remained beside her now, no doubt out of a misguided sense of duty. "How's your breathing? Feeling any better?"

"Much better." She wanted him to take her into his arms and protect her from her own idiocy.

She was such a coward!

She let out a light, laughing groan. "I will admit, I've had better moments."

"You'll do better next time. In truth, you scared the hell out of me. What happened? You were in serious distress."

She sighed. "I panicked. But you were quite heroic in coming to my rescue."

His haunted gaze bore into her, no sign of teasing humor, as though he'd seriously risk his life to save her if it ever came to that.

Oh, crumpets again! "Lady Withnall scares me. I was so afraid I'd let slip what happened last November, I accidentally bit down on the sardines. I can't abide them and they don't like me either. I acted purely out of fear. Unbridled terror, if you must know the truth."

"If it's any consolation, I was quaking in my boots, too." He grinned and dabbed at her chin with his handkerchief again. Then he took her hand and held it in his warm grasp. "There, all better. Well, almost."

Her eyes narrowed. "What do you mean by *almost*?"

He tweaked her nose. "Your hair's a little out of place. A lot, actually."

"Oh, not again!" Her hands shot to her hair. Most of the pins she'd stuck back in place after Ivy had pulled them out were now dangling amid her curls again.

Ian stopped her as she tried to put them back in place. "Let me," he said in a husky rumble that stole her breath away. The pulse at the base of her throat began to pound as he leaned in close. Oh, he smelled so good, the scent of sandalwood so pure and fresh against his skin.

She smelled of sardines, spittle, and drool.

"You smell of peaches and heaven," he said with a soft chuckle, easily reading her thoughts. She'd have to work on masking her expressions better. Men liked mysterious women, right? In any event, she couldn't let Ian know just how much she liked him.

Her heart began to flutter as he took out all her pins and slowly ran his hands through her unbound hair. *Oh, that feels sinfully good.* But she couldn't let him know that either.

"Your hair's soft as silk. Seems a shame to put it back up."

She was a grown woman. She couldn't go about with her hair wild and unbound, though she often did so when at Coniston. There was something about the pure country air and unspoiled lakes and hillsides that freed one from society's restrictive conventions. "Help me pin the last of it up, you wretch. You promised you would."

He arched an eyebrow. "Why am I a wretch? I thought I was

behaving myself." He turned her slightly away. "Here, tilt your head a little. That's it." He tucked the last of her pins firmly in her hair. "You're all put together again. Back to your prim and proper self."

He spoke as though there was something wrong with the notion. "It's the only way I know how to be." However, she wasn't really offended or even angry with Ian. He'd been wonderful to her throughout the tea. She grinned. "Except when I'm maniacally deranged, as I was in front of Lady Withnall."

He cast her another surprisingly tender smile. "No, you're perfect. You're Dillie Farthingale, often sensible, sometimes scared. Always enchanting. Don't ever let anyone tell you otherwise."

She hated when he was nice to her. He made her body parts tingle. More than tingle. They were on volcano-about-to-erupt alert.

He fished into the inside pocket of his jacket. "Here, I have something for you." He handed her a slender box.

A gift? From Ian? She closed her eyes a moment to cool her overly heated senses. "What is it?"

"Open it and see. I promise, it's no trick. Just as you were thinking of my firm and golden buns," he teased, "I was thinking of you. I was going to stop by your residence sometime later this week, but since we're here right now, there's no point in waiting. Go on, open the box. I think you'll like what's inside."

She nodded and smiled up at him, but was worried that he'd bought her an expensive trinket, the sort of elaborate jewelry that a man would purchase for his mistress. She could never wear something like that. Nor would she accept it. And what would her family say? "You don't owe me anything, Ian. I'm glad you've recovered and look so fit. I—oh, Ian! It's beautiful!" She gazed up at him and laughed. He'd bought her a silver brooch fashioned in the shape of an elephant gun. It wasn't fancy at all, didn't even have any precious gemstones worked into it. "I love it. It's perfect."

"Am I forgiven for teasing you?"

She nodded. "You're forgiven for everything."

He arched an eyebrow in confusion. "What else have I done wrong?"

"Nothing." And that was the problem. As far as she could tell, he had no faults, except for his desire never to marry.

That counted as a fault, didn't it?

CHAPTER 4

SEVERAL WEEKS LATER, Ian was comfortably ensconced in one of the overstuffed leather chairs in the larger club room at White's, nursing a finely aged Madeira port and contemplating his latest problem. The mahogany wood-paneled male sanctuary smelled of finely cured cigars, worn leather, oil polish, and newsprint.

He'd just ordered another glass of port when Graelem and Gabriel strode in. If Graelem was back in town, then the entire Farthingale clan could not be far behind. Cousins, aunts, and uncles from Oxfordshire, Yorkshire, Derbyshire, and heaven knows where else would all descend on the Farthingale residence on Chipping Way, eager to celebrate the start of this year's season.

He knew Dillie would not mind the noise or be dismayed by the lack of privacy, for she loved every single member of her unruly family. Quite a contrast between the Farthingales and his own miserable excuse for relatives.

"There you are," Gabriel said from across the room, earning frowns from the older gentlemen hunched in their chairs, reading their newspapers. "Where have you been hiding?"

"In plain sight." It was early April, still a little too soon for the marriage mart to fully hit its stride, but there were plenty of dinner parties, musicales, and soirees to keep those already in town entertained. He'd attended a few of those events, mostly those known to attract a faster crowd. He knew Dillie would not be permitted to attend these more risqué gatherings.

Ian set down the crystal wine glass he'd been absently twirling in his hand and rose as his friends approached.

"You weren't at Eloise's last night."

He shrugged. "Something came up. I couldn't make it."

Gabriel arched an eyebrow, but said nothing. He'd mellowed since his marriage to Daisy, no doubt due to her influence; she was the middle Farthingale daughter and the one who always strove to keep peace in the family. Graelem had married Laurel, the hot-tempered daughter. Graelem had a bit of a temper himself and needed a strong-willed woman to keep him in check, though it was Laurel's soft side that seemed to do the trick more often than not.

Dillie, the youngest of the Farthingale girls, although by only several minutes, seemed to have taken snippets of the best qualities from her sisters. She was as artistic as Rose, the eldest. She was spirited, but not as quick to anger as Laurel. She was as caring and loving as Daisy, and almost as clever as her twin, Lily. In truth, Lily was a freak of nature. No living being came close to her intelligence. Yet Lily always turned to Dillie first for advice.

Hell. He was thinking of Dillie again. He hadn't meant to, for he had bigger problems at the moment. Apparently Graelem and Gabriel were worried about something as well.

"We've just come from the Prince Regent. Those blackguards who tried to kill you last November weren't Napoleon's agents. No connection whatsoever. He's worried about you, wants to know who else might want you dead," Gabriel said, drawing him into a quieter corner of the club room.

Ian frowned. "I have plenty of enemies." *Including my own family.*

Graelem glanced around to make certain no one was standing close enough to overhear them. "That doesn't narrow it down much."

He'd told his two friends and the Prince Regent of the attack. Of course, he'd had to report it in full to Prinny, but hadn't gone into quite the same detail with his friends. If they ever found out that he'd recovered in Dillie's bed, or that she'd nursed him back to health, he would be a dead man.

He would tell them eventually. Now was not the right time.

"Forget about the incident. My only concern is that it represented a possible threat to the royal family. If it's just some husband after me for a supposed wrong, then leave it alone. I was hurt. That ought to be enough to satisfy the old clot who sent those blackguards."

Gabriel rubbed a hand across the back of his neck and sighed. "I still don't like it. You're being far too casual about the incident. You almost died."

He shook his head and crossed his arms over his chest. "First of all, I'm still alive. Second, no one would care if I did die."

"We would," Gabriel insisted.

"So would the Farthingale family," Graelem added. "You helped to save Lily when she was abducted and they're forever grateful."

"I didn't do all that much. Ewan and his Bow Street runners were the ones who saved her."

"What you did was important," Graelem insisted, getting that stubborn look about him. "Lily's parents, not to mention Dillie, were in unbearable pain. Those twins practically share one heart, and when they were forced apart, Dillie felt every painful rip. You stayed beside them the entire time, gave them hope that Lily would be found alive."

He arched an eyebrow. "Never realized I was quite that magnificent."

Gabriel punched him on the shoulder. "You aren't. But the Farthingales think you are."

Ian cuffed him back with a laugh. "I'm sure I can count on both of you to assure them that I'm an utter ass."

Several of the older members ruffled their newspapers and let out angry harrumphs.

Gabriel glanced around and caught the attention of a club steward. He pointed to the glass Ian had set down when they'd first walked in. "This is a woman's drink. We need a bottle of fine aged whiskey. Your best. Spare no expense. And three glasses sent to the billiards room. Put it on the duke's account."

Ian let out a laughing groan.

"Make that two bottles," Graelem added, but his grin faded once the ancient steward slowly shuffled off to do their bidding. "We have another matter to discuss with you. It concerns Dillie."

Ian's laughter faded. Had someone hurt her? He'd rip the blackguard apart with his bare hands.

"She has a suitor," Gabriel said once they'd reached the privacy of the billiards room and shut the door behind them. "Lord Ealing's eldest son, Charles. The Farthingales believe he'll ask for her hand in marriage soon."

Ian said nothing, for his body had just taken a hard slam to the ground. It was ridiculous, of course. He didn't plan to marry. He didn't want Dillie. So why didn't he want anyone else to have her? He was like the dog in Aesop's fable who didn't want the food in the stable trough, but wouldn't let the other animals have it either.

He ought to have been overjoyed for Dillie. Charles Ealing was a good man. A decent man. A simple man. Too bad Dillie would be bored to tears within a month of their marriage. "Give her my congratulations. I'm sure she'll make him a fine wife."

Graelem frowned. "She would, but he'd make her a terrible husband. We need your help to stop the wedding."

Ian had been in ill humor all day. The news about Dillie only put him in fouler temper. Dillie in love and getting married? He couldn't wrap his brain around it. He didn't want to think of the girl in another man's arms. He didn't wish to think of the girl at all. "There's nothing to stop. He hasn't asked her yet. Right?"

"That's right," Graelem said.

Ian lifted a cue off the rack and pretended to study it. In truth, he had the violent urge to break it over Ealing's head. Good thing the clunch wasn't at White's. Ian wasn't sure he'd let him escape this stodgy establishment alive. "Why are you two so eager to meddle in Dillie's affairs?"

"Bugger," Graelem muttered. "It isn't us. It's our wives. Dillie's sisters. They've got it into their heads that Dillie can't possibly love him. They're worried that she's feeling lonely because they're all married and out of the house. They don't want her to make a mistake she'll regret for the rest of her life."

"She's a clever girl, not likely to make such a blunder." But he'd seen the way Dillie had looked at little Ivy, the way she'd lovingly held her and inhaled her baby scent. Dillie was all about love and nurturing. She must have felt terribly alone these past few months, rattling about the empty halls now that all her sisters were gone.

He understood about loneliness. He'd spent most of his life feeling as though he were entombed in a coffin, trapped in a breath-stealing nothingness while everyone around him went about with their lives.

Dillie's sisters were busy leading their own lives, raising their own families. Dillie no longer knew how she fit in.

But how could he help? He wanted Dillie out of his life, out of his thoughts. How else would he ever regain control of his traitorous body? "There's a simple solution. Buy her a dog."

"Dillie needs a husband. The *right* husband," Graelem said, "not a damn dog."

"You're wrong. Dillie needs something to occupy her attention. A pet will do the trick." But Ian's heart was a pounding, thrumming riot as they stood glowering at each other in the private gaming room. The steward chose that moment to enter with their drinks. It was about time. Why couldn't he have come a little sooner, preferably before the conversation had turned to Dillie?

Ian was certain he heard the old man's knees creak as he doddered in. More creaking as he set down the bottle and glasses, then ever so slowly made his way out. How much time had elapsed? Hours? Weeks? Eons?

Well, perhaps he was a bit impatient. Patience had never been one of his virtues. Not that he had any virtues. Rakehells never did. So why were his friends dragging him into a Farthingale problem?

Graelem settled into one of the soft leather chairs while Gabriel grabbed one of the cues and set the balls on the table.

"Care to place a bet?" Ian asked.

Gabriel shook his head. "No. You always win. I prefer better odds when I wager."

Ian led off, giving his ball a sure, swift strike so that it hit the others with a precise spin. One ball rolled into the left corner pocket. Another caromed off the maroon felt backing and fell into the right corner pocket.

Ian called his next shot, made it, and then walked around the billiards table to face Gabriel. "Out with it. Why did you tell me about Dillie? And when did you two turn into a couple of old women? I'm not getting involved. I won't meddle in a wedding that may never take place." He turned to concentrate on his next shot, but struck his ball so hard it almost flew off the table. "Sorry. I've had a bad few months. Don't need more troubles piled on."

It wasn't a lie. Ian had recently discovered he had a half-sister, the result of his late father's illicit affair with "a woman of no consequence," as his mother had put it.

He might have felt sorry for his mother were she the sweet, caring sort, but she had ice in place of a heart and had never cared for anyone but herself. His father had been little better, a cold and bitter man who'd shown little love toward his family.

A far cry from the boisterous Farthingales, who obviously adored each other.

Ian stifled a sigh. Not long after he'd learned about his sister, she had died while giving birth to a married man's child. His friends didn't know about Mary because she had been born on the wrong side of the sheets. Illegitimate. His father's bastard. A scandal his mother had struggled mightily to quell, but not because she'd loved his father and been hurt by his straying. No. Celestia Markham loved only herself. She thought only of herself and hadn't wished the image of perfection she'd created in her own mind to be tarnished.

Ian and Mary had never met. Now she was dead, leaving behind a child. He had arranged to provide for Mary's daughter, just as his father had provided for Mary when he was alive. But seeing Dillie and the way she'd doted on Ivy had convinced him that he needed to do more. Arranging for a proper house and hiring a reputable nanny weren't nearly enough. The child needed affection, something he was ill equipped to provide.

Yet he couldn't turn to anyone for help.

Certainly not his family. In her typical twisted fashion, his mother blamed him for his sister's demise. No surprise there. She managed to blame him for all the ills, real and imagined, that had befallen their family. Two siblings dead now. Both deaths blamed on him. His father was dead, too. All he had was a mother who hated him and an illegitimate six-month-old niece who needed his protection. His mother would surely turn the child against him at every opportunity.

That was it. That was his family.

And his friends wanted him to save Dillie? Chances were, he'd be dragging Dillie into his little acre of hell.

Gabriel shot him a pained grin. "Our wives were hoping you would court her."

Ian's breath caught in his throat. He paused a long moment, and then threw his head back and laughed. "You're jesting. Right? They want her saved, not ruined. She'll never escape the tarnish if her name is ever associated with mine."

"She only needs to be courted by you long enough to discourage Ealing. Once he's out of the way, the plan is to have Dillie break off the courtship. You'll quietly retire to nurse your wounds and Dillie will be available once again."

"I can think of a hundred reasons why the plan won't work."

Graelem drained his glass of whiskey and poured himself another. "Such as?"

"Everyone knows that I don't intend to marry, so my intentions toward Dillie will be suspect." He raked a hand through his hair, wondering why they were even having this discussion. "Everyone knows what I am, so how can my attentions ever be considered honorable?"

Gabriel nodded. "I was never keen on the idea either. That, coupled with your stay in Dillie's bed last November—"

Graelem shot out of his chair. "What?"

Ian set down his cue and took a step toward Gabriel. "What the hell? Who told you that?"

Gabriel shrugged. "George did. Yesterday. He was in on the discussion with Dillie's sisters."

"*Hell and damnation!* And now her sisters know?" He shook his head and groaned. "They're not looking for my help. They want me to marry Dillie."

Graelem's hands were fisted at his sides as he approached Ian. "Can you blame them? You were in Dillie's bed."

"What's wrong with you? She wasn't *in* it at the time. I filed a complete report with the Prince Regent. Read the damn report. George can verify every word of it. I'm not marrying Dillie."

Graelem's expression remained ominously dark. "She never mentioned a word about you to her sisters. What does that signify?"

"Nothing, because there's nothing to tell," Ian insisted. Thank goodness, she hadn't blabbed the rest of it. If a Farthingale sneezed, the entire clan, from as far south as Portsmouth to the far north Scottish Isles learned of it within the hour. Farthingale news traveled faster than a North Sea wind. Farthingales did not keep secrets. Farthingales had diarrhea of the mouth.

Graelem wasn't halfway convinced. "Game over, Ian. Have a seat."

Ian could have told him to go to hell, that he was through with this conversation, but Graelem was big. Strong. And Gabriel was also frowning. He could take on one Dayne, but that would still leave the other.

He pulled back one of the chairs and sank into it. "As I just said, read the bloody report. Dillie and George saved my life last November, as you well know since the two of you have been investigating the matter. What is not relevant, and no doubt why no one mentioned it, is that George stitched me up in the only available bed at that moment. Dillie's bed." He glanced from one to the other. "Again, Dillie wasn't in that bed with me. Satisfied?"

Graelem's hands balled into fists. "Not nearly. What else haven't you mentioned?"

He wasn't insane. He wasn't about to let them know he had been naked in her bed. Or that Dillie had seen him naked. He wouldn't get out of White's alive if that little detail ever slipped out. "The point is, even a pretend match between me and Dillie is a bad idea."

He couldn't mention the kiss either. Or the one that had happened two years ago.

He turned to Gabriel. "Dillie has already had one dismal encounter with Lady Withnall. The old harridan will never let up if her name is ever associated with mine. You saw how Dillie responded at Daisy's tea. She's an innocent. Lady Withnall is a wolf on the prowl. She'll eat Dillie alive. So you see, putting us together in any way is a bad idea."

He sensed Gabriel was wavering, so he pressed on. "Are we done now? Good. Go back to your wives and tell them not to meddle in Dillie's affairs."

Though Graelem's eyes were still blazing, he finally cracked a smile. "Spoken like a confirmed bachelor. Tell Laurel what to do? Not if I value my life—or my husbandly rights. No way in hell. I'm keeping my mouth shut and letting Laurel do whatever she feels she must do to protect Dillie."

Ian rolled his eyes. "And you, Gabriel? Are you as big a coward as your cousin? Does Daisy rule your household?"

"I'm utterly whipped and proud of it. Submission has its rewards."

Ian groaned. "Bloody hell. I don't wish to hear any more. It's obvious you both lost your testicles when you acquired wedding bands." He polished off his glass and rose to leave. "There is a reasonable compromise to be had, however. I'll keep an eye on Dillie and Ealing. She did save my life, after all. I owe her. But I'm not going to court her."

HELLFIRE.

Ian grabbed his cloak and had just walked out of White's when Gabriel came chasing after him. "Hold on, Ian. We have to talk."

Ian turned to face him on the busy street. The sky was darkening and a cool breeze swirled around them. Ladies and gentlemen passed by with heads ducked against the wind, hands on their hats and fisted about their cloaks to hold them down as they hurried to their destinations. Had he been a little faster, he could have drawn his own cloak and disappeared into the crowd, just another gentleman hurrying down the street before the April skies opened up. "Didn't we just finish talking?"

Gabriel nodded and drew him aside. "We've been friends for a long time, been through some very bad times together. Friends look out for each other. You like her, don't you?"

"Who?"

Gabriel arched an eyebrow. "Dillie, of course. But she scares you."

Ian tensed. "If you knew me as well as you claim, you'd know that nothing scares me."

"I know. Not even death," Gabriel said with an indulgent nod. "But we aren't speaking of death here. This is far more serious. What you feel is something far more frightening. I know that look. Same look I had when I first met Daisy."

"You're wrong." Gabriel had been ready to marry. Meeting Daisy had made him realize how much he'd wanted to find love. Ian wanted to run as far away from love as possible. Love brought pain and disappointment.

He turned to walk away, but Gabriel held him back. "Why are you really in town?"

"I've already told you. Business."

Gabriel regarded him thoughtfully for a long moment. "If you have no intention of courting Dillie, then you can help her best by keeping away from her. Disappear for a while. Surely you have estate affairs to keep you occupied up north."

"I don't. Can't leave London for at least another month." Outright lie. He'd never lied to Gabriel before. Dillie was in London and he wasn't leaving. He needed to see her. He'd keep his distance. He just needed to see her openhearted smile. He needed her warmth to pierce his cold heart. Just once. Perhaps a little more than once. Maybe a dozen times. She had a great smile. She also had the gentlest hands. They'd felt so good against his skin. That's all he wanted, just a little more time with her. "Why are you now asking me to leave London? A moment ago you were asking for my help."

"Our wives were asking," Gabriel corrected, and leaned forward so that his voice would not carry on the blustery wind. "Frankly, I thought it was a decent plan, but I'm not so sure anymore. Don't get me wrong, Graelem and I would be delighted to have you as a brother-in-law. But your feelings for Dillie are dangerous. Something's going on between the two of you, whether or not either of you realize it or are ready to admit it. Your manner changes when you speak of her."

"My manner? What the hell does that mean?"

"I don't quite know. It's different, that's all. So I don't think you can manage a pretend courtship with her. More important, if you court her, I'm not sure she'll rebuff you."

"I'm the one who declined to court her, if you will recall. In any event, it won't come to that." Ian frowned. "I thought you said she liked Ealing."

Gabriel sighed. "She does. But he isn't you. And Dillie never said a word about caring for you in her bed. Not to anyone, not even to her sisters."

Second time he and Graelem had mentioned that. Ian understood that the Farthingale girls were close. They had a big, loving family. He'd wished for that when he was a boy.

It hadn't happened.

When his father died, his mother had summoned him. He'd gone to Edgeware ready to console her. She wasn't sad. "I hate you," she'd told him. "I wish you were the one dead."

She'd thought it important for him to know. He knew it, all right. He'd known her feelings for him since he was a child of four. That's when his brother had died. That was the first time she'd told him that she hated him. That's the last time she'd ever held him in her arms. And the last time his father had ever spoken to him.

"I won't hurt her, Gabriel. In truth, I'll do my best to keep away from her. But if Laurel and Daisy are worried that Dillie's about to do something foolish, let me know. I'll do what I can to help—short of marrying her, of course. I'll be available if they need me. As I said, I just can't leave London at present." Yet more lies told to his best friend.

The conversation put Ian on edge. Dillie wasn't in any danger of losing her heart to Ealing. She couldn't be, could she? And what of Ealing? He would have to be an utter clunch to resist Dillie, probably was already deeply in love with her. Hence the impending marriage proposal.

Ian's insides twisted. What could he offer Dillie? He had no intention of ever marrying. No, he was just that damn dog in the manger, ready to bite anyone who came too close to Dillie.

She wasn't his. He had no right to interfere with her happiness.

But he was going to do it anyway, just for this month.

He'd be careful.

No one would be hurt.

DILLIE SET DOWN the book she was reading and looked up as Rose burst into the Farthingale library, her eyes sparkling and her breaths coming in soft gasps, as though she'd run the entire distance across the park that separated their fashionable neighborhoods. "Dillie, there you are! I've been looking all over the house for you. What are you doing hiding in this musty library? Have you heard?"

Dillie closed her book and rose to greet her sister. "I love this room. There's nothing wrong with it. It's the coziest in the house. What's the important news?"

"It's about the Duke of Edgeware. His mother, the dowager duchess of Edgeware, is in town."

"Ian's mother?" Dillie's heart began to beat a little faster. This was her chance to learn more about him. Not that she wished to pry, but he had a penchant for getting into trouble, and it would be helpful to know whom to summon to his side the next time he lay close to death. Of course, this time she'd make certain he was dressed for visitors—even if she had to dress him herself.

Though it seemed an awful pity to cover up his gloriously hard body.

She let out an *eep* and forced herself to pay attention as Rose replied. "Eloise was paying a call on us when Lady Withnall stopped by with the news. Goodness," she said with a roll of her eyes, "that woman hears everything. I haven't a clue how she manages it, but she has everyone with secrets quaking in terror. She's worried about Edgeware."

Dillie tipped her head, confused. "Lady Withnall? I didn't think she cared about anyone."

"No, not her. Lady Withnall hurled that fireball, then dashed off to tell the rest of the world. *Eloise* is the one who's worried. She wouldn't say much, other than to reveal that there's bad blood between him and his mother. They don't get along. In fact, his mother detests him. She refuses to be within a hundred miles of him."

Dillie frowned. "Then why is she here?"

Rose shook her head and sighed. "I don't know. To cause mischief? Because she wishes him ill? I wonder what happened between them. No doubt his fault. He must have done something to insult his mother."

"Why would you ever suggest such a thing?" Dillie's frown

deepened and she felt the urge to clench her fists. Instead, she clasped her hands behind her back to hide her anger. "He helped us immensely when Lily was abducted, stayed beside us the entire time. He did everything for us, even used his vast resources to help track down her abductors. He didn't ask for a single thing in return. He calmed Mother and Father. He was strong and protective, stayed by my side even as I fell apart. If his mother hates him, it must be her fault. Ian isn't a beast. He's... nice."

Rose's eyebrows shot upward. "Holy crumpets!"

"What?" But Dillie felt the heat rise in her cheeks. She'd said too much. Now her entire family would know that she felt something for Ian. She didn't quite know what that something was, but he didn't deserve to be thought of as a horrid beast.

Rose raised her hands as though in surrender. "Daisy and Laurel said you liked him. I don't think they realize quite how much."

"Don't be ridiculous." But her ears were burning and so were her cheeks. Why had she defended him? She didn't know anything about him or his family. In truth, the little she knew of him was bad. He was a rakehell. He seduced other men's wives. He ran with a fast crowd.

On the other hand, Gabriel and Graelem liked him. More than that, they considered him a loyal friend. He was also very brave, having worked with Gabriel and Graelem to protect king and country from Napoleon's army, quietly risking his life and making no fuss about his valor.

She hadn't pressed Gabriel or Graelem about their exploits during the war years, for neither liked to speak of those difficult times. Still, she could ask them about Ian's exploits, couldn't she?

She dismissed the notion at once. No, not a good idea.

She wanted to believe Ian was a dissolute rakehell, because if Ian was something more, something better... well, she'd be utterly lost. Ian made her heart flutter.

A noble, heroic Ian... oh, she'd lose her heart to him faster than a hummingbird could flap its little wings. Fast and hard, that's how she'd fall for him.

"You're blushing," Rose accused. "You never blush."

"The library's musty. I feel a sneeze coming on." She did a

pathetic job of faking a sneeze.

Rose pursed her lips, a sign that her married brain was working up a plan. She began to slowly walk around Dillie. *Ugh!* She definitely had a plan in mind. "Have you seen Lord Ealing lately?"

The little pulse at the base of her throat began to throb. "Stop prowling around me."

"I'm doing nothing of the sort." She continued to circle her in a slow, deliberate manner that Dillie found most irritating.

"Yes, I saw Charles Ealing yesterday and will likely see him this evening at Lady Wakeford's ball." She wasn't particularly looking forward to it, but couldn't admit it to Rose. Everyone liked Charles. Her parents thought he was a perfect gentleman. She liked Charles, as well. She wished to like him more than she did. She wanted to fall in love with him and be in raptures when he proposed marriage.

However, he didn't make her skin tingle or her heart skip beats. She didn't think he would look very good naked. He was soft and lumpy.

Ian was hard and smooth.

She sighed. She had to stop thinking of Ian, for he could offer her nothing. As nice as he was at times, there was nothing to recommend him as a husband. Falling in love with Ian would condemn her to a life of loneliness and disappointment. And how would he be as a father? He'd been nice enough to Ivy the other day, but that required only a few moments of his time. How would he behave toward his own children? Would he bother with them at all?

Rose regained her attention by giving her a hug. "You let us know what you want, once you've figured it out for yourself. We'll support you, whatever your decision."

She returned Rose's hug. "I wish it were that easy. I'd love to have what all of you have with your husbands, and I don't simply mean marriage. You've all found love with the one partner in life who makes you happy, who believes in you and brings out the best in you, just as you bring out the best in him."

Rose cast her an indulgent smile. "You'll find it, Dillie."

She drew away slightly and sighed again. "When?"

"You're young still. It will happen. Don't be so impatient." But her smile slipped as she added, "If your heart leads you to the Duke of Edgeware, be careful. Learn all you can about him before daring to open your heart to him. It is a rare mother who hates her child as openly as the dowager duchess hates him. There must be a reason. Find out what it is as soon as possible."

CHAPTER 5

A GRAY MIST fell as Dillie stood on the steps in front of the Farthingale residence with Rose later that afternoon, watching Rose's sleek carriage draw up to the townhouse gate. "I enjoyed our time together," Dillie said, a little wistful as they hugged farewell. These visits were a rare pleasure, for Rose now had a thriving glassware business, a doting husband, and beautiful children who commanded her attention.

"Remember what I said about Edgeware," Rose whispered before scrambling up the carriage steps and climbing in. She stuck her head out of the window as the carriage began to draw away. "I love you, Dillie!"

"Love you, too." She grinned and tucked her shawl more securely about her shoulders to ward off the chill in the air and then glanced up at the sky again. The clouds were thickening. She sighed. This light mist would soon turn into a hard rain. She hoped it wouldn't ruin Lady Wakeford's ball this evening. She had been looking forward to it all week long. Her sisters, all of them save Lily, would be in attendance. Goodness, she missed them. It was no fun clattering about alone in this big house.

There was no help for it—she simply had to find herself a husband. How difficult could it be? She already had two men under consideration. The first was Charles Ealing, an amiable lord who genuinely seemed to like her. He had much to recommend him as well. The second was Ian Markham, who was not amiable in any way, and she didn't know why he'd even slipped into her thoughts.

He had no intention of ever marrying, didn't want the complication of a wife.

So why was she thinking of him? The Chipping Way curse was stuff and nonsense. They weren't destined to marry.

Goodness, the mere possibility made her shiver.

Dillie walked back inside. "Pruitt," she said as the Farthingale butler hurried forward to close the front door, "where's my mother?"

"Retired to her quarters for a nap. Your aunts have retired to their quarters as well, no doubt to refresh themselves before the Wakeford ball."

"Where are my cousins? Sleeping as well?"

Pruitt rolled his eyes. "I doubt it. Last I saw of them, they were upstairs in the children's quarters being read stories by their nannies. I hope these young ladies last longer than the pair they replaced."

"I'm sure they will. The younger boys aren't as wild as they were last year. They're growing into little men, and Lizbeth has turned into quite the young lady." She shook her head and let out a gentle laugh. "Amazingly, I'm sure they'll be no problem."

Pruitt nodded. "Truth be told, it is a little disconcerting to have the house so quiet. At first, I was afraid I was losing my hearing."

She shook her head and laughed. "But you haven't." Then she turned serious, nibbling her lower lip in thought. Pruitt had been in the family since before she was born and knew her family better than anyone else. He was loyal, clever, and a good judge of character. Though he never voiced an opinion, he always seemed to be standing close by whenever one needed him. "Pruitt, what do you think of the Duke of Edgeware?"

His eyebrows arched upward, an obvious sign of his surprise. "It isn't my place to say, Miss Dillie."

"But say it anyway. Please, Pruitt. It's important for me to know how you feel about him."

"No," he said, leveling a gentle, grandfatherly gaze on her. "What matters is how *you* feel about him. However, I can tell you that he isn't the sort to steal the silverware."

She frowned at him. "That isn't very helpful. I know he's honest. But what else is he?"

He shook his head and sighed. "You'll have to ask him. However, I don't think *he* knows the answer to that question yet."

Dillie thanked him and walked off to retrieve the book she had been reading in the library. Her thoughts were as muddled as ever as she made her way upstairs and retired to her bedchamber. She wished someone had answers to give her. Her twin had always been the one she turned to for advice.

She missed Lily.

By eight o'clock that evening, she and her parents were stepping down from their carriage into the cool evening. They made their way slowly up the grand steps of the Wakeford townhouse in the queue of guests to be announced. The rain had swept through London hours ago, leaving a starry sky overhead and a cool, but dry, breeze.

The receiving line moved quickly. Either that or Dillie was more distracted than she realized. They soon entered the hall and Dillie took a moment to glance about while their names were called out. The Wakeford home was ablaze with light. There were long tapers dripping wax from a row of crystal chandeliers lining the ceiling. The flames from the tapers reflected off the crystal fixtures in glistening bursts of red and amber. More candles blazed in decorative sconces along the walls, casting the elegant Wakeford home in a warm, golden glow.

Ladies and gentlemen chatted and merrily greeted friends as they removed their wraps and handed them to waiting footmen. Dillie stood back a moment to take in the display of finery, the breathtaking shimmer of silks and satins on the women and the fine black coats worn by the men. She glanced down at her own attire. She wore ivory silk trimmed with a pale blue ribbon immediately below the bodice. Her gown was quite simple compared with some of the more lavish designs worn by the older ladies—no bows or ruffles, no intricate lacework to complicate the style.

Her jewelry was simple as well. A strand of pearls adorned her throat, the necklace a family heirloom. Every Farthingale girl was expected to wear it at some point during her debut season. Being a twin, she'd had to wait until now, for Lily was several minutes older and had been given the pleasure last season. In truth, it was less of a pleasure and more of an ordeal, for neither she nor her sisters ever wanted to be the one to lose those precious pearls, something that could easily happen during the mad crush of a *ton* party.

Her sister, Daisy, had actually lost the necklace once. Fortunately, Gabriel had found it for her, and none of the family elders had ever learned about the incident. Dillie closed her eyes and silently prayed that she'd make it through the evening without any mishaps. When she opened them a moment later, Charles Ealing stood before her. "Miss Farthingale, you're looking as lovely as a gardenia blossom."

She smiled back at him. She disliked gardenias almost as much as she disliked sardines, but Charles had no way of knowing that. He looked surprisingly handsome. The black of his formal jacket slimmed his slightly round frame, making him appear taller and less lumpy than usual.

"My cousin is visiting from Little Dorking. Do you know her? Lady Mary Abbott? She was widowed last year and has finally rejoined the living, so to speak. I'm duty bound to offer her the first dance, but will you save the second for me?"

She nodded. "That will be lovely."

"Good. Good." He bowed over her hand and made a hasty retreat to the opposite side of the ballroom where his family stood in wait for him. Among them was a delicately built blonde beauty who appeared to be searching the crowd for someone in particular. No doubt she was the widow, for Dillie recognized all the other members of his family.

Dillie craned her neck for a better view. She couldn't see the Ealing family very well, for other guests kept getting in the way. However, she couldn't help but notice the widow break into a beaming smile as a gentleman approached her.

Dillie's heart sank. It was Ian.

Lady Mary was obviously pleased to see him, and her smile was in no way innocent. Foolishly, Dillie felt a small pang to her heart. Had she thought Ian would change his rakehell ways? Obviously, he had no intention of it.

"What matters is how the duke feels about her," Rose said, reaching her side and drawing her away from their parents. "My, he looks handsome. But doesn't he always? Anyway, that widow isn't the sort to hold his attention for very long."

"How do you know?" Dillie frowned at her. "You could be wrong."

Rose grinned. "But I'm not. Look, he's already moving away from her."

"That signifies nothing. He's probably arranged to meet her elsewhere and is now discreetly moving on."

"Trust me, he isn't going to meet her later. He isn't interested in what she's offering." They hadn't taken three steps before Rose began to unload more pearls of wisdom. Dillie hadn't asked for her sister's opinion; however, Rose was a Farthingale and therefore felt compelled to give it. "True, the widow is obviously moon-eyed over him, but look at the tension in his stance. Something's troubling him. His mother, no doubt. I wonder if she'll show up here this evening."

Dillie shook her head. "I hope not."

Rose let out a light, mirthless chuckle. "And Lady Withnall hopes she will. The tiny terror thrives on the misery of others. She adores ugly scenes. I'm sure the duke will slip away from the party if his mother does show up. He'd rather be thought of as a coward than ever allow their family troubles to be put on public display." She paused to study Dillie. "Not that anyone would ever consider him a coward. He's proved himself in battle. He can also be ruthless when pushed too far, so don't you go running to his rescue. He doesn't need your help. He doesn't need anyone's help."

Dillie didn't bother to reply since no response was necessary. However, she was grateful for the reminder about Ian. Rose's words were painfully true. Ian didn't need anyone. He didn't want anyone to complicate his life.

He didn't need or want her.

She took a deep breath and let it out slowly. "Charles has claimed the second dance. I had better write him into my dance card."

"Who's taking the first? Father?"

Dillie laughed. "No, his gout is acting up. Uncle George isn't here yet, and our cousin William has already disappeared into the card room. I suppose you'll have to keep me company in the meanwhile."

Rose locked arms with her. "Good, I haven't seen nearly enough of you lately. Gives us more time to find out about the duke's mother."

Dillie gazed at her in confusion. "You must be jesting. Didn't you just warn me not to get involved in his family woes?"

Rose rolled her eyes. "I warned you not to get involved with *him.* Hearing the latest gossip about him and his family is quite a different matter. Ah, there's Daisy. Laurel's with her. Oh, they're talking to Lady Withnall. I can see her egret feather madly bobbing in front of them. Utterly perfect. Let's join them. I'm sure the old snoop has plenty to tell us all. No doubt she spent the entire afternoon prying every sordid detail from the dowager duchess."

"Who was more than willing to disclose every rotten thing she could think of about her son." Dillie felt another small pang to her heart. What had Ian done to make the old dowager detest him so much? She thought of what her father often said. *People don't change.* But if that were true, how could one reconcile the detestable son and the Ian she knew?

Rose nudged her forward. "Come on. Let's greet them. It's the polite thing to do."

"Engaging in gossip, *encouraging* gossip, is in no way polite."

Rose shrugged. "Fine. I'm a snoop. So are you, though you're not ready to admit it. Stop dawdling. Lady Withnall, that bloodhound, must have spilled everything to Daisy and Laurel by now."

Rose grabbed Dillie's elbow and propelled her to Lady Withnall's side, where they exchanged warm greetings with their sisters, the feared harridan, and Aunt Julia, who had joined them. Though Julia had merely married into the family, she was just as much a snoop as any Farthingale and fit in perfectly. She was always at the ready with unasked for advice. Yes, a true Farthingale in spirit, though not a blood relation.

In truth, Dillie liked Julia and would always consider her a part of the family. Her husband, Harry Farthingale, had died years ago in Napoleon's war, and after a long period of mourning Julia had remarried. She seemed content in her new marriage, but had remained as close as ever to the Farthingale family. Dillie hugged her and received an equally enthusiastic greeting in response.

Another woman none of them recognized stood beside Lady Withnall. She seemed to be an old and dear friend of hers, for Lady Withnall was smiling broadly and appeared eager to make introductions.

As usual, the old harridan's gaze shot straight to Dillie. "Ah, my dear. You're just the one I was hoping to see."

Never a good sign. Dillie suddenly felt quite uncomfortable. Both Lady Withnall and her companion were staring at her intently. The pair looked like brilliantly colored birds of prey, dressed as they were in their dark silks. They sported matching egret feathers in their hair, and each was armed with a Spanish fan to cool herself as the ballroom began to warm.

Dillie wished she had thought to bring one along, for the heat of their gazes was quite suffocating. She glanced toward the open doors that led onto the terrace, resolving to escape into the Wakeford garden as soon as possible.

Daisy nudged her as Lady Withnall introduced the woman standing beside her, who turned out to be the dowager duchess of Edgeware. *Ian's mother!* Her name, ironically, was Celestia. Yet there wasn't a trace of heavenly kindness or warmth in the woman.

The dowager had Ian's gray-green eyes, but hers held no brilliance. She had Ian's honey-blonde hair, but hers did not appear natural. No doubt the strands had turned gray years ago, but dyes had been around for centuries and did wonders for those who wished to cling to their youth.

Dillie silently chided herself. Was she judging the woman too harshly?

There were no laugh lines at the corners of her mouth or crinkles of merriment at the corners of her eyes. This was a cold, bitter person who felt disappointed by life. Perhaps she had cause to be bitter, but Dillie simply didn't know enough about her yet to form an opinion.

Rose took no time in lighting a fuse. "A pleasure to meet you, Your Grace. We know your son, and are quite grateful for the friendship he's shown our family."

"Friendship?" She arched a haughty eyebrow and waved her gloved hand in arrogant dismissal of Rose's claim. "Then I doubt you know him very well at all."

Dillie clutched her dance card a little too hard, crumpling it in her tightening fist. *Keep silent. Ian doesn't need your protection.* "Oh, but we do," Dillie couldn't help but respond. "His closest friends are my brothers-in-law." She nodded to Daisy and Laurel. "Lord Gabriel Dayne is Daisy's husband. Lord Graelem Dayne is Laurel's husband."

Her sisters smiled back sweetly. She wanted to throttle them. Why weren't they jumping to Ian's defense? *Ugh!* Laurel never kept her mouth shut about anything. Why was she turning into a tight-lipped clam now?

"They also happen to be Lady Eloise Dayne's grandsons," Lady Withnall explained blithely.

"Of course, I know Lady Eloise. I hear her grandsons are charming boys," Ian's mother said, bestowing her own, cold smile on Dillie. "Both have turned out quite well. She must be awfully proud of them."

Lady Withnall nodded. "She is, though they did worry her for a time."

The dowager duchess nodded sympathetically. "My son's doing, no doubt. He must have been a terrible influence on them, but they've moved on and bettered themselves." She cast Daisy and Laurel smiles of acknowledgment. "Unfortunately, my son isn't capable of improvement. It pains me to speak ill of him, but his latest scandal cannot be overlooked."

"What scandal?" Julia—bless her—asked when all of Dillie's sisters seemed to have grown mute.

Dillie shot each a glower, but they merely responded with mawkishly innocent grins. Oh, why had she allowed Rose to drag her to Lady Withnall's side? No good would come of it. And why had she remained? She had legs, after all. She could walk away.

But she wasn't going to do it. She *wanted* to stand here and entertain their gossip. In truth, her actions were unpardonable.

"Well," the dowager began, her voice lowering. Dillie tipped her head forward and perked her ears. Ian would be livid if he knew what she was doing. She wouldn't blame him if he never spoke to her again.

On the other hand, if there was a scandal attached to Ian, she needed to know about it. How else could she help him? Lady Withnall would surely spread the shocking details across London before the night was out and someone had to stem the damage. She was that someone, for Ian wouldn't do anything to help himself.

The orchestra opened the dancing with a lively waltz, and the chatter in the ballroom grew louder as more guests arrived. Dillie moved a step closer to the two matrons, eager not to miss a word, though she knew Ian's mother couldn't be trusted to tell the truth. After all, she detested her son.

"Well, it's no longer a secret, so I may as well speak of it." The dowager's eyes took on a keen brilliance, as cold and bright as the diamonds she wore. She cleared her throat, as though hesitant to reveal the latest scandal attributed to her own son, but her eyes gave away her delight. "He's fathered a child and taken that child from its mother."

Dillie and her sisters exchanged startled looks. In truth, she had expected to hear some nonsense about his dallying with a married woman. Or a complaint about his being tightfisted with her allowance. But this—this surprised her.

"The mother's a nobody, but that doesn't excuse my son's actions. He simply wrenched the child from the poor woman's arms, turning a deaf ear to her pleas." She paused to heighten the effect, and appeared a little disappointed when no one uttered a disparaging comment. In truth, Dillie was in shock. Her sisters were as well. Not even Laurel could fashion a response. "Can one blame the poor young woman for what she did next?" she continued.

Rose was the first to find her voice. "What did she do?"

Ian's mother shook her head and sighed. "It is never easy for a woman to lose her child, but my son showed no mercy. That is so like him. Cold, cruel. He abandoned her to fend for herself. She had nowhere to go, no funds or family to take her in. She's dead now—"

Dillie gasped.

Daisy grasped her hand and gave it a little squeeze. She supposed the gesture was meant to calm her. Perhaps it was meant to convey doubt about the dowager's tale, for what sort of mother spilled gossip to strangers about her own son? Dillie wasn't certain about the reason, but she was glad for her sister's touch. That was Daisy in a nutshell. The thoughtful middle child, the conciliator. Daisy also knew how hurtful lies about one's honor could be, for she'd endured a tarnish to her own good reputation. Fortunately, Gabriel had seen beyond the lies and fallen in love with her. They'd had their happy ending.

She knew Ian would never have his happy ending, not if he continued on his current path. But how could she get him off that path? He didn't trust women. She glanced at the dowager. Her eyes were avidly gleaming, as though preparing for another attack.

She sighed inwardly. This woman had shaped Ian, doomed him to loneliness.

"My son will deny responsibility for her sad fate, just as he's denied responsibility for the other deaths he's caused."

"Other deaths?" Dillie repeated, her entire body now numb.

"Celestia, enough," someone angrily spoke from behind Dillie. She didn't need to turn around to recognize Eloise's gentle but commanding voice. That she'd referred to the dowager by her given name, and not *Your Grace* or other courtesy title, meant she was beyond angry. She was livid.

"Lady Dayne, so nice to see you." Rose leaned forward to buss her cheek.

Dillie did the same, adding a quick hug, for she was glad to have her join them and take Ian's mother to task. Eloise was the voice of reason. Eloise was all things kind and gentle. Yet, she was no fool. If Ian had done wrong, she would have been the first one to take *him* to task for it. "You don't know any of the facts. He's your son. Hear him out before you encourage the ugly gossip."

"Do you think I wish these horrid rumors to be true?" Ian's mother put a hand to her throat as though pained. Again, the cold gleam of her eyes proved otherwise. "He brings it upon himself. He shames our noble family. He's destroyed our good family name."

She added something more, but Dillie couldn't hear it. The Wakeford ballroom was now packed to the rafters with guests and much too noisy to continue discussion of this delicate subject. An elegantly clad couple bumped into her as they passed by, tossing apologies as they moved through the sea of bodies.

Noise and laughter filled Dillie's ears so that her head began to spin. She could hardly hear Ian's mother and the bitter words she was still spewing. "I cannot bear to speak of him," she continued, her voice half lost amid the growing din. "The mere thought of him, of his wanton ways and casual disregard of others, reduces me to tears."

However, Dillie noticed that she'd shed no tears. Was she being unfair to the dowager? Years of sorrow could have drained her of all feeling, wrung her out so completely that she had no more tears left to shed.

People don't change, Dillie reminded herself, struggling to shake off the dread that threatened to overwhelm her. Ian was either the worst human being alive, or horribly wronged. Was it possible that Ian had fathered a child? It would explain his fascination with Ivy. He'd been watching her play with the child several weeks ago at Daisy's house. He had definitely been studying them. Perhaps hoping to learn how to be a father?

Dillie exchanged desperate glances with her sisters. Were they thinking the same thing? They'd talk privately later, preferably after Dillie had spoken to Ian. He deserved to be heard, and she had so many questions to ask him. Would he bring the child to London? Was the child in London now? Was the child really his?

More important, was he properly caring for this precious innocent who deserved to be protected no matter how he or she had come into the world?

Dillie scanned the crowd, hoping to find Ian, for he would easily stand out amid the powdered faces in the ballroom. She wanted to slip away to talk to him. Now that Eloise had arrived, there would be no more gossip about him. She was relieved. She'd heard more than enough for one evening.

The orchestra, hidden in the balcony overlooking the dance floor, continued to play the opening waltz. Lord Wakeford was still dancing with his wife, and though they were a little on in years, they seemed to enjoy being in each other's arms. No wonder the waltz was all the rage in London. Who wouldn't adore being in the arms of someone they loved?

The choice surprised some of the older ladies who were expecting a traditional quadrille, but it delighted the younger ones who were eager to be swept into the arms of handsome suitors. She noticed Charles and his cousin among the dancers and knew they'd be occupied for the next half hour.

Dillie's legs felt weak. She politely excused herself and hurried through the double doors that led onto the grand terrace. A gentle breeze blew through her curls as she stepped outside. She expected to be alone, for it was early yet. The music had just started, so there hadn't been time for the room to heat up. Ladies and gentlemen were whirling and swaying in time to the music, too busy enjoying themselves to consider walking away from the gaiety.

Dillie wasn't feeling very festive at the moment. She needed time to think, to compose the questions she wished to ask Ian. She wondered where he was. Perhaps dancing? Or playing cards? Then she noticed a gentleman standing in a dimly lit corner of the terrace, his elbows resting on the stone balustrade as he gazed up at the stars.

Dillie shivered. It was a cool, clear night. A half moon cast its silver glow across the Wakeford garden. Thousands of stars twinkled brightly against the black sky. She slipped beside him and joined him in staring at the stars. "Good evening, Your Grace."

Ian laughed softly. It was a curt, mirthless laugh. "You shouldn't be out here, Daffy."

He'd called her Daffy, as he always did when trying to push her away. She gazed at him, wanting to ask questions and not knowing where to start. She had no right to pry into his affairs. She would have been quite put out if he'd meddled in hers. Not that she had anything going on in her life that would interest anyone. Nothing of interest whatsoever. Quite dull. Intensely boring.

She sighed.

He shifted his stance, now straightening to his full height as he returned her stare. "Are you going to gawk at me all evening? I assume you've heard the rumors."

She nodded. "Your mother told me about the child."

"My mother?" He tensed. "I see. She doesn't waste time."

"In cutting you to ribbons? No, she's rather good at it." She placed a hand on his arm and felt the ripple of his taut muscle beneath her fingers, as though he were steeling himself against her next words. "We Farthingales have many faults, but raising children isn't one of them. If you need any help with... goodness, I don't even know if it's a boy or a girl."

"A girl. Felicity."

Dillie smiled. "What a lovely name. So much nicer than mine. Daffodil. Ugh!" She let out a mock shudder. "If you need any help with Felicity, please ask. I'm not as experienced as my mother or sisters in caring for children, but I've stepped in and cared for several of my cousins whenever we've lost nannies, something that happens fairly often in the mad Farthingale household."

"Mad is an understatement." His lips curled ever so slightly at the corners and his gaze seemed to soften.

She blushed. "I don't mean to pry, but I'd like to offer my help. We're friends. It is what friends do... help each other out when asked. Though you haven't asked me. Perhaps you were afraid to impose, but it isn't an imposition at all." She was rambling now and couldn't seem to stop. "The point is, the child is innocent and shouldn't be blamed for what you and... er, her mother did. Not that I'm judging you. I don't even know what really happened. Nor do I expect you to answer to me. You don't owe me explanations."

She sighed, and then closed her eyes a moment to gather the thoughts still muddled in her head. "What I'm trying to say, and doing a rather bad job of it, is that I heard Felicity's mother died. I'm so sorry, Ian. No matter what your mother says, I don't believe you abandoned her or ripped the child from her arms. You'd never hurt the mother of your child."

He shook his head again. "Mother of my...? Is that the gossip? That I'm Felicity's father." He let out a deep, groaning laugh. "That's rich."

"You're not?" Dillie's heart leaped into her throat. "Why would your mother spread such a cruel rumor about you?"

He shrugged. "Don't know. Don't care."

"Of course you care. Anyone would care." Unbidden, she repeated what his mother had told her. She watched his expression, but it remained unreadable. His mother had maliciously distorted the truth in order to damage his reputation. Not that Ian had much of a reputation to protect. Still, he wasn't the beast his mother made him out to be.

"At first, I didn't know what to believe. That's why I went in search of you. Pruitt believes you're an honest man."

"Your butler?" He shrugged again. "High praise indeed."

"It is. He's never wrong. That's why I had to seek you out. I know you'll tell me the truth." Her hand was still resting lightly on his arm. She felt another twitch of his muscle beneath her palm. She could feel the tension flow through him like the angry flow of molten lava. "Will you talk to me?"

"No." He returned his gaze to the stars.

"Please look at me. Please, Ian."

"No. You shouldn't be out here. People will make something of it. Your reputation will be in tatters. You don't want to be caught on the terrace with a murderer, do you?"

She wanted to pummel him for his obstinacy. "I'm not out here with a murderer. I'm gazing at the stars with you."

He surprised her with a sudden, harsh laugh. "So, you think you know me?"

"Actually, not at all. And I don't wish to know you, because I may end up liking you more than is safe for me. Though you're doing your best to make yourself unlikeable right now."

"It's what I seem to do best."

"It's the way you defend yourself from pain. I understand that now, for after a few moments with your mother, my head is aching and my entire body feels numb."

Though he said nothing, she felt the slightest easing of his tension. She took it as a small sign of encouragement and continued. "I don't believe the rumors, and I don't understand why you're allowing them to circulate. You're a fighter, not a coward. Why aren't you defending yourself?"

"Because it's pointless to do so. And I don't really care what anyone thinks of me." He turned to her once more, staring down at her as he crossed his arms over his chest. "At least those marriage-minded mamas will turn their attention elsewhere. Not even the most desperate ones will encourage their daughters to marry a heartless killer."

She shook her head and sighed. "You know as well as I do that nothing, not even the hint of murder, will stop them. You're a rich duke, too good a catch to slow down their chase even for a day." She crossed her arms over her chest, mimicking his stance. "I know you didn't hurt anyone. I know you wouldn't ever harm an innocent. That's why I came to find you. I thought it important to let you know that you have friends. You don't have to fight every battle on your own."

"Consider the news delivered. Now go back inside and leave me alone."

"What you need," she said with a deflated grumble, "is a swift kick to your backside. However, what you need more is someone to put their arms around you, to hug you fiercely and let you know that they believe you. That they believe *in* you."

"You're not that person, Dillie."

The comment hurt, but she refused to let it show. "Perhaps not, but you'd better allow someone good into your life or you'll become just like your mother. Cold and bitter."

Oh, I've really crossed the line this time.

He moved close enough to take her by the arms and shake her soundly. Surprisingly, he didn't. His own arms remained folded over his chest, which only accentuated his broad shoulders.

"Go away, Dillie." His arms were like a closed gate through which no one would be allowed to pass.

Would Ian ever allow anyone in?

IAN WAS SO HUNGRY for Dillie he wanted to devour her. She wasn't a typical *ton* beauty, tall, blonde, and elegant with boring conversation and a calculating heart. She was a soft-hearted little snoop with big blue eyes that set his heart pounding whenever she glanced at him. She had a body that made him ache to hold her, and dark, silky hair he yearned to slip through his fingers.

He didn't want to think about that soft, kissable mouth of hers.

Unfortunately, all he could do was think about that mouth and how soft it would feel against his lips as he kissed her into eternity. *Hell.* He wasn't merely thinking days, months, or years with Dillie. He was thinking a lifetime and beyond. *Eternity.*

This was bad. He hadn't even slept with the girl. Nor would he. Not ever.

He kept his arms crossed firmly over his chest, fighting the urge to give in to all his damn urges and sweep her into his embrace, plant his lips on hers, and pour his heart and soul into one long, wild kiss.

More than one long, wild kiss.

Plenty of them. Wickedly wild, hot kisses.

She mistook his silence for disapproval. He knew by the way she sighed and dejectedly slumped her shoulders. In the next moment, her gentle hand was on his arm again. What was wrong with the girl? It would take nothing for him to ruin her reputation. Merely being caught alone with him, as they were now, would be enough to raise eyebrows. It could destroy her chances with Charles Ealing. The clunch would not be pleased to find them together.

Apparently, Dillie wasn't concerned. Was she even thinking of Charles?

She gazed up at him again, and he knew what she was going to ask before she'd opened her mouth to speak again. The girl loved family. The girl had a big, generous heart. She was thinking of Felicity.

He had to redirect her mothering instincts. He'd buy her a cocker spaniel to nurture, one with big, chocolate brown eyes and a happily wagging tail.

"If Felicity isn't your child, then whose is she?"

"None of your business."

"But—"

He fully turned to face her, now so close he could smell the scent of peaches in her hair. He felt a surge of anger—not aimed at her, of course. She squeezed his arm lightly, as though sensing his anguish. He was desperate to suppress all feeling. He was hurting. Dillie made him hurt. Dillie made him wish for things that were impossible.

Dillie almost made him feel good about himself.

He hated the feeling.

He wanted her to believe the lies his mother had been spewing. He wanted her to be angry with him, to condemn him and call him a lying bastard. He'd dealt with hatred all of his life. He knew how to handle it. He'd never received support and assurance. Until now.

Until Dillie. She believed in him.

He didn't know how to respond to that.

He was *afraid* to respond to that.

If he let her in, he'd inevitably disappoint her as he'd disappointed all who had ever mattered in his life. "Stop trying to save me, Dillie. I don't give a bloody damn what anyone thinks of me."

She sighed. "But I do. I can't seem to help myself. Do you want to know why?"

He kept silent.

"I'll tell you anyway. It's these words my father often says—though they're meant to apply to his business dealings, the caution is appropriate for friendships and other matters of the heart. He says that people don't change." She paused again, obviously hoping he'd respond. He wasn't going to encourage the girl.

"So," she continued, "I've given quite a bit of thought to what you are. Would you care to know what I think?"

"The answer is still no. Stop meddling in my business."

She let out a short, sweet laugh. "You forget that I'm a Farthingale. I can't help meddling. It's what we Farthingales do best. Snooping, prying, it's in our blood. Taking care of family is also in our blood. I can help. We all can help. Felicity—"

"Not this time. I know you mean well, but you needn't worry about the child. I have a capable staff to attend to her every need."

She shook her head. "That's where you're wrong. The child needs more than a roof over her head and food for nourishment. A child needs love. Lots of it. Something I suspect you've never had." She arched an eyebrow and cast him a gentle grin. "See how pitifully you turned out. Is that what you wish for Felicity?"

Despite his efforts, he laughed. "Did I mention you were stubborn and insufferable?"

She rolled her eyes. Lord, she had beautiful eyes. "Too many times to count. How old is she?"

He groaned inwardly. "You don't give up, do you?"

"No, not until I have my way. I'll stay here as long as it takes." She glanced toward the ballroom. The first dance of the evening was about to end. Guests were starting to drift to the doors and would soon be on the terrace, seeking the cool outdoors. "I'm not worried about my reputation. My family is too wealthy to be snubbed. So am I, though I won't come into my funds until I'm twenty-five, or sooner if I marry."

He held up his hands, as though in surrender. "Very well. I'll answer the question, if only to be rid of you. Felicity is about six months old now, just a little younger than Ivy. She isn't mine, though no one will believe it because of the family resemblance. Felicity is my niece."

"Your niece," she repeated in a whisper, the very softest expression written on her face. She didn't know anything about his family, yet she believed him.

"Felicity's mother is my half-sister. Her name is... was Mary Rose. We shared a father, though Mary was the result of an illicit affair. I didn't know her, never even knew she existed until fairly recently. My father's solicitor told me about her. She'd gone to him asking for my help and I gave it."

"How did she die?"

"Giving birth to Felicity. I don't know who the father is. She refused to reveal his name. I expect he's a married man."

"Probably a pillar of the community," Dillie remarked with a snort. "Isn't it always the way? I'm so sorry. I know you did your best to protect her. I'm glad you told me. Let me know if you need my help. In truth, I've been feeling lost lately, not quite sure what I'm supposed to be doing or where I belong in that big, empty house."

He arched an eyebrow. "Empty? Isn't it filled to the rafters with Farthingales now that the season is underway?"

She winced. "Yes, but it's different. Lizbeth and Charles are quite grown up now, and I hardly recognize them. Aunt Julia is married, so she and Harry are happily residing with her new husband. None of the Yorkshire Farthingales have arrived yet, and I doubt the Devonshire Farthingales will join us this year."

"Poor Daffy."

She poked his shoulder. "Stop calling me that, you ungrateful wretch. I came out here to help you."

"I know." His expression turned serious. "I also appreciate your desire to help Felicity. I'll take your suggestions into consideration."

She nodded. "Just remember, you don't have to be perfect. You just have to love her. She'll respond to that. And if you happen to bring her down to London, please think of me. I'd love to have my earrings tugged on and my fashionable hairdo destroyed."

He gently tugged on her ear. "Duly noted."

"Well, I had better go back inside." She held up her crumpled dance card. "Charles Ealing has claimed the second dance. Would you care to claim me for a dance?"

He arched an eyebrow. "No."

"I see. Of course." She looked so disappointed, as though she were a little cocker spaniel and he'd just kicked her.

He tugged on her ear again. "It isn't safe for you. That's all. Otherwise, I'd claim every damn one of them. Now that would set the gossips in a frenzy."

She appeared startled. "You would?"

He cupped her chin in his hand and tipped her head up so that their gazes met. "I would. Every dance."

And with those words, he felt the granite-hard shell he'd so carefully built around his heart begin to crack and crumble. He watched Dillie as she hurried back into the ballroom, her steps light and movements graceful.

He had to repair that protective outer shell. Fast.

He couldn't let Dillie in. Not ever.

He seemed to be saying that a lot. Yet she was getting in anyway.

CHAPTER 6

IAN HAD UNDERSTOOD long ago that his mother didn't love him and never would. His father hadn't loved him either, his method of showing his disdain perhaps crueler, for he never shouted at him or beat him. He treated him like a ghost. Invisible. Beneath his notice. As dead to him as his brother actually was.

His parents' contempt had been obvious to all in the Markham family. Unlike the Farthingales, his was a small family. One uncle and two male cousins on his father's side. Two spinster aunts on his mother's side. Since they all took their cues from his delightful parents, none of them liked him or cared a whit about him. Not a one, even though he had never shown them any discourtesy while growing up.

He rarely thought about them now. Until this week. Something was going on, some new plot hatching, and he needed to find out what it was. His mother hadn't visited London in years, preferring the quieter life at Bath with her sisters. Yet, here she was, attending the Wakeford ball escorted by his cousins, Simon and Edmund.

She'd wasted no time in efficiently spreading lies about him.

The attacks to his reputation were commonplace. He'd endured the rumors and snide gossip for years, had often gone out of his way to prove them true. He wasn't a saint. But the war years had changed him. As strange as it sounded, he'd gained a purpose to his life in fighting Napoleon's army, and actually liked doing the right thing, protecting king and country.

Still, nothing was going to change the way his family felt about him. Not medals, not royal honors. What were they hoping to accomplish by coming to London? He had the support and trust of the royal family. If anything, his scheming family would only land themselves in trouble.

Of course, they'd blame him for their woes.

They always blamed him for their woes.

He returned to the ballroom, preferring to remain by the open doors to the terrace in the event he wished to make a quiet departure. He wasn't enjoying the ball and had no intention of exchanging pleasantries with most of the Upper Crust in attendance. In truth, he planned on leaving shortly.

From his vantage point beside the ballroom doors, he watched his mother make her way into the Wakeford dining room for midnight sweets and other refreshments. She was escorted by his younger cousin, Edmund. Simon, the elder of his cousins, was now emerging from the card room. No doubt he'd lost a tidy sum, for he seemed angry. A desperate sort of angry. A dangerous mix of desperate and angry.

Ian had never thought much of his cousins. They were arrogant young men, and he trusted them not at all. Had one of them hired the ruffians who had tried to kill him last November? Perhaps both had been in on the plan, no doubt with his mother's blessing. Or at her goading. It would be easy enough to find out. He simply hadn't bothered to investigate.

In truth, he hadn't wanted their involvement confirmed. It was one thing for his mother to detest him, but to actually undertake to kill him? The thought made his stomach churn. What would she have to gain by it? Only Simon would benefit by his death, for he was next in line to the dukedom.

Simon shot him a malevolent look and stalked across the dance floor toward him. "Good evening, *Your Grace*. Seems you've disgraced the family again."

Ian caught the stale scent of whiskey on his cousin's breath. No surprise there since his cousin had been drinking all evening. *Great*. Desperate, angry, and drunk. Should make for a lovely conversation. "I'm surprised to see you here, Simon. Can't say I'm pleased."

"Didn't think you would be. I can't stand you either." Simon's insult might have been more effective had he been less drunk. He'd slurred his words so that they were almost unintelligible. "Never thought you'd kill a woman."

Ian arched an eyebrow. The man before him was falling-down drunk, had probably paid to have him killed, but *he* was the disgrace. Ah, his family was an endless font of joy. "I didn't, as you well know. Don't tell me you're starting to believe the lies you've been spreading? I might have to do something about that."

He returned Simon's gaze with an icy one of his own, pleased when his cousin paled and took a small step back. Simon was a big man, built like a bull. He had the temperament of a bull, as well. Easy to rile, always stomping and angry.

Ian wasn't in the least intimidated by him. He was almost a head taller than Simon and much stronger. A lot angrier, too. A cold, quiet anger. Far deadlier than Simon's bluster.

"You're a bastard, Ian."

That's clever.

"Been down to the docks lately, Simon? You ought to get your advance back from those wharf rats. After all, they didn't accomplish their task. I'm still alive. Still duke."

His cousin shot him a glower, his Markham green eyes showing no warmth. "Not for long, I hope."

Ian put an arm around Simon's shoulder, a gesture that might appear friendly to others who were passing by but wasn't. Simon was desperate to inherit the dukedom. Ian wasn't about to hand it to him on a silver platter. The man was a wastrel. He'd never worked a decent day in his life. Yet he knew how to spend. Mostly, he knew how to lose at the gaming halls. He'd destroy the Edgeware holdings within a few short years of acquiring them.

Ian tightened his grip on his cousin's arm. "Try that little stunt again, Simon, and I'll cut off your bullocks and stuff them down your throat. I know it was you and Edmund who planned the attack on me. He's a little toady, always ready to do your bidding."

Since his hand was still on Simon's shoulder, he felt the shudder that ran through the arrogant sod. *Sniveling coward.* Edmund, without Simon to lead him astray, might have made something of himself. But he was the younger brother and worshiped his older sibling. Much as Ian had worshiped his own brother.

"You got away with it because I let you get away with it. I won't be so generous next time." He tightened his hold on Simon until he saw his cousin flinch. "Understand me?"

"You're breaking my arm," Simon said in a harsh whisper. "Let go of me."

"Give my regards to Edmund and my mother." Ian released his cousin and watched him scurry into the dining hall, no doubt to complain of his mistreatment. He reminded Ian of a frightened, squealing pig.

"You all right?" Gabriel asked, coming up beside him and offering him a glass of champagne.

"Never better." He wanted to step outside to cool down, but Gabriel would know he was rattled and ask questions that Ian had no desire to answer. He drank the offered champagne and turned away, pretending to watch the dancers as the orchestra struck up a lively gavotte.

Hellfire.

He saw Dillie amid the dancers, stepping and twirling to the music in the arms of Charles Ealing. The bastard had claimed her for a second dance. "Bloody great ball. So glad I came. Having a wonderful time."

Gabriel arched an eyebrow. "Surlier than usual, aren't we? It's those stupid rumors. What can I do to help?"

"Get lost, Gabriel." His gaze remained on Dillie, who appeared to be having a glorious time. Damn the girl. Damn him that he cared. "Who appointed you my nursemaid?"

"No one, you ass. But you look like hell. I thought I'd offer my help."

Ian sighed and turned to face his friend. "Sorry. I appreciate the offer. No need to help. I have it under control."

He drained the contents of his glass, set it on the tray of a passing servant, and started for the terrace once again. He was in need of cooling down before he did something stupid like flatten Simon, Edmund, and Charles Ealing. Not that Ealing was doing anything wrong. He wasn't. But Ian didn't like the way he had his hands on Dillie.

He didn't like the hungry way Ealing was eyeing Dillie.

Until this moment he hadn't considered Ealing the sort to take a step out of line, but the clunch had been drinking, and Dillie looked breathtakingly beautiful. Innocent and beautiful.

Any man would want to put his hands all over her.

Of course, he'd have to kill Charles Ealing if he tried.

He knew he was being surly, just as Gabriel had said.

"I know what you're thinking, Ian. Not a good idea."

He turned to face Gabriel, only now realizing that his friend had followed him outdoors. He frowned. In truth, he was out of sorts and thinking the worst of everyone, whether or not deserved. Still, Ealing was in his cups and obviously feeling randy. His hands kept sliding down Dillie's back. Dillie wasn't liking it. She kept easing out of his grasp.

Ian suddenly felt possessive.

He knew he was being unreasonable. Behaving as though Dillie was his. Not that he planned to do anything about it. Still, he didn't want anyone else touching her. *Dog in the manger again.* He couldn't have her. Didn't want anyone else to have her. Didn't like that Ealing had her. He wanted to flatten Ealing. One punch. That's all it would take.

"Ian?" Gabriel's hand was now on his shoulder.

He shook his head and sighed. His family hated him, had tried to kill him, yet he was mad as a hornet because Ealing was dancing with Dillie. *Damn.* He'd earlier told Gabriel that he had matters under control.

It wasn't true.

He was a shambles. He didn't have anything under control.

DILLIE REALIZED THAT she ought to have been paying more attention to the gavotte. She'd stepped on Charles' feet at least twice so far, but he'd forgiven her each time. He was a little drunk and probably feeling pleasantly numb, which was a good thing since he hadn't noticed that she'd just stepped on his foot again.

His hand slipped a little lower on her waist so she moved it back up. He apologized, obviously doing his best to concentrate, though the champagne and whiskey he'd imbibed throughout the evening had obviously fogged his brain.

He must have knocked back quite a bit more than a few drinks.

She'd had three or four glasses of champagne herself, which explained her inability to concentrate on Charles or their dance. Her gaze constantly flew to Ian, who was standing against the wall, arms still folded across his chest, looking quite daunting. He stood alone, stiff as a crossbeam, as though propping up the wall.

He unfolded his arms as Gabriel approached and handed him a drink.

Charles let out a yelp.

Dillie returned her attention to him. She really had to be more careful. "I'm so sorry! I've stepped on your toes again."

"You're forgiven. I think you're tired," he said gently.

She nodded. "I'm not used to all the dancing and excitement."

Charles held her a little too closely as they continued the gavotte. "The London season can be quite overwhelming, even to those of us who have experienced it over the years. This is your first. You'll get through it."

"Actually, this is my second season."

He shot her a blank stare. "You were in town last year?"

"Yes, I'm certain we discussed it." No matter, most society conversations were vapid and easily forgotten. "But I am quite spent," she admitted. "We country girls aren't used to these late hours."

His eyes brightened and he cast her an odd, rakish smile. "Ah, I've heard that country girls quite enjoy their beds at night."

Dillie agreed, for the cool breezes and outdoor activities had a way of tiring one out. "Quite so. Nothing better."

"I love country girls. They're lots of fun. Lots of fun indeed."

She nodded, not sure why his eyes were suddenly gleaming like two bright lanterns and his smile was now an open-mouthed, toothy grin.

"Perhaps we should end this torture and take a stroll on the terrace," he suggested. "My cousin is out there and will be grateful for the company."

Dillie agreed without hesitation. The scent of hot, sweating bodies now permeated the ballroom and left an unpleasant tickle in her nose. Charles had a pungent air about him as well. The promise of a lilac-scented walk in the cool of the evening sounded perfect. There was nothing untoward about a casual stroll since they'd be joining Lady Mary. He'd mentioned her several times during their dance, obviously concerned for her welfare.

The torch-lit terrace was crowded as they stepped out onto it, but Dillie enjoyed the pleasant breeze. At least thirty guests stood about in small groups, the ladies fanning themselves while some gentlemen smoked cigars. Others held drinks in their hands. "I don't see Lady Mary," Dillie remarked, craning her head to search beyond the immediate crowd. She leaned over the balustrade to look across the flower beds. It was early spring and only the lilacs, primroses, and bluebells were in bloom.

Charles also looked around. "She may have walked to the fountain. She mentioned earlier that she might. Let's have a look."

"It's awfully dark back there. Do you think she would have strayed so far on her own?" In truth, the garden wasn't very large and most of it could be seen from the terrace, but there were a few dark nooks, no doubt where lovers hid to do all the naughty things she had been warned never to do.

"This is her first ball since her husband's death. I'm worried about her. Will you help me find her?"

Dillie hesitated. She trusted Charles, but didn't wish to walk into one of those dark places with him. Yet he seemed genuinely concerned for his cousin.

He took her hand and pressed it lightly. His fingers felt hot and clammy. "She might be feeling lonely. I wouldn't know what to say to comfort her. I'd be most grateful if you stayed with me."

She agreed for several reasons. First, he truly appeared concerned. Second, he wasn't likely to make it down the steps on his own, for he was swaying and in danger of falling flat on his face. She placed her other hand under his arm, bracing his weight against her shoulder. "Of course. I'll be glad to help."

Charles smiled that odd, drunken smile again.

She managed to guide him down the terrace steps and endure his overly enthusiastic gratitude. He leaned close. He still felt clammy and smelled pungent. He reached for her hand again, and missed when she hastily stepped back.

He tried again and wound up giving her hand a sloppy, wet kiss.

Ugh! She felt as though Jasper, her brother-in-law's enormous sheepdog, had slobbered over her fingers, for Charles' tongue was that wet and sticky. She extricated her hand from his grasp. "Stand still. You keep falling on me."

He giggled.

Crumpets, perhaps he's a little more drunk than I realized. She sighed. "Come on, let's find Mary."

They made their way onto the pebble pathway between the flower beds and yew shrubs, and he began to call out his cousin's name. Then he made a lewd rhyme out of Mary's name.

Dillie frowned. "Be quiet, Charles."

"Why should I?" Another giggle. "You're a country girl. You've said so yourself."

What did that mean? A little prickle ran up her spine. Being out here alone with him suddenly didn't seem quite so sensible. "Why don't you stay right here while I look for her? I think it will be easier if I search on my own."

"Can't let you do that. It isn't safe. I must protect you." He swayed as he spoke, back and forth like a tree branch on a stiff breeze. His speech was slurred, and his grin was little more than an unattractive leer. He hiccupped. Lily had once explained to her the intensifying effect of cold air on an inebriated person. Something about the fermentation process within one's body. She hadn't paid attention at the time. Her mistake.

Charles still had that odd glint in his eyes.

"Don't move," she commanded. "I'll find her. Wait right here."

He nodded. "Right here," he said, pointing to his toes.

She rolled her eyes. Would this evening never end? For the most part, Charles was an amiable fellow. She tolerated him when he was sober. She didn't like him nearly so much when he was drunk, for he was far cruder and more... uninhibited than she'd realized. He also believed himself to be irresistible to women.

Ugh! He wasn't.

Dillie turned a few corners and came upon the fountain. It was surprisingly dark here, no moonlight glistening on the water, for the moon was presently shrouded in a passing cloud. The terrace was no longer in view.

The strains of a waltz filtered through the gently rustling lilac leaves, and Dillie suddenly realized that the music from the ballroom would drown out any noise from the garden. The guests taking air on the terrace wouldn't hear her if she cried out.

But why would she? She was in no danger.

"This way," Charles urged, suddenly coming up behind her. "I think I see her sitting alone on a bench."

Dillie gasped.

She didn't see any bench, or anything remotely resembling the outline of a woman. "I told you not to follow me." She curled her hands into fists.

Charles frowned. "You took too long. I was worried about you."

"I can take care of myself."

He took a step closer, seemingly offended. "How was I to know that? Don't you trust me?"

"I had better go. My family will be worried about me." She tried to step around him, but he grabbed her hand and forced her up against him, his breath now unpleasantly hot against her neck.

"Not yet. Stay with me, country girl. No need for pretense." He emitted a silly laugh that nonetheless felt dangerous. "You've been playing coy with me all evening. I know what you really want. Mary told me so. She said I ought to do something about it. Are you hot for me, Dillie? Shall I do something about it?"

She tried to push him away, but he was heavier than she'd realized. "Actually," she said with a grunt, shoving at him with all her might, "Mary's wrong. I don't find you pleasant at all. You're disgusting and I'd like you to go away."

He seemed surprised, but not at all deterred. He bent to kiss her and managed to land his tongue in her ear. "I don't believe you." He tried to kiss her again, and this time his wet mouth landed half on her eyelid and half on her nose. *Ew!*

"Let go of me. Now!" She drew her hand back, and then swung it forward with all her strength, resulting in a resounding slap across his face.

Perhaps not the best idea.

He was on her again, this time angry. His hands clamped around her back and moved downward to cup her buttocks. "No need to play hard to get. I know how you like—" She slapped him again. Hard. Too bad she didn't have a decent stick to use as a club to pound him over the head or shove up his—*Ow!*

His grip tightened painfully on her arms. "Did you expect me to believe your innocent act? I know I'm not your first."

"What?"

He laughed. "How many before me? Mary said you were no virgin. In truth, I don't care. You'll find me most accommodating."

"You're attics-to-let if you believe your cousin's drivel. Why would she say such a wicked thing about me?"

He jerked her backward, pinning her against a tree. She felt the painful prickle of rough bark against her skin. She tried to escape, but he had her trapped between his arms. "And now to claim what's mine."

"No!" She poked him in the eye, and was about to raise her knee to kick him in his male parts when he suddenly peeled away with a shriek. She heard a splash, and then heard him sputter. He must have landed in the fountain. How?

"I believe the lady said no." *Ian! Crumpets, I'll be in for a lecture now. From him of all people!* "I suggest you go home and dry off, Ealing. Don't let me catch you near Miss Farthingale again."

Charles staggered to his feet, soaked from head to toe. "So that's how it is? You and Edgeware? Mary warned me. I ought to have listened." He turned to Ian. "You can have the deceitful bitch. She's good for nothing but her dowry."

"I wish you hadn't said that." Ian left Dillie's side. She heard his fist slam against Charles' jaw and heard Charles yowl in response. Then she heard another splash as Ian tossed him back into the fountain. More sputtering as he staggered out of it.

"I'll get you for this, Edgeware! You'll be sorry."

"Get in line," Ian snapped back. "There are others ahead of you."

Charles, soaking wet and angry, started back toward them. Ian nudged her behind him and took a step forward, fists raised. "You really want to do this, Ealing?"

Dillie heard the snap of twigs and rustle of bushes as Charles came to his senses and ran off.

"Odious man," Dillie muttered after him.

Ian turned to face her. It was too dark to see his rage, but she sensed it. "Damn it, Dillie," he said, the words coming out as more of a groan than a shout. In truth, he wasn't shouting at her at all. "What were you doing out here alone with Ealing?"

She cast him a weak smile, though she doubted he could see it in the darkness. "Obviously, I was doing my best to fight him off. He lured me out here on the pretense of searching for Lady Mary. I don't suppose she was ever out here. I feel so stupid." She heard the gentle trickle of water in the fountain and the soft breeze dancing through the leaves. She heard Ian's quiet breaths as he brushed a stray curl behind her ear.

"Did he hurt you?" There was something achingly sweet in the way Ian touched her. Then the moon slipped out from behind a cloud and she saw the concern etched in his handsome face.

She felt her eyes well with tears and knew she was about to cry. She struggled to keep those tears from streaming down her cheeks. "Only with his words. I'm fine. Truly. I ought to have realized that he only wanted me for my trust fund."

Ian took her trembling hands in his, holding them gently against his chest. His heart was beating calmly, not pounding or racing as hers was. "He didn't mean it, Dillie. He was hurt and not expecting to be rebuffed. Now that Mary's free to marry again, she's taken a closer look at the Ealing fortune that Charles will soon inherit. Probably didn't like that he was interested in you, so she did her best to undermine your courtship. He might have seen through her lies had he been sober."

"He's horrid. He ought to have known better. How could he believe her? How could he think I was that sort of girl? I'm going to hit him again when I see him."

Ian let out a soft laugh. "You'll only break your hand. He isn't worth the effort."

"I suppose not. Still, he made me feel dirty." She shuddered. "But you were wonderful. Thank you for coming to my rescue."

"You would have managed to extricate yourself," he said, his manner still gentle. He smelled of sandalwood and a hint of spice, not at all stale or pungent. "I just made certain it happened sooner."

She eased away to sit on the stone rim of the fountain. She was still trembling and needed to hold onto something hard and firm. Just not Ian. He felt too good. She wasn't certain she'd ever let go of him. She wanted to breathe him in. She wanted to feel his warm skin against her palms. Instead, she gripped the hard stone. "This has been an awful night for you. I'm sorry I made it worse."

He eased his large frame beside her. "You didn't. I felt like hitting something. You gave me the opportunity. I ought to be thanking you."

She shook her head and laughed.

He took her hands back in his and held them loosely. "You're cold. I'll walk you back inside."

She took a deep breath. "I think I need another moment. Do you mind?"

"Take as long as you wish."

He kept hold of her hands, lightly rubbing them to keep them warm. However, he maintained a loose grip. It was his way of showing her that she could pull away at any time. Unlike Charles, he had no intention of forcing her to do anything she didn't wish to do.

He was being Good Ian again.

Good Ian was dangerous.

Good Ian made her want to be very, very bad. Only with Ian, of course. It wouldn't be fun to be bad with anyone else.

"Charles is bigger and stronger than I realized, but I wasn't afraid of him. I was thinking of Lily and how she must have felt when she was abducted, carried out of London, and held captive by a man she'd always considered a friend. Her ordeal lasted for several days. Mine lasted less than a minute, yet I'm still shaking."

Her eyes began to water again. "Lily kept her wits about her, escaped some very dangerous ruffians." She took a ragged breath. "I know it happened almost a year ago, but it feels like yesterday. She was the one in danger, but look at me. An inebriated lout tries to kiss me, and I can't stop trembling. I think I'm about to cry. I'm such a ninny."

"No, you're not."

"Then what am I? Other than a bank account to be courted by an amiable clunch who, it turns out, is not so amiable after all?" She drew another ragged breath. "I ought to be disappointed, but in truth, I'm relieved. I've never felt anything for him. Try as I might, I couldn't summon up the least bit of excitement." She rested her head against Ian's shoulder. He felt warm and inviting. "I think I'm doomed to be a spinster."

Ian let out a deep, rumbling laugh. "Dillie, there'll be a dozen young men at your doorstep by tomorrow, all of them eager to court you. They'll want you, not your trust fund."

They sat side by side a little while longer, Ian gently holding her hands and she still leaning her head against his shoulder. She liked this. Felt safe beside him. His arms were hard and strong.

He cleared his throat. "Ready to go back inside?"

"No. This is nice. I could sit like this for the rest of the evening. Perhaps forever."

"Forever," he repeated softly. "That word seems to come up often around you."

She turned to him, confused by his comment.

He cleared his throat again. "We had better go inside."

CHAPTER 7

DILLIE AWOKE LATE the following morning, nursing a headache. She was still out of sorts and dreading the arrival of friends and acquaintances who would call upon the Farthingale family within a few hours. The day was cool and overcast, but the guests would come even if the skies threatened a hard, wind-driven rain. There was too much juicy gossip to be discussed, dissected, and distorted around the fashionable salons of London.

Horrid weather was no impediment when the peccadillos and scandalous perversions of the nobility were involved.

Dillie joined her mother and Aunt Julia in the breakfast room. The pair sat at the table, enjoying a late breakfast of sausage and kippers, their quiet chatter punctuated with the occasional gasp, soon followed by "no, you don't say!"

Dillie managed a cheerful greeting, though she felt certain dragons had slept in her mouth last night, their flames aimed at the back of her throat. She walked to the sideboard and stared at the smoked fish resting on the silver salver. Its lone eyeball ghoulishly stared back. *Oh, I feel ill.*

Her stomach voiced protest as she was about to spoon a hefty serving of that fish onto her plate. She reconsidered her breakfast strategy, set down the spoon, and grabbed a delicate teacup, though she wasn't certain she could hold down even that gentle liquid this morning.

Since she had to eat something to stop the angry rumbles gurgling inside her, she decided to nibble on a scone, take it slow, and pray she was able to hold it down.

"Sophie, you must tell her before she hears it from anyone else," Julia said, exchanging a woeful glance with her mother.

"I know. I know." Her mother sighed softly, and then motioned for Dillie to take the seat beside her.

Dillie obeyed, dragging a raisin scone and cup of tea along with her. Once seated, she waited for the news that her mother so obviously dreaded having to tell her. "Is everything all right? Father? My sisters?"

"They're fine. No, this isn't about our family." She took a deep breath and then let it out slowly. "He isn't for you. In truth, I've never liked him."

"Nor did I," Julia chimed in because, no doubt, her opinion mattered as well.

Her mother nodded. "But we didn't know how to tell you. Nor did we think it right to interfere—"

Dillie choked on her tea. *You always interfere!* Of course, she wasn't going to accuse them of it since she was just as determined to meddle in Ian's affairs. For his own good, of course. Someone had to save him. He'd thank her for it later. Meddling? Yes, Farthingale curse. "Who are we talking about?"

"Oh, dear." Her mother batted her long, dark eyelashes over expressively sad eyes.

Dillie had always loved her mother, even those times when she was so overwhelmed with the never-ending parade of visiting relatives that she forgot she'd ever given birth to her five daughters. "You! I think you're one of mine," she'd sometimes call out in her dizzier moments, struggling to recall that her name was Dillie, or that yes, she'd popped out of her mother with the other daughter whose name she also couldn't recall.

Not that Dillie ever blamed her. How could she? Her mother managed a household constantly filled to the rafters with family from all parts of England single-handed, made them all feel loved and welcomed, tolerated the horde of young cousins who constantly crawled underfoot, and took care of their father—Dillie loved him dearly as well—who was always calling out to her for help in finding one object or another that he'd just set down and that was obviously still in front of him.

This morning it had been his mustache clippers.

It was to be expected. Apparently, male eyeballs didn't know how to look down, unless it was to stare—with eyes bulging—down a woman's bosom. Her father, to his credit, never looked down anyone's bosom but her mother's. He was wildly in love with her, came alive whenever he caught sight of her even after thirty-five years of marriage, even though her dark hair was now dappled with gray and tiny lines were etched at the corners of her gentle blue eyes.

"Who are we talking about?" Dillie repeated when neither her mother nor her aunt seemed able to find her voice.

"Lord Ealing," her mother said, letting out another long breath.

"Charles?" *Crumpets!* What had they heard about the incident at the fountain? Did they know she was the girl involved? Dillie's instinct was to panic. Had Lady Withnall seen her and Charles by the fountain last night? Had she seen Ian tossing Charles into the fountain? Or seen Ian comforting her?

Then again, nothing untoward had happened between her and Ian. She had nothing to be worried about in that regard. In truth, she wished that she did have something to be worried about, because having Ian's arms around her and his lips planted on hers, probing the depths of her mouth, would have been great fun.

But nothing had happened. Not a blessed thing. Ian hadn't felt the slightest urge to conquer or plunder her.

No, he'd been a perfect gentleman.

Drat.

"Seems Charles and his recently widowed cousin—"

"Lady Mary Abbott?"

"Precisely." Her mother cleared her throat. "Seems they are rather *close* cousins."

Julia leaned forward. "Tell her just how close."

"Oh, Dillie! My sweet, innocent child. They were caught in one of the Wakeford bedchambers in a most embarrassing position."

"Lord Ealing's clothes were off and thrown wet on the floor," Julia intoned.

Dillie felt her cheeks grow hot. "Poor man," she said, feeling not a whit of remorse. She dared say no more, for her mind was as scrambled as the eggs she usually ate in the morning. Not this morning. Her stomach was in full revolt. "Wet, you say? He might have fallen into... oh, who knows? Perhaps the Wakeford fountain. He imbibed quite heartily last night. Accidents happen." She tittered.

Ugh! She never tittered.

"Perhaps so," her mother said with a slow nod, "but that doesn't explain why Lady Mary was caught naked beside him."

"Or why her clothes were lying beside his, bone dry," Julia added.

THE GOSSIP WAS repeated later that afternoon in front of their visitors, among them two attractive eligible bachelors, Lord Randall Whistlethwaite and the honorable Geoffrey Harding. Neither was anywhere near as handsome as Ian, but Dillie was pleased to see them nonetheless. Ian had predicted that other suitors would come forward now that Charles was no longer in the hunt, so to speak.

Still, she was suspicious of these new characters. Neither young lord had shown her the slightest interest before today.

They told her she looked lovely. They expressed their horror at what Charles had done, confirming that he was a base ogre and she was fortunate to be rid of him.

She smiled prettily. She was very good at smiling prettily, having perfected the art after a mere dozen years of training. She could also walk across a room balancing a book on her head, something Lily had never mastered. That book would be in Lily's hands and she'd be reading it before she was halfway across a room.

Dillie glided to the door in her fashionable tea gown of palest rose velvet to greet more callers. She wore velvet because it was a chill, damp day. A simple wool or muslin gown would have been too plain for the occasion, and silk would have made her look overdressed. "Good afternoon, Gabriel," she said, greeting Daisy's husband with genuine warmth. She adored Gabriel. He wasn't quite as good-looking as Ian—was any man?—but he came close.

"I just saw Lady Withnall's coach draw up in front of the house," he said in a whispered warning, leaning close to buss her cheek. "She was gazing out of it, her beady eyes as bright as hot, red embers. Someone's about to get burned this afternoon."

Dillie's heart sank. "Oh, no."

Gabriel eyed her curiously. "The blood just drained out of your head. Calm yourself, Dillie. It isn't you." He arched an eyebrow. "Right? You've been on your best behavior, haven't you?"

She nodded.

He let out a breath. "Good, otherwise I'd have to kill the man who led you astray."

"I haven't been led anywhere," she assured him, rolling her eyes. "My days are as dull as ever."

"Poor child." He patted her head. "Eloise and Ian will be joining us. Stay close to Eloise. She'll protect you from that tiny harridan."

Within moments, Pruitt strode in to announce Lady Withnall's arrival. All conversation ceased, and guests who had been smiling only moments earlier began to exchange worried looks. Dillie scanned the crowd. If she wasn't to be Lady Withnall's next victim, then who among them was?

Whistlethwaite and Harding made hasty apologies and took themselves off. "Strike them off the list," Dillie muttered under her breath.

"I wonder what she's doing here," Julia said in a reverent whisper as the *thuck, thuck, thuck* of Lady Withnall's walking cane struck the polished wood floor.

Her mother shrugged. "We'll find out soon enough." She stepped forward to embrace Lady Withnall. "How nice of you to drop by. Do join us. Would you like a cup of tea?"

"Lovely," the old harridan said, taking a seat beside Dillie, who had just dropped onto the settee that her supposed suitors had vacated. "Was that Whistlethwaite and Harding I saw dashing off?"

Dillie nodded.

"Good. Dullards, the both of them. You ought to thank me for my visit. I hope I sent them packing for good. Very dull gentlemen, indeed. Can't think of a nice thing to say about either of them. They're quite unremarkable. Not suitable for you, Dillie. Neither one will make you happy."

Dillie was about to toss back a noncommittal response, but Lady Withnall wasn't finished yet. "They're lazy and reckless. But now that they've gone, let's speak of more interesting subjects. Tell me what happened to you at the Wakeford ball."

Once again, Dillie's instinct was to panic. She was saved by the timely arrival of Eloise and Ian. More greetings, a slight shuffling of the seating arrangements, meaning Dillie had shot out of her seat and offered it to Eloise in the hope that her neighbor would keep the tiny demon beside her under control.

Ian greeted her mother and Julia, acknowledged their other guests, and turned to her last. His lips were slightly curled upward as he bowed over her hand. "Your eyes are wide as saucers and your cheeks are a bright scarlet," he said quietly.

She let out a soft moan. "Lady Withnall went straight for me."

"Why? You haven't done anything wrong. Stay calm. Don't you dare *eep*," he warned, casting her a gentle glance that made her bones melt.

"Can I fake an attack of sneezing?"

He laughed softly. "No."

"I don't know why she's so interested in me, unless she saw me and Charles by the fountain last night. Maybe she saw you toss him in."

"So?"

Or saw Ian comforting her. Then again, nothing untoward had happened between her and Ian. He was right. She had nothing to be worried about.

Why hadn't Ian kissed her last night? Come to think of it, she ought to have been insulted that he hadn't tried. He was a rakehell, after all. He had a sordid reputation to uphold, yet his behavior had been above reproach. He'd been valiant and noble. That was quite rude of him. Didn't he like her? Did he find her so unappealing?

She frowned.

His lips broadened into a smile. He re-melted her bones. Was that even a word? Could bones melt more than once?

He gave her hand a light squeeze. "Just answer truthfully. You have nothing to fear from her."

Oh, he was so wrong! "What if I stumble?"

He suddenly turned serious. "I'll catch you. Always," he said in that husky, crumble-a-woman's-resistance voice of his.

Holy crumpets! With sugar on top! Good Ian had put in an appearance again and was playing havoc with her heart. "And I'll do the same for you," she assured, though he didn't seem to need her help. He handled all manner of adversity with a confident ease. Had her family spoken of her the way his family had spoken of him, she would have been in tears for days.

He went about his day as though nothing had happened.

Did nothing affect him?

Ian cleared his throat and turned away.

Lady Withnall picked up exactly where she had left off before Ian and Eloise arrived. She cast Dillie a beady-eyed glance and smiled. "As I was saying, what happened to you at the Wakeford ball, my dear?"

Dillie's tongue seemed to swell within her mouth. Her throat began to close up tight. She didn't know why this woman struck such fear in her heart. She hadn't done a blessed thing worthy of eternal damnation. Were mere thoughts sufficient? She often dreamed of doing sinful things to Ian's body. But thoughts didn't count. How could they? She didn't even know how to be sinful. She merely *wished* to be sinful with Ian.

He would have to show her how.

Lady Withnall reached across the tea table with her cane and nudged Dillie to regain her attention. "Answer me, gel. It's a simple question. Or do you have something to hide?"

The remaining guests tipped their heads toward her, eagerly awaiting her response. They were all settled in the Farthingale parlor, a light and airy room decorated in pale blue silk. The drapes, the settee, and chairs were in compatible patterns of blue silk fabric. The carpet was a lovely, hand-woven floral on a background of pale blue wool. In contrast, Dillie's gown was a pale rose with a simple white lace fichu at her bosom.

She looked quite elegant, she didn't mind saying so. "I danced and took a walk on the terrace to cool down afterward."

Lady Withnall eyed her shrewdly. "Twice, I believe."

"Perhaps. I wasn't paying close attention. I had a full dance card. The ballroom was quite crowded." Dillie began to breathe heavily.

Ian sighed.

Dillie's mother shot her a worried glance. "You didn't eat sardines today, did you?"

"No." She was now panting as rapidly as a dog on a hot summer's day.

"Your Grace..." Lady Withnall said, her attention now trained on Ian, her eyes small and narrow as though she were aiming down the barrel of a musket.

Dillie cringed, waiting for her to mention the lies Ian's mother had spread last night. Her hands curled into fists. *It isn't fair. He hasn't done anything wrong.* He'd been wonderful to her last night.

"Your Grace," the old harridan repeated. "I hear that—"

Dillie shot out of her seat, knocking over the tea tray and spilling cups, teapot, and cakes onto the very expensive carpet. "Mother, I'm so sorry!" She cast a scowl at Lady Withnall, who returned the glare with an innocent gaze of her own. Too bad there were only dull butter knives at hand. She would have neatly dispatched the old troublemaker had she a real knife at her disposal.

"Dillie!" her mother cried in a fluster. "Summon Pruitt! Be quick about it. Goodness, what's wrong with you today? I've never seen you so out of sorts."

Dillie dashed into the entry hall in search of their ever reliable butler. He must have heard the crash of silver and china, for he was already armed with a dustpan and had two maids in tow. "Pruitt, it's all my fault. I've destroyed the carpet and overset the tea table."

His expression was achingly gentle as he said, "We'll set it back in order, never you worry." Then his gaze moved beyond her. "Your Grace, oh dear."

Dillie turned to look behind her. Ian had followed her out. The sleeve of his elegant gray jacket was soaked with tea. She grabbed his hand. "Come into the kitchen with me. We need to get those stains out fast."

She had led him as far as the dining room before realizing that all she needed was his jacket. "Oh." She stopped and tried to release his hand, but he held fast. She liked the enveloping warmth of his fingers entwined in hers.

"I'll let go in a moment," he needlessly assured, for she was in no hurry to separate from him. "I'd like you to calm down and tell me what has you so overset. Did something else happen to you last night? Anyone hurt you?"

"No."

He let go of her hand—*drat*—and then gazed searchingly into her eyes. *Crumpets! Eyes like his ought to be outlawed.* "Then why are you as jumpy as a frog? Lady Withnall was merely making polite conversation."

"She was not! Did you see the way she was looking at me? Then she looked at you in that same beady manner." She squinted her eyes to show him, but he merely chuckled. "It isn't funny. Didn't you notice? I'm certain she saw us together last night."

He sighed. "So? We were merely speaking to each other."

"In the garden. Under the moonlight. I rested my head against your shoulder. You warmed my hands."

He was still reveling in his amusement, his mouth curved in a delicious grin. "Sounds rather romantic."

It was. You should have taken me into your arms and kissed me. Have you no pride? Why didn't you uphold your rakehell reputation? "Give me your jacket, Ian. I only need it, not you."

He shrugged out of it. Dillie leaned against one of the dining chairs, certain her legs were about to give way. His shoulders ought to be outlawed as well. And his broad chest. Banished from the kingdom! "Oh, the tea soaked into your shirt sleeve."

He arched an eyebrow. "Are you asking me to take my shirt off as well?"

"No, you idiot." Her heart would stop if he did. Perhaps it would explode. Shirtless Ian would do serious damage to her bodily organs. Not to mention her eyeballs. They might never settle back into their sockets. "I suppose I'll have to take you with me after all."

She turned and walked ahead to the kitchen, doing her best not to think of him or look back as he followed her. Mrs. Mayhew and her scullery maids looked up from their preparations and smiled, mildly surprised when she walked in, and then began to buzz and flit like bees about a hive when Ian strode in behind her.

"Your Grace!" Mrs. Mayhew bobbed a curtsy as did the scullery maids, who wouldn't stop bobbing until Ian urged them to ignore him and apologized for the intrusion.

Dillie handed his jacket to Mrs. Mayhew. "It was all my fault. I knocked over the entire tea service and made a mess of His Grace's garments."

"Not to worry, lamb. I have two pies baking in the oven. They're almost done. I'll have them sent to the parlor as soon as they've cooled." Mrs. Mayhew ordered one of her girls to put on more water for tea, took Ian's jacket, and lumbered to the pantry to begin cleaning the stains out of it.

Dillie ordered Ian to sit on a stool beside the kitchen's window ledge where the pies would have been set to cool if it weren't raining. The rain was still coming down hard, but the window had been left open a crack to allow in the draft. Fortunately, the wind was blowing the rain away from them so that the droplets fell outside instead of pattering in.

The ledge was one of the few bare spots in the kitchen. Every spare table and countertop was covered with pots, utensils, serving trays, and food to be cooked for this evening's supper.

"Rest your arm here," she instructed once he'd settled on the stool. He obediently propped his elbow on the ledge. Though she was distressed by the damage she'd caused to his clothing, he remained amused and took far too much delight in her discomfort. "I'll have to remove the cuff link so I can get under the sleeve."

"I never refuse a woman wishing to take off my garments."

She rolled her eyes. "It's just the cuff link, you clunch." But his jest brought home all the reasons why she and Ian would never make a good match. She needed a husband who would be faithful. He would be off and cheating before the minister closed the Bible on their wedding vows.

She tried to remember that as she worked on the stain, but it was a struggle. All she could think of was the strength of his body dangerously close to hers and the heat of his skin beneath her fingers. Whenever she breathed, she caught the sandalwood scent of him mingled with the delicious scent of cinnamon and apples wafting from the oven. She tried not to breathe, but that didn't work.

She made the mistake of glancing at him. He looked at her as though he ached to hold her in his arms and never let her go. It was a devastatingly tender look. It was a forever look. But that's what made him so dangerous. Experienced rakehells knew how to toss that look even while plotting their next conquest.

"THERE. ALL DONE. Give it a moment to dry, then I'll put the cuff link back on," Dillie said, the sweet sound of her voice wrapping around Ian's heart. *Damn it.* She had no business being anywhere near his heart. She was as hopeless a debutante as he'd ever met.

She'd proved it again today, making a mess of her mother's salon, upsetting an entire platter of cakes and a large pot of tea, shattering her mother's favorite cups and saucers, damaging his shirt and jacket (not that he cared—those were easily replaced), and scalding his forearm.

Wild ferrets caused this sort of mayhem.

Wild ferrets and Dillie, apparently.

To make matters worse, she had insisted on tending his forearm, rubbing butter on the burn while she moaned and softly called his name. *"Ooh, Ian. Ian. Am I hurting you? Ooh, tell me if I am,"* she'd purred.

She couldn't have made him hotter if she'd stuck her hand between his thighs and... well, no. That delight would have killed him.

She'd take a meat cleaver to him if she realized what he was thinking.

"Ian, where is it?" She was purring again. Driving him insanely hot again.

"Where's what?"

"The cuff link, you clunch. What else would I be looking for?" She raised the square of linen she'd used to rub the tea stains off his sleeve and dabbed at the beads of perspiration now coating his forehead, no doubt mistaking the overheated kitchen as the cause of his discomfort. In truth, it was his raw, rampant lust to blame.

She met his gaze and let out a gentle laugh. "You're a hot, buttered mess. I think I like you better this way. You aren't so dauntingly perfect." Her tongue darted out to give the butter remaining on one of her fingers a light, curling lick.

Every organ in his body began to throb. His groin had been throbbing all along, but now it felt as though it were stuffed with gunpowder, fuse lit. Detonation in five seconds. Four. Three. Two.

Thuck, thuck, thuck.

Thank the angels! Lady Withnall's arrival was like a barrel of ice water poured straight down his pants. "What brings you into the dungeons?" he asked, genuinely surprised she'd found her way here. Few women of her stature ever visited their kitchen, and certainly never visited a friend's kitchen.

"Came to check on the gel." Her gaze practically bore into Dillie.

Dillie gulped.

Ian wanted to take her hand, give it a light, reassuring squeeze, but he knew it was the worst thing he could do in front of an audience, even though that audience consisted of only one person. But that one person was the most meddlesome in existence. *Damn.* Lady Withnall was purposely riling Dillie, taking forever to make her way across the kitchen to their side, her gaze never wavering and trained on Dillie.

He heard Dillie sneeze twice, and wasn't certain whether she was faking. He rose to stand beside her, ready to protect her if the need arose.

"The pair of you look quite cozy in here. Good thing I came along."

"She's only treating my wounds," Ian replied before Dillie could open her mouth and make matters needlessly worse. He stuck out his forearm to show her the burn.

"Hmmph. Scalded you with the tea, did she?" She continued to gaze at Dillie. He moved protectively closer. Probably shouldn't have, for it put ideas into Lady Withnall's head. "Gel, you seem to be making a habit of repairing the Duke of Edgeware."

Dillie let out a shaky breath that blew softly against his shoulder. "I don't know what you mean."

"Of course you do, and you've done a fine job of keeping it a secret. An admirable trait in a young woman. But I know that the Duke of Edgeware spent a week in your bed last November."

Dillie suddenly seemed to stop breathing.

Ian let out a soft growl and put his arm around her, his protective instincts surging to the fore. "Phoebe, what are you playing at? You know I don't care what's said about me, but Dillie is innocent."

The old harridan shook her head and sighed. "You ought to have thought about that before you landed in her bed." Having said that, she turned and walked out.

Thuck, thuck, thuck.

DILLIE WASN'T IN any danger of swooning. True, the air had built up in her lungs and she hadn't released it yet, but for the most part she was fine. Fine and angry. Her fists were tightly clenched. She stepped in front of Ian, glaring at Lady Withnall's turned back as she attempted to follow after the tiny troublemaker.

"Don't you dare," Ian warned, holding her back by the skirt of her gown. "You'll only make matters worse. I'll speak to her. She and I are friends. She won't spread that ugly rumor. I won't allow it."

Dillie shook her head, certain she had misheard. "Friends? And you think you can buy her silence? What sort of friend extorts another?" She felt her eyes water. They were glistening with anger. "I don't care about myself. You had better not give her so much as a ha'penny to protect my reputation. My family trusts me and will never believe her lies. No one who matters to me will ever believe her, but your family is another matter. They're looking for any reason to hurt you. I can't believe Lady Withnall means to give it to them."

"She won't."

"How can you be sure?" Once again, she started for Lady Withnall, but he held her back. "What's the matter with you, Ian? You can't let her hurt you like this. You've never taken advantage of me. Quite the opposite, you've been a perfect gentleman. And you've never harmed anyone or stolen any infants. Why won't you allow me to defend you?"

"I'm asking you to leave it alone. You're not my friend," he said with a quiet determination that made her heart catch in her throat.

"But—"

"Leave it alone, Daffy." That said, he strode to the opposite end of the kitchen to retrieve his coat from Mrs. Mayhew, and then strode out without a backward glance at her.

Dillie turned to the slightly open window, needing the draft to cool the heat of her anger. Lady Withnall wasn't the only object of her ire. She was just as angry with Ian for holding her back, for refusing to defend himself. Mostly, she was angry with herself. She had allowed Ian to get to her heart. For a moment, she'd believed that he actually cared for her, but he only knew how to push people away. Is that why his family despised him?

Still, she'd hoped that she mattered to him a little. He'd just made it painfully clear that she didn't.

The clunch!

CHAPTER 8

SEVERAL DAYS LATER, Ian's carriage drew up in front of the Belgrave Square townhouse his mother and cousins had let for the season. It was a large house, built of gray stone, and had lots of windows to allow in sunlight. The drapes were drawn, of course, for his mother hated the sun's glare. It exposed her physical flaws, those hideous age spots that she strove so mightily to conceal.

He descended from his carriage and walked up the stairs to the front door, a large, wooden door that was painted a bright, garish red, like the rouge his mother had taken to painting on her cheeks in the mistaken belief she would appear young and ruddy cheeked. She was wrong. She was aging, and not well.

It was on the early side, not quite noon. He had decided to pay his mother this unannounced visit in the hope of surprising her. Not in a good way. Their encounters were never friendly, though he was always cordial to her. She was the one who tensed and bristled, and then attacked. She wanted nothing to do with him. Had she known of his arrival, she would have slipped out the back way.

The meeting was necessary. He needed answers about that November attack. He also needed to rein in his mother. He was used to her venomous words and no longer cared about the insults hurled at him. But he wouldn't allow her to insult Felicity. Truly, this was a new low even for his mother, stooping to destroy a defenseless infant.

Hence the reason for his visit. The cold, proud Duchess Celestia was never that brave when forced to speak to him in private.

He decided to discuss the November attack first, for it was

uppermost on his mind. He didn't think his mother had come up with the scheme, but she must have approved of it. His cousins would not have paid those wharf rats to come after him without consulting her first.

Why attempt to kill him? There was nothing to be gained. Neither Simon nor Edmund cared to work, and they ought to have been satisfied with the allowance he gave to each. Had he not been generous enough with them? He set aside the thought as the door opened and a butler stepped forward.

Ian usually gave only passing notice to servants, but this man caught his attention. He wasn't sure why. Perhaps it was the shape of his eyes or their unusual color, brown with flecks of amber. The man appeared to be about fifty years old. He had a trim build, graying hair, and an unmistakable air of refinement.

"Your Grace," he said with a respectful bow, obviously recognizing him though he hadn't presented his card. Perhaps he'd noted the Markham family emblem engraved on his carriage door.

When he introduced himself as Badger, Ian wanted to ask the man whether they'd ever met before but dismissed the notion. Why should he care? "Let's spare the polite conversation, shall we?" he said instead. "No, the dowager duchess is not expecting me. No, I will not leave until I see her. I don't care if my cousins join us or not. They're free to slink off and hide out at their club if they so choose. I'll hunt them down when I wish to see them."

Badger merely nodded and led Ian into the parlor to wait. "I'll have refreshments sent at once, Your Grace."

"No need, Badger." He liked that name. Liked the cut of the man as well. No doubt he came with the townhouse, for neither his mother nor his cousins would ever have engaged his services. He didn't appear to be a toady. "I won't be staying long."

"Very good, Your Grace."

"And Badger, let my mother know that if she's not down here in ten minutes, I'll come up there and drag her downstairs."

The man didn't blink, didn't change the stony expression on his face. "Very good, Your Grace," he repeated, but Ian noted the subtle glint of amusement in his eyes.

Upon closer inspection, the parlor furniture wasn't quite as elegant as it had first appeared. Though well made, it had a patina of faded gentility that must have rankled his mother. She was used to the finest of everything, and although he never stinted on her maintenance, it never seemed to be enough for her.

Nothing was ever good enough for Duchess Celestia. She hadn't been satisfied with her husband. Certainly had never been satisfied with her sons, until the death of his brother. Then James had become the golden child, the one upon whom she proceeded to bestow her love, posthumously of course.

In truth, Ian had been too young at the time of his brother's death to understand about maternal love or the lack of it. Perhaps she had loved James as deeply as she proclaimed, but he doubted it. She wasn't the sentimental sort. If she bemoaned his death, it was because she thrived on the attention of others. She wasn't selective about who offered her sympathy. Anyone would do. A friend. One of her lovers. Even the household servants. It was attention she craved.

He might have believed her sincere had she been less theatrical about *her* torment. She never considered that anyone else might have mourned James. No one else mattered to her, or had ever mattered to her.

To Ian's surprise, he didn't have long to wait before his mother made her appearance. She glided in, dressed in a gown of yellow satin, her blonde hair perfectly done up in the latest style. The three fat curls dangling by the side of her ear looked awkward, but the style of her hair didn't matter. Nor did the pronounced downturn of her mouth bother him. He was used to her sour expression, the tight purse of her lips, as though she'd eaten something unpleasant. Or seen something unpleasant. Namely, him.

The train of her gown billowed as she made a sweeping turn and sat on the stiff divan. "Why are you here, Edgeware?" She rarely called him Ian, couldn't bring herself to call him by his given name lest it be mistaken for affection.

He remained standing, not that she cared. She hadn't offered him a seat. "For the truth. I know that you, Simon, and Edmund have forgotten what that is."

"Did you come here to insult me? If so, then I must ask you to leave."

He paid her no mind. "Five months ago," he started. "Who came up with the brilliant idea to end my life? You? Simon? I doubt it was Edmund. He hasn't had an original thought since the day he was born."

"Don't be ridiculous! We wouldn't—"

"Stop. There's no use denying it. I've already had the scum you hired to do your dirty work tracked down and questioned. They'll be punished." He paused a moment to watch her squirm, which she did a little, but mostly she glared at him. "I don't plan to do anything about my loving family—yet. You'll all keep your allowances and your heads this time."

"How generous of you," she remarked dryly.

"It is. Damn generous, though you don't deserve it." He rubbed a hand across the nape of his neck. "I just want to know why. Why last November?"

She shrugged, as though to say the time line didn't matter. She hated him, always had, and never wanted him around. "If you must know, we didn't really think it through," she admitted. "You're a horrible son, but you know how to grow the family wealth, and of course, you've shared it with us, as is your duty."

"Right. My duty." He struggled to suppress a hearty laugh at that remark. Those were love scars crisscrossing his arms and slashed across his stomach, placed there by the knife-wielding ruffians hired by his beloved family. He owed them nothing.

"It *is* your duty," she insisted. "After all, I devoted the best years of my life to raising you."

Odd, he thought he'd been raised by strangers. A governess, a tutor, the housekeeper at Swineshead, a fitting name for the place. In truth, it was a beautiful house, but isolated. The relatives rarely visited unless they were in need of funds. They reminded him of pigs at the trough. "Of course. I remember all those cozy nights we sat beside the fire, drinking hot cocoa while you or Father read to me. Wonderful memories. Brings tears to my eyes."

Her lips pursed in that sour lemons expression she'd perfected. "You always were a sarcastic bastard."

"Not to mention a constant trial and a disappointment." He

shrugged. "Go on. What put the idea into your head to have me killed?"

She paused a moment, her manner as unaffected as though she were about to comment on the unpredictable London weather. "It didn't start out that way. We never meant to have you seriously hurt. We heard you intended to marry."

He said nothing for a moment, stunned. "Me? Take a wife? Bring a sweet, young thing into *this* family? That will never happen."

"Why not? You're a wealthy duke. Any girl would be flattered by your proposal, no matter how loathsome you are. We only meant to prevent the marriage from taking place. We like things as they are. Didn't want the greedy bitch urging you to cut us off."

"Warms my cockles," he said, a familiar numbness sweeping through his body. Since childhood, he'd endured his family by creating a hard shell around his heart. He was like a turtle, ducking into that hard shell whenever danger approached. He'd managed to survive the brutal kicks and punches because he was protected by that thick outer covering.

Sometimes he was kicked so hard the shell cracked a little. However, it would quickly repair itself. His shell would take only a day or so to recover from this kick. "So what you're saying is that you preferred to have me dead rather than possibly losing your allowance. I'm moved, Mother. I feel more tears coming on."

"We never meant to end your life, just interfere with your wedding plans." She tipped her nose into the air and made a little sniffing sound. "What did you expect to hear? That I love you? That I'm glad you're my son? Well, I'm not glad. You're a murderer and I rue the day I gave birth to you."

Which is how most of their encounters ended. "Good day, Mother. I hope I won't see you around." Which was his way of telling her to leave town immediately, before he changed his mind and had them all clapped in irons.

"London is surprisingly dull this year," she said, her nose still tilted upward into the air. "I think I shall return to Bath with your cousins."

"A wise decision." He started for the door, and then halted. "By the way, if you or my cousins ever make mention of Mary or Felicity again, I will cut off your funds." *In addition to cutting off my cousins' balls.* He hadn't bothered to issue that threat because if given the choice of which to lose, their manhood or their money, his cousins would have sacrificed their manhood. "You will mention it to Simon and Edmund, won't you?"

She rose with a start. "You wouldn't dare cut us off! Who cares about your father's by-blow or her wretched offspring? The infant is an affront to the sanctity of my marriage. Your beloved father—"

"Right, my sainted father." The man who hadn't spoken to him since the day James died. The man who'd cheated on his mother, just as she had cheated on her father throughout their perfect marriage. He pinned her with a warning glare. "The rumors stop. Starting now."

DILLIE HAD ARRANGED to pick up Daisy on her way to their monthly sisters meeting, which was to be held at Rose's townhouse. The monthly meeting had lately become a weekly meeting, and would have become a daily meeting if Dillie had her way. She was in desperate need of advice from her all-knowing married sisters.

Despite Ian's assurances that the *ton's* most eligible young men would be tripping over themselves to court her—well, he'd been right about that—none of them were in the least interesting to her. Was she the problem? Or were they? She needed to be told whether her standards were unrealistically high or her suitors as unimpressive as she'd thought them.

"Unremarkable" was the term Lady Withnall had used. It was an apt description of the gentlemen calling on her. However, Dillie gave a small shiver, for she hoped never to end up as withered and mean-spirited as that old woman.

"Play us a song before you leave," her young cousin Charles said, tugging on her arm. She'd brought him and a few other cousins along for the ride to Daisy's. They would remain in the care of Ivy's nanny while she and Daisy visited Rose.

Her other young cousins, Lizbeth and Harry, chimed in with their pleas. "The shoemaker song," Lizbeth said, referring to a silly tune Dillie had made up on a lark last year. The children adored the easy refrain. *Clip, clop. Clip, clop, went the shoemaker's wooden shoes.*

Dillie quickly gave in, for she couldn't refuse them anything when they stared at her with their big, innocent eyes. She knew there was plenty of time to indulge the children, for Daisy was still in her morning gown and had run upstairs to ready herself only moments ago.

She soon found herself in Daisy's music room, walking over to the piano. Charles, Harry, and Lizbeth began to squeal in anticipation the moment she sat down and tickled the keys. Lizbeth jumped up and down in front of her. Dillie laughed. Ah, she loved her adoring public, even if that public comprised three youngsters who were family and therefore required to feign raptures over her talent. "There was an old shoemaker," Lizbeth began to sing.

Harry, the youngest, joined in.

Dillie counted only two voices. "Charles, won't you sing along?" Charles, all of eight years old, had suddenly turned quite serious.

In truth, it was in his nature to be quiet and reserved. One rarely got a squeal out of this young man.

Lizbeth, on the other hand, was rarely quiet. She was now about twelve, approaching that awkward age between child and young woman, and as to be expected, responded to everything with joyful excitement or abject tears of sorrow. Dillie hoped she would grow out of it in time.

Harry was the youngest and a very grownup five. Unfortunately, he'd been forced to deal with serious matters quite early on, for his father had died in Napoleon's war. Gabriel and Daisy had helped him get through the loss. Harry chose that moment to cast her a beaming smile. Dillie felt a happy twinge in her heart.

"May I sing?" Charles asked, as though he required permission to let loose with his vocal talents.

"Of course you may. The song is meant to be sung by a trio."

"But Aunt Sophie," he said, referring to Dillie's mother, "told us not to be a bother."

Dillie returned his earnest gaze with one of her own. "You never are to me. I love having you with me."

"Are you certain?" Speaking to Charles was like being put on the witness stand and hounded with questions. He'd make a fine barrister someday. "You were told to bring us here," he said in his precise way, "because we've lost our nannies again. We're to stay with Ivy and her nanny for today."

"So you see, it worked out perfectly. I wanted to bring you along. I didn't need to be asked."

Lizbeth's smile faltered and her eyes began to water. "I thought we'd been good this year. I don't know why the nannies hate us."

Dillie reached over and hurriedly gave her a hug. "It isn't your fault. You've all been wonderful and I'm so glad you're here. In truth, you three are my salvation. I'd be bored to tears without you."

"We love you too," Harry assured her, throwing his little arms about her waist and giving her a big hug emphasized by an effusive grunt. His hands were sticky, but what did it matter when she had his love?

Dillie hugged him back. "I have a game I know you'll enjoy."

The children squealed, their sadness quickly forgotten. "What is it?" Charles asked.

"It's a musical game."

Their ears perked.

"I'll play the shoemaker's song while you three walk around the piano. When I stop playing, you have to stop in place and stand as still as statues. Anyone who moves is out of the game. Then I'll start playing again and the remaining players can start walking around the piano again."

"And when you stop, we have to stop and pose as statues," Lizbeth said, her eyes brimming with excitement.

Ah, children are so easily satisfied. Too bad men are not so easily handled.

She began to play the shoemaker song. It was a lively, skipping sort of tune. Lizbeth walked like a lady, nose in the air as she glided in front of the boys. Harry and Charles, being boys, were not required to take walking lessons. They hopped, jumped, skipped, and *clop, clop, clopped* around the piano, taking delight in the thuds they made upon the wood floor each time they landed. Harry, being quite little, did an admirable job of making noise. His little feet came down with the heft of a fat old man.

Dillie suddenly stopped playing. All three immediately stopped in their tracks, but as for posing as still as statues? It didn't happen. They were fidgeting and giggling, but she wasn't going to call them out. "Oh, you're all too clever for me!"

She began to play again. Lizbeth resumed walking like a lady, her nose back in the air. The boys resumed hopping and clopping around the piano.

Once again she stopped playing. More laughter. More giggles and squirms.

They were so adorable, so intensely engaged in the game, that she couldn't help but burst into ripples of laughter herself. The game continued, none of the children called out, and by now they were running and stomping around the piano as she played—until all of a sudden, they broke the circle and raced toward the door.

Dillie turned to call them back, but the words caught in her throat.

Ian was standing in the doorway. He looked devastatingly handsome as always, calm and composed even as the children slammed into him in their haste to welcome him and have him join in their game. Ivy's nanny bustled in upon hearing the commotion, sparing Dillie the need to make excuses to the children as to why Ian could not join in.

The nanny clapped her hands to gain their attention. "Children, come along. It's time for milk and biscuits."

That halted any protest contemplated by the boys.

Lizbeth cast Dillie a shockingly mature grin, and then followed the boys out of the music room, leaving her alone with Ian. Dillie shook her head, laughing gently. "How long were you standing there?"

"Long time," he said with a slight rasp to his voice. He shot her another one of his heart-melting smiles. If handsome were a crime, Ian would be imprisoned for life. "Harry left his handprints on your gown."

She glanced down to inspect the outline of little fingers on each of her hips. "Oh dear, I hope it's just chalk."

When she looked up, Ian had an intensely scorching look in his eyes. Was he going to kiss her? He was staring at her lips. "What are you doing?"

"Studying you." There was something in the way he spoke, a sensually husky whisper that stirred the butterflies in her stomach into their usual Ian-induced frenzy.

"I can see that. But why are you studying me?" *And not kissing me with reckless abandon.*

He bent his head closer, so that their lips were almost touching. "Can't help myself. You're beautiful."

"I suppose you say that to all your conquests." She couldn't help but be disappointed. Honestly, he'd just spouted an uninspired, and rather stale, line of seduction. He must have told thousands of women that they were beautiful, and then kissed them.

"Yes, I've said it before. Lots of times," he admitted. "There are plenty of women who are outwardly beautiful, but..." His voice trailed off and he suddenly seemed to be struggling for words. Ian never struggled over anything. "I was watching the gentle way you handled the children. The way you played with them. The way they giggled and hugged you. They adore you. You're so honest, so patient with them. That's what makes you so incredibly beautiful."

He cast her a look she'd never seen before, one that she doubted anyone had ever seen cast during Ian's entire life. He was letting down his barriers, allowing her to see the pain he carried in his heart because of his unhappy childhood. Dillie wanted to cry. There was so much pain reflected in his gray-green eyes.

"Ian," she said in a whisper, her heart aching so badly she could hardly speak. She reached up and lightly touched her mouth to his. "Thank you. I've never received a lovelier compliment."

He said nothing, just circled his arms around her and drew her into his gentle embrace. She was up against his body. Big, muscled body. But it wasn't a seductive embrace. She didn't know what to think of it, for it seemed as though he were drowning and needed to hold onto something safe to keep from sinking underwater.

A hot tingle shot through her, even though he wasn't trying to seduce her. But she always responded this way when she was in his arms. Or hoping to be in his arms. Or thinking of his muscled arms. Or thinking of him. She slid her hands up his chest and rested them on his shoulders, tugging on them to draw him even closer. It wasn't nearly enough.

Crumpets!

She didn't wish to ruin the moment, but couldn't help herself. She raised on her tiptoes and touched her lips to his again. Lightly.

He responded with a low, feral growl, taking control of what had started as a simple kiss. He deepened it, teased her lips open with his tongue, and plunged in, each thrust of his tongue powerful and at the same time gentle. Each thrust commanding and at the same time protective. Suddenly, no one existed for her but Ian. No one mattered more to her than Ian. He knew just how to coax the breathy moans out of her, and knew how to ease the pressure of his lips at just the right moment, knew how to heighten that pressure again for exquisite effect. Yet, it wasn't his mastery that made the kiss so spectacular. It was him.

She was mindless and out of control, but so was he. He was allowing himself to lose control. He was trusting her. *Trusting her.* Now that was something special.

Then he did something even more special. When he ended the kiss—because she wasn't going to be the one to pull away, ever—he kept his arms around her and simply hugged her. A long, gentle hug that felt pure and innocent. Well, not quite innocent. Ian was far too handsome, far too dangerous, far too experienced ever to be considered innocent. The hug was pure and heartfelt.

That was it. Heartfelt.

And anyone who knew Ian knew that he always hid what was in his heart. But not this time. Not with this kiss. Tears welled in her eyes. She began to sniffle. Ian sighed. "What's wrong, Daffy?"

He eased her away slightly to look at her. And he'd called her Daffy, which was his way of closing himself off again. She wasn't ready for that yet. "Nothing."

"Then why the tears?"

She sighed. "The kiss rattled me, if you must know. It was the best kiss ever."

He chuckled. "Ever?"

"Yes, in the entire universe of kisses. In every kiss that has occurred since the dawn of man's existence," she insisted. "It was the best."

She expected Ian to dismiss the remark as ridiculous. After all, she had been a little theatrical about it. Quite over the top about it, truth be told. He knew that she'd never been kissed by anyone else. So how would she know if someone else was better at it than he was? She couldn't compare him to anyone else. *Ugh!* Why had she mentioned the dawn of man's existence? She could have kept the time period shorter. Best since last week. Best kiss since the start of the season.

His gaze turned tender. "Yes, it was. Best ever."

And that was the problem with Ian. He kept saying nice things to her and making her feel as though he meant them. He wasn't safe for her. She had to tell him to stop.

She would tell him. Soon.

Just not yet.

"IAN, THERE YOU are," Gabriel said, striding into the club room at White's later that evening. "I've been looking all over for you. Heard you came around to see me earlier today. Why didn't you wait?"

Ian set down his newspaper and motioned for the bartender to send over two glasses of whiskey. "Problem got solved. Didn't need to disturb you. Where were you, anyway? I thought you'd be home."

Gabriel shot him a smug grin and settled into the overstuffed leather chair beside him. "I was upstairs, about to come down when Daisy delayed me." His grin broadened. "She needed my help to change out of her morning gown. Couldn't manage those pesky buttons on her own. I'm ever the obliging husband."

Ian winced. "You ass. I don't want to hear about how you undressed your wife."

"Fine. Then I won't tell you the rest of what I did to her."

Ian let out a laughing groan. "Get out." He took the two drinks off the butler's tray and held Gabriel's out of his reach. "All this talk of marital bliss is making my ears bleed."

"Never realized you were so delicate. Just like a woman. Not as soft or pretty though."

"Weren't you just leaving?"

"You had better not swoon. I'm not going to catch you." Gabriel grabbed the glass out of his hand, and though he was still grinning, Ian saw the concern in Gabriel's eyes as he settled back in his chair. "What's troubling you?"

Ian took a sip of his drink. Nice. Smooth. "As I said. No longer a problem."

Gabriel's expression revealed his doubt. "So from the time you arrived at my home until the time you left, let's say that was about fifteen minutes, you worked it all out?"

Ian nodded. *Damn.* He knew what was coming next.

"Interesting." Gabriel leaned forward. "Did Dillie have anything to do with fixing your problem?"

Everything. "No."

"Because she and that adorable rabble of Farthingale cousins were at my house when you arrived."

"They could hardly be overlooked." He and Dillie had never figured out what substance Harry had managed to stick on his hands. Their only clue was that it wouldn't wipe off Dillie's gown. "Dillie was playing the piano. The children were jumping up and down, doing their best to smash holes in your expensive floor with their little feet."

Gabriel threw his head back and laughed. "So that was the pounding noise I heard downstairs. I wondered what that was about. Wasn't going to run downstairs though. I had my own pounding—"

"Stop! You're roiling my stomach. No man should lust after his own wife the way you do."

"Actually, I was talking about my armoire. I was repairing the spindle leg that had loosened on it." He was still grinning like a hyena. "Want to know how that leg got loose? It happened last night. Daisy—"

"You're still a monumental ass. Stop talking about how often you make love to your wife. Or where. Or how. Breaking furniture while you're in the 'throes' doesn't earn you any points."

"Daisy seems to think it does." He took a gulp of his whiskey and set it down quickly. "I know. I know. I'll stop talking about her. Let's work on fixing your problem."

Ian stifled a groan. "You're not listening to me. There is no problem."

"That's where you're wrong." Gabriel shot him that well-meaning *we're more than friends, we're brothers* look. "I know you, Ian. You're hurting."

"Wrong again. I'm feeling fine." But his hand was clenched around his whiskey glass, which was probably a hint that things weren't as smooth as he wanted them to appear.

"Now who's acting like an ass?" Gabriel leaned back, the gesture significant. He was assuring Ian that he wouldn't dig too hard to get at the information he sought.

Ian liked that about Gabriel. He knew how to be a friend. They'd remained close even after Napoleon's war. Gabriel was always there to support him, but respectful of his need for privacy. "It wasn't just Dillie," Ian admitted, "but the cheerful chaos that was going on around her. That's what solved the problem." His smile turned humorless. "I'd just come from my beloved mother's house. We had another of our warm and cozy chats. You know how it is with me and my family. They're always so loving. Fairly suffocate me with their tender care."

Gabriel wasn't smiling either. "Bloody hell. I'm sorry, Ian."

"Don't be. I'm used to it. Or thought I was. Sometimes they get to me. Sometimes their foul taint crawls under my skin." He took another sip of his whiskey, and then let out a bitter laugh. "I was feeling that way until I walked into your house. The children ran to me and hugged me. Dillie smiled when she saw me, a happy sort of smile that reached into her eyes."

"Yes, the Farthingale smile. And those incredible Farthingale blue eyes. They suck you right in, don't they? Next thing you know, you're drowning in those magnificent blue pools. Same thing happened to me when I first met Daisy. I remember how you'd warned me not to walk down Chipping Way if I wished to remain a carefree bachelor."

Ian nodded.

"You were going on about the Farthingale daughters and the Chipping Way curse. I thought you were attics-to-let, but Lord, you were right. Thank goodness. I've never been happier." Gabriel leaned forward again. "If Dillie's smile slams into you the way Daisy's smile slammed into me, then let nature take its course. Let it happen, Ian. You won't regret it."

But Dillie would. Every damn day of her life.

CHAPTER 9

SEVERAL WEEKS HAD passed since Lady Withnall had practically stopped Dillie's heart in the Farthingale kitchen by revealing she knew Ian had spent a week in her bed. In truth, Dillie had been on edge ever since, dreading the day the axe would fall, though Ian had assured her that it wouldn't.

She knew it was inevitable, for the gossip was too juicy to remain a secret. Yet Dillie was stunned when her so-called loss of innocence finally did happen. After all these weeks, she had almost been lulled into believing Ian's assessment had been right.

She couldn't have been more wrong.

The evening had started out harmlessly enough. She'd just descended from the Farthingale carriage with several members of her family on a beautiful April evening, preparing to attend Lord and Lady Cummerfield's ball. She was rather proud of the way she looked. Her gown was a simple, white silk concoction, the sort appropriate for an unmarried young woman attending a fashionable ball.

Madame de Bressard had outdone herself. London's most popular modiste had fit the gown to her perfectly, the smooth fabric draping over her curves so that each fold and sway fell in a way that flattered her body. The feisty Frenchwoman had designed gowns for her and her sisters as each had made their entrance into society. The gowns were exquisite, but her prices were exorbitant.

Dillie wore the Farthingale pearl necklace around her throat, and more pearls had been wound into her stylish chignon, enhancing the dark sheen of her hair. Again simple, yet elegant.

Her mother commented favorably on Lord and Lady Cummerfield's exquisite Belgravia home, and Dillie quite agreed. The residence was charming, a large townhouse painted in cheerful yellow with white trim around the windows and doors.

Then the heavens came crashing down atop her.

While standing in line, waiting to be introduced, the gaudily gowned and indiscreet Lady Bascom leaned over to her companion, Lady Aldritch, and whispered rather loudly, "Edgeware came to her each night!"

At first, Dillie thought she was commenting on one of Ian's new conquests, which would explain why she hadn't seen him in weeks. The kiss they'd shared in Daisy's music room must not have been as satisfying for him as it had been for her, though he'd politely agreed it had been at the time.

She stifled her disappointment. Ian wasn't going to change his rakehell ways. He was a confirmed ne'er-do-well. Perhaps it was for the best that he'd moved on to someone else, for she had grown to like him more than was safe. Good Ian, that is.

She'd seen a lot of Good Ian lately.

But he also had a wicked side, the rakish part of him that used women and discarded them without a second thought. She'd momentarily forgotten that side of his nature, the dissolute, confirmed bachelor who wasn't going to change his ways for any woman.

"For an entire week!" Lady Aldritch confirmed. "Right under our very noses."

"Right under her family's very noses," Lady Bascom corrected with a cold laugh. "Not one of them realized he was sneaking onto Chipping Way each night."

What?

Dillie heard a startled buzz behind her. *Oh, crumpets!* Her family must have heard every word, for Lady Bascom was never one for discretion. She could not have whispered louder had she shouted the news from the ramparts.

Dillie turned toward the buzz and groaned. Every blessed Farthingale in existence happened to be standing behind her. Well, perhaps not all five thousand of them, but certainly a good twenty or thirty.

She prayed for Lady Bascom to be struck mute.

Apparently, not hard enough, for Lady Bascom continued, her voice resounding as clearly as a church bell. "Who would have guessed? The Duke of Edgeware and Dillie Farthingale."

Lady Aldritch expressed shock and embellished the rumor by adding a trellis outside her window that had never existed. "I must say, I was surprised. She didn't strike me as the sort the duke would notice. She's a quiet girl."

"Isn't it always the quiet ones?" Lady Bascom replied. "She was doomed to scandal the day her parents named her Daffodil. It's an impertinent flower, if you ask me. Not easily controlled. And it wasn't a trellis. I heard the duke climbed a tree to reach her bedchamber. That's why her father had the thing cut down. Too late, of course. He ought to have thought of it sooner."

Dillie stepped forward to glower at both ladies. "What utter rubbish! Nothing of the sort happened. Who told you this malicious drivel?"

Both women paled.

"Who?" she demanded when they seemed to have lost their tongues. Her hands curled into fists, and she must have appeared ready to do them bodily harm, for they both gasped and scurried off as though she'd just drawn a pistol and threatened to shoot them.

She turned to her parents, expecting to find them as angry and indignant as she was. "It must have been Lady Withnall who started the disgusting rumor. I'll speak to her and..."

Her mother had tears in her eyes. "It won't do any good, Dillie. The damage has been done."

"No," she said, emitting a mirthless laugh. "It's all been a terrible mistake. I can fix this." She waited for her family to agree. Her sisters and their husbands were standing right behind her. Thank goodness. She could rely on her sisters for support. But a glance in their direction revealed that this time, they wouldn't come to her rescue.

"I can fix this," she insisted, and she would as soon as she stopped shaking. Anger. Fear. Dread. Defiance. All these sensations clashed within her body. She felt helpless and utterly out of control.

She'd also felt helpless and out of control whenever Ian kissed her, but it wasn't at all the same thing. Ian's kisses made her feel good. Right now, she felt nauseated. Her head began to spin.

Her father was looking at her as though she had just died. So was Uncle George.

Her brothers-in-law exchanged glances with each other.

"Oh, no. No, no, no! I know that stupid 'we protect our women' look!" Dillie's entire body was now shaking and her heart was slamming against her chest. "Don't you dare lay a hand on him! He didn't do anything wrong. *I* didn't do anything wrong. You all know what really happened."

Graelem folded his arms across his chest. She turned frantically to Laurel. "Knock sense into your stubborn husband. This gossip will pass. You know I never... that he never..." She closed her eyes and groaned. "Not you, too. Laurel, don't look at me that way. Farthingales marry for love. I will not marry a man who doesn't love me."

"But Dillie, this is really bad. This isn't about you and just any man. This is about you and the notoriously wicked Duke of Edgeware."

"He isn't wicked. He's..." She was going to say that he was kind and decent, but he really wasn't that way with everyone. Many people were afraid of him, perhaps with good reason. Yet, Gabriel and Graelem liked and respected him. Well, perhaps not at this moment.

Julia stepped forward, took her hand and gently patted it. "You could do a lot worse. He is a duke, after all."

"But he doesn't love me." She swallowed hard. Her hands were trembling and her legs felt as though they were about to buckle. She glowered at all of them. "If you confront him, then everyone will believe the rumor is true and I'll certainly be ruined. But if you go on about your business as you always have, if you accept him and continue to treat him as the friend he's always been to us, this will pass. People will follow your guidance. See? Easily solved. This problem will go away in time."

"No, it won't." Her father sighed. "Let's go home."

George nodded, signaling his agreement.

A horrid sensation swept over Dillie, that same, curdling

discomfort she got whenever she ate sardines. Her tongue began to swell and her throat grew tight. "You can't do this to me. If we run, everyone will believe the worst of me."

She wanted to stomp her foot, rant and rage, behave like a petulant child. Her heart and happiness were at stake. Why couldn't anyone understand that? She tried to control herself. She spoke with calm and dignity, perhaps a touch of indignation. Perhaps more than a touch. "I will not go home. *I haven't done anything wrong.*"

Just when she thought the situation couldn't get worse, Ian made the mistake of walking in. Graelem and Julian grabbed him.

"Don't hurt him!" Dillie cried out, and then let out a shriek when George and Gabriel grabbed her. They crisscrossed their arms and scooped her into the makeshift chair. "Stop! Put me down!" Though she struggled, they effortlessly carried her back to the family carriage.

The entire Farthingale clan followed after them. So did Lord and Lady Cummerfield. So did most of their guests, though the Cummerfields and their guests made it only as far as the street corner before more Farthingales cut them off. She heard mutters of "family business" and "give us privacy," as though she and Ian had been caught doing something horrible and they were all now mourning her fate.

The outrage hadn't been nearly this awful when Charles Ealing and Mary Abbott were caught naked at the Wakeford ball. *Naked.* Ian hadn't even seen her without her clothes, yet everyone was treating him as though he had. So unfair!

She craned her neck to search for him amid the wall of Farthingale busybodies. "Where's Ian? What have you done with him?"

"Ian, is it?" her father growled.

"Well—*ack*!" Dillie was shoved into the first Farthingale carriage with George, Gabriel, and her parents. She found herself squeezed between George and Gabriel, pinned between their annoyingly broad shoulders. "Have you all gone mad?"

"Be quiet, Dillie," her father said in a voice that drew her up at once with its barely leashed anger. Her father had never used that tone with any of his daughters, not even with Daisy when she'd fallen in love with Gabriel, and his reputation had been as bad as Ian's at the time. Perhaps worse.

She closed her eyes as a shudder ran through her. This wasn't happening. It was only a bad dream. She'd wake up and all would be well. The sun would be out and birds would be chirping outside her window.

Please.

The carriage in which she rode—or more aptly, into which she had been pushed—was the first to turn onto Chipping Way and make its way through the gate at Number 3. The tree in front of the house was still standing, though short a couple of branches that had been blown to pieces by the elephant shot last November. The tree had not been cut down and there was no trellis outside her window.

All these were discrepancies that ought to have cast doubt on the ugly rumor. Only no one was paying attention. No one wished to be confused by the facts. They'd rather believe the unsubstantiated rumors.

She glowered at her parents, still furiously angry with them.

Her father ordered her into the parlor. "Wait there until I call you into the library."

"I will not! Where's Ian?"

He repeated the command.

She refused again, so he threw his hands into the air and muttered something about his "five plagues" that probably referred to her and her sisters, none of whom had managed a traditional courtship.

The entire Farthingale clan piled into the library. Honestly, they'd all suffocate if one more person attempted to enter the room. Perhaps an exaggeration, but the library was crowded. There was a small commotion as Julian and Graelem strode in, their giant, brutish paws on Ian as they hauled him in. Yes, she was definitely suffocating. Perhaps the cause was dread and not the throng of Farthingales gathered around her.

She was trying not to be theatrical, but this was a dramatic moment. Perhaps the most dramatic of her life. Her future happiness depended upon the outcome of this evening. She turned and wound up face to face with Ian, who was still in the determined clutches of his captors. Did they think he'd run away? Dillie knew he wouldn't. It wasn't in his nature. He was a rakehell, not a coward.

She noticed that Ian's jacket was missing. One of his brutish captors (also known as her ape-like brothers-in-law) must have ripped it off him at some point between the Cummerfield residence and here. Perhaps he'd taken it off himself, preparing for a fight.

She'd seen him wearing it earlier. He'd looked quite splendid in his formal black attire and white tie. Now, he looked as though he'd been kicked, punched, and thoroughly pummeled during the short ride.

His shirt and tie were in disarray. His right eye was swollen and so was his lip, which appeared to be cut and lightly bleeding at the corner. Julian and Graelem looked worse. She didn't care. They deserved the pounding obviously received courtesy of Ian.

She reached out to touch Ian, and then thought better of it and instead began to wring her hands. "I'm so sorry."

He stood proud and unbending. "Don't be. Not your fault, Dillie."

He had every reason to be furious with her, but he'd merely responded with patience and understanding. *Not your fault.* He spoke the words softly, each word falling upon her like a protective caress. She inhaled lightly. He wasn't going to do something stupid, such as agree to marry her, was he?

She stepped closer to study his eyes. *Oh, crumpets!* "Don't do it, Ian. You don't have to marry me. I don't want you to."

He let out a mirthless laugh and shook his head. "I don't think the choice is ours to make."

Her mouth dropped open. "It is. Farthingales marry for love. I refuse to be the exception. You can't give in to this rabble."

His smile faded. It wasn't a joyful one in the first place. More like a gallows smile, the sort that quickly fades when the noose is put around one's neck. "Do you think you can ever love me, Dillie?"

Her tongue once again began to thicken and her cheeks grew hot. Flaming hot. Choking-on-a-sardine hot. "How is that relevant? You don't love me. You'll never love me." She turned to face her sisters, hoping they would understand and come to her rescue. "How can you stand there and let this happen to me? Were any of you saints before your wedding day? I hardly think so. Why, your husbands couldn't keep their hands off you before—"

"This isn't about us," Laurel said in a sudden rush, her eyes widening and a blush now staining her cheeks. Rose and Daisy coughed as though to clear their suddenly parched throats. So did several of her aunts. Interesting. Her mother's face was the deepest shade of crimson. So deep, it was almost purple. Now, that was even more interesting.

Her father, whose face was also red, though most likely from anger, frowned at her. "Enough of this nonsense. I want to hear the truth."

"I've been telling you the truth, practically shouting it at you till I'm hoarse. Ian... His Grace... has always been a gentleman. He came to my rescue when Lord Ealing tried to lure me into a compromising position. He threw the clunch into the Wakefords' fountain. That's how Lord Ealing got his clothes wet."

She glanced at Rose. "And I suppose Rose was right when she said Ian... His Grace, wasn't interested in Lady Mary Abbott, because she immediately set her sights on Lord Ealing and got *him* into a compromising position. They deserve each other."

One of her Oxfordshire aunts came forward, shaking her head. "I thought you liked Lord Ealing?"

"No, but I wanted to. I tried to. I simply couldn't. In truth, I was relieved when he and Lady Mary were caught." She sighed. "But my problem isn't with them or with the duke." She shot Ian another glance. "Don't worry, I'm not going to marry you. As many times as they beat you into saying yes, I'll say no."

Ian cast her an appealingly lopsided grin, which was all he could manage with his lower lip swollen. "I'd rather avoid those beatings." Then he laughed and shook his head. And laughed harder.

Obviously, the Farthingales had driven him to madness. She scowled at her family. "I'm ashamed of you all. Your behavior has been reprehensible."

"Our behavior?" her mother, her father, and at least six Farthingale relatives said in unison.

Dillie nodded. "You acted as though the rumors were true. Had we all stayed and ignored the whispers, the matter would have blown over in a few days. But you panicked and ran, as though ashamed of *me*."

Her mother stepped forward. "We're only trying to protect you."

"But you aren't protecting me." Where was Lily to explain it to them? Oh, how she wished her brilliant twin were here. "You've made things worse. You see, by running away—"

"Strangers can be cruel," Julia said. "We didn't want them to make you cry."

She shook her head in dismay. "I see. Only my family has the right to make me cry. Well," she said, as the tears began to spill from the corners of her eyes, "you've succeeded."

Ian shook off his captors and stepped toward her. "Dillie, it's all right—"

"No. It isn't," she said between sniffles, searching for a handkerchief and not finding one. Her father reached out to offer his. She tilted her chin into the air and refused it.

Ian sighed. "Here, take mine."

"Thank you." But he didn't step back. He stood close and watched as she dabbed the tears now streaming down her cheeks.

"Can you ever love me?" he asked again, his voice deliciously soft against her ear. She wasn't going to respond to the question. She refused to consider the possibility. No, she wasn't going to think about it. Ever. Her feelings for him—assuming she had any—wouldn't solve anything.

"What of you? Do you even like me? Enough to be saddled with me as your wife? *Forever,*" she shot back.

He frowned.

She had her answer. He wished to remain a confirmed bachelor. He didn't want a wife, and didn't want *her* as his wife. He didn't love her. Didn't need her. She was in a terrible scrape. She was tarnished. Ruined. And the worst part of it was that she had missed out on all the fun, for she hadn't actually done anything wicked with Ian.

But she would next time.

Oh, yes. Indeed. She would indeed.

Next time Ian landed in her bed, she'd take full advantage of his big, gorgeous body.

"I'm sorry. I don't mean to be ill-tempered with you." She shook her head and sighed. "I'm angry and... scared, if you wish to know the truth. Oh, not for me. I know you'd never purposely hurt me. I'm worried about you. I don't wish to ruin your chances of finding happiness. Not that you're a happy person. In truth, you're about the unhappiest person I know. And I've just made things worse for you."

Ian's expression was unreadable. Unlike hers. She was disgustingly easy to read, every thought and feeling revealed at a glance. He kept himself closed off, didn't share his heart with anyone. He kept all his secrets to himself, especially the horrid ones that had scarred his soul.

She didn't know any of his secrets, other than the one about Felicity's existence, which wasn't really a secret. Anyway, it wasn't *his* secret. He'd merely acted as any loving brother would, stepping in and doing the honorable thing to save a child.

Yet his family hated him. What had he done to make them despise him? And why did he despise himself as deeply as they did?

And why did she secretly wish to marry him?

No! No, no, no!

But the butterflies in her stomach were doing their Ian-frenzied happy dance.

She let out a sob and ran from the library.

IAN SHOVED HIS way through the crowd of Farthingales and warned them to stay back while he chased after Dillie. He caught up to her as she hurried up the staircase in the entry hall. "Dillie, stop."

But she wouldn't.

He reached her on the third step and took her into his arms, trying to be as gentle as possible while she struggled to break free. Her feelings had been badly bruised by her family's distrust and he wasn't about to add physical bruises. "Calm down and listen to me. It's going to be all right."

"How? By your being beaten into a loveless marriage? By my destroying your freedom and happiness?" She continued to struggle, but he wouldn't let her go. Finally, she gave up and set her hands on his chest. She leaned into him and moaned. "Oh, Ian. Why did you come after me?"

"As you said, I was never all that happy." He wrapped his arms around her, wanting to hold her close, determined to protect her from the ugliness she would surely endure for the rest of her life unless he fixed things.

She gazed at him a long moment, saying nothing.

His heart tightened and began to pound hard within his chest. He'd been surrounded by a sea of unfriendly faces, been pummeled by Julian and Graelem. He'd stood alone... as always. None of it had frightened him.

However, the look in Dillie's eyes right now had him shaking in his boots.

She looked delicate and beautiful. There was a magical, ethereal quality about her with those pearls shimmering in her luscious dark hair. She was young and incredibly vulnerable, yet at the same time, brave. The way she had chased off his attackers last November was quite something.

He knew what he had to do. "This is my fault. I'm not going to run from the consequences." He tipped her chin upward so that her gaze met his. There was only one possible solution to this problem. "I owe you, Dillie. You saved my life."

He released her and bent on one knee, a gesture that could not be mistaken by her or the horde of relatives watching them.

Dillie gasped and let out another sob. "Ian, you idiot! Get up."

Not the response he expected. "No. Let me do this."

"But you don't owe me anything. I don't need you to save me. I'll save myself."

"How?" He was offering to marry her. He was willing to make the sacrifice, a rather noble sacrifice. A monumental sacrifice for him. Perhaps she was too overset to realize what he'd just offered to share. His name. His title. His wealth.

She tugged on his shoulders to yank him up, but he refused to budge. "There must be a better solution. There has to be," she insisted.

He glanced at her family. The women were all silent and holding their breaths. The men had their fists curled, itching to do him bodily damage if the outcome was not to their liking. He turned back to her, hating the look of misery in her eyes. "There isn't. Death-by-angry-family is a most unpleasant way to die. I'm not keen on ending up that way."

She dabbed at the tears still streaming down her cheeks. He noticed that she was still holding tight to his handkerchief and she had her hand on his shoulder, clinging to him for support. She liked him, felt comfortable with him. This could work. She might even love him, if her response to his kisses was any indication. Of course, Dillie, being who she was, would never admit that she loved him. Not to him or to herself.

She let out a shaky breath and sat on a step in order to meet his gaze as he knelt. He loved the soft way she looked at him, the gentle warmth of her eyes, and the beauty of her hesitant smile. "You're not going to die at the hands of my family. In any event, you're a wealthy duke. You can survive anything." She placed her hand against his cheek, caressed it. "And you're handsome, too. And brave. And wonderful."

"Is that a yes?" Because he was seriously starting to rethink this marriage issue. Avoiding it like the plague wasn't working out too well for him. Having a wife had its benefits. For one thing, the scheming, marriage-minded mothers and their insipid daughters would stop chasing him.

Her hand slipped off his cheek. "No."

The men in her family started toward him.

"Stay right there!" Dillie commanded them. "No one sets a hand on the duke." There was a glint in her eyes that warned she'd take an elephant gun to anyone who dared cause him more harm. *Him.*

Him.

She was fighting to protect him. She stole his breath away.

"Your Grace, go home," she said with purposeful formality, obviously hoping to end the discussion. "I'll be fine. Thank you for offering to marry me. I truly appreciate the gesture. In truth, it's quite something coming from you."

He could barely make out the soft blue of her eyes for all the tears she had spilled. Her voice was shaking and her breaths were ragged.

She was trying to remain composed for his sake. She was strong, but despite her protestations, she wasn't at all fine. She was scared.

"It isn't merely a gesture. The offer is real," he said, allowing instinct to guide him. He didn't want to think about what he was saying or what he was offering. He'd been running from marriage for most of his life. As Dillie had said, he was one of the unhappiest men she'd ever met. "Take all the time you need." To emphasize his point, he leaned forward and kissed her lightly on the cheek. *Softest cheek.* "I'll be here for you whenever you're ready. I'll always be here for you, Dillie."

There it was. He'd said it again. *Always. Forever.* These strange words kept tripping from his tongue as though they were the only ones he knew. As though they were the only words that could be said to Dillie. These sensations—affection, sharing, concern—were strange to him. In truth, they frightened him. He was opening up his damn turtle shell and inviting her in. There was a risk to it. She might not like what she found buried deep within.

His brother had died because of what he'd done. He could never take it back. "Always."

The magic would end once she found out about James, and her affection would turn to disgust. He'd still protect and take care of her, of course. He owed her that. He'd provide all the advantages that came with the title of duchess, for she deserved the best.

As for him, he'd go back to being alone.

It was the only way of life he'd ever known.

CHAPTER 10

DILLIE SIGHED AND tossed in bed, unable to sleep, as sunrise neared. She finally gave up, throwing off her covers to walk to the window. She hoped to find Ian standing in the garden below, his handsome frame outlined in the gray wisps of dawn. But he wasn't Romeo and she wasn't Juliet. He wasn't standing beneath her window with a love-struck expression on his face, eager to spout sonnets to her beauty. He'd gone home... or possibly elsewhere to seek the comfort of another woman.

She knew he had a mistress.

She knew his mistress was exquisitely beautiful.

Oh, she would turn into a watering pot if she didn't stop crying over Ian. Or wondering where he was. Or whether he had his arms wrapped around another woman.

She turned away from the window and settled on the bench beside it, her head swirling with the one decision to be made, the most important of her life. It should have been easy. Any other young lady would have been waltzing about her room after receiving an offer of marriage from a duke. Even if that duke were Ian.

Especially if that duke were Ian.

Dillie sighed, knowing she was different for wanting love and fidelity. No one else would have demanded it of him. No other would care about Ian's discreet *amours*. Indeed, most young ladies would have been delighted at the prospect of acquiring a noble title and the riches certain to accompany said title. As for sharing Ian's bed, most would have been shocked if he required it, for everyone knew that dukes and duchesses retired to their separate quarters. It wasn't a hard and fast rule, but simply done that way.

Dillie had never been very good at following rules. She wanted to share Ian's bed, wanted his strong arms about her on cold winter nights. Any other young woman would have been content to wrap her arms around her newly gained title, allowing it—and not the man—to keep her warm and cozy.

Indeed, Dillie knew she was different. She needed Ian beside her not only on those wintery nights but on warm summer nights, too. And cool spring nights. Also on mild autumn nights. She wanted *him*. Not his wealth. Not his title.

Had she just made the most idiotic decision of her life in rejecting his proposal? He'd spoken to her father before leaving, probably repeated what he'd said about waiting for her consent. His offer was still open. *Always.* For Ian, "always" meant about two weeks.

Her heart tightened. She was going to cry again. "You can't spend the entire season in tears," she muttered to herself. The sun would soon rise, giving way to a bright new day, and she had accomplished nothing. Not that she had much to accomplish, now that she was temporarily ruined. At least she hoped it was temporary. In any event, this season was over for her. She wouldn't be invited into any respectable salons while scandal swirled about her. If she were by chance invited, it would certainly be to be put on display and mocked for the amusement of others.

No doubt she'd lose her composure and poke some old biddy in the nose, making matters worse. Then she'd be considered not only loose with her morals but violent to boot. Not that she cared. However, her parents would be heartbroken.

There was no help for it. She had to return to Coniston, for how could one think amid the mad London whirl? There, she could immerse herself in peaceful isolation, take long walks down country lanes, and gaze for hours at Coniston's scenic splendor. Indeed, she needed to be alone and away from her meddling, although well-intentioned, family. Away from Ian, for she couldn't hold a thought when he was near. He overwhelmed her senses.

She'd give herself two weeks to come to a decision. In that time, Ian might lose interest and effectively make the decision for her. No, she realized at once. He was determined to protect her, and a determined Ian was not easy to overcome. He'd be ruthless in getting his way, using his considerable powers of seduction to lure her into accepting his proposal.

She was so close to surrendering. The butterflies in her stomach were already flitting about inside her, cheering and shouting, *Yes, my love! My dearest! Yes, yes, yes!* By tomorrow, they'd be dancing to the tune of a wedding waltz.

The only holdout was her heart.

She sniffled, realizing she was still holding Ian's handkerchief and had held on to it all night. Crumpets, she was a pathetic creature for needing a piece of Ian beside her, even something as inconsequential as a small square of cloth. *Ian, I wish you loved me.*

Her tears began to flow again, confirming that she had officially turned into a watering pot. She was misty eyed, red nosed, and a blubbering, sputtering mess. She cried until morning. She cried until the sun shone brightly through her window. Then she dried her tears, dressed, and rang for Gladys. "Pack my trunks."

The sweet girl's eyes popped wide. "Where will you go?"

"I'm returning to Coniston."

She announced her plan to her parents when they came down to breakfast later that morning. Dillie had been waiting for them and was already seated at the dining table, an untouched glass of milk in front of her. She hadn't eaten any food. She hadn't the appetite, for her stomach was twisted in a painful knot. "I don't want anyone to accompany me. I'm going alone."

Her father, who had just filled his plate with sausage and kippers and then sat down beside her, threw his napkin onto the table and rose. "Sophie," he said, pushing back his chair, "our daughter is determined to put us into an early grave. Alone, Dillie? Are you jesting? Isn't it what got you into this scrape in the first place?"

Dillie's mother left her plate on the sideboard and hurried to his side. She patted him on the shoulder. "Now, John, you know none of this is Dillie's fault. The duke was hurt. Dillie and George saved his life. I'm quite proud of her. You ought to be as well."

Dillie smiled for the first time in what felt like centuries. "Thank you, Mama."

"And the duke is willing to marry her. He could offer nothing less, of course. After all, she did save him." She nibbled her lower lip as she turned to Dillie. "So why won't you marry him? Is there something you aren't telling us?"

"No. I simply don't wish to be the only Farthingale trapped in a loveless marriage."

Her mother shook her head. "I still don't see the problem. I've noticed the way you look at him, child."

Of course, because she didn't know how to hide her feelings. Especially about Ian. She turned into a tongue-dragging, stumbling, bumbling idiot whenever he was near. "It isn't that simple."

Her mother cast her the gentlest smile. "Yes, it is."

Perhaps for her mother. She glanced from one parent to the other. Her mother had always had her father's loyalty and affection. He'd loved her from the moment he'd set eyes on her. Not on Chipping Way. He'd met her in Coniston. She hadn't needed the Chipping Way curse to catch a husband.

"I just need time alone to think, time without everyone looking over my shoulder and commenting on everything I do or say. Abner can drive me up in one of our carriages. Or I'll take a hired coach."

Her father slapped his palms on the table. Dillie jumped at the resounding *thwack*. "The devil you will! You'll take a Farthingale carriage. And your aunt Imogen will accompany you."

"Aunt Imogen?" Dillie groaned. "Oh, not her! Anyone but her. She reeks of rosewater and never stops talking."

Her mother let out a small gasp. "That isn't a nice thing to say." But she was pursing her lips and trying her best to hold back a grin.

Dillie raised her chin in indignation. "But it's true."

"John," her mother said softly, "perhaps Rupert can escort Dillie most of the way. Didn't you just tell me that he must go to Carlisle on family business?"

He nodded. "An important meeting on Wednesday. He won't have time to drop her off and still make the meeting."

"He would if we went straight to Carlisle and dropped him there first," Dillie said. "Abner can then take me down to Coniston. It's an easy day's ride from Carlisle, and even if we're delayed, we know the area well. If we have any difficulty, I'll take a room at the Black

Sail Inn in Penrith. It's a respectable establishment. You've often said so yourself."

"What do you think, John?" Her mother was still at his side, soothing him as no one else ever could. "It sounds like a workable plan."

He shook his head and sighed. "I think," he said, sighing again, "that I ought to have thrown each of my daughters into a dark dungeon and not let them out until I had betrothal contracts firmly in hand."

Her mother reached up and kissed him on the cheek. "Your daughters managed quite well on their own. Even Dillie. She has an offer of marriage from a duke. A young and handsome one at that."

But one who doesn't love me.

"Very well. I'll give you a week. Abner brings you back to London by the following Wednesday."

Which was an enormous concession, and Dillie knew better than to press her luck, but she tried anyway. "I need two weeks. Not a day less."

Her father now had a stubborn set to his jaw. "One."

They settled on two weeks, but her father would spend the second week with her in Coniston. It was a workable compromise. By late morning, she and Uncle Rupert were passing through the Farthingale gate in the carriage, drawn by a pair of sturdy horses in the capable hands of Abner Mayhew, their longtime coachman.

Abner was a most pleasant fellow, older than her father by a good ten years. He had a full cap of white hair and round, ruddy cheeks. The Mayhews had worked for the Farthingales for generations. Mrs. Mayhew was their long-time cook. Abner was their coachman. Amos, the youngest, who was about Dillie's age, was one of their footmen. Various Mayhew nieces had worked in the Farthingale household in the positions of nanny, maid, and governess.

Which was perhaps why Abner felt it was his place to comment on her situation when they stopped near Northampton. The carriage clattered to a halt in the courtyard of the Hawkshead Inn just as the sun faded over the glistening rooftops. Rupert descended and strode ahead to arrange for their quarters while Abner grabbed his step stool and set it in front of the carriage door. "Let me help you down, Miss Dillie."

She smiled her thanks.

She could see that he was simply bursting to tell her what was on his mind. "Are ye sure ye want ta be runnin' from a duke, Miss Dillie?"

"No, Abner. I'm not sure at all."

"Then why are ye runnin'? Is it because of them ugly rumors?" he asked, releasing her hand and taking a step back.

"My supposed scandal? It's utterly ridiculous. The duke always behaved as a gentleman—"

"*Ech!* I never believed that stuff and nonsense about you and him. Ye're a good girl. We all know that." He nodded to emphasize his point. "I meant those other nasty rumors. The ones about him."

Her heart suddenly beat a little faster. "Tell me, Abner. Please. No one else will talk to me about his past. What have you heard? Is it something important?"

"I think so, Miss Dillie." He paused and swallowed hard. "They say he murdered his own brother."

IAN RODE FOR Swineshead the morning after the disastrous Cummerfield ball. Of course, he hadn't actually attended the ball, just been tossed into a Farthingale carriage and beaten into submission by his own best friends. He supposed he deserved it. After all, he'd run down Chipping Way the night he was attacked, ignoring the Chipping Way curse, and now he was suffering the consequences.

The sky was overcast and threatening rain, but he hoped to get in several hours of hard riding before the skies opened up. No matter the weather, he needed to leave town. It wasn't for his sake, but for Dillie's. She needed time to calm down and think, time to realize that her prospects were dim unless she married him. She would come around in time. He just needed to keep away and give her that time alone to consider all the possibilities.

In this, he was a patient man.

He wasn't in any hurry to be leg shackled. Truth be told, he hadn't planned on ever taking a wife. He certainly wasn't about to offer for anyone other than Dillie, for he wasn't fit husband material for any woman. He'd try his best for Dillie's sake, though. It might work. She had a way of easing the pain he carried in his heart, of making him laugh, and she never bored him.

That counted for something, didn't it?

He was not expecting miracles. Dillie could never completely heal his wounds or bring back the brother he'd loved deeply. He'd been scarred by that one bad moment and had never felt good about himself since. Indeed, he would never forget what he had done to James, nor would his detestable family ever allow him to forget, making certain to twist their verbal knives deep into his heart each and every time they met.

Hence that turtle shell he'd built around his heart.

As he rode off, he considered another problem. Once he and Dillie were married, it would be difficult to keep her and his family apart. Having been raised in a close and loving household, Dillie would feel duty bound to bring him and his relations together, just as her twin, Lily, had done with her husband's family. That effort had ended happily, but any effort on Dillie's part to reconcile him with his family would not. The Markhams were different. His mother and cousins would do their best to poison the marriage.

He wouldn't allow it, but what if he weren't around to protect Dillie? She'd chased off a pair of base ruffians and saved his sorry life. Still, his wretched family would not hesitate to tear her to pieces if given the opportunity. *Damn them.* Celestia and her toadies could say or do what they wished to him, but he'd hunt them down and kill them in cold blood if they ever attempted to harm Dillie.

He shook his head and sighed, wondering whether he was fretting needlessly.

What if Dillie refused him?

Hell, she'd be better off.

He rode on, ignoring the biting wind against his cheeks and wanting to get as far away from London as possible. This gave him the perfect opportunity to visit Felicity in Swineshead, for he needed to make certain she was being treated well. He also needed to tend to several Edgeware matters he'd put off because he'd tarried too long in London.

Until a few months ago, he'd used Swineshead as a hunting lodge. The land, with its abundant forests and well-stocked streams, was a perfect hunter's retreat. The ponds, lakes, and streams attracted all manner of freshwater fish and game, and the dense forests provided shelter for birds, deer, and wild boar.

Felicity's arrival at Swineshead had changed everything. He'd ordered improvements made to the lodge since she was to reside there, and he wanted her to be comfortable and happy. He was now eager to see the changes.

He released the breath he'd been holding and let out a wry laugh. Within the month, his life might never be the same, a fast descent from rakehell to married family man. He'd made the necessary arrangements with Dillie's father. The only thing lacking was Dillie's consent.

She would give it. She had to. He owed her for saving his life and he always repaid his debts. It could work. Dillie would make it work, for her kisses were delectable and she had a sunshine smile that always warmed his cold heart. Felicity would love her, for she had a gentle way with the Farthingale children that made him ache every time he watched her play with them.

No one had ever been gentle with him. Not once in his life.

It rained steadily on and off for the first three days of the journey. Ian finished his business in Coventry with surprising ease and continued north toward Swineshead, but he was hindered on the fourth day by a brutally cold rain that began to fall hard as he approached the market town of Penrith.

All of a sudden, the skies opened up with a vengeance and buckets of fat raindrops quickly muddied the roadway. It was early evening and the sun had yet to set, but thunderous black clouds covered the sky so that it appeared as ink-dark as a starless night. "This looks to be a bad one. We had better find shelter," he muttered to Prometheus, the handsome gelding he'd acquired at Tattersalls.

He wasn't far from the Black Sail Inn, a decent establishment situated on the outskirts of Penrith. Since he often stayed there while attending to business in Carlisle or across the border in Scotland, he headed for the inn, resigned to continuing his journey the next day once the weather cleared. He wasn't about to risk injury to Prometheus.

The horse suddenly grew skittish, forcing Ian to concentrate on the road. He drew lightly on the reins, easing him from a canter to a walk across a particularly slick patch. The temperature had taken a swift dip, and sleet now mingled with the rain that fell with torrential force. *Bloody English weather.*

The wind kicked up, now tossing that rain straight into his face, but the Black Sail Inn was just up the road and he looked forward to warming himself in the common room beside the well-stoked fire. He'd dry off first, then imbibe a much-needed tankard or two of ale. However, he had to put those thoughts of comfort aside for the moment. The road was suddenly a dangerous mix of mud and ice requiring all his concentration.

Ian's tension eased as the inn's thatched roof came into view. "Do you see it, Prometheus?" He dismounted and walked his gelding the short distance through the mix of cold, pelting rain and hailstones. The temperature had dropped even more precipitously, and the courtyard would soon be a treacherous expanse of ice.

"Yer Grace! I'll see ta yer rooms at once," the proprietor said, bustling out of the inn and walking precariously on the slick ground to greet him. "Good ta have ye with us again. 'Tis not a fit night for man nor beast. Haven't seen conditions this dangerous in years."

A stable boy hurried forward and took his horse. "I'll take good care of 'im, Yer Grace. Never ye worry. Gaw! He's a big one. What's 'is name?"

"Prometheus. He looks fierce, but he's a lamb to handle. Just give him a few gentle strokes and some soft praises."

"Gaw! Just like a woman."

Ian let out a startled laugh. "Aren't you a little young to know about such things?"

The boy tossed him a smug grin. "I've seen things. And I'm almost fourteen."

"That old? My, my." Ian slipped the pouches off the saddle and hurriedly carried them in while the boy took Prometheus to the stables.

The proprietor, a portly man by the name of Gwynne, began to fuss over him the moment they were inside. He summoned several servants, and with the quick clap of his hands ordered one to ready Ian's bedchamber and another to carry wood upstairs to light a fire in his hearth. He then ordered another two servants to heat water for Ian's bath. A tub was already in his chamber, Mr. Gwynne explained. "'Tis our finest room, and why shouldn't I offer m'best guests every modern comfort?"

Ian nodded. "You'll find no argument from me. My stays here are always pleasant. In truth, I made for your inn the moment I saw the darkening sky."

Mr. Gwynne puffed out his chest with pride. "Will you be dining downstairs, Yer Grace?"

Ian was cold and wet, and his back was stiff from the long ride. "I'll come down for a drink later, but have my meal brought upstairs."

With another efficient clap of his hands, Mr. Gwynne called to one of the serving maids. "Elsie, His Grace is in need of a tankard of ale and a hearty chicken stew. Bring a tray up to him at once."

Elsie was a young, attractive girl who had warmed Ian's bed a time or two on past visits. She cast him a look that indicated she was eager to do so again. "I'm always at yer service, Yer Grace."

"Stew and ale is all I'll need tonight," he said, politely refusing her offer.

"I'm available if ye change yer mind." She purposely grazed her breasts against his arm as she left to obey the innkeeper's instructions. A year ago, he wouldn't have needed any encouragement, for that had been his way of life. Wherever he went, whenever the urge struck, there were always women eager to share his bed.

He no longer found these meaningless encounters appealing. Dillie made him hunger for something more. He wasn't certain what that "more" was, but he knew it would be something more substantial than the casual satisfaction of a tumble in the sack.

Ian slung the pouches over his shoulder and turned for the stairs. He was eager to get out of his wet clothes and didn't care to wait for the servants to ready his quarters or offer to carry his bags upstairs.

The pouches were light in weight, containing only a change of travel clothes and some private business papers.

He strode past the common room, which was purposely situated near the stairs so thirsty travelers would be enticed as they walked to and from their sleeping quarters. Ian heard the sound of clinking tankards and laughter. He glanced into the room and noticed the rows of empty tables. There were no more than a dozen stray travelers who had sought shelter from the storm.

A few locals also appeared to be enjoying the usually crowded tap room. Mr. Gwynne shook his head and sighed. "The storm's bad for my regular business. Hope it passes quick."

"I'm certain it will." A fire blazed in the common room's massive fireplace. Wisps of smoke drifted toward Ian, carrying the scent of burning wood and a pork roast that must have been glazed with honey as it cooked over the flames earlier in the day. His stomach growled. He was hungry, not only for Dillie but for actual food.

The other guests didn't seem to notice him, for their backs were turned. In any event, Ian had no wish to engage in pleasantries this evening. The common room was inviting enough, but he was spent. He ran his fingers through his wet hair. Pieces of ice slipped through his fingers. Ice in April? These late storms were particularly treacherous, for travelers were often ill prepared for them.

Mr. Gwynne led the way, huffing and lumbering up the stairs. "Yer Grace, I hope ye find yer quarters satisfactory. Elsie will bring ye that tankard of ale and a bowl of chicken stew. It isn't fancy, but it will warm yer innards."

Ian nodded. "It's most appreciated."

He was pleased to see a plump mattress on the bed and a fire blazing in the hearth. A tub stood near the hearth, and there was a side table with chair on the far wall beneath the window. The shutters were rattling, no doubt loosened by the fierce wind. "Blasted weather. My apologies, Yer Grace. I'll fix them at once."

Ian removed his oilcloth and cloak and hung them on a hook beside the hearth. He crossed to the window to assist the innkeeper, who was wrestling with the shutters. Eager to be left alone, he was about to offer to take over the chore when he saw a brilliant bolt of lightning strike the courtyard. It was followed by a roll of thunder.

He blinked his eyes. Surely the light was playing tricks on him. Was that a girl he'd seen trudging through the rain? He turned to Mr. Gwynne, but the man was still fussing and muttering, his attention fixed on the rattling shutters.

Another crack of lightning lit up the courtyard and was quickly followed by another roll of thunder. He *had* seen someone. Definitely a girl out there, struggling. She'd fallen to her knees in the cold mud. "Forget the shutter, Mr. Gwynne," he said with sudden urgency. "There's someone in peril. A girl. I think she's just fainted."

"Lord love me! I'll get my men to help at once."

But Ian had already grabbed his oilcloth and hurried downstairs, taking the steps two at a time. He tore out of the inn and into the courtyard, quickly making out a slight, limp body lying amid the icy puddles. He put the oilcloth around the girl and lifted her into his arms. "Miss, I—" His heart suddenly shot into his throat. He knew this girl, recognized the slender curve of her body. No. She was in London. Safe. "Dillie?"

It can't be.

His damn limbs froze and his mind began to reel. The icy rain continued to pelt them. He shifted her more securely in his arms. "Dillie, can you hear me?"

Lord! What in blazes is she doing here?

"Hurt. Abner's hurt. Carriage... must save him," she mumbled, struggling in his arms though she was obviously dazed. "Overturned. Must... show you the way."

He would have laughed were the situation not so serious. This was typical Dillie. Spirited. Independent. Ready to take action, no matter that she was on the verge of fainting. She'd obviously hurt her leg. He'd seen her hobbling as she came into the inn's courtyard.

He carried her inside, his heart now pounding so hard it threatened to burst within his chest. She continued to struggle, not yet recognizing him. Her eyes were unfocused and he knew that she was in pain. "No... not here... north road!"

He set her down on one of the long benches in the common room, the one closest to the warmth of the fire, and knelt beside her. A stern glance warned away the patrons who'd come to gawk. "We'll take care of Abner," he said gently. "Don't worry about him, Dillie.

I'll gather a search party. North road, you say? But London is south."

"We... Carlisle. North. North. Not London."

She tried to say more, but he stopped her for she was merely rambling, most of her words now incomprehensible. He caught only a few, enough to know others were still out there and probably hurt. Why did she insist they were coming from Carlisle? It made no sense. He'd left her in London only a few days ago.

To be safe, he decided to order the innkeeper's servants to search in both directions. "How far did you walk, Dillie? Did the carriage overturn by the sharp bend in the river?" That bend in the river was north of here. One passed it coming from Carlisle, as Dillie had said. The road from London was a straight approach.

She managed a nod.

He wasn't certain what that nod meant, or whether she was responding to his question.

"Anyone else with you besides Abner?" He knew the route from Penrith to Carlisle fairly well, having traveled it quite often. He wasn't convinced she'd come from there, but it was possible, assuming she'd left London the same day he had. He'd traveled by horse, spent three days in Coventry. She'd gone by carriage. Had she gone straight to Carlisle and then come back south? It didn't seem likely. No matter, he'd unravel the details afterward.

More important, he didn't think her father would allow her to leave London without a proper companion. There had to be another passenger. "Who else rode with you?"

"Abner... Abner," Dillie insisted when he asked her again. She was ashen, not quite lucid. Her tears blended with the icy raindrops on her cheeks. Could he trust what she was saying? "Uncle Rupert... Carlisle."

"Your uncle was with you?"

She nodded. "This morning."

Which made sense of a sort, although he didn't understand why Rupert Farthingale would be dropped in Carlisle first. If Dillie was traveling to Coniston, she should have been taken there before her uncle proceeded north.

She sniffled. "He wanted to stop earlier, but I refused."

It took Ian a moment to realize she was once again referring to

Abner. She buried her face in her hands, and though her words were muffled, he understood most. "Must reach... Black Sail Inn. Abner said it was too dangerous. My fault. I made him drive on. All my fault. I'm to blame."

She paused and took a deep breath. Her shoulders began to rise and fall, as though she were silently sobbing. Ian took her hands in his and gently drew them away from her face, giving her no choice but to look at him. "It's all right, sweetheart. You're safe now."

She took another quivering breath and gazed at him with misty eyes. Or rather, seemed to gaze *through* him, for her eyes were glistening and unfocused. "Abner isn't. I'm at fault." She began to ramble again, but he managed to understand that their horses had been spooked by lightning. They must have reared and then raced off when the carriage broke apart, skidding off the road when they hit an icy patch. "I'm to blame. We tipped over. The horses ran off." She slipped her hand out of his grasp and put it to her brow. "He's hurt and it's all my fault."

Ian cautiously wrapped her in his arms, not quite certain yet how badly she was injured. "It was an accident. No one's fault. You have a lump on your forehead. You've injured your foot. Or your leg. Sit still, Dillie. Let me have a look at you."

"No!" Her gaze was still unfocused. Strands of her wet hair were sticking to her cheeks. Her gown was soaked and muddied. She looked like a drowned water rat. One with big, frightened blue eyes. "Abner... I promised to rescue him."

She was injured and in no condition to go anywhere.

Ian glanced at the innkeeper and the small group of servants who had donned their cloaks and oilcloths and were now heading for the door. "Search the north road, by the river's bend." He pointed to three of the servants. "You three search south—it's possible Miss Farthingale is mistaken. Her driver is injured. Their carriage overturned." He would catch up to them later. Right now, he needed to ask more questions, needed to be certain there was no one other than Abner thrown from the carriage and lying injured in the storm. Most of all, he needed to be sure Dillie was all right.

He ran his hands over her body, trying to think medically and not like the besotted idiot he always seemed to be around her. She had no broken bones, thank goodness. Still, he used special care when lifting Dillie into his arms.

He called to Elsie, the maid who'd earlier offered to warm his bed, feeling a qualm as he did so for this had been his way until now. Casual enjoyments. No promises. Somehow, it didn't seem right that she should tend Dillie. Yet, there was no help for it. "I'll settle Miss Farthingale in my quarters. I have a dry shirt in my saddle pouch. Get her out of these wet clothes and into my shirt. It'll have to do for now."

"Aye, Yer Grace."

"And have Cook prepare a broth. No chicken stew for her yet. She'll be in too much pain to hold down any solid food. She has a lump on her forehead and her foot is badly sprained." That lump on her forehead worried him.

The girl began to wring her hands. She looked scared, but Ian needed her to care for Dillie while he joined in the search. "Once you've dried her off, seat her in a chair beside the fire. Toss more logs onto the fire if it starts to die out. She's still shivering and needs to warm up. Tuck blankets around her legs and shoulders."

"Her lips are blue."

He carried Dillie upstairs and into his quarters, still issuing orders. By this time, he'd gained the attention of two other maids, neither of whom he'd entertained in bed. He dismissed Elsie, sending her off to fetch the broth while the older maids remained to attend Dillie. "Drag that stool near the chair and prop a pillow on it, Hilda. Set her foot on the pillow, but be very gentle. She's certain to be in a lot of pain."

"Poor lamb," Hilda muttered, placing the wooden stool as he'd commanded. She appeared to be the sturdy, reliable sort who could be counted on to carry out his orders. He certainly hoped so.

Ian set Dillie down on the chair, and then left her side to toss more logs onto the fire. He was too impatient to wait for the servants to take care of it. In truth, he was jumping out of his skin. Dillie was here. Hurt. Still too dazed to realize that he was at her side.

When the innkeeper's wife rushed in, Ian's tension eased. Mrs. Gwynne was a most capable woman. "Miss Farthingale is not to be left alone. Do you understand?"

Her white mob cap bobbed up and down. "Aye, Yer Grace."

He turned back to Dillie and knelt beside her. "Who else rode with you?" He'd already asked her the question downstairs, but he wasn't confident of her answer. He needed to be certain that the search party wouldn't leave anyone behind.

She didn't respond.

"Damn." He wouldn't get much out of her in her present state. "Mrs. Gwynne, watch her carefully. She isn't to fall asleep." He knew this sort of head wound could be dangerous.

He rose, reluctant to leave Dillie but knowing he was of little use here. He would be of more help searching for Abner. In any event, Dillie would never rest until the old man was safe. He would attempt to talk to her at length later, once she was out of her wet clothes and had some warm broth in her.

He cast Dillie one last look and ran his knuckles gently along the curve of her jaw. "We'll find him," he said softly. "I'll look in on you as soon as I return."

She glanced up, her eyes suddenly bright with recognition. "Ian," she murmured, taking hold of his hand as it lingered on her cheek. She didn't remove it, but closed her eyes and let out a sob. "Am I dreaming? Am I dead?"

"Very much alive, sweetheart." However, her cloak was soaked. So was her gown. So was her hair. Her lips were now a purplish blue, and her teeth were chattering worse than they had been downstairs.

He drew away and went to his saddle pouch that was hanging over the footboard, digging out his only remaining clean shirt. He handed it to Mrs. Gwynne. "It'll have to do for a nightshirt. She'll take my room, of course. Ready other quarters for me."

Since the maids immediately took off to prepare his new room, he reached down to remove Dillie's shoes. He'd seen her hobbling, which likely meant a bad sprain. There would be swelling. She let out a soft cry. "I've twisted my ankle. My shoulder's sore, but I don't think it's broken. Abner's badly hurt. He's unconscious and still out there. I was so stubborn and stupid. It's all my fault. Our carriage overturned. His leg is crushed beneath one of the wheels. I couldn't pull it off him. The horses broke loose and galloped off."

She assured him there was no one else but Abner, then tried to rise. He caught her as she stumbled. "I'm fine. I'll show you the way."

Ian's heart was in his throat. Dillie might have been killed. What other injuries had she sustained? "There are men searching. I'll join them. You trust me, don't you, Dillie?" Why had he asked that? How could she trust him?

She smiled up at him, a small, weak smile. "Oh, Ian. I do."

It was good enough for him. Not just good. It sent his heart soaring. He gazed into her eyes, breathing a sigh of relief that they now appeared clear. "Get those clothes off you and soak in the tub. Then put on this shirt and stay by the fire. Eat something. The maids will tend to you. Ask for whatever you need. Anything, Dillie. Don't hesitate to ask."

He raked a hand through his hair. His heart was still slamming against his chest. Dillie here? Injured. He'd meant to give her time to think about his offer of marriage. What cruel twist of fate had thrown them together? If word ever got out that they'd spent the night together at the Black Sail Inn, there'd be nothing for her to think about. Her family would be at his door, pistols pointed down his throat.

She stared up at him, those big, blue eyes of hers wide with fright.

He turned to leave, and then stopped and returned to her side. He planted a solid, possessive kiss on her lips that drew a gasp from Mrs. Gwynne. *Hell.* He probably shouldn't have done that. "I'll be back with Abner."

CHAPTER 11

BY THE TIME Ian reached the innkeeper and his servants, they had already found Abner and were working to lift the carriage off his crushed leg. Ian added his strength to the endeavor, relieved when they managed to raise the carriage just enough to pull Abner out. The old man was unconscious, but traces of vapor that formed about his mouth meant he was still breathing. "How are we ta carry 'im, Yer Grace?"

Ian knelt beside Abner and checked him for broken bones. The old man's neck and spine were what concerned him most, for he'd taken a nasty spill. Nothing appeared to be broken other than his leg. Abner was fortunate. The muddy grass had somehow cushioned his fall. "I'll carry him. Help me lift him over my shoulder."

The icy rain continued to pummel them. Mr. Gwynne held his lantern high, but it offered very little illumination against the unrelenting sheets of rain. Thunder rolled and another bolt of lightning struck too close for comfort. Ian quickly secured Abner on his shoulder and then he and the search party walked as fast as they dared in the treacherous conditions, no one uttering a word until they reached the safety of the inn.

One of the maids must have been on the lookout for them. She opened the door as soon as they entered the inn's courtyard, ushering them in as they trudged up the two steps to the entry. "Lud! Is he alive?"

"Barely," one of the searchers muttered. "Pray for 'im, Louisa."

Ian shifted Abner off his shoulder and carefully stretched him out on one of the sturdy wooden tables in the common room close to the fire. He ordered Louisa to boil water and bring clean cloths. Then he turned to Mr. Gwynne. "I'll need slats of wood to bind his leg. It's easiest done down here. We'll move him up to my quarters afterward." He'd already given up his first room to Dillie and would give up the second to Abner.

Mr. Gwynne appeared surprised. "Yer quarters, Yer Grace? To a coachman?"

Ian frowned. "Is it a problem, Mr. Gwynne?"

"No, Yer Grace. Never ye worry. We'll rearrange things." Ian suddenly realized that all the rooms at the inn were likely occupied due to the foul weather, and he might very well be forced to spend the night in the common room, stretched out on a makeshift pallet by the hearth. Or rather, some poor sod who'd just made himself comfortable in one of those upstairs chambers would be tossed down here while he took over that sod's quarters.

"You needn't move anyone on my behalf," he called out as the innkeeper was about to leave to gather the slats of wood he'd requested. "I doubt I'll get much sleep tonight." He also knew that the Gwynnes would give up their own bedchamber to accommodate him, if it came to that. He wouldn't accept, of course. Even a duke could survive one night on a hard floor. He'd survived far worse.

After quickly stoking the fire, Mr. Gwynne scurried off to find pieces of wood suitable to fashion a splint. Ian took a moment to examine Abner again. His first attempt had hardly been sufficient in the dark, amid pelting ice and rain. He'd do a better job of it under the amber glow cast by the fire's leaping flames.

He studied the old man lying so still upon the table and frowned. Had he suffered more than a broken leg? It didn't appear so, but Ian couldn't be certain, for he wasn't properly trained. His medical knowledge had been gleaned over the course of many battles against the French during Napoleon's war. The Peninsular battles had been particularly bloody. Lots of broken bones suffered by his soldiers.

Fortunately, Ian knew how to set and securely bind a break. Apparently, he was the only man in this establishment who did, for no one else stepped forward to volunteer for the task. He removed his oilcloth and wet jacket, rolled up his equally wet shirt sleeves, and took a step back while the innkeeper's men removed Abner's cloak and jacket. "Careful. Be gentle with him. Better cut open that left boot," he instructed. "His foot must be swollen to twice its size. Don't tug on it. Go easy. He's an old man."

Abner let out an anguished groan.

Ian heard a soft gasp come from behind him. He turned, as did the other men in the common room, and saw Dillie standing in the doorway, barefoot and wearing his nightshirt, with a blanket carelessly wrapped about her shoulders. Her dark hair was still damp, left loose and falling to her waist. His heart began to hammer within his chest. She was an intoxicating mix of waif and angel. He wanted to wrap her in his arms and... *Bloody hell.* "What are you doing down here?"

Her eyes began to tear. "Is he alive?"

Ian nodded, unable to take his gaze off her. She looked beautiful. Bedraggled, but beautiful. "Let me take you back upstairs."

"No. Please. I must see him." She began to hobble toward Abner.

Ian let out a soft oath and strode to her side, uttering another soft oath as he lifted her into his arms over her tepid protest. She felt soft and warm. He was soaked to the skin, but her blanket was between them and would keep her dry enough. "Put your arms around my neck."

She did as ordered, and then leaned her head against him so that her cheek rested against his shoulder and her lips nuzzled his throat. Had he been cold a moment ago? Not anymore. His body was as hot as those flames blazing in the hearth.

"Sit quietly," he warned Dillie, more annoyed with his body's immediate and intense response to her nearness. Would it always be like this? He fervently hoped not. He hated this lack of control, wasn't used to it at all.

"May I hold his hand?" She spoke against his throat, her lips achingly soft against his bristled skin. He hadn't washed off the dirt from the long day's ride, and wouldn't shave until morning.

He settled her on the bench nearest Abner, almost dumping her on it, for his need to hold her was so strong it scared him. "May I?" she repeated, now casting him a devastatingly anguished plea.

"Of course." Ian recalled the gentleness of her touch and how much he'd enjoyed having her close when he'd been stabbed and struggling to survive all those months ago. Dillie's touch was something special and had meant everything to him at the time.

"Abner," she said in a whisper, gently stroking his arm.

He didn't respond.

She glanced uncertainly at Ian. "What have I done to him?"

"You?" Ian knelt beside her and lightly brushed a damp curl off her brow. "This isn't your fault, Dillie. You were caught in a vicious storm. No one's to blame."

"I am to blame," she quietly insisted. "It's all my fault. I was so stubborn. So foolish. Will he die because of me?"

"No." A lump rose in Ian's throat. Those were the exact words he'd said after he and his brother had been pulled out of the icy pond and taken back to the manor. James had been revived and was breathing when put to bed. Later that evening, his mother had come into Ian's room and stared at him with unmasked hatred, as though she wished he'd been the one trapped beneath the ice and not her precious firstborn. *Will he die because of me?* The answer had been yes. James had died later that night. "No, damn it!"

If Dillie was surprised by the vehemence of his response, she didn't show it. Instead, she reached for Abner's hand and squeezed it. "You have a broken leg," she said in that soft, melodic voice of hers. "And a fat lump on your forehead." She leaned forward. "It matches mine. See?"

Abner lay quiet.

She glanced once more at Ian, her expression swinging like a pendulum from anguish to despondency. "He can't die." Tears began to slide down her cheeks. "I couldn't live with myself if he did."

Ian wasn't going to let it happen. Abner was going to live. He would make certain of it. Dillie was happy, gentle. He refused to allow any darkness into her life, refused to allow her to experience the pain he'd endured when his brother had died, the haunting pain he still endured every damn day of his life, the tormented dreams that came to him every damn night. Sunrise did not bring relief, but the anguished reminder that he had lived another day while his brother had died.

It wouldn't happen to Dillie.

Mr. Gwynne returned with a makeshift splint. The maid brought in fresh cloths and boiling water. Ian attended to Abner with renewed determination. He made quick work of binding his leg, and then ordered the innkeeper's servants to carry Abner upstairs. "Get him out of those wet clothes. Cut his trousers off him. I don't want you disturbing the injured leg. Place a warm brick between his sheets. Keep his fire well stoked."

"I'll stay by his side," Dillie said, her voice little more than a rasp.

Ian frowned. "No. You need to get into bed yourself. Have you had your broth? Your lips are still blue."

"I'm in the pink." She shivered just then, but did her best to hide it.

"And your ankle is a vivid shade of purple," he replied, since they were sparring with colorful descriptions. "Come on, I'll carry you upstairs. You can look in on Abner in the morning. There's nothing you can do for him this evening."

"Is he that bad?"

Ian wanted to lie to her and tell her Abner would pull through, but that would only make her devastation worse if he didn't. In truth, Ian didn't know what the outcome would be.

"Let me stay with him if he's going to die." She let out a ragged breath, and then buried her face in her hands and began to cry in earnest.

Hell.

He turned to Abner, studying his limp form. *Open your eyes, damn it! Don't do this to Dillie.*

He glanced up at the ceiling, wanting to rage. He had prayed so hard for his brother to survive all those years ago. His prayers hadn't been answered, so he'd stopped praying from that time on, and stopped believing in goodness and hope. But Dillie still believed. *Answer her prayers! You can't destroy her. Do what you want with me. Don't hurt her.*

The servants carefully lifted Abner, preparing to carry him upstairs.

Ian took Dillie into his arms and kissed her on the forehead when she buried her head against his throat, still crying. Which explained why she didn't immediately hear Abner call out to her. It sounded more like a mumbled groan, at first. "Miss... Miss Di... Dillie."

Ian gave her shoulder a light squeeze. "Dillie, listen." But she was too distracted, leaning her head against his chest and sniffling. "Hush, sweetheart. Do you hear him? He's calling to you." He ordered the men to put Abner back down on the tabletop. "Give us a moment," he said, knowing Dillie needed to see that the old man had regained his senses.

He settled her on the bench beside Abner once again, her expression so hopeful it made Ian ache. "Abner? Can you hear me?"

"Where am I?" He tried to rise, but Ian held him down.

"Careful, you have a broken leg."

Abner let out a snort. "So that's what hurts like the devil."

"You're a fortunate man. Your leg appears to be the worst of your injuries. You have a few bruises and scratches, and a thick lump on your head. How does your neck feel? Don't move it just yet. Let me see you wiggle your fingers first."

He managed it quite easily. "How did I do, Miss Dillie?"

"Excellent. Perfect, as always, Abner." She cast him a smile so bright it lit up the entire room. "I have a little bump on my forehead, too." Of course, she'd neglected to tell him about her badly sprained ankle, but it didn't seem important to mention it now.

"Wiggle your toes," Ian said. "Just the right foot. Your left one is in bad shape. We've bound it, but the break is a bad one. You'll be in pain for quite some time."

"I'll endure it," he assured. "So long as Miss Dillie is all right."

"She is." Now that Abner was conscious, Ian took the opportunity to conduct a more thorough examination, or as thorough a one as somebody with his limited medical experience could manage. He had to be careful. Abner was an old man, and there was no telling what damage might yet be hidden.

When he glanced at Dillie, he saw that her eyes held hope but her lips were tightly pursed and chin quivering. "I'm so sorry, Abner," she said with a noticeable ache to her voice. "It's all my fault. If I hadn't forced you to—"

"What? I'll hear none of that, young miss." Abner furrowed his bruised brow. "I ought to have known better. I would never 'ave forgiven myself if ye'd come to harm. Can ye ever forgive me?"

Ian allowed the old man and Dillie to trade recriminations a while longer. In truth, it was music to his ears, knowing they both felt horrid about what had happened to each other and were obviously relieved that they'd both survived. They were fortunate to be alive, only a little worse for wear. They'd taken a horrific spill.

He watched Abner, looked carefully at his eyes. Ian had been in the thick of Napoleon's war and had learned more than he'd wished through experience. He'd seen all sorts of injuries, had come to know which ones would lead to death. He'd learned to tell by the look in a man's eyes whether or not that man would survive.

Abner would survive.

Thank the Graces!

Dillie was now smiling through her tears. Smiling. Ian glanced upward, knowing Dillie's prayers had been answered. Not his. Never his. Nonetheless, Ian was grateful. *Thank you.*

"I'll engage one of the servants to tend to you through the night," Ian said, interrupting their joyful reunion and motioning for the servants to resume carrying Abner upstairs. "I'll have broth sent up to you." He had no spare clothes to give Abner, but hot soup and a warm fire would keep him safe enough. The old man could sleep naked.

He tried not to think of Dillie naked.

Of course, that's all he could think about now that the immediate danger had passed. Abner would survive. So would Dillie.

His own survival was in serious doubt. Dillie was out of her blanket and back in his arms, nestled against his wet shirt and wearing nothing underneath her nightshirt. He could feel the light heave of her breasts against his chest. He could feel *everything*.

The servants carried Abner to the second room that had been prepared for Ian, while Ian carried Dillie into the room he had turned over to her. She looked up at him with her big, blue smiling eyes. "Will you stay with me a little while?"

"As long as you wish." He was soaked to the skin and hadn't eaten a bite. He was cold, dirty, and fatigued. At the same time, he was fires-of-hell hot, lusting so badly for Dillie that every inch of him was in hard, throbbing agony.

"I suppose you ought to change out of your wet clothes. Where's your room? Close to mine?"

"I don't know. I'll worry about it later. Time to get you to bed."

He kicked the door shut with his booted foot.

They were suddenly alone in her chamber. He'd leave soon, but he just wanted a moment alone with Dillie. He didn't quite know what he was going to say or do now that he had her all to himself. He knew what he *wanted* to do. Of course, he didn't expect *that* to happen. He'd never take Dillie against her wishes.

Dillie's arms were still wrapped around his neck. "Ian, you were splendid with Abner. Brilliant, wonderful, brave. With me, too." She touched his cheek, her fingers light against the bristled skin. "I can't believe you're here, but I'm so glad you are. Was it an act of divine providence that brought you to me when I needed you most?"

Her lips were at his ear, her breath warm and sweet. He caught the scent of peaches on her skin. Not mud or ice or smoky common room, just sweetest peaches.

He loved her scent.

"I happened to be on my way to Swineshead when the storm broke. This inn is known to be the best around, so I made for it." He shook his head and let out a mirthless chuckle. "I left London for your sake, to give you time away from me to think about my offer."

"And I was on my way to Coniston, to be away from you and my meddlesome family while I gave thought to my future." He felt her lips curve into a smile against his neck. "But I'm glad you're here. I know you were sent to me from heaven, so don't even think to deny it. No one else could have done what you did for Abner tonight."

"You were the brave one, sweetheart," he said with a mix of gentleness and pride, "limping through the storm, determined to do whatever you had to do to save Abner."

"And I found you," she said in a whisper, her voice achingly ragged. "Latch the door. I don't want us to be disturbed."

Ian's heart began to pound through his ears. He wanted to spend the night with her, hold her in his arms. He wanted to do much more, explore her body and understand the workings of her beautiful, generous heart. What did she intend?

Her smile slipped a little. "Stay with me, Ian."

"Dillie—"

"I couldn't bear it if you left me now."

"Very well, a little while longer." He settled her in the chair beside the fireplace, and then strode to the door and latched it, closing them in. This was madness. The two of them alone and cozy in this chamber while the storm whistled and howled outside. Scary how good it felt to be alone with her. What in blazes was he doing? Did Dillie understand what she was doing? She'd struck her head in the spill. Was she thinking clearly?

He certainly wasn't.

He returned to her side, still soaked to the skin and not caring a whit. And though she was no longer in his arms—a problem he would soon remedy—the sensation of her perfect breasts rising and falling against his chest was etched into his memory. He could still feel those soft mounds, her taut, puckered nipples. *Hot, buttered crumpets*, as Dillie would say. He could still feel *everything*.

He started to turn away, but she protested. "I like the warmth of your body against mine."

He shouldn't have shut the door. Or latched it. Dillie hadn't accepted his offer of marriage yet. If they spent another minute alone, there would be no turning back for Dillie. *Lord help me!* He couldn't possibly spend the night with her. Come morning, she'd have no choice but to marry him or forever remain a ruined spinster.

"I'm glad you stayed," she said, another soft breath tickling his ear. "We have to talk."

"Good. Talk. That's what we need." He carefully eased her foot onto the pillowed stool, for he needed to do something to calm himself. He refused to look at the invitingly enormous bed, nor did he dare settle Dillie in it yet. Far too dangerous for her. They'd talk for a short while, and then he'd walk out and find somewhere else to sleep.

Not that he wanted to do anything of the sort. He wanted to stay with her, put her in that big bed, and never let her out of it.

As ever, he was hot and aching for her.

Hard and aching.

"I just want you to know..." She paused to let out a soft, quivering breath. "No matter what Abner says, it was my fault. I think it's important for you to know that I made a terrible mistake.

Abner almost lost his life because of it."

He knelt beside her, angry that she still cast blame on herself. He understood all too well the terror and disgust gnawing at her insides. He still felt that same disgust over what he'd done to James. "Am I supposed to think less of you, Dillie? I don't. Accidents happen. That's all it was. You both survived. It's over. You're both on the mend. I won't hear another word about it."

"But it was my fault. We'd passed another inn earlier. I didn't like the look of the place and insisted we move on. What if he had died? Or been maimed for life?"

"He's very much alive, no doubt enjoying an excellent whiskey at my expense." He took her hands in his. They felt cold. His ought to have been cold, but every part of him heated whenever he was near Dillie. "He suffered nothing more than a broken leg." Arching an eyebrow, he cast her a small smile. "And a lump on his forehead to match your own."

She didn't smile back, and instead began to nibble her lower lip. "Ian, is this how you always feel?"

He stiffened. "What do you mean?"

"That sick, churning feeling in your stomach. That terrible ache in your heart, because you were to blame for something dreadful. Is the rumor true? Did your brother die because of you?"

So that's why she'd been carping on about Abner's injury and blaming herself. That's why she'd lured him into staying. *Latch the door.* He, like the idiot that he was, had fallen for it. She had been trying to draw him out, hoping he'd speak of James. *Damn her.* She had no right. He was mostly angry with himself for allowing her to shoot that cannonball straight through his heart. He'd let down his guard, and she'd blown a hole straight through him.

He rose and turned to storm out, but she hobbled to her feet and clutched his arm with both of her hands to hold him back. "Please, Ian."

She winced, the mere effort of standing obviously painful to her, but she had that stubborn Dillie look on her face and he knew she'd follow him into the fiery pits of hell to find her answers. "I'm so sorry. I went about this all wrong. I didn't know how to broach such a painful subject. I never realized until today just how horrible a burden you've carried all these years. We have to talk about it. I need to know the truth."

"No, you don't." He'd been poked and prodded all his life, the family knives twisting into him with rapacious glee, tormenting him in the hope he'd break. He never had, even as a child. He never would. Not even the French had succeeded, torturing him for information on English invasion plans. He hadn't spilled those vital secrets either. No, he wasn't ever going to break.

She eased her grip, but the gentle look of determination in her eyes held him close. He loved that look, loved her gentleness. He couldn't pull away even if he tried, even when angry with her as he was now. "I'm not trying to hurt you, Ian. You must believe me."

He did.

"I'm trying to understand you. More precisely, I need to trust you if I'm to be your wife."

"Who said my offer was still open?" But he smiled and arched one eyebrow so that she knew he was jesting. She probably knew it anyway. Dillie had a way of reaching his heart, soothing his heart, as no one else ever had.

"Take off your clothes," she commanded, shifting out of the blanket he'd made sure to tuck securely about her, for he didn't trust himself when all that stood between him and a naked Dillie was his last clean shirt. "You're soaking wet and I'd hate for you to catch a chill."

She handed him the blanket.

Firelight glowed behind her, illuminating her slender body through his spare shirt. Big shirt covering a little body. She looked good enough to devour.

The hem of the shirt reached only to her knees. She had spectacular legs, even that left leg with its swollen, purplish ankle. He wanted to see the rest of her, wanted to slip the shirt off her body and kiss his way down her skin.

She must have noticed his look, for she cast him a scowl that warned "we're still talking" and nothing more was going to happen until he'd bared his soul.

"How can I truly trust you when you don't trust me?" she asked as he continued to study her.

"What makes you think I don't trust you?"

She rolled her eyes. "You don't trust anyone. You keep everyone out. Those walls around your heart are thicker than the walls of Jericho. But I have a proposition for you."

He crossed his arms over his chest, knowing he ought to refuse but wouldn't. "Go on."

"I propose that we trade intimacies." She hurried to explain as his eyebrow shot up in surprise. "You tell me a secret. In turn, since I haven't any secrets whatsoever, having led an exceptionally dull life until you came along... well, the point is, I will do a favor for you in return."

"A sexual favor?"

She blushed. "Yes, I suppose that's the point of intimacy. But you had better reveal big, important secrets if you ever hope to see me naked." She paused a moment and her blush deepened. "You do wish to see me naked, don't you, Ian?"

He was down-on-his-knees-begging desperate, but it wouldn't do to let her know how thoroughly she affected him. "It has crossed my mind a time or two."

She let out the breath she'd been holding. "Good. I thought so, but I wasn't quite sure. You've been a gentleman with me all along. I'm glad the notion crossed your mind. More than once or twice, I hope."

"Quite a bit more." He removed his shirt and spread it out on one of the small tables in the room, the one closest to the hearth. If they were to talk and exchange sexual favors—did she understand what she was suggesting?—he may as well be comfortable. As she'd said, he'd catch a chill if he remained in his wet clothes. Lord, he was feverish already.

He took a moment to tug off his boots, but kept his trousers on. Perhaps he'd allow her to unbutton them. She might enjoy it. He certainly would.

She let out a little *eep* when he turned to face her. She was still standing, gripping the back of her chair for support. "Ian, you're supposed to cover yourself with the blanket."

"No." He wasn't about to wrap that itchy thing about his bare shoulders when she'd already seen him naked in her bed, and now they were once again up to their eyeballs in trouble. Even if nothing else happened tonight, they'd already given Lady Withnall enough material to fill her scandal sheets for years.

"No?" Dillie let out a soft laugh. "Not even to spare my delicate sensibilities? Although I haven't been very delicate, have I? Asking you to latch the door. Asking you to remove your wet clothes. Demanding that you allow me into your heart." She paused and swallowed hard. "Ian, I want to know you better. I want you to know me. I suspect you already do. I'm not very complicated. But you are. Do you think you can ever let me into your heart?"

He'd been alone for so long, his defenses were too deeply embedded. "I don't know, Dillie. I realize it isn't the answer you hoped for, but it's the best I can give you right now."

He expected her to end the game. Instead, she cast him the gentlest smile. A log splintered and crackled on the cozy fire. Then silence. The noise of the raging storm seemed to disappear into the background. The shutters no longer rattled, and all that could be heard was the low howl of the wind outside and the muffled *pick-pock, pick-pock* of the icy rain that struck the shutters' thick slats.

So quiet he could hear himself breathe.

A bottle of whiskey and serviceable glass had been set out on the small table beside the window for him, and it hadn't been removed when he'd given the chamber to Dillie. The whiskey glowed, a dark, rich amber against the glow of firelight that filled the room. He dared not take a drink. He was already too besotted for his own good.

"Honesty is good, Ian. I'll be honest with you, too." She glanced at the canopied bed, its blue velvet curtains drawn back with matching velvet ties. "I want to be in that big, comfortable bed. I want you in that bed with me and doing all sorts of delightfully wicked things to me." She held up a hand, as though to stop him from carrying out her wishes. "But you'll have to work hard to earn your way into that bed."

He shook his head and laughed. "Dillie—"

"We're not getting out of this scrape, are we? You and me. Alone at the inn. Alone in this room."

He agreed. "We're done for."

Her smile slipped a little. "The choice should be an easy one for me. Do I marry a handsome, wealthy duke, or do I remain a ruined spinster for the rest of my days?"

He put his hands on each side of her waist and gently drew her close. "It is easy. Marry me."

"I want to, truly I do. But I don't know anything about you or the secrets you keep locked away. I don't know if you'll break my heart. I think you will, because you can have any woman you want, and I don't see you reforming your rakehell ways after we're married. I'm not good at sharing. I never was, Lily can attest to that." She cast him a wan smile. "Knowing that you're satisfying your... base, manly urges on other women while I sleep alone in my elegant apartments in Belgrave Square isn't for me. I suppose I could discreetly take on a lover as other duchesses do." Her eyes began to water. "But I couldn't ever do such a thing."

Hence her proposed game. Ian groaned inwardly, not only understanding her concerns, but wishing he could put her mind at rest. She needed to be happy in her marriage, just as her parents were. Just as her sisters were. She needed to know that he wasn't a bastard who would destroy her life as he'd destroyed the life of his brother. She wanted it all. Love. Commitment. Happiness. Forever.

"Dillie, you're making too much of this marriage business."

She took a stumbling step back, as though he'd physically struck her. He reached out to steady her, but she'd already taken another step back and now stood with the chair between them, as though using it as a shield against him. "Brutal honesty. Well, I asked for it, didn't I?"

He sighed. "No, Dillie. I'm an idiot, as you well know. I didn't mean it as it came out. I don't know what I meant by it."

She brushed a hand across her cheek to swipe at a stray tear. "Of course you do. You've answered my question. Thank you. And you can keep your secrets."

He sighed again. "Dillie—"

"No, you needn't fret." She swallowed hard. "We needn't continue this game, although it isn't really a game, is it? Not when hearts are involved. I'm not going to boot you out, Ian. Not yet, anyway. I actually have a secret to reveal to you." A light blush stained her cheeks. "After our scandal broke, I promised myself that if you ever landed in my bed again, I would take full advantage. You aren't quite in my bed yet, but I hope you will be before too long. Right now, it seems that I'll end up a spinster for the rest of my days. All the more reason for me to have this night with you. I want this night. *My night.* To treasure always."

"Damn it, Dillie." He ran a hand along the nape of his neck. When was he ever at a loss for words? He wanted her. Ached to have her. Not this way. "You're right. We don't need the bloody game. Just marry me. Don't try to break through my walls. Ignore the gossip about me. You don't need to know about an event that happened over twenty years ago."

She frowned. "Wait. What? Your brother died over twenty years ago? How old were you when it happened?"

"It doesn't much matter. He died."

She clutched the chair's high back, as though needing to steady herself. "How old were you? Six? Eight? You were only a child." She looked angry, as though she wanted to pound his chest. She wouldn't cause much damage, for her hands were small and hardly able to grasp his shoulders. Her little fists wouldn't even bruise his thick skin.

"I was four. The incident happened about twenty-five years ago, to be precise. Satisfied?" He turned away, crossing the room to stride to the door, though he didn't wish to leave. He couldn't leave, dressed as he was. Or rather, undressed as he was. He hadn't a shirt on. Didn't have on his boots. He was clad only in his trousers. And there was a hard bulge between his legs that Dillie would have noticed if she hadn't been so busy staring at his face.

"Four!" She let out a yelp. Then he heard a thud. Damn it, had she just fallen? She must have been chasing after him.

He returned to her side, his heart lodged in his throat. "For pity's sake! You're a stubborn little baggage. Are you hurt?"

"I'm fine. I landed softly," she said with a laughing groan. "No harm done."

He made certain of it before he scooped her off the floor. "You're attics-to-let. You know that, don't you?"

"I didn't want you to leave me." She wrapped her arms around his neck, leaned into him so that her breasts heaved against his skin.

"Dillie, I—" He was about to tell her that he'd never leave her. But how could he be sure? "I had better put you into bed."

She stiffened in his arms. "Only if you'll join me."

"You don't understand what you're asking. I'm not sure I do either. You have me spinning in circles, first demanding that I spill my secrets if I ever hope to marry you or have you naked in this bed, and in the next moment, asking me to join you in bed. Does this mean I'm to be allowed access to your delectable body without the need to marry you or spill any of my secrets?"

She nodded.

"Not a single damn requirement or consequence?"

"Why is it so hard for you to comprehend? To put it in mathematical terms, sharing secrets equals marriage plus sex. Not sharing your secrets equals no marriage plus sex. Either way, you get to have your wicked way with me. So, do you wish to save me from spinsterhood or not? Because I won't ever marry you if you walk away now."

He glowered at her, not liking the game she was still playing, and not liking the way she was manipulating him. Doing a bloody good job of it as well. She knew he'd never allow her to remain a spinster. He wouldn't give up until she married him. For her own good. He owed her for saving his life. "I'll stay."

"Thank you, Ian. Climb into bed with me. I want to be in your arms, feel the weight of your body against mine."

He didn't know what else to do with the bossy bit of goods, so he agreed. Well, he knew what to do with her. Kiss her. Peel the shirt off her. Bury himself inside her sweet, naked body. Lick and touch and tease every beautiful inch of her. Make her hot and slick for him. Make her scream out his name while in the throes of ecstasy.

Make her agree to marry him.

Dillie Farthingale was not going to be a one-night dalliance for him.

CHAPTER 12

A SUDDEN GHASTLY thought struck Ian as he lay stretched atop the covers on the bed beside Dillie, certain his rod would permanently ossify if it grew any harder. She still wore his shirt. Thin shirt. And she had a dreamy expression in her eyes that made their spectacular blue depths seem even more spectacular. "Did someone give you medicine for the pain while I was out searching for Abner?"

Dillie nodded. "The innkeeper's wife gave me laudanum." She glanced at her sprained foot. "She said it would ease the throbbing."

"Damn it." He was on his back, Dillie nestled into the crook of his arm, her arm thrown over his chest as she snuggled beside him. He eased her off him and rose slightly to face her. "Here's one of my rules," he growled, putting his weight on one elbow to prop himself up. "I'm not bedding you until the damn medicine wears off. Then you can ask me again. I won't say no. I've wanted you in my arms, in my bed. *Naked* and in my bed, longer than I care to admit."

"Me, too. That's how I've always felt about Good Ian. But everyone keeps saying there's a bad side of you. Even you think so." She shook her head slowly. "I know my mind's a little fuzzy, but I still want to know. What did you do that was so awful? Why do you hate yourself so?"

Great, he was about to bare his soul to a slip of a girl who'd been drugged and now lay injured in bed beside him. Would she remember any of their conversation once the drug wore off?

"I didn't take any of the laudanum yet," she said, as though reading his thoughts. "I wanted to keep my head as clear as possible.

I'm still a little muddled, but that's because of the bump on my brow. I'll take my medicine afterward."

"After you've had your answers?"

"I'd like those, but no. After you've had your way with me. And since this will likely be the most memorable moment of my life, I don't want to be too drugged to remember it clearly."

He fell back and sighed. The girl had him turned upside down, twisted in knots. "Does this mean we're done talking?"

"Heavens, no. Your ordeal isn't nearly over. You haven't told me anything that I didn't know already. Oh, you did tell me that your nightmarish event happened when you were only four years old." She propped up on her side, resting on her own elbow as she faced him. "I suppose it counts as a secret. Now I owe you a sexual favor. Name it, Ian."

"No. I thought we'd ended your silly game. You're playing with fire, Dillie. You don't know what you're doing."

"We did end it, but I thought it important to try again for your sake. You need to talk about what happened. You can't carry the pain inside of you forever."

"Yes, I can. I've managed to do it all these years."

"No, you haven't. You're the unhappiest man I know." She shrugged when he didn't respond. "Have it your way. I'll play with myself."

He groaned. Yes, that would be a great sexual favor, watching her touch herself... rouse herself. Watching her run her fingers over the engorged tips of her firm, pink breasts. Watching her writhe as she stroked the sensitive nub that lay between her thighs until she was wet and hot and ready for him. The thrill would stop his heart.

"What are you doing?" she asked.

"I think I just took my sexual favor." Laughing at her confusion, he drew her atop him so that her splendid breasts, and their soon-to-be-engorged tips—for real, next time—were pressed to his hot skin. The nightshirt was still between them, of course. It wouldn't be for long. "Your turn."

"I want to ask you more about your brother."

"Not yet, Dillie," he said quietly. "Please."

She studied him a long moment, and then nodded. She rolled off

him and nestled once more in the crook of his arm, shifting and squirming until she was once again comfortable. She turned away from him so that they were almost spooned, her back to his front, and then turned again, apparently preferring to face him. She was like a kitten in his arms, squirming this way and that until she found the right spot.

She smiled as she trailed her fingers softly across his bare chest. "Your skin is like gold silk. You're all muscles and silk, Ian." She ran her thumb across his taut nipples. "And the gold hairs across your chest shimmer like rays of sun striking the water."

His body jerked.

She smiled again, a devilish smile as she ran her tongue across one nipple in a slow, sensual circle.

He let out a low, throaty growl. "Where did you learn to do that?"

"Do you like it?"

Hell, yes.

"That's how I lick the clotted cream off my strawberries."

"I love strawberries. Clotted cream, too. My turn." He eased her onto her back and ran his hand under her shirt. *His* shirt, she'd only borrowed it.

Dillie stayed his straying hand. "Not yet. It stays on until you tell me a big secret."

"Or you change your mind." He dipped his head to her breast, at the same time cupping it in his large hand. She had great breasts. The soft mound nicely filled his hand. He stroked his thumb lightly over her nipple, pleased when it quickly peaked. He took the hard tip into his mouth and used his tongue to tease through the crisp linen fabric.

He had a mouthful of the fabric. He wanted to taste Dillie's skin, not the damn shirt. She shuddered, obviously not expecting the sensation, and arched toward him, scraping her fingers across his bare shoulders. "Ian, wait! Oh, blessed crumpets, stop!" She paused a beat, twisted her hands in his hair and held him to her breast. "No, don't stop. Not yet."

He swirled his tongue across her nipple.

"Wait!"

He drew back slightly, but did not remove his hand from her breast. Her heart was wildly pounding beneath his palm. She was excited, confused. This was her first time, so he was going to be patient. He didn't wish to scare her. But so far, making love to Dillie was like playing with a wild ferret. Frustrating and unpredictable. "Dillie, we don't have to do this."

She groaned and laughingly kissed the top of his head, for her hands were still twisted in his hair and his head was at eye level to her breast. He liked the view. Would like it better without the shirt between them. "Yes, we do. I want to. Problem is, I don't know what I'm doing. Will you help me, Ian?"

It took him a moment to catch his breath, for her casual kiss had sent him reeling. It was a careless, affectionate kiss. Gentle. Accepting. "I'll help, but you must let me take control. You said earlier that you trusted me. Do you, Dillie?"

She let out a breathy sigh that ruffled his hair. "I do."

Now, if only she would repeat those words when the minister read their vows.

"You can't question me," he warned.

Another breathy sigh. "I won't."

"Or talk at all."

"But—"

"No talking. You just said you trusted me."

"I still do, though I'm reconsidering," she said with a teasing grin. But she had that Dillie tender look in her eyes, and her body was leaning toward his, so he knew that she wasn't going to refuse him anything.

"One last thing. There is one word you can always say to me, and I'll stop immediately. Just a simple no. All right?"

She nodded.

"Good." He wasted no time in slipping the shirt off her body, his hands riding up her thighs, and then over her waist and higher to push the fabric off her slight shoulders until there was nothing to impede his view.

He let out a soft breath. She was perfect, soft and round in all the right places, yet sleek and firm wherever she should be.

He brushed his fingers over one nipple. It turned pebble-hard

within a few strokes.

He tossed the shirt to the foot of the bed, not caring where it landed. He was too busy staring at Dillie. He even liked the blush that ran from her cheeks to the tips of her ears. "Don't cover yourself," he whispered when she tried to draw the counterpane over her shoulders.

"But Ian—"

"Sweetheart, you're beautiful." He ran his hand through her long, damp hair, brushing it back so that it fell over her shoulders and across the mattress. He trailed his fingers along her soft, pink throat and downward over her breast. "Beautiful," he repeated in quiet awe, and meant it with all his heart, for she had an innocent sensuality about her that he found irresistible.

He took her nipple into his mouth, and swirled his tongue over the smooth, peach-scented skin. He eased her flat on her back and carefully moved his leg between hers, always aware of her injury and the fact that she hadn't taken anything to stem her pain.

When she tried to reach for him, he took her hands in one of his and pinned them over her head because he knew she'd otherwise distract him, asking what she should do and where she should put her hands to pleasure him. It wasn't his turn to be pleasured. Not yet. He'd fly off like a cannonball shot from the massive cannon of a frigate if she touched him, he was that hard and ready.

He returned his attention to Dillie's body, teasing and nipping and running his thumb over the now engorged bud of her breast, and then taking it into his mouth again and teasing some more.

"Oh, Ian. I'm tingling all over. Hot tingles."

So much for not talking, but he didn't mind. These were new sensations for her and he loved her innocent wonder and responsiveness. She wanted him, trusted him, and he didn't wish to disappoint. That would come later, after they were husband and wife. Even if he managed not to muddle things, his family would do its best to destroy the marriage.

He didn't know what would happen in the future, but tonight was his and Dillie's.

He slid his hand between her thighs and gently dipped his finger into her moist opening, knowing she was ready for him. She gasped and arched her back as he stroked her hot, sweet core. "Ian, I want to touch you." She struggled weakly to free her hands, but he wouldn't allow it.

"No, sweetheart. Not yet." He needed to taste and savor her first, to make her feel the wondrous sensation of passion. He wanted to watch her soar to the stars when she reached her ecstasy.

Afterward, he'd allow her to touch him. Hell, he couldn't wait. But he would have to, for he knew his limits, and Dillie had him dangerously hot and wanting, too damn close to the edge. She would push him over the edge if she touched him now. Next time would be different. Next time, they'd soar together.

"Ooh, Ian."

His mouth was on her breast and he could feel the wild beat of her heart against his lips. Her skin was deliciously hot and pink, so soft against his mouth. He stroked between her thighs and felt the pulsing throb of her nether regions as he teased her to mindless bliss. Dillie was eager and passionate, holding nothing back as she bucked against his fingers, her slender body undulating to the motion of his strokes. *"Oh! Oh, heavens! Ian!"*

He loved the breathy moans emanating from low in her throat, loved the way she writhed against his hand and the frantic passion in her voice when she called out his name. *"Ian. Ian! Oooh!"*

She opened her beautiful eyes and turned to him, ready to take him inside her. He ached for it, too. Soon. Not yet. "It gets better, sweetheart." He moved down her body, dipping his head lower and taking her with his tongue, his onslaught gentle but relentless against her nether lips, licking and suckling until she was beautifully wild. She arched her back, called out his name, and then he felt the rolling waves of ecstasy begin to engulf her, felt the heave and shudder of her glistening body against his mouth. *"Ian! Ian!"*

He loved the raspy softness of her voice.

He drew her up against him, holding her securely in his embrace until her passionate shudders abated and she slowly began to calm. He slid his hands along her hot, damp skin and inhaled her scent, an intoxicating mix of sex and peaches.

He'd pleasured women before and had received sexual pleasures in return, but those had been mere carnal acts, involving nothing of himself. He'd never lost control. Never cared about the woman, just the act of satisfaction. And he'd been careful to choose women who never cared about him either.

Dillie was different. She mattered to him.

"I wasn't very quiet, was I?" She rested her head against his shoulder, her unsubdued breaths tickling the short hairs sprinkling his chest.

He ran his fingers through her hair, brushing the damp strands off her cheek as he caressed her. "No, you were quite the noisy Farthingale. I didn't mind."

She smiled against his ribs. "So, you're not irritated with me for breaking your rules and talking?"

"No. I liked the breathy way you called out my name."

He felt another smile against his ribs. "I couldn't help myself," she admitted. "I *love* the way you touch me. I never knew it could be like this. No wonder my sisters are so happy with their husbands."

He chuckled.

"I'm about to ask a stupid question. Promise you won't laugh."

He kissed the top of her head. "I promise."

"Is there more? You see, the way Lily explained it to me... but that was before she'd met Ewan, and her knowledge was only from books—"

"You're still a virgin, if that's what you're asking. There's so much more to be shared between us. This is only the beginning of our journey."

"*Our* journey? Sounds nice. How long before we reach its end?"

Never, I hope. The errant thought surprised him, but it shouldn't have. He'd been having these thoughts about Dillie for quite some time now. She was his forever girl, if only he could convince her of it. If only he could be sure of it himself. He'd never felt like this with anyone before. He kissed her softly again. "Sweetheart, be patient. We're just getting started. The journey will last a lifetime, if you'll let it." Or unless he did something cruel to break her heart. He never wanted to hurt her.

"Seriously? Even when we're old and gray?"

He arched an eyebrow and grinned. "Yes."

Her eyes were still wide and brimming with wonder.

"Seriously?"

"If you wish it."

"Ian, I can't think beyond tonight."

"Then don't. Just feel. The night is young, and I'm not anywhere near done with you yet."

She snuggled against him once more, her body wrapping around his as he continued to hold her in his embrace. She was slight and slender, yet there was something heavenly in the way she fit beside him. Something perfect. She wasn't too big. Wasn't too small. She was Dillie, the temptress of his fantasies.

Exploring Dillie's body, finally seeing her in all her naked glory—and her body was undeniably glorious—had been his wish for longer than he cared to admit. He'd thought the fulfillment of his fantasy would satisfy his curiosity and allow him to move on. He'd marry her, of course. Provide wealth and respectability. Most important, he'd regain control of his wits, no longer aching for her as he had been these past few years.

He couldn't have been more wrong.

He wanted Dillie.

More than he ever had before.

And he damn well wasn't going to be satisfied with just one night.

She nudged him, bringing him back from his thoughts and casting him a soft, Dillie smile. "I'm ready for the next step. This is rather a lot of fun."

THE BUTTERFLIES IN Dillie's stomach had always fluttered in a frenzy at the sight of Ian, but as he lay beside her, holding her close in his muscled arms, they were beyond frenzied and caught in paroxysms of delight. Never in her wildest imaginings had she ever thought this moment would arrive, nor had she expected it to be so wonderful.

Nor had she expected Ian to be so wonderful, but he was.

She could see that he had been affected as well. There was a gleam of confusion in his eyes, those beautiful gray-green eyes that never revealed more than amused disdain but tonight revealed a small corner of his hurt and empty heart.

She reached up and kissed him softly on the lips, loving the warmth of his mouth. He'd touched her as intimately as a man could touch a woman—as far as she knew—and despite his rakish reputation, she'd never felt used, never felt that her body was merely a vessel at his disposal, to be discarded once he'd had his fill.

He'd touched her, kissed her, slid his tongue inside her and teased her over the edge, always with affection and consideration. "What comes next, Ian?"

"This." He ran his fingers through her hair again, brushing the long strands over her shoulder and then easing her onto her back against the soft horsehair mattress. He removed his trousers, revealing the hard, manly length of him, and allowed her to look her fill before he moved atop her. He propped most of his weight on his elbows so that they sank into the mattress on each side of her.

She smiled as she felt the weight of his hard body pressing down on hers, his chest against her breasts, his long legs covering hers, and then all rational thought fled as he lowered his lips to hers and kissed her with enough heat and passion to set the entire inn afire. *Blessed saints and holy crumpets!*

He smiled when he ended the kiss, the smoky emerald gleam of his eyes promising something wonderful, promising to guide her to someplace she'd never been.

In that moment, Dillie knew she would follow Ian anywhere. Across a windswept sea. Atop white-crested waves. Along green valleys and majestic mountaintops capped with snow. She wanted to be with him for the rest of her life.

But Ian wasn't the forever sort.

He would lose interest in her eventually; perhaps he had already lost interest. Perhaps he had never been interested. Rakehells were good at convincing women they were special. Yet all of this felt real to her.

She wasn't certain what *this* was. For the moment, she had Ian to herself, but for how long? Only tonight? She refused to think beyond the next sunrise. However, if there were consequences to this night, she would write to him at once and agree to marry him. It was one thing for her to remain a ruined spinster, but quite another for her to bring a child into this world out of wedlock. She wasn't that foolish.

Nor was he. In truth, she knew he'd be at her doorstep with special license in hand before the ink had dried on her letter. He didn't love her, but he felt he owed her. Ian was the sort who always paid his debts.

His tongue scraped lightly against her teeth. She parted her lips to allow him entrance, eager to surrender to his promise of pleasure. "Dillie. Sweetheart," he said in a moaning whisper, and then his tongue was in her mouth, plundering and probing her depths. She wasn't exotic or mysterious. She wasn't intriguingly deep. She was simple and obvious, often walking around with her heart exposed.

He was the real mystery.

He was the one who held secrets and hid behind the thick walls built around his heart.

She grasped his big, sinewy shoulders, responding to his kisses with a fervent hunger the like of which she'd never experienced before. She touched and swirled and rolled her tongue with his, returning his urgent thrusts with those of her own, until the pleasure overwhelmed her and she dug her nails into his back, slid her hands down his body to cup his firm buttocks. *His golden buns.*

She was so hungry for him. He tasted much better than food.

He began to gently knead her breast, his fingers so magical that she melted at his touch. She let out a moan as he began to tease her nipple with his thumb, and moaned again when he teased it to a hard bud that peeked out between the cascading strands of dark hair that he'd earlier brushed over her shoulder. The wondrous sensation of her hair and his thumb rubbing across her now-engorged tip sent waves of heat coursing through her body. "Ian, I'm on fire."

He smiled against her lips. "So am I, sweetheart."

She loved his smile. She saw it so rarely, but tonight he had lots of smiles for her. And she loved the way he touched her, sometimes gentle, sometimes urgent, but always seeming to know what she needed and exactly when she needed it. There was a natural, manly grace to his movements, the way his muscles bunched and corded, the way they tautened and strained.

She wanted to watch him, but her eyes closed of their own accord and she felt him instead, felt the skim of his body against hers, felt his strong, solid arms around her. Felt the pucker of the vicious scar that stretched across his belly.

It wasn't the only one. He had many scars on his body, a sign that he'd endured much cruelty, but all she felt was the gentleness of his touch and the hard heat of him against her fiery skin as he settled between her thighs and poised himself at her entrance.

She wanted so badly to take him in, as though her entire life had been building up to this one moment. "Ian, please." She arched against him. "Tell me what to do."

"Your body will tell you. Close your eyes, sweetheart. Feel the way we move together." She didn't argue, for he seemed to know what he was about, and she liked the way he began to rub against her slick opening. He let out a low growl that emanated from the back of his throat, a manly growl of arrogant satisfaction.

He thrust inside her, his movements cautious at first, but with each thrust, he went a little deeper, moved a little more urgently, until he'd fully embedded himself inside her.

She wrapped her legs around his waist to better take him in.

"Sweetheart, am I hurting you?"

"No." She blinked her eyes open to meet his gaze. "I love the feel of you." He'd been calling her sweetheart all evening long. She liked it. So much nicer than "Daffy," although he hadn't called her that in a while. Did it mean he was no longer pushing her away?

She gave no further thought to the matter. Instead, she closed her eyes and reveled in the delicious sensation of Ian's body as he continued his thrusts. He reached deep into her soul. He stole her heart.

How could her heart ever belong to another now?

Ian made her tingle. Ian made her hot. Ian made her soar higher than she'd ever dreamed possible. Ian made her dream.

His skin felt hot and damp to her touch. His breaths were coming faster now, though she couldn't quite tell because she was also panting with need. She heard his grunt as he moved deep inside her, and felt his thrusts, now commanding and urgent.

They were on a precipice and she was about to slip over the edge of the volcano and fall into its crater. An intensely satisfying heat swept over her body, just as she'd experienced the first time, when his mouth had been on her most intimate part. *"Ian!"*

He kept up the relentless pressure, each thrust sending her closer to the edge, so close she knew she was going to fall. *So close.* The sensation was powerful and exquisite. She wasn't frightened, for Ian was holding her tightly in his arms. He wouldn't let go of her. They'd tumble over the edge together. Together. That's what he'd said he wanted.

That's what she wanted too.

And then she did fall. Hot waves of sensation flowed over her, drew her upward in their forceful volcanic crests, each molten wave higher than the one before, hotter and more powerful as they coursed through her body with wild abandon.

Ian thrust into her twice more, and then let out a deep, throaty growl as his body pulsed and shuddered against the powerful force of his own release, his muscles so taut they appeared to be sculpted on him.

"Dillie," he said in a whisper, spilling his seed inside her.

She loved the feel of him inside her.

She loved the scent of his hot, damp skin.

He let out another animal growl, and with one last shuddering heave, collapsed atop her.

The full weight of his big, handsome body came to rest on her. She held onto his shoulders, desperate to cling to him for as long as possible. She wanted to hold on to their journey, for it might be their last. She might never experience this perfect joy again. This was Ian, the man who wouldn't give his heart to anyone. Would he leave her now that he'd satisfied his curiosity?

Oh, she knew that he would marry her. But did he truly want her?

Ian took another moment to recover his strength, then eased onto his elbows and cast her a tender smile. "How do you feel, sweetheart?"

She laughed. "Womanly."

He kissed her lightly on the nose as he pulled out of her, and then his gaze suddenly turned serious. "How about wifely?"

"As in, will I stop being an idiot and marry you now?"

He rolled her atop him. "Something like that, except I'm the idiot. You're perfect."

"Flattery will get you everywhere." Although her tone was light, she felt overwhelmed and confused. She wanted him. He was determined to marry her. He simply didn't love her. "Ian, let me sleep on it. You know this isn't about me. I want to be your wife. Now that I know what happens in the marriage bed, I want it more than ever. Our mating was quite spectacular, but you knew it would be. You're confident in your prowess."

He groaned. "Our mating? My prowess? Now you sound like Lily when she lectures about her baboons."

She laughed again. "I don't know what else to call it."

"How about lovemaking?"

"Love." She nodded. "That's how I felt when I was in your arms and you were inside me. I felt safe. Protected. Loved. I suppose it's the right thing to call it, because I did feel all those things. You made me feel wonderful. What about you, Ian? What did you feel?"

He put his arms around her and kissed her on the nose again. "I'm feeling desperately hungry. How about you, Daffy? Care for some more broth?"

"Only enough to dump over your head." However, she wasn't really angry with Ian for changing the subject and making a jest of something so important. And calling her Daffy again. He was purposely shutting her out. She'd chipped at the walls surrounding his heart and he didn't like it. This was his Ian-back-in-hiding response.

She knew that he wasn't trying to hurt her. He would marry her. Out of a sense of duty, of course. Yet, sometimes he looked at her in a loving way. Even now, he was holding her in his arms and seemed in no hurry to let her go.

When he finally did ease away and rose from the bed, she shook her head and sighed. His lean, golden body was now on glorious display, but so were his scars. The raw, ugly one across his stomach was most prominent. "I'll scrounge up something for us to eat. I'm famished. How about you?"

"Ravenous. You had better be quick about it, Your Grace, or I'll take a bite out of your firm, golden buns."

IAN AWOKE THE next morning to the sounds of servants stirring downstairs. He glanced at Dillie, who was curled up against his body, her arm thrown across his chest and one leg wedged between both of his.

She looked innocent as a kitten, a sleeping kitten with long, dark hair that cascaded over the pillows in a splendid, silky waterfall. And she was naked. Gloriously so. He skimmed his hand along the length of her arm. Her skin was pink and felt warm.

"You're beautiful, sweetheart," he said in a whisper, kissing her on the cheek. He slipped out of bed as quietly as he could manage and crossed to the hearth to add more logs to the fire that had died out sometime during the night. The shutters were closed, but he could hear the icy rain still pelting the slats without letup. He and Dillie would be trapped here at least another day.

He glanced upward. *Thank you.* Another day with Dillie would be heaven.

He glanced back at her luscious, sleeping form. A sudden thought struck him. He'd slept last night. At least five hours straight between the last time he'd... with Dillie... and then he'd fallen asleep and not stirred until now. No nightmares to jolt him awake. No terrors to leave him in a sweat and gasping for breath.

The logical explanation was that he'd simply been bone weary last night. After all, he'd traveled all day in a miserable rain that had turned hard and icy, and then carried Abner from the overturned carriage back to the inn. The long day and foul weather would have been enough to make any man weary.

He knew that his tortured dreams would return tonight. He'd been spared only the one night. That was the logical explanation.

Then there was the Dillie explanation.

He had pleasured her. Twice. But she had worked her magic on him as well. There was something about her smile that grabbed his heart, and something about her touch that he always found soft and soothing.

She had a way of easing his pain.

He didn't know how she managed it, she just did. Even last night, the way she'd cuddled against him to seek his warmth, had made him feel so good. Peaceful. Contented. He hadn't felt that way since his brother's death.

She must have sensed his gaze on her, for she opened her eyes and sat up in bed. She cast him a sleepy, vixen smile that made his heart soar. "Good morning, naked Ian."

He threw back his head and laughed. "Good morning, Daffy. You're looking rather naked yourself."

She glanced down. "Oh, dear." She drew the covers over her breasts. "Have you seen my nightshirt?"

"My shirt, to be precise. I'll look for it in a moment, though it's an awful pity to cover up your heavenly body. You look much better with nothing on."

She blushed. "That isn't the point. The innkeeper and his staff are stirring downstairs. We'll have to let them in sooner or later."

"But not yet." He tossed some kindling into the hearth to get the fire started, and once it began to burn, tossed in several logs. Then he turned to inspect the clothes he'd hung up to dry last night. They were still a little damp, but would be dry within the hour. "It's still early. We have time before anyone bothers us. How do you feel?"

She cast him another soft smile. "Very wifely. I enjoyed... you know."

"So did I," he said with a chuckle, "very much. But I meant your foot. You didn't take any laudanum before you fell asleep. Does it still hurt? The lump on your brow seems to have subsided."

She touched her hand lightly to her forehead. "It's much better. I hardly feel it now. The foot's still sore." She drew back enough of the covers to show her leg. Her ankle was swollen and a deep purplish blue.

He grabbed two pillows and carefully tucked her injured foot atop them. "Try not to put your weight on it, at least for today."

"But I must see Abner. Will you carry me over to his room later? I wonder how he's doing."

"He's safely on the mend, I think. We would have been alerted otherwise. I instructed Mr. Gwynne to let me know at once if Abner took a turn for the worse."

She nibbled her lower lip. "That was before you shocked the poor man by locking yourself in with me." She sighed. "At my behest, no less. What must he think of me?"

"Are you regretting last night?" *Damn.* He shouldn't have asked the question, for he might receive an answer he didn't wish to hear.

She glanced at him in surprise. "No, of course not. Last night was wonderful."

He nodded. "I thought so, too."

"I know. You're strutting around like a dominant male baboon. See, even now you're casting me a baboon grin, that I-satisfied-my-woman, smug sort of grin." Then she made a silly monkey face and uttered a monkey sound, and Ian burst out laughing. In that moment, he was happy. Unrestrained. Heartfelt. Happy.

Happy because he was with Dillie.

There was no artifice about the girl, only genuine warmth. She'd given him everything last night and demanded so little in return. He owed her, but not out of a sense of duty. He owed her because she meant something to him. Because he cared about her and didn't ever wish to hurt her.

He cleared his throat as he picked up the shirt that had lodged between the mattress and the footboard. He handed it to Dillie.

"Will you help me to put it on?" she asked with an impish, glowing smile that reached into her eyes.

"No. If I help, you won't ever get it on you. I love the way you look right now." *Had he just used the word love?* "You're prettier than a perfect sunrise." He turned away before he spilled the rest of his thoughts, most of which had to do with his immediate sexual urges. Last night hadn't been nearly enough for him. He wanted more time with Dillie. Hell, he wanted Dillie.

The frightening part was that he wanted *only* Dillie.

Not just for now.

Possibly forever.

CHAPTER 13

BY LATE MORNING, Dillie was propped in bed, tended by Mrs. Gwynne and Hilda, a sturdily built older woman with thick, curly hair that appeared quite orange against her mob cap. She recognized Hilda as one of the maids who had taken care of her the night before. "Eat up now, Miss Dillie," she said with a motherly concern in her bright green eyes. "There isn't much meat on yer bones."

She'd set a hearty breakfast of poached eggs and sausages before Dillie, and once Dillie had devoured it—she was the first to admit she was famished—Hilda and Mrs. Gwynne had helped her to prepare herself for the day. One brushed her hair and braided it. The other assisted her in washing.

Neither mentioned that both sides of the bed were rumpled.

Or that she was still wearing Ian's shirt.

Or that Ian, the Duke of Edgeware, could have asked on her behalf to borrow a gown or robe or something similarly suitable from Mrs. Gwynne or any of the maids. He would have compensated them handsomely.

She glanced at her own gown draped over one of the chair backs. It looked torn and stained, not at all fit to be worn by a young lady of her genteel upbringing. No matter, for Ian had ordered her to remain in bed today. She would worry about what to wear tomorrow... or the day after... or day after that.

The storm would have to pass eventually. What would happen then?

Mrs. Gwynne and Hilda were still smiling at her. She thought it quite odd, for they appeared cheerful and not at all disapproving of her when the evidence of what had taken place between her and Ian was all around them.

Her father would learn of it shortly. There would be no arguing with him afterward or stopping the men in the Farthingale clan from coming after Ian. Not that Ian was resisting. She was the one who had been reluctant to wed, but not anymore. "Has His Grace returned yet?"

Her soon-to-be husband, as she was now beginning to think of Ian, had promised to carry her into Abner's chamber for a short visit after he'd returned from scouting the site of the accident.

"No, Miss Dillie," Mrs. Gwynne replied, casting her yet another kind smile. Dillie had expected curious looks and condescending frowns, but both ladies were exceedingly polite. She didn't know what Ian had said to them, but he'd obviously told them something outrageous. What was it? "He and Mr. Gwynne are still out in that storm, hoping to salvage some of your baggage. They'll try to recover the carriage as well." She shook her head and grumbled. "Never seen such beastly weather in m'life."

"Please let me know when he returns."

Mrs. Gwynne chuckled. "Oh, ye needn't worry about His Grace. I think he'll come straight up to see ye. I doubt ye've been out of his thoughts since he first set eyes on ye."

Dillie struggled not to blush, but her entire face heated, including the tip of her nose and tips of her ears. The women either didn't notice or politely pretended that they hadn't.

Hilda busied herself by clearing off the remains of her breakfast while Mrs. Gwynne crossed to the shutters and opened them to peer out. She must have been concerned about her husband battling his way home even though it was now daylight. The storm was a dangerous one, blinding snow and thick ice mingled with torrential spurts of frigid rain. It seemed as though the skies had opened up and launched all manner of weaponry in the celestial arsenal at them.

Dillie was concerned as well.

"No letup yet," Mrs. Gwynne muttered, but a moment later she let out a soft gasp. "Oh, heavens be praised! The men are returning."

"Do let them in, Mrs. Gwynne. You needn't stay to fuss over me.

I'll manage."

"Thank ye, Miss Dillie." She bobbed a curtsy and bustled out of the room.

Hilda remained, but not for long. "I'll bring up a pot of freshly brewed tea and some cakes. His Grace will surely need something to warm 'im up, though I'm sure the sight of ye will be enough for 'im."

Dillie shook her head and smiled. *What in heavens had he told them?*

Her heart beat a little faster when she heard the appealing rumble of Ian's voice downstairs and then recognized his confident stride as he marched up the steps. Within moments he was at the door, entering their chamber. *Their* chamber, as in the one they were still sharing. His expression was serious until he saw her, and then it seemed as though his entire being lightened. He grinned at her. "I missed you."

Her heart took a small leap. This was Ian. Duke Ian. The Duke of Edgeware. The rakehell all mothers warned their daughters about. *Her* Ian, and he'd missed her. "I missed you, too. Warm yourself beside the fire, then you can tell me what you found. Hilda's bringing up tea and cakes for you. I'll ask her to bring up something more substantial if you're hungry. Some chicken stew or... Ian, you're still grinning at me."

"Am I?" He hung his oilcloth and cloak on hooks beside the hearth, and then ran his fingers through his wet hair. His normally deep honey-gold hair appeared darker because it was wet, more the color of chestnuts.

"Yes, you are. What are you thinking?"

He shrugged. "That you look quite content in that enormous bed. Is it because of me?"

She rolled her eyes. "The inn contents me. It's warm and inviting and I'm being well cared for. You, on the other hand, confuse me. What did you say to the innkeeper and his staff? I'm being treated like a princess."

"And not a fallen angel?" He ran a hand once more through his hair. "You ought to be treated with utmost deference, for you and Abner are in my care. I would expect no less from them. I needn't say a word. I'm a duke. Dukes do not explain themselves to anyone but the royal family."

"Most odd. Well, make yourself comfortable and tell me what you found."

He brought a chair to her bedside and settled his large frame onto it. "The carriage is destroyed," he said with a shake of his head. "The frame is twisted and bent. The seat cushions are not only soaked, but muddied and torn. The roof is cracked. So are two of the wheels."

"Oh, dear. Father won't be pleased, though I suppose it'll be the least of his concerns once he finds out how I've spent these past two days."

"You needn't dwell on your father's response. A wedding band on your finger will cure all ills." He studied her, appearing to steel himself against her protest.

She made none. "You're right. Were you able to save any of my gowns?"

"I'm right?" He made no effort to mask his surprise, and seemed pleased by her decision. She supposed it was better than seeing a look of resignation on his face.

"You are," she admitted, casting him a soft smile. "However, I refuse to be called Duchess Daffy. Merely being addressed as *duchess* will be disconcerting enough."

He shook his head and laughed. "I'll add it as a condition to the betrothal contract. I suppose I'll have to add a clause about your clothing allowance. You're going to need a new wardrobe, since the contents of your trunk were mostly washed down the river. What remains is ruined rags."

"Madame de Bressard will be pleased," she said, referring to London's most sought after modiste, who had designed most of her gowns.

Ian arched an eyebrow, his expression devilishly appealing. "Until then, you're stuck with my shirt... or nothing. I prefer you with nothing. In that bed. Right where you are now. Wearing nothing at all."

He shifted his gaze and suddenly rose. "Ah, Mrs. Gwynne. Let me help you with that tray. The cakes look marvelous, particularly the gingerbread. It's Miss Farthingale's favorite. How thoughtful of you."

Dillie wanted to shrink under the covers. Had the woman heard their conversation?

"We aim to please, Yer Grace," she said, her manner remaining polite and respectful as she bustled into the room and set the tray on the table beside the shuttered windows. The room was darker than usual because the shutters were once again closed, but Dillie didn't mind at all. There was ample light from the hearth fire, the flames casting a delightful amber glow about the room. Indeed, everything felt warm and cozy now that Ian was beside her. "Tug on the bellpull should ye need anything."

"We will, Mrs. Gwynne," Ian said and winked at the woman.

Mrs. Gwynne hastily made her way toward the door, and then turned and winked back at Ian.

He quietly shut the door and latched it.

Hot, buttered crumpets! She and Ian were alone again. She'd caught the wink between him and Mrs. Gwynne. What was the meaning of that exchange? "You did tell them something."

He cast her an innocent glance. "Would you care for a gingerbread cake?"

She supposed it wasn't important. Whatever he'd said had turned the innkeeper and his entire staff into his private little band of conspirators, their fiendish plot to make her as comfortable and well cared for as possible.

She watched Ian, the mastermind behind that plot, cross to the table and set a slice of that gingerbread cake on a plate. "This one's for you. Would you care for some tea?"

"No, thank you." He returned to her side and handed her the plate. "Ian, how do you know that this is my favorite cake?"

He'd already walked back to the table to pour himself a cup of tea. He looked quite ruggedly handsome by firelight—broad shoulders, trim waist, and long, muscled legs. His gold hair was damp and curling at the nape of his neck. "You and I have been to many of the same society affairs. Parties. Teas. It's the first thing you ever reach for."

She laughed. "You noticed?"

"I noticed *you*. Always."

The room began to heat. Or was it just her? "Why?"

"For starters, you were usually the prettiest girl at any party. You also have a propensity for getting into mischief."

She quickly swallowed the bite she had been chewing. "I do not. I'm quite proper."

His eyebrow shot up. "When you're not deceiving everyone. You spent most of last season pretending to be Lily. I found your acting abilities quite entertaining. You had some alarmingly close calls, but you managed to outwit everyone for months."

"Apparently, not you."

He cast her a teasing smile and walked back to her side. "I'm not quite the idiot you make me out to be."

"Oh, Ian. You're not an idiot at all. I only said that to keep you at arm's length. I was afraid of you. Rather, afraid of how much I truly liked you. There, I've revealed my only dark secret."

He brushed his fingers lightly across her cheek. "It wasn't ever much of a secret. I'm a scoundrel, remember? I can sense when a woman is attracted to me."

"You knew? How is it possible? I didn't know it myself until... never mind. You couldn't have known."

He set his untouched cup on the nightstand beside her. "Here, why don't you have it? I think I'll pour myself a whiskey. I need the liquid fortification."

"Of course, to get the chill out of your bones."

"Not quite." He turned to meet her gaze. "To fortify me for what I'm about to tell you."

"WHAT ARE YOU about to tell me?" Dillie asked Ian. Her smile faded as Ian drew his chair even closer to the bed and sank into it with a heavy sigh. He'd poured himself a glass of whiskey and had begun to swirl the amber liquid, absently watching it gleam within the glass while he considered the wisdom of dredging up a pain that would not be numbed no matter how much he drank, even the entire contents of the bottle.

Dillie set her tea and partly eaten cake on the nightstand, and then leaned close. The look on her face revealed that she was ready to swallow him in her arms and offer him comfort if the need arose. That's what set Dillie apart from the peahens with whom he often dallied, those ladies who clucked and fussed around him but never seemed to accomplish much. Dillie, once she set her mind to it, could conquer kingdoms. Or scare off ruffians. Or melt a duke's icy heart.

Lord! He hardly believed he'd heard right. She'd agreed to marry him, just like that, no longer fighting him or resisting the wishes of her own heart. It wasn't just their lovemaking that had swayed her. Something had happened between them, something wondrous that went beyond the carnal act itself. Somewhere between his grunts and her breathy moans, they'd forged a bond that would connect them forever. A bond of silk, for the fabric of life that bound them was delicately spun and exquisitely rare. He'd felt the connection just as she had.

In truth, asking Dillie to share his life, and knowing she would probably turn it upside down, felt good. Damn good. But that's how Dillie always made him feel. The sun shone brighter when she was near. The air smelled sweeter. He always heard laughter. Sometimes his own. He *felt* alive whenever Dillie was by his side.

But how would she feel once she learned the truth about him? She would eventually find out. Better that she hear it from him. "The gossips say that I killed my brother," he started, taking a deep breath that did nothing to stem the ache in his heart. "They're right. I killed him as surely as if I'd taken a knife and stabbed him through the heart."

"Oh, Ian!" Dillie glowered, but her glare wasn't aimed at him but at everyone who had ever maligned him. It felt odd to have an ally. He'd never had one growing up. "You told me you were only four years old when he died. A mere child. A child that age can't hurt anyone, not intentionally. Would you tell me what happened?"

He took a sip of whiskey and felt the heat of it slide down his throat. "It was winter." He took another sip, needing a moment to collect his thoughts. He'd never confided in anyone before, not even his closest friends. Hell, this was Dillie. She was going to be his wife. She'd earned his trust. "Being boys and cooped up indoors, James and I were misbehaving. James is... was... my big brother, all of six years old at the time."

"A perfect age for mischief." She cast him a soft, encouraging smile.

"So our nanny always claimed. She'd had enough of our antics that day and decided to take us for a walk along the pond on our estate, hoping the cold wind and long trudge through the snow would rid us of our wildness. It was a particularly brutal winter that year, and the pond had frozen over—or so we thought."

Dillie's eyes began to glisten and she let out a ragged breath. She'd soon be crying. He took her hand to warm it in his, or perhaps she'd taken his hand. It didn't much matter. "The ice was thin in spots, mostly where the water ran deepest. It all happened so quickly. I don't recall everything that happened. All I know is that I was on that pond, falling through the ice and calling out for James."

"Oh, Ian." She let out another ragged breath.

"I reached out for him. I remember that, too. At some point, we both fell through the ice and went under. I saw him as we sank below the surface, somehow managed to grab his coat to pull him toward me." He tightened his grip on the whiskey glass to keep his hand from shaking, but it shook nonetheless. "We couldn't have been underwater very long, but it was long enough for me to black out. Next thing I remember, I awoke in my bed, my nanny seated by my bedside and crying. I asked her about James. She told me to get some rest and she'd see me in the morning. She said that James needed her more. She was right. He never made it through the night. James was dead within a matter of hours."

Dillie made no pretense of being brave. Tears were streaming down her cheeks. "You must have loved him very much."

He nodded. "He was everything to me. Our parents never paid much attention to us. We saw them only occasionally. James and I saw each other every day. He was the best. Loving. Protective. So damn softhearted. We were brothers and the best of friends. Then I killed him."

Dillie frowned. "No. You fell through the ice."

"And he ran out to rescue me. I was someplace I shouldn't have been, and he paid the highest price for my mistake."

"The mistake of a four-year-old. Where was your nanny? Why

didn't she stop you?"

"I was told that she tried, but I slipped out of her clutches and tore onto the pond. It doesn't matter what happened. James died and I lived. From that day on, I was dead to my family. James, who had mostly been ignored until then, as I was, suddenly became the adored child."

"That isn't fair. Oh, Ian! Your parents were wrong." Her fingers were entwined with his, her hand so soft against his cold palm.

"I'm not looking to blame anyone, Dillie. I understand that I was a child. Had I been older, I would not have run onto that fragile ice." He set his drink aside and took both of her hands in his. "James was all I had. From that day on, I was on my own. I never saw my nanny again. No doubt, she was discharged. I don't know what happened to her. She had been good to me and James, but James had died under her watch. I suppose I ruined her life as well."

He sighed. "After that day, my father never spoke to me. He refused to *see* me, even if we were standing in the same room. I was a ghostly apparition. My mother only spoke to tell me how much she hated me. The rest of the family followed suit. That was my joyous upbringing."

Dillie squeezed his hands, her expression anguished as she gazed at him. "No wonder you refused to speak of it earlier. I'm so sorry I tried to make a stupid game of it."

"You don't owe me any apologies, Dillie. I ought to have told you about James months ago. I'm not used to confiding in anyone. But you're to be my wife now, so it's only fair that you should know. I ought to have told you last night before I latched the door. I took advantage of your trust, gave you no chance to toss me out on my ear."

Dillie shook her head. "I wouldn't have tossed you out."

"The point is, I didn't give you the choice. I purposely boxed you into a corner, trapped you into consenting to the marriage. It wasn't well done of me. Yet I feel no remorse. I'd do it all over again."

"To protect me from scandal?" He noticed that her fingers were still entwined in his and he took it as a hopeful sign.

He nodded. "That's one reason."

"Is there another reason?" She shifted closer. Any closer and she'd be on his lap, but he didn't mind. He wanted to feel her soft curves against his body.

"Hell if I know." He'd spent his life alone and hadn't needed anyone until now. He didn't want to need Dillie, but at the moment, she was more important to him than air to breathe.

She pursed her lips and glanced off into the distance. "I think we've both lied to each other and to ourselves. We've always been drawn to each other. Oh, blame it on the Chipping Way curse, if you will. I think it has little to do with such superstition and all to do with fear of falling in love. We're both fighting so hard to deny the attraction." She laughed lightly, and there was a gentle look in her beautiful blue eyes. "You needn't worry. I'm not going to ask if you love me. Having been raised in that loveless household, how can you possibly understand what it means? But I hope you will grow to understand it in time. I hope one day you'll say those words to me. Ian, I'll cherish the moment."

The conversation went no further, interrupted by a sharp rap on the door. Ian released Dillie's hands and pushed back his chair. He strode across the room and opened it. Mr. Gwynne stood in the doorway. "Beg pardon, Yer Grace, but the coachman's askin' for Miss Dillie."

"Abner?" Dillie called from behind him. He heard the shift of her covers and knew she was already climbing out of bed. Her feet must have hit the floor, for she let out a soft cry.

"Your ankle must hurt like blazes," he muttered, returning to her side. He grabbed one of the blankets off the bed and wrapped it around her body for modesty's sake. "Duchesses don't walk around inns in bare feet and skimpy nightshirts." He scooped her into his arms.

Abner's quarters were located across the hall from theirs. *Theirs!* They weren't married yet, and he was already thinking of them as a couple, of her as a necessary part of his existence. Lord, it felt odd. Good. But odd. He set her down on the stool beside Abner's bed. "I'll give you a moment alone." He expected that Abner wanted to know for certain whether Dillie was all right, for although the old man was in a laudanum-induced languor and hopefully feeling no pain, he considered Dillie his responsibility and would not rest until certain she was on the mend.

At some point, Abner would realize that he and Dillie had shared the neighboring quarters, shared everything that could be shared between a man and a woman. By then he'd also know that Dillie would marry him.

He left them, but made certain to keep the door slightly ajar in order to hear her when she called out to him, for he didn't want her hopping about needlessly. He remained close by, returning to their chamber and leaving that door open as his thoughts turned to obtaining the special license. He would procure it as soon as the weather cleared, for he wanted a quick, simple ceremony without fuss or bother. However, if Dillie wanted a fancy wedding, he would not deprive her of it.

As for him, he was a man. He couldn't care less about the celebration, only the girl. The sooner Dillie shared his bed, the better.

The sooner he introduced her to Felicity, the better. He wanted Dillie to meet his young niece, spend time with her to make certain she was not being neglected, for he knew nothing about raising children and didn't trust himself to know the difference.

He strode across the chamber to open the shutters and peer out the window. The surrounding trees were coated in a thin layer of ice, their leaves glistening against the meager light. It seemed as though the entire countryside had been turned into a forest of ice. A thing of shimmering beauty, yet treacherous. Rain and snow were still falling in a sleety mix, but a little lighter now. He doubted the storm was ending, perhaps just a lull, for the distant clouds were a bleak, dark gray. A thick layer of snow covered the icy cobblestone courtyard and the stable's thatched roof. He watched the fat, wet snowflakes as they fell, and lost himself in his thoughts.

He wasn't certain how long he stood beside the window watching the storm rage outside, but for the first time since his brother's death, he felt the violent storm that had always raged within his heart begin to ease. Healing would not come easy, he knew that much. But he would have Dillie to help soothe the ache over time.

He sighed, realizing that he hadn't told her about his nightmares. She would find out soon enough, and most certainly choose to sleep apart from him during their marriage. Few married couples ever shared a marriage bed. He understood and would accept it. Just not yet. He wanted Dillie in his arms tonight.

"Yer Grace," he heard someone call out softly from behind him.

He turned, confused as he heard his door shut quietly. The pretty maid who'd warmed his bed a time or two now stood alone with him in the chamber. Door closed. *Hell.* "Elsie, you shouldn't be in here."

"But Yer Grace, I'm ever yer obliging servant." She tossed him a seductive smile and began to unlace the ties at the front of her gown. "I'm at yer call should ye need... anything."

He strode to her, frowning as he turned her around and opened the door to boot her out. "Who sent you up here? I'm not in need of your services." He put a hand on each of her shoulders to give her a gentle nudge down the hall when she appeared reluctant to obey.

And then he noticed that Abner's door was wide open.

Dillie was standing beside it.

Staring at his hands on Elsie's shoulders. Staring at Elsie's unlaced ties.

Damn.

She looked as though he'd just shot her through the heart.

DILLIE FELT HER entire body go numb. She couldn't move, not even to turn away from Ian because at this moment, she wanted him out of her sight.

"Elsie, go downstairs and don't come back up here," Ian said to the girl in his arms, but his gaze remained firmly fixed on Dillie as he spoke. Elsie cast Dillie a smug smile as she sauntered downstairs, leaving Dillie alone in the hall with Ian.

She was still unable to budge. Her mind was a whirl of confusion. What had just happened? She'd been with Abner only a few minutes. Ian had made a point of keeping both doors open so that he would hear her call out when she was ready to return. Had he planned to dally with the pretty maid in the meantime? Thinking he could finish with the girl and send her on her way before anyone noticed? Obviously, he'd miscalculated.

"Dillie, I know what you're thinking and you're wrong."

"Oh, I see. She came up here unbidden and untied her laces all by herself." He was a rakehell, and until this very moment, she hadn't quite understood what the word meant. She understood now. Rakehells were the depraved sort of men who sought their pleasure whenever the opportunity presented itself, no matter the circumstances and no matter who they hurt.

"In fact, she did." He spoke softly, his voice calm and even. However, Dillie saw the thunderous swirls of gray in his eyes and knew he was angry. When at peace, Ian's eyes were a beautiful, deep grayish-green. The haunting gray that swirled in them now tugged at her heart.

"Oh, Ian. I want to believe you, but I don't know if I can." Yet he wasn't stupid. He must have known that he might be caught. Was that risk a part of the thrill? It seemed so opposite his nature. He was a careful, deliberate man, one who needed to be in control of his surroundings at all times.

Nor did it seem in his nature to be cruel, especially to her, and not after what they had shared last night. She'd felt safe and protected in his arms.

Still, the evidence could not be overlooked. "I just want to know the truth."

He reached out his hand and took a step toward her, but she backed away.

"So that's the way it is." He dropped his hand to his side. "Your mind is made up. I've been found guilty."

"No. I don't know. The problem is, I don't know *you*." Her needs were simple. She wanted a happy marriage to a man she loved and respected. Was she now condemned to life as the ignorant spouse of a man who would spend his nights cavorting with any woman who caught his fancy? She closed her eyes and took a deep breath to calm her thoughts. Her head was spinning, and her heart felt as though it had been cut to ribbons. What she'd seen made no sense, yet the girl had been standing beside Ian with her lacings untied and Ian's arms had been around her shoulders.

She waited for him to explain, but he said nothing further, so she hobbled past him with her head held high and made her way toward her bed. Her foot was swollen and painful, but that did not compare to the ache of his betrayal. They weren't even married yet, and he'd already been caught dallying with the girl under her very nose.

Her eyes welled with tears.

No! She refused to cry in front of him.

"Damn it, Dillie." He scooped her into his arms and carried her the remaining distance to the bed. He set her down gently in the center of it, and then stepped away and ran a hand across the back of his neck. "You have to trust me."

Her eyes widened in surprise. "Why? Give me a reason."

He crossed his arms over his chest, now appearing quite indignant, which would have been hilarious had it not been so tragic. Then his manner softened. "Because you're the last person on earth I'd ever purposely hurt. You must know that."

"I want to. I'm trying, but I don't know if I can."

"Is this how it's to be between us? My groveling at your feet, begging for forgiveness for every perceived slight? I'm a damn duke. You're to be my wife, not my judge and jailor." That said, he stormed downstairs.

CHAPTER 14

DILLIE SPENT THE next half hour angry and stewing in her chamber. She'd been too unsettled to remain in bed, so she'd moved to the chair beside the fire and propped her foot on the stool that Ian had ordered placed there. The pillow Ian had also ordered for her was atop the stool, cushioning her bruised and swollen ankle.

She took a deep breath to stem her ache and caught the scent of gingerbread. Ian had ordered those gingerbread cakes brought up to her as well. Was this the sort of care a rakehell offered to just any woman?

She simply didn't know. Her parents had always made marriage look easy. Oh, they bickered at times, but only over small matters. She couldn't recall any of their arguments ever starting with "What were you doing with that woman in your arms?" Her sisters seemed happy with their husbands as well. In any event, none of them were here to offer guidance.

In truth, it seemed important that she work the problem out by herself. She wondered what Lily would do, and decided to start by making a list in her mind of Ian's strengths and weaknesses. It was a logical and methodical approach. Very much like Lily.

If only she were more like her twin!

"Right, let's start." She decided to count Ian's strengths on her hands and his weaknesses on her toes. First, Ian protected her and made her feel safe. A definite strength. She stuck her thumb up.

Second, he was clever and she enjoyed his company. He'd rescued her from the ardent attentions of Charles Ealing and been a gentleman about it. More strengths. She held out two more fingers.

He'd tried to protect her from Lady Withnall. He'd been by her side after Lily had been abducted, offering his quiet assurance and using his considerable resources to help find the culprits. She'd been terrified that she would lose her twin. He'd taken charge and kept up her spirits. She loved him for that alone.

Yes, she loved him.

There was more. She'd used up the fingers on one hand to count all his wonderful attributes and was about to start on the other, but it was shaking. In truth, both hands were shaking. She was a fool. She didn't need to count. What Ian had done for her and her family after Lily had been abducted was worth at least a thousand points in his favor.

Had she been wrong to doubt him?

She shook off her concern and pressed on. Those horrid rumors circulating about Ian had also been false. He wasn't a murderer. He didn't kill his brother, even though he insisted on blaming on himself. His family had heightened his anguish with their heartless disdain and vicious lies. Yet he'd borne their cruelty and hurtful insults with noble grace.

And the night he'd been attacked outside the Farthingale townhouse, he'd—

Crumpets! She was an idiot.

She shot out of her chair and hobbled to the bed to grab one of the blankets. *Ugh.* She really needed to find some decent clothes. She started to wrap the blanket around her body and then changed her mind. More people were milling about downstairs. She could hear their voices carrying up the stairs. Either the storm was letting up—though it didn't seem so—or the locals had grown tired of waiting for the wintery mix of snow and icy rain to let up and had braved the forces of nature for the sake of a pint of ale.

No matter the reason, the inn was filling up. She slipped off Ian's shirt and donned her gown and stockings. They were torn and stained, but at least dry. She tucked her good foot into one of her boots. Hilda had taken them yesterday to be cleaned, and they now appeared to be in passably good condition. She didn't bother with the other boot, for her foot was so swollen she doubted more than her big toe would fit inside.

She wrapped her now-dry cloak about her shoulders, grabbed one of the larger fireside irons to use as a cane to steady herself, and left her chamber. A quick peek in Abner's room showed that the old man was alone and sleeping comfortably. She hopped along the hall, trying to make her way downstairs without falling down the flight of stairs that now appeared as daunting as a cliff wall.

No doubt Ian was sitting alone with a large tankard of ale in front of him. She firmed her resolve, knowing she was about to make a spectacle of herself. The sound of laughter and conversation emanated from the common room, an indication that the inn was now bustling. She took several deep breaths, ready to face the patrons who would be gawking at her while she limped in on a foot that was too swollen to allow her to wear proper shoes.

As she neared the bottom landing, she heard two women conversing in quiet but insistent tones. "Elsie, are ye mad? Ye could have been sacked for that little stunt. Be grateful that His Grace didn't report the matter to Mr. Gwynne."

"How was I to know, Hilda? He's asked for me before," the younger of the two replied. Her sniffles and quavering voice revealed she had been crying. "But he wants nothing to do with me now. He was angry and steered me out of the room."

"Ye should have realized that he wasn't interested when he asked Mr. Gwynne to keep ye working downstairs. But ye didn't care. Ye purposely tried to cause trouble between 'im and Miss Farthingale."

"So what if I did? She's just a passing fancy for him."

Hilda seemed to grow angry. "Ye're a fool if ye think so. She's the girl he'll be marrying and he said those exact words to me and Mrs. Gwynne before he left to scout the accident site this morning. And he meant 'em. No more mischief, I'm warnin' ye. Keep out of his way or I'll toss ye out into that storm m'self. I'll be watchin' ye closely, Elsie. Ye'd better behave."

Dillie did her best to shrink against the shadows when she heard light footsteps approach. She saw a tearful Elsie disappear down the hall, and then she heard heavier footsteps as Hilda marched into the common room to tend to the bored and stranded patrons.

Oh, no. Dillie remained leaning against the wall, suddenly needing support. Ian had been telling her the truth. She'd trusted him on everything else and ought to have trusted him on this. In her own defense, she'd already realized her mistake and had been on her way to tell him so.

However, she was also grateful that she'd overheard the conversation between the two maids. When dealing with Ian, she had to be confident and relentless. He'd put up those thick walls around his heart and only a battering ram—lovingly wielded, of course—would knock them down.

A quick inspection of the common room revealed he wasn't there. She frowned. He hadn't been in Abner's room either. Nor was he in the inn's private dining room. Nor in the kitchen or entry hall. Mrs. Gwynne bustled toward her. "Miss Dillie! What are ye doin' out of bed?"

"I'm looking for His Grace. Have you seen him?"

She clucked and shook her head. "Oh, ye must 'ave been asleep and he didn't wish to wake ye. He's in the stable checking on his horse. I'm sure he'll be back soon. Shall I help ye up to yer quarters?"

"I'd rather wait down here."

Mrs. Gwynne glanced toward the common room and frowned. "I don't think ye ought," she said in a whisper. "A few travelers arrived early this mornin'. I don't like the look of 'em. They were askin' questions about our guests. Tryin' to be casual about it." She tapped the side of her nose. "But I've seen enough of 'em squirrely sort to know that I should have m'guard up. I told 'em they were welcome to take a hearty meal in the common room, but couldn't stay the night."

Dillie tried to peer over the portly woman's shoulder. "Which ones are they?"

"Them two over there."

She pointed to a pair of men who were dressed decently but appeared quite rough around the edges. "They do look squirrely."

"You keep away from 'em, Miss Dillie." She tapped her nose again. "They're fidgeters. See how their eyes dart from their tankards to the door? And how they duck their heads whenever someone approaches their table? They're up to something, mark my words."

"Has His Grace been warned about them?"

"Not yet. I'll warn him as soon as he returns."

They heard a commotion at the door. "That must be 'im now."

But it wasn't Ian, just more squirrely knaves, as Mrs. Gwynne would say. "Inn's full," she told the pair. "Ye're welcome to a hot meal and then ye'd best be on yer way. There's another inn up the road a little ways."

One of the men fished a shiny coin from his pocket, which surprised Dillie. The pair were poorly dressed, even accounting for the bad weather, and appeared more suited to a dockside tavern than a respectable inn. She hadn't thought them capable of raising thruppence between them. "Ride off in this storm?" one of the men questioned. "Here's for yer trouble. We'll stay the night in yer stable."

Mrs. Gwynne was about to refuse, but her husband chose that moment to pass by. He saw the silver coin and nodded. "Of course, gentlemen. Have ye eaten?" He glanced into the common room and seemed pleased that it was filling. He motioned to a passing maid. Dillie held her breath, realizing who it was as the innkeeper summoned her over. "Elsie, come here. Take care of these gentlemen."

The girl bustled to him, saw Dillie, and stiffened. "At once, Mr. Gwynne." She hastily led the men to a table—or rather, the men pointed to their desired table, which happened to be near the other two shady-looking knaves. Elsie took their orders and then glanced at the entry where Dillie still stood. She appeared angry and hurt, but not at all remorseful for the mischief she'd caused.

Dillie had hoped the girl would take Hilda's warning to heart, but from the look of her, she doubted it. Sighing, she considered returning to her room, but decided against it. The walk down those steps had exhausted her. More important, the newly arrived knaves had just made eye contact with the other two men, as though passing a signal. She wasn't well versed in the art of intrigue, but something was going on. Those men had taken pains to avoid everyone else's gaze.

A shiver ran up Dillie's spine. Were they a ring of thieves? Even so, they wouldn't be so bold as to carry out a theft in broad daylight. Certainly not in front of the inn's patrons, most of whom could later identify them. Mrs. Gwynne had made no bones about being on to them. Surely they realized it.

"Miss Dillie, are ye certain ye wouldn't rather be upstairs?" Mrs. Gwynne asked, interrupting her thoughts.

"Truly, I'm fine right here. I'll stay out of your way."

The woman gave a little cluck and rubbed her hands on her worn apron. "Ye aren't in my way at all, m'dear. I'll check on the kitchen staff and be back in a trice to tend to ye."

"You needn't hurry." Dillie returned her attention to the newly arrived men. She watched Elsie set a tankard in front of each, but they had barely touched their drinks before one of them rose and sauntered back into the entry hall where she still stood.

She pretended not to notice him by studying a painting displayed on one of the walls. However, she tightened her grip on the iron shovel she'd been using as support, ready to use it if he came too close.

Fortunately, the man ignored her. His companion followed him out a moment later. Elsie hurried after them. "Sirs! Shall I set yer drinks aside?"

The pair glanced at each other. "Aye, lass. We won't be long," one of them said with a smirk.

Dillie did not like that ugly smirk.

She scurried to the window as soon as they walked out, her heart beating a little faster as she watched them stride toward the stable. Then the two gentlemen who had arrived first and been sitting in the common room avoiding everyone's glances walked past her and out the door. They moved with purpose, also toward the stable. Ian was in there. "Elsie," she said in a rush, casting aside her anger toward the girl, "find Mr. Gwynne. Tell him there's trouble brewing and I need him to meet me in the stable. He'd better bring a couple of his men."

"I'm sorry, Miss. I'm busy. Ye'll have to find 'im yerself."

Dillie grabbed the girl's arm as she was about to turn away. "I think those scoundrels mean to harm the duke."

That caught Elsie's notice. She gasped and took off in a hurry, calling for Mr. Gwynne.

Dillie took off as well, moving as fast as she could toward the stable, though a turtle could have outrun her in her present state. She leaned on the shovel, trying not to howl with each painful step. Her injured foot, which had only a stocking for protection against the elements, was soaking wet and throbbing by the time she reached the stable.

She walked in carefully, trying to make not a sound even when she saw the boy who tended the horses sprawled on the hay-strewn ground. "Get help," he said in a pained whisper, carefully rolling to his feet. "I think they've killed His Grace."

ALTHOUGH NAPOLEON'S WAR had long since ended, Ian's senses had remained on heightened alert. He'd always been cautious and distrustful of others, even more so after being carved up in front of Dillie's townhouse on Chipping Way, courtesy of his loving family.

Damn.

Ian knew something was wrong. Young Harry, the talkative boy who'd greeted him when he'd first entered the stable, was suddenly nowhere to be found. The boy had followed him into Prometheus' stall, chattering like a magpie the entire time. Wanting a moment's quiet, Ian had sent him off on a made-up errand to fetch another bucket of oats. The lad had gone off some time ago and not yet returned. And now the horses were agitated, particularly Prometheus, who whinnied and kicked the wooden boards of his stall. "What's wrong, fellow?" Ian held out a hand to stroke his nose, but the beast would not be soothed.

Damn again.

Trouble.

Could it be local ruffians? He dismissed the notion. Mr. Gwynne would ban them forever from his taproom. No, locals seeking to do mischief would wait until he was on the road to accost him.

He felt a tug at his heart, realizing what was about to happen. He'd warned his family against further attempts to harm him, but it seemed they hadn't been dissuaded. Did they hate him so bitterly? Wasn't the generous allowance he'd granted each of them enough?

Sighing, he reached into his boot and withdrew the knife he always carried for protection. The two characters who'd come after him on Chipping Way were now languishing in prison. His family must have retained other vermin to do their bidding. It really didn't matter who'd been sent or how many of them were now about to attack him, for he knew who'd sent them and that's what ate him up inside.

He strained to listen for footsteps, but the earthen ground was soft and damp, muffling all steps. Then he heard a soft creak to his left and knew that at least one of the assailants had crept to the adjoining stall. He heard another creak to his right. In the next moment, both men came at him with knives in hand.

He narrowly avoided being slashed by the first man and managed to slam a nearby empty bucket into the second man's face, causing him to curse and fall backward into Prometheus' stall. He whirled and cracked that same bucket over the first man's head as the bastard attempted again to slash him. The knife flew out of the man's hand, and as he knelt to retrieve his fallen weapon, Ian gave him another good, hard crack over the head with that bucket and knocked him out cold.

One down.

Ian grabbed the fallen knife and then turned to the second man in time to see Prometheus rear in panic and land both front hooves hard on the man's chest. He heard the sharp crack of bone and then the man's sharp gasp. *Crumpets!* as Dillie would say. That had to hurt.

He was about to rescue the undeserving wretch from Prometheus' hooves when another two men suddenly appeared. These men had pistols drawn. Ian dove behind a bale of hay as one got off his shot. He heard it whizz past his ear. Too close. The bullet narrowly missed his head. But now Ian realized he was pinned between two bales of hay and had no way out.

The other blackguard stepped in front of him and raised his pistol. Ian knew there was no chance he'd miss. *Dillie, I'm sorry. I won't be there for you.*

The shot rang out and somehow struck an overhead rafter instead of him. He heard a dull thud, and then the man fell atop him unconscious. "What the—"

He shoved the motionless body off him and scrambled to his feet in time to see Dillie swing an iron shovel hard at the knees of the last man left standing. That blackguard howled and crumpled to the ground. "My knee! You bitch! I'll get you for this!"

She raised the shovel to swing it again, but Ian grabbed it from her hand before she accidentally struck him—or Mr. Gwynne and the sturdy helpers who'd just come running in to save him. He no longer needed saving, of course. Dillie had managed to complete the job, just as she had the last time he'd been attacked on Chipping Way.

"Lord love me! Mrs. Gwynne suspected these knaves were up to no good! I ought to have listened," Mr. Gwynne said, shaking his head at the bodies littering the stable. "What a mess! And they coshed young Harry over the head pretty good, but he'll be all right. That boy has a thick skull." He ordered his men to tie up the assailants, sent one off to summon the magistrate, and then grinned at Dillie in obvious admiration. "Good thing ye alerted us, though ye don't seem to have needed our help." He turned to Ian. "Yer Grace, are ye injured?"

Ian shook his head and let out a soft laugh. "No. I'm well, thanks to my valiant defender." His smile faded a little as he studied Dillie. She had on her stained gown and her equally stained cloak, and she wore one boot. At the moment she was leaning against him, looking quite uncomfortable as she tried to keep her injured, unshod foot in the air. She was covered in a sleety snow that clung to her hair and cloak. "Bloody hell," he said quietly. "You might have been killed. Are *you* all right?"

She nodded and leaned closer. "About our earlier conversation," she said in a whisper, "I have something I need to say to you… concerning Elsie."

Bloody hell again.

"Dillie, can't it wait?" This was hardly the time or place for the discussion. He wanted to question those men first and have his suspicions confirmed. No doubt his family had sent them and they had been following him since London.

"No, it can't." She had that stubborn, Dillie look of determination on her face, completely ignoring that he had almost been killed. That *she* could have been killed. Apparently, facing death was no more daunting for her than a stroll in the park. Lord, he didn't stand a chance. Napoleon's armies would have surrendered to her if faced with that stubborn look.

Ass, she just saved your life again.

He owed it to her to listen to whatever she had to say. Obviously, finding Elsie unlaced beside him had distressed her more than facing death at the hands of these fierce assailants.

He carried Dillie off to the side where several bales of hay were neatly piled and set her down on one of the bales. He hoped the small, makeshift wall of hay would lend them some privacy, for he expected her to unleash some stunning blows. He'd take whatever she wished to dish out. He owed her that much and more.

"Go on, tell me what's on your mind." He folded his arms as he stood beside her, waiting for the barrage of angry accusations. However, he kept his gaze on Mr. Gwynne and his staff as they worked, for he needed to be sure the blackguards were securely bound and unable to cause more harm. Only then would he carry Dillie back to the inn, before she did more damage to her injured foot.

She tugged on his jacket. "You have to look at me."

He sighed, knowing he ought to face his punishment like a man. "Very well." Reluctantly, he gave her his full attention.

She squared her slight shoulders and cast him a hesitant smile. "I'm so sorry, Ian. Can you ever forgive me?"

"What?" He shook his head, certain he'd heard wrong. Where were the insults and accusations?

"I owe you an apology and I hope you'll accept it." She placed her small hand on his arm. "I'm not very good at this courtship thing. I don't suppose anyone would consider this a proper courtship anyway. We seem to leap from one scandal to another, from one adventure to another. A little too adventurous for my tastes, by the way."

He let out a soft, groaning laugh. "For me, too."

"What I'm trying to say, perhaps ineptly, is that you've never given me reason to doubt your honor. I'm truly sorry that I ever did."

"Dillie, you don't owe me—"

"But I do," she insisted. "Elsie caught me by surprise, I will admit. Seeing you with her brought all my fears rushing to the fore."

She glanced at the bales of hay piled up around them. "Won't you sit down next to me? I'm getting a crick in my neck looking up at you."

"As you wish." He settled beside her, trying not to respond to the softness of her body against his, or the sweetness of her smile. She had his head spinning. He'd expected an argument, at best a heated conversation. But she was apologizing to him. Was he dreaming? "Daffy—"

"You're still angry with me. You called me Daffy."

"I'm not at all. I'm grateful to you for saving my life. A second time, no less. I'm surprised, but grateful, for your apology. I didn't expect it. I didn't expect *you* in my life." The stable smelled of wet horse manure, wet hay, and wet chicken feathers. The place was damn cold, too. Yet it felt like paradise now that she was here beside him. He called her Daffy whenever he felt the urge to call her something far more dear, such as "my darling." *My love.*

She had found her way so deeply into his heart that she was firmly etched in there. Forever. The depth of his feelings for this snip of a girl frightened him. A little unsettled, he rose again and propped his foot on the bale of hay where she sat. He leaned toward her, wanting to kiss her. Wanting to do so much more, but that would have to wait until he got her back into bed. "You turn me upside down and inside out."

She grinned. "That's progress, I think. Just try to see it from my position." Then her grin faded a little and she shook her head. "You're wonderful and perfect. Too wonderful and perfect. At times, you overwhelm me. I don't know what I have to offer you. I'm still not sure why you'd want to chain yourself to me for the rest of your life. You're a duke. You can do anything you wish. You can have any woman you desire."

"And you thought I wanted Elsie?"

"In that instant. I allowed doubts about myself to cloud my reason. I have four brilliant and talented sisters, but I don't have any particular brilliance or talents. My musical abilities are passable at best. I had an uninspired debut season, save for you landing in my bed at the very end of it. In short, I'm quite unremarkable. That's what scares me the most. I want a man who will love me, but what do I have to offer a man to make him love me?"

Ian gaped at her in surprise. Did she truly not realize how wonderful she was? "You're jesting, right?"

She frowned. "Seeing you with Elsie left me reeling. I didn't know what to do, so I tried to think of how Lily would solve a particularly thorny problem. She always made lists. I began to make a list of your good attributes and your bad, only I couldn't come up with any bad ones. As I said, you're perfect."

He shook his head and laughed. "Good to know." He'd never had this sort of conversation with any members of his family, or any of his mistresses. His family simply hated him. His mistresses only wanted expensive gifts. Past mistresses. He no longer had any. Dillie was all he could handle at the moment.

Not just for the moment.

She was his forever girl.

"Well, that's all I wished to say." She gazed longingly toward the door and sighed. "I wish this horrid weather would end. My foot's not only swollen, but half frozen."

He reached for her hands and held them in his palms. "Your hands are cold, too. I had better get you back to the inn. Come on, Daffy. Put your arms around my neck. Let's get you warmed up."

"Why are you still calling me Daffy?" She continued to stare at him, her lips adorably pursed and aching to be kissed. So he did kiss them, but only a short, sweet kiss. He doubted he could hold back if it were to last longer.

She repeated her question. "Why?"

"Because you still have me off my stride." He never thought he would ever feel this way about anyone. In truth, he never thought he would ever feel again. He'd watched his friends fall in love with the other Farthingale sisters, had seen them turn into besotted dolts, and been so certain the same would never happen to him.

In all his life, he had never expected to follow suit. But he had. Dillie overwhelmed his senses. Dillie overwhelmed his heart.

"You're brave, smart, and beautiful. Kind. Gentle. Yet, at the same time, fierce. There's no one in the world like you."

She rolled her eyes and laughed. "Other than my identical twin sister!"

But I love you.

Bloody hell.

He loved Dillie.

CHAPTER 15

THE WIND WAS still howling and rain still pelted them when Ian finally carried Dillie from the stable to their shared quarters. Dillie snuggled against him, rather liking this mode of transportation and thinking that she ought to have sprained her ankle a lot sooner, perhaps the night Charles Ealing had made those untoward advances and Ian had come to her rescue. *Ooh, Ian. Take me into your manly arms. Ooh, ooh, I'm so helpless!*

Too bad she hadn't thought of it back then. Well, she was enjoying the warmth and strength of his arms now. If only they could stay like this forever, except without the cold and rain. Except that she ought to be wearing a nicer gown. *Ugh!* She was going to burn these wretched clothes as soon as she reached Coniston.

She chided herself for allowing her thoughts to drift along this nonsensical path instead of concentrating on Ian. The attack in the stable had affected him quite profoundly. She could feel the thunderous pounding of his heart against her own chest. Ian's heart never thundered or pounded. He was always in complete control.

Obviously, not now.

He hadn't carried her back to the inn immediately after she'd apologized to him, although he had intended to do it. But Dillie knew he would have dropped her in bed and hurried back to the stable to question the scoundrels Mr. Gwynne and his men now had securely bound, so she'd insisted on remaining with him in the stable until he'd completed his inquiries.

In truth, she was itching with curiosity and eager to know what those scoundrels had confessed. For this reason, she had been more than willing to sit in wait on the cold, wet hay. To her dismay, Ian had been just as eager to keep the questions and responses to himself. He'd purposely kept her out of earshot, sticking her as far away from him as possible, forcing her to sit on one of those prickly bales while he'd interrogated the culprits.

Her time had been completely wasted.

How could one snoop from that distance? One simply couldn't. No matter how hard one tried. It was quite disappointing. She'd just saved his life, hadn't she? How was she to protect him if he kept her ignorant of the dangers?

As they reached the inn and Ian carried her inside, she tugged on his ear to gain his attention. His jaw was still tightly clenched and his thoughts seemed far away. In a dark place, which concerned her. "Will you tell me what you learned from those vile men?" There had been a dangerous look in his eyes when he'd returned to her side after questioning them, and that look was still there. Haunted. Pained. Angry.

Wordlessly, he carried her up the stairs to their room. He closed the door but did not latch it, which meant he wasn't going to have his wicked way with her. She stifled her disappointment, but knew that Ian was hurting terribly. Perhaps he didn't trust himself in this state and feared doing something that would harm her.

She had to soothe him, but how? What could she say or do when she didn't know what was wrong and could only guess at what he'd learned from those scoundrels?

He set her down carefully on the chair beside the hearth and propped her foot on the pillowed stool, but instead of moving away, he knelt beside her and took her cold hands between his palms to rub them lightly. "I'll be leaving you for a little while—"

"You're going to leave me? Why?" She wanted to leap out of her chair, but Ian put his hands on her shoulders and pressed her down gently.

"Sit still." He kissed her affectionately on the nose. "I won't be gone long. I promise."

"Is it because of those men? The magistrate will be here soon to take them off your hands. What did they tell you?" She held her breath, hoping he'd confide in her. She was to be his wife, after all.

He shrugged. "It isn't important."

"Or rather, so important and so distressing that you can't bear to speak of it." She sighed. "Ian, let me help you. Won't you please talk to me? It breaks my heart to see you aching so badly."

"I'm not aching."

She rolled her eyes. "You will be after I club you over the head for that stupid comment. You're the most stubborn man I've ever met, and that's saying something because Farthingale men are quite impossible at times."

He shook his head and laughed. "And Farthingale women are the snoopiest women I've ever met. You were leaning so far off that bale of hay, straining so hard to catch a word, I was certain you'd tumble off it."

She blushed. "True, but we snoop with the best of intentions. How can I help you if you won't tell me what's wrong? I love you, Ian." *Oh, crumpets!* "Oh, dear. Did I just say that?" She let out a little *eep*.

His expression softened. "You did. Care to say it again?"

She *eeped* again. Honestly! What was wrong with her? She'd just taken down two assailants without so much as a hitch in her breath. But now, she was in full blush, her tongue thickening in fear, and she couldn't seem to stop *eeping*. "I didn't mean to let it slip out, but it's no secret. You must know how I feel about you. I do love you, Ian."

"Which makes me doubt your sanity." He cast her a wry grin, but there was such turmoil in his expression that it tugged at her heart. He was a damaged soul, unable to believe that anyone could care for him, and if someone ever did care, then something awful was bound to happen.

"I suppose that's why you call me Daffy." She maintained her smile, wanting to keep their conversation as casual as possible, even though she'd just exposed her heart and had no illusions about the chaos her words were causing him.

Nor did she expect Ian to take her into his arms and profess his undying love for her. Still, she was disappointed that he'd simply made a jest of it and now looked like he'd rather be anywhere but here beside her. She was not going to force him to say more, for affection and caring were new sensations to him and he must find them overwhelming. "I'm not the only one who's a little out of sorts right now," she said. "You're rather a shambles at the moment, too. What did those men tell you?"

He drew away and moved to stand beside the hearth, resting his arm on the mantel as he gazed into the flames. "They just confirmed what I already suspected."

"Which is..." she prompted when he didn't immediately continue. She was afraid to push too hard, for he might walk out and she was in no condition to chase after him. Her race to the stable to save him had sapped her strength and been quite enough excitement for one day.

He remained silent, still staring into the fire. She took the opportunity to study him while he appeared distracted. That look in his eyes... so haunted and angry. He was capable of murder. Was he actually contemplating it? "You know who ordered the attack, don't you?"

He nodded.

She shoved out of her chair to hobble to his side and wrap her arms around him. "You can tell me anything. I'll keep it in confidence, which is saying quite a lot since Farthingales never keep their mouths shut. But you know I can. Please let me help. Please don't run away from me."

He arched an eyebrow in surprise. "Why would I run from you?"

She eased back to study his face. His torment was still evident on his handsome features. That was quite something, she realized with a start, for Ian wasn't trying to hide his feelings from her. Quite the opposite, he was allowing her to see into his heart. For Ian, that was as close to an admission of love as he was capable of giving. "I don't know. You're the one who said you had to leave."

"Among other things, in order to obtain the special license and engage the minister. I'll bring him back here to perform our wedding ceremony. I'm not wasting any more time on courtship. Not that I've spent a whit of time properly courting you."

"And not that I care a whit about it either. I've accepted the fact that we'll never do anything the ordinary way. I can't wait to meet Felicity and make the three of us a family." But he'd said "among other things," and that was the part that worried her. What else did he intend to do before he returned with the special license and the minister?

"Felicity will love you at first sight," he said, stroking a finger across her cheek as he cast her a tender smile.

"As I'll love her." She sighed and shook her head. "Mother will be disappointed. Five daughters and not a decent courtship among them. Lily's wedding was a beautiful affair, though. I suppose my mother will have to be satisfied with that. I'll ask her to throw us a party. She'll enjoy planning it. Aunt Julia will help. Thank you for wanting to marry me, Ian. I don't think I could ever love anyone but you. In truth, I know I couldn't."

She paused a moment, hoping he might return the compliment. "It's quite fortunate matters worked out the way they did," she continued, swallowing her disappointment when he kept silent, "except for those attacks on your life, of course. Those were terrible. I'm glad you weren't hurt this time. I'll stop rambling now."

He surprised her by lifting her into his arms. "Thank you for saving my life. Second time. It hasn't escaped my notice that I seem to need you by my side."

She melted once more at the tender, lopsided smile on his face. Perhaps there was hope for their married life. She returned it with a hopeful smile of her own. "As much as you need air to breathe and water to drink?"

He shook his head and laughed. "More so." Then his laughter faded. "It's time I stripped you out of those wet clothes and got you into bed."

She liked the direction this conversation was taking. He still had her in his arms and she had no intention of protesting. "Will you be joining me?"

He settled her in the center of the bed, sat beside her, and then ever so slowly began to roll down her stockings. Oh, heavens! The sensual touch of his fingers along her thighs was shockingly delicious. A sigh escaped her lips. Her skin grew hot and her thoughts wanton. She loved the feel of his hands upon her body.

He grinned as he rose from the bed and hung her stockings by the fire. Then he walked to the door and latched it. *That's a promising sign.* He returned to her side and deftly slipped the gown off her body. She could still feel the heat of his hands on her skin after he'd undressed her.

But instead of removing his clothes, he reached for the shirt she'd been using as a nightshirt and put it on her. "What are you doing?" she asked.

"Getting you settled. Get under the covers and I'll tell you a story. Go on, Dillie. I can't concentrate while your luscious body's in plain view."

She did so reluctantly, worried that he hadn't been completely honest with her. Oh, she never doubted that he meant to obtain the special license and return to her with a minister in tow, but she also suspected that he was going to do something reckless and dangerous beforehand. Perhaps confront the enemies who had ordered the attack on him. Perhaps kill his enemies.

He knew who wanted him dead. She simply had to get the truth out of him before he set his rage free and destroyed his future. "Give me your hand, Ian. I want to hold it."

"I'm not a little boy. I don't need you to worry about me."

"I know you don't." She cast him a smile, hoping her strain did not show through. She didn't give him the chance to draw away and simply reached for his hand. She was trying to encourage him, not browbeat him into confiding in her.

He was used to working things out on his own, used to keeping all the hurt and disappointment bottled up inside. This second attack had affected him quite badly. Would his anger finally erupt? She didn't know how much he would reveal to her, but she would listen to whatever he had to say, hoping that in time he would learn to trust her with all his confidences. "Go on. I'm listening."

"You know the beginning already. My brother drowned. My family never forgave me. Ever since that fateful day, I've been made to suffer for surviving that accident. I haven't forgiven myself either. I doubt I ever will."

"Oh, Ian—"

He gave her hand a little squeeze. "No, Dillie. It's all right. I've managed."

"Quite well, I think. You've built a thriving dukedom, earned the respect of the royal family and the Duke of Wellington for your bravery during the war years. Even Gabriel and Graelem admire you. Gabriel claims that you saved him numerous times from Napoleon's grasp."

"I wasn't brave. I never cared whether I lived or died. I'm amazed that I did survive Napoleon's war. In truth, I never thought I would. But I did, and I was angry that I had. James was dead, and here I lived, no matter how many battles I'd fought, no matter how many enemies I'd faced, no matter how many enemy cannons were aimed directly at my chest."

Because James was watching over you.

She couldn't reveal her thought to Ian. He wouldn't believe it. Since he blamed himself for his brother's death, he'd never understand that his brother would not feel the same way. James was surely an angel in heaven, and angels were all about compassion and forgiveness, or so she'd always been taught.

"There I was, still alive and enjoying all that society had to offer. Meaningless parties, meaningless trysts. Then suddenly one night I kissed the wrong girl." He paused a moment to cast her the softest smile. "She was snooping in her neighbor's garden around midnight, poking about where she should not have been."

Dillie blushed. "I never forgot that kiss." He was still smiling at her, making her heart melt. Good thing she was seated in bed, for she doubted her legs would have held her up had she been standing. Her entire body had turned to pudding.

"Nor did I. I never forgot the kiss, or the girl I mistakenly kissed. You, Dillie. I knew you'd be a danger to my heart the moment our lips touched. Yours were so soft, they just drew me in. I would have gone on kissing you if you hadn't stepped back and slapped me."

"You'd startled me, that's all. I didn't really want you to stop. I liked it rather a lot. I still like your kisses."

"The night I was attacked on Chipping Way," he continued, absently running his hand along his stomach and the scar that stretched across it, "I think now that I must have been running toward you. I wasn't aware of it at the time. As it turns out, it was the smartest thing I could have done for many reasons."

She nodded. "Uncle George was there to save you."

"That, too. But most important was catching a last glimpse of you... the girl I'd mistakenly kissed. You took my hand that night and never let go." He swallowed hard. "For the first time in my life, I felt that someone cared. It felt good. Damn good. That night, I knew my time on earth had not been wasted because I'd met you."

He shook his head and leaned back. "I know you're afraid that I'm about to run off and do something foolish. I won't deny that I want to, but I'll let my man of affairs take care of my enemies. It's a simple matter, really. I need only cut off their funds. Toss them out of their homes... *my* homes."

She shook her head. "You support these enemies of yours? I don't understand. Who are they?"

"I thought you would have guessed by now." He shrugged his shoulders. "My family was behind this latest attempt. I imagine it was for the same reason that prompted their first attack."

"*They* ordered the Chipping Way attack?" She frowned, trying to make sense of what he'd just told her. "Why?"

"Come on, Dillie. Why the confusion? Think mean, petty reasons. My mother would rather see me dead than happily married. My eldest cousin always thought he would inherit, and now he's terrified that I'll sire an heir to displace him."

Her heart twisted in a painful knot. How had he survived his childhood? She thought of the nights he must have spent alone, a small child left to fend for himself, lying heartbroken and alone in the dark. Despite the lack of a mother's love, despite the lack of any love at all, he'd turned into an admirable man. "I'm so sorry, Ian."

"So am I," he said in a quiet manner that revealed the extent of his torment. "I'd love to wring their bloody necks, but I won't. I'll do something far more painful to them. I'll cut off their funds and remove them from England. Perhaps ship them off to Jamaica or India. Since I support them, own their beautiful homes, and have been maintaining them all these years, it will be easy for me to do. My terms will be generous. I'll continue to support them, because as bad as they are, they're all I have—but I won't give them enough to pay for more assassins—so long as they remain away from England."

He sighed, and his voice broke just a little as he said, "I was a fool to hold out hope, to believe they might one day forgive me."

She wrapped her fingers in his, but glanced away. Her eyes were watering and she didn't wish Ian to see her crying, for he would mistake her tears for pity. Ian was too proud to ever accept anyone's pity or help. "They're the fools. Your entire family."

"Perhaps, but they're still my family. I can understand my cousins' greed. But my mother?" He leaned back and let out a bitter laugh. "She knew this second attack was planned. Didn't consider warning me. Now, that's a mother for you."

Dillie was speechless. She couldn't imagine a single Farthingale ever behaving so abominably. Farthingales might smother with love, but never with apathy or hatred.

"And then there's you," he said softly. "My guardian angel. Your eyes sparkle whenever you look at me. They always have. Even that first night in Lady Eloise's garden. I'm glad you were the wrong girl and glad I put that sparkle in your eyes."

He tipped a finger under her chin and turned her to face him. "I meant what I said the night I lay dying. I'm glad it was you by my side." *I've never wanted anyone else beside me. Only you. You're all I've ever wanted.*

One day he'd find the courage to tell her.

IAN SENT A messenger off to Swineshead with a warning note to his staff to keep alert for strangers prowling about, and then made straight for London. At times, he rode in sunshine that warmed the air, but mostly he rode in a light mist, the stubborn remnant of the powerful storm now moving upward into Scotland.

The roads improved as he made his way south, but his rage seemed to churn and grow with each stride closer. He stopped at his townhouse before visiting his solicitors, for he needed a hot bath to wash away the layers of dust and mud caked on his clothes.

He needed a change of clothes as well, and Ian hoped that once he was properly groomed and dressed he'd feel nobler than he did right now. All he felt now was a mounting, unstoppable fury aimed at the people he laughingly referred to as his family. It was all he could do to contain the urge to load his pistols and hunt down the sorry lot of them. He knew that in his present state he was capable of taking cold, dead aim and shooting them.

His valet hurried toward him as he made for the stairs. The poor man's eyes rounded as he gaped at Ian's sorry state. "Your Grace! Has something dreadful happened?"

"Not yet, but it's about to."

Ian took the stairs two at a time. Ashcroft did his best to follow and was noticeably short of breath by the time he reached Ian's bedchamber. "I'll order a bath brought up for you," Ashcroft said, inspecting him as he shrugged out of his jacket and began to remove his shirt. "And you appear to need refreshments. I'll order those brought up as well." Then he shook his head and sighed. "Your clothes, Your Grace. I had better burn them."

"I do believe you're right." As his valet continued to fuss about him, Ian took a moment to glance around his immaculately maintained quarters. The big bed dominating his chamber caught his attention. Dillie would soon be sharing that bed, sharing his life, assuming he didn't go off and do something immensely idiotic, such as get himself killed.

While his bath was wheeled in and servants began to carry in buckets of water to fill it, he strode to his desk, withdrew a sheaf of paper and quill pen from one of the drawers, and hastily penned a note to his solicitors, Dumbley and Sons. It was early afternoon. He had time to collect his thoughts before making decisions that would impact the rest of his life. "Have this note delivered to the senior Mr. Dumbley. I'll stop by to see him within the hour."

"Very good, Your Grace." However, he hesitated a moment before turning away.

"Ashcroft, what's troubling you?" His valet rarely appeared this perplexed.

"I don't wish to presume," he began, clasping his hands in front of him and staring at his toes. "But if this has something to do with the dowager duchess Celestia, then you ought to know... she has returned to London."

Every aching bone in Ian's body stiffened. "Returned?"

"Indeed, Your Grace. Only yesterday. Your cousins as well."

"Damn it," he said softly. He'd banished them to Bath earlier in the season, but here they were back again, no doubt confident their second plot would succeed. Too confident. He was about to disappoint them. "Where have they set up residence?"

"Same townhouse they'd let for the season. Or rather, that *you'd* let for them. I must say, we were all surprised, for they'd only recently left, and at the time of their departure you did not appear inclined to allow them back."

"That's putting it politely." Ian didn't know whether to roar with laughter at their presumption or pound his fists on his desk in anger and frustration. Either response would have frightened his valet. He kept his manner even and controlled, as he had for all of his life, no matter the insults, no matter the hurt and disappointment. "No, I was not inclined to let them back at all. Nor am I now. However, their presence in town will make my task all the easier. Thank you for letting me know, Ashcroft. You've just saved me a lot of time and trouble."

He nodded. "I'm adept with weapons, Your Grace. Of course, you know that. Just thought I'd mention it again, for I take my responsibilities to you seriously."

"Thank you, but laying out my clothes and making certain my cravat is properly tied before I step out onto the street is all I require of you just now." He noticed the look of disappointment on his valet's face and realized he'd just taken the wind out of the poor man's sails. No doubt insulted his loyalty, too. "Keep your weapons at the ready. The day isn't over yet, and who knows what might happen?" Ian was spoiling for a fight himself, and knew he'd have it before the sun set over the muddy Thames. "Your offer is much appreciated."

Ashcroft puffed out his chest. "Thank you, Your Grace."

Ian washed and dressed, then made his way to the Inns of Court where Dumbley and Sons maintained offices. He quickly finished his business with the senior Mr. Dumbley, arranged to meet him later at his mother's townhouse, and then made his way to a less fashionable side of town to engage Homer Barrow, the Bow Street runner of excellent reputation he'd used on occasion before. He liked Homer. The man was sharp-witted and reliable.

The church bells of St. Paul's were ringing in the distance by the time Ian, his trusted man of affairs Henry Matchett, his elderly but feisty solicitor Mr. Dumbley, and Homer Barrow and his Bow Street runners reached his mother's townhouse. Mr. Barrow was an amiable-looking, portly fellow with a bulbous nose, but looks were deceptive. He and his companions, Mick and Bert, were quick to action and doggedly attentive to their purpose. They earned curious looks from the passersby, who were not used to such gatherings along the fashionable square.

"Just give us the word, Yer Grace," Mr. Barrow said with a nod, waiting for permission to march in and haul Ian's cousins out of London and onto the next packet ship sailing somewhere far, far from England.

The task of arranging that passage had been assigned to Mr. Dumbley, who already had the tickets in hand. In truth, Ian was surprised by the enthusiasm with which his solicitor had agreed to take on the task. "About time you got rid of those wretches," he'd muttered.

Long past time, Ian knew. "I'll go in first. Wait for my summons."

He knew that his decision to bring along his man of affairs and his solicitors when confronting his family was the right one. He would leave those cooler heads to finalize the details of their banishment.

He sighed.

Dillie had cause to be concerned about him. He wasn't used to thinking of anyone other than himself, and were it not for her and Felicity, he'd be ruthlessly pummeling his cousins, pounding his fists into them until they were bleeding and could no longer breathe. If he were the sort to accost women, he'd do the same to his mother. But that was one thing he'd never do, for he could never bring himself to strike a woman, no matter how evil she was.

Ian strode into the elegant townhouse unannounced and found his mother, as expected, sipping tea with his useless cousins. "Good afternoon, Celestia. Simon. Edmund. How convenient to find you all together. But you've all turned pale. What, have you just seen a ghost?"

The teacup slipped from Celestia's hand and clattered to the floor. "It isn't possible."

Simon bent to reach into his boot. Ian withdrew his pistol and aimed it at Simon's heart, his grip calm and steady though he was still a muddle of fury and heartache. His own family! And now it had come to this. "I'd reconsider if I were you."

Simon held out his hands as he straightened back up, obviously sensing Ian's rage and afraid to make a wrong move. "Bastard."

"Alas, Simon, it isn't the case. Otherwise, you would have been duke. But you're not, and never will be." He called to Mr. Barrow, and didn't have long to wait before he scuttled in with his runners right behind him. "Escort my cousins to their rooms and help them pack. Be quick about it. Their ship sails at the evening tide."

"A ship?" Celestia rose to her proud height, her eyes widening in obvious surprise as Matchett and Dumbley entered the salon. She stiffened her spine. "I'm not leaving England. You can't make me go."

Ian arched an eyebrow. "No, the journey is only for my cousins." He turned to them as they were about to be hauled upstairs, his expression as cold as his heart now felt. "There's hope for you in a new land, away from Celestia's poison. If you think to step foot on English soil again, just know that the Prince Regent has issued warrants for your arrest. He's holding off enforcement of those warrants until tomorrow. You'll both be hanged if you're ever caught in England again. Keep that thought in mind."

Celestia glared at him. "You're a beast." She turned and rang for her butler. "Badger! Badger!" She cast Ian an imperious smile, as though expecting her servant to stride in and toss him out.

Badger. Ian remembered the man, still felt that odd tug of recognition. Where had he met him before? "He won't respond, Celestia. Nor will any of your staff. Sit down and learn your fate."

She hesitated, her eyes darting to him and his companions, then to the entry door, and finally to the fashionable silk chairs beside her. She took a seat, making a dramatic sweep of her gown as she settled in. "Am I to be put to death, as you did to your brother?"

Lord, she never missed an opportunity to stick her knife in him. "There's no warrant issued for your arrest. I planned a better punishment for you."

"No doubt devised by that Farthingale bitch you ruined. Have you turned soft? Are you going to marry that—"

"Don't say it." Ian reached out and pointed his pistol at her head. Damn. She'd rattled him, just as she'd intended. Indeed, by her gloating smirk, it seemed as though she wanted to goad him into shooting her. Then he'd have the deaths of both his brother and his mother weighing on his soul. Did she truly prefer to be dead than ever see him happy?

"Your Grace, it isn't wise," Mr. Dumbley quietly said as Ian continued to take aim at Celestia.

Ian let out a mirthless laugh as he put away his pistol, not yet trusting himself. He wasn't in control of his temper, for she'd finally done it, made him hate her as much she had always hated him. He understood the twisted workings of her mind. *Damn.* "I alone devised your punishment. That pleasure was all mine."

Though he'd truly taken no pleasure in it. He would have given anything for one smile, one nod of approval from her or his father. "One of the Isles of Scilly is where you'll spend the rest of your days. On St. Mary's, in a little house on an isolated hill. Mr. Dumbley will provide the details. Mr. Matchett will escort you there."

She curled her hands and raised them at him, like a cat with claws bared. "You can't make me go there. I won't stay."

"Indeed you will, make no mistake. You're not Napoleon and have no loyal minions to rouse. No one will come to your aid. There'll be no escaping your new home." He paused and shook his head. "You won't find any of the *haute monde* in residence on the island, but you can make friends among the lesser society who will be your neighbors."

She tipped her head up and sneered. "I'll never stoop to that level. Still, I suppose I can manage for a few months. I'll write to my friends, let them know I'll return to Bath by Christmas. I'll require a lady's maid, of course. A cook and a housekeeper. A proper butler. I'll need a large house with rooms enough for my sisters when they visit." She stared at him, casting a cold, soulless smile. "I wish you ill, Ian. I hope your wife recoils from you in disgust. I hope she takes on other lovers and makes you the *ton's* laughingstock. I hope your children hate you."

"I get the point, Celestia. Oh, and if you do attempt to escape, I'll have you confined to an asylum. So think on it, the Isles of Scilly or Bedlam? What's it to be?"

THE SUN SHONE unbearably bright as Ian left London and rode to Swineshead the following day. He was in a foul, dark temper, his mind awhirl and the blood coursing through his body cold and thick. Nothing seemed to warm him. He felt strange. He felt soiled. He'd disowned his family, but it had been at great cost to his heart. He'd never see them again. There would never be a reconciliation. His cousins were now on a ship bound for Goa, on the western shore of India. His mother and Mr. Matchett were in a coach bound for Cornwall, and then a boat to the Isles of Scilly.

He ought to have felt elated, but he simply felt a terrible, hollow sadness. He was in part to blame for the family's downfall. He couldn't shake the thought, nor would he ever absolve himself of blame. At least Dumbley and Matchett were delighted by this turn of events. They had assured him all would be well from now on.

He knew they were right.

He would make damn certain of it.

He tapped a hand to his chest and felt along the inner pocket of his cloak. The special license was safely tucked inside, the little piece of paper resting against his heart, as though a blanket protecting him from the hailstorm of rage and sorrow swirling within him. Soon, he and Dillie would be married. The thought was like a tether, holding back his dark side, that empty part of him capable of violating most of the Ten Commandments. *Honor thy mother and thy father.*

That would never happen.

Dillie's family, however, was something special. He'd stopped by the Farthingale residence earlier to speak to Dillie's father, but was told he was already on his way to Coniston to meet his daughter. No doubt he'd stop at the Black Sail Inn and find her there. Ian considered riding straight to the inn to protect Dillie from her father's wrath, but John Farthingale was nothing like Ian's parents. John would sooner cut off his right arm than ever hurt one of his girls.

Ian rode for Swineshead instead, eager to visit Felicity and make certain she had not been harmed. He knew he was being overly cautious. His family didn't give a fig about the infant, and probably assumed he didn't either. However, they might have set a plan in motion, intending a bad end for the helpless innocent.

Once he'd seen to Felicity's protection, he'd attend to the other pressing matter, marrying Dillie. Lord, he wanted to wrap her in his arms and never let her go. Love and hate. It felt odd to harbor these dramatically different sensations within his heart, and odd how easily he was able to separate them. Hatred still dominated his heart... no, that wasn't quite right. All his life he'd felt achingly empty. Emptiness wasn't the same as hatred. His family hated him, to be sure. But he hadn't reciprocated the feeling until now.

Quite the opposite, he'd yearned for their approval, had wished so hard for their forgiveness as a child. He'd died a little inside each time they'd withheld it. But no more. That part of his life was over and would no longer haunt him. He now had Dillie's love and would work hard to earn that gift.

The air turned cool as Ian approached Leeds. Night was falling and a stiff breeze cut straight through him. He drew his cloak securely about his shoulders, but it did little to help. Prometheus had been traveling at full gallop, but Ian now held him back to a canter. These northern roads were still a dangerous mix of mud and ice.

Giving in to darkness and fatigue, he stopped in Leeds for the night, determined to catch only a few hours of rest and resume his journey at daybreak. He kept to his schedule and was off at the rooster's first crow. Once again, the sun shone brightly throughout the day. In truth, he hadn't seen this beautiful a stretch of days in years. Broad patches of blue dominated the sky, as though some force above was watching over him, assuring him of a brighter future. No swirls of gray in sight. "What do you think?" he muttered to Prometheus. "Is our luck changing?"

The hours passed quickly and before he knew it, the dark stone walls of his hunting lodge came into view. Swineshead was a sturdily built structure, erected centuries ago by one of the earlier dukes of Edgeware. Its simple, rough-hewn exterior had been designed to blend in with the natural forest surroundings, and for this reason Ian felt more comfortable here than at his much grander ducal estate at Edgeware.

The roof was made of a sturdy, dark slate. Vibrant green ivy covered the outer walls. The lodge hadn't changed much in almost a hundred years, and Ian was determined to keep it that way. Despite the recent improvements to its interior, necessary to accommodate Felicity and her caretakers, he'd ordered the exterior to remain untouched.

He'd also authorized some changes to the rear garden, ordering a stone wall built to separate the garden from the stream that ran along its northern perimeter. He couldn't have Felicity toddling too close and falling—

He changed the direction of his thoughts. No, one death by drowning in the family was quite enough.

"Yer Grace! Welcome home." His groomsman, a stocky, bow-legged Irishman by the name of Quinn, hastened from the stable toward him with a big smile on his face. "Oh, 'tis good to see ye. Will ye be stayin' a while?"

Ian dismounted, handed the reins to Quinn, and then patted him on the shoulder in greeting. "Nice to see you, too. How are things? Quiet?"

The old man rolled his eyes, and then shook his head, all the while laughing. "Not since Miss Felicity arrived. She has a set of lungs on her, that's fer sure, but other than her occasional outburst, all has been well."

Ian strode with him toward the stable. "No strangers lurking about?"

Quinn halted in his tracks and regarded him quizzically. "None. Are ye still concerned about 'em not so friendly visitors?"

"I hope not, but one can never be too careful." Four assailants were now in the magistrate's custody, and there was no telling if his family had hired others. Homer Barrow would find out, but his investigation could take weeks.

"We've been vigilant, Yer Grace, but if it'll help matters," Quinn said, his brow furrowing, "I have a few friends nearby who might be willin' to visit for a spell. Can't hurt to have a little extra protection around, and we've plenty of rooms above the stable to house them.

They'll help me out in exchange for a warm bed and a few square meals."

Ian nodded, liking the idea. "Send for them today. I can't stay long this trip, and I'd like them here before I leave."

Quinn patted Prometheus' neck. "I'll tend to this fine beast first, and then head off to fetch them. Will that suit Yer Grace?"

Ian thanked him and then strode to the lodge, eager to set eyes on Felicity. He'd walked no more than two steps in the door before he saw Miss Poole, the thirtyish woman he'd engaged to care for the child, scurrying toward him with a welcoming smile on her face. She was a plain-looking woman, but that smile on her face spoke volumes. "Your Grace, I'm so glad you're here. Felicity will be delighted to see you. Be prepared to cover your ears, for she can be quite expressive at times."

He laughed softly. "So I've been warned by Quinn."

"Her Highness is sleeping now, but she'll soon wake from her nap and demand to be fed. I was just on my way to the kitchen to collect her supper."

"Then I'll not delay you." He glanced around. "I'll take a quick look in on Felicity and then inspect the changes made to the lodge."

Miss Poole appeared to have no objection to his plan, not that she had any right to countermand him. Still, it eased his concern to see her so comfortable in his presence, for it boded well for Felicity's care. He'd hired the woman because she appeared efficient, and warm and engaging as well. She had come highly recommended, had sterling references, and even so, Ian had worried that he was doing the wrong thing in leaving Felicity in a stranger's care. It seemed he had fretted needlessly.

Eager to see Felicity, he climbed the stairs and walked into the nursery, taking extra care to be quiet. The room was sparse, but charming. A white armoire decorated with yellow roses stood in one corner, and a white high chair also decorated with yellow roses stood in the corner nearest the window. White lace curtains billowed at the corners of the window. A small carpet in hues of dark red, azure blue, and golden amber covered the dark wood floor beside Felicity's crib.

Ian's heart caught in his throat as he peered into the crib and saw the sleeping infant. Her angelic face was pink and smooth, and her little lips were puckered and moving as though she were suckling on a nipple. "My favorite dream, too," he said in a whisper, thinking of Dillie and her glorious breasts. "Most men never outgrow that dream."

Felicity had the good sense not to respond to his wayward remark.

Ian continued to study her. She was dressed in a clean, white gown decorated with pink ribbons, and lay sprawled on her back with arms raised above her shoulders, as though she hadn't a care in the world. This is what he'd wanted, had hoped for. He let out a breath, relieved he had managed to get this one thing right.

Miss Poole bustled into the room carrying a bowl of what looked like mashed fruit. She set the bowl down on a table beside the high chair, and then tiptoed toward him. "She's an angel, isn't she?"

Ian nodded.

Felicity let out a little squawk. Then another.

Miss Poole winced. "Oh, goodness. Here it comes," she warned, just as Felicity let out an ear-splitting wail and burst into anguished tears. "Hush, Your Highness! Is this any way to greet your uncle?" She lifted the crying child into her arms and gently rocked her until she calmed. "Well, at least her bottom's dry. Won't be for long though, will it Your Highness?"

Felicity fisted her little hands and rubbed them along her dripping nose. Miss Poole laughed. "We'd better clean that little nose before you eat. The hands too. Now, where is that wet cloth I always keep close?"

"I'll hold her while you look for it. I've been riding through rain and mud for most of these past few days. She can't do my clothes much more harm."

She appeared surprised, but pleased. "As you wish, Your Grace. But don't say I didn't warn you."

A feeling of contentment washed over Ian as he held his young ward. He planted a kiss on her head, his lips gentle against her soft, dark curls. Indeed, he'd gotten this part right. Dillie would approve, of that he had no doubt.

A short while later, once Felicity's attention was firmly fixed on her food and no longer on him, he strode out of the room and made his way about the lodge to inspect the general improvements. He was pleased with the results. Sturdy new windows, solid wood floors in good repair, hearths and chimneys also in good repair. Carpets cleaned and new furniture in place so that the lodge had been transformed from a rough and tumble bachelor's hunting retreat to a home suited to accommodate a family.

Ian remained the following day at Swineshead as well, deciding to spend a little extra time with Felicity and make certain that Quinn's friends, who had arrived last night, were familiar with the grounds and what was expected of them concerning Felicity's protection. His instincts told him there was no danger, that neither his family—nor the wharf rats they'd hired to do him in—would show up on his doorstep to abduct Felicity.

Likely, there had only been those four assailants, all of whom were now securely in the magistrate's hands. So why was he lingering here, making excuses to avoid returning to Dillie? He wasn't certain and could come up with no good reason. He knew he had to marry her. He truly wished to marry her. The sooner the ceremony took place, the better.

"Don't be an idiot," he muttered to himself, suddenly understanding his reluctance. He'd been alone all of his life. Detested by his family. He wasn't yet in control of his anger. What if he unleashed his barely leashed rage on those he cared for most? He wanted to be a good husband to Dillie, but wasn't certain he knew how.

He'd just entered the stable and approached Prometheus' stall looking for Quinn when the feisty Irishman hurried in behind him looking quite perturbed. "Yer Grace! There's a carriage rattling up the drive. It could be them unwanted visitors."

Ian tightened his grip on the stall gate and nodded. "Summon your friends. I want them in the lodge, guarding Felicity, their weapons at the ready." Had his gut instinct been wrong? Were more assailants on the loose?

"No worries, Yer Grace," he said as they walked out to intercept the approaching carriage. "They're in the kitchen as we speak. I'll take care of 'em interlopers while ye get yerself to safety." He raised a fist and shook it at the advancing carriage to emphasize his point.

The morning sun shone on the gleaming black conveyance. Ian shaded his eyes with his hand and gazed into the distance. He grinned. "Quinn, forget my instructions. These are welcome guests." Though how Dillie managed to obtain a Farthingale carriage and find him here was beyond him. The note he'd left in London with George Farthingale had only mentioned that Dillie and Abner were at the Black Sail Inn due to bad weather and difficulties with the carriage, and that Ian would escort them to Coniston within the next few days.

He stood with arms folded across his chest, waiting for the conveyance to draw to a halt, and then moved to the door as it opened. Dillie fairly flew into his arms. "Ian, you're here! Thank goodness. I was afraid you'd gone off to... well, I wasn't certain what you planned to do, just knew it would be something dangerous."

He frowned, but kissed her soundly on the lips because—damn it—he'd missed her. One look at her and all his concerns simply fled. She was sunshine and meadow flowers. She loved him. It felt so good to have her in his arms. "You ought to be resting your foot. And where did you get these new clothes?"

She had on a simple, blue wool gown, several shades darker than the blue of her eyes. Her hair was pulled back in a bun at the nape of her neck, but some curls had broken loose in the light breeze and now framed her beautiful face.

"The gown is mine. We stopped at Coniston first so I could pack some belongings, and then we came straight here." He bent to kiss her again, but John Farthingale chose that moment to descend from the carriage. *Oh, hell.* He did not look at all pleased. No doubt, he'd learned about Dillie's carriage tipping over and seen Abner Mayhew recovering from his broken leg.

Ian was curious to know just how much else Dillie had told her father. By his angry scowl, Ian figured she'd told him far too much. He had no intention of deceiving the man about what had happened between him and his daughter, but that conversation was better held after the wedding ceremony, when pistols were less likely to be drawn. Specifically, her father's pistol pointed at his throat. He stifled a sigh. A little discretion on Dillie's part would have been helpful.

No, the fault was all his. A little restraint on his part would have done the trick. Unfortunately, he'd shown not a whit of it when seducing Dillie and still felt not a whit of remorse. "Welcome, Mr. Farthingale."

His greeting was met with a grumble. "Good morning, Your Grace."

Dillie rolled her eyes. "Oh, Father. I asked you not to growl at him. He'll obtain the special license and marry me as soon as Mother arrives." She returned her gaze to Ian, and then nudged him. "I think my father needs some reassurance." He noticed a tinge of apprehension in her eyes as well. "I thought we might have a quiet ceremony at Coniston in a week's time. We've sent word for my mother to join us there. Do you mind?"

Did she doubt that he'd marry her? "It suits me fine. Is that what you tracked me down to ask?"

"No, I had no idea you'd be here." A light blush stained her cheeks. "You caught me being meddlesome again, but after all that happened at the inn, I grew concerned for Felicity's safety and thought it a good idea to stop by for a visit. How is she?"

Ian laughed. "Very noisy. She'll fit right in with the Farthingale clan."

He wanted to sweep her into his arms and kiss her again. She had been worried about Felicity, realizing as he had that his family might wish to harm the child. She'd dragged her father across the Lake District to offer their protection.

Indeed, she was ridiculously meddlesome. And wonderful. He ought to have been angry, but wasn't in the least. Dillie cared about him and Felicity, and for a man starved of all affection for most of his life, her caring felt like heaven. "I have the special license with me. We can marry today if you like."

John Farthingale looked obviously relieved.

"See, Father. I told you all would be well." She cast Ian a beaming smile, one that came straight from her gentle heart. "Next week will do."

Perhaps for her, but the week-long wait to hold her in his arms, to run his hands along her naked body and feel the tingle of her soft, warm skin... too damn long.

He led her and her father into the lodge, rang for refreshments, and then summoned Miss Poole. "Her Highness has callers," he said with a chuckle. "Please bring her down to meet our guests."

Miss Poole smiled and bustled off to do his bidding.

Dillie, he could see, was practically leaping out of her skin with excitement. He'd expected her to accompany Miss Poole upstairs, and then realized that despite her obvious desire to do so, she wasn't about to leave him alone with her father.

Bloody hell. Had she told him everything?

What a difference between the Farthingales and Markhams. He would never trust his family as Dillie trusted hers. In truth, Ian was glad he'd taken care of banishing his loathsome relatives. He hadn't wanted them in England when he married, hadn't wanted the remotest possibility of their foul taint touching his soon-to-be duchess.

It didn't take long for Miss Poole to return with Felicity. While Dillie and her father fussed and cooed over the child, Ian kept his gaze on Dillie and simply soaked in her genuine warmth. Felicity responded with glee, adoring the attention and squealing with delight at Dillie's playful manner and John Farthingale's obvious experience with boisterous children.

Ian thought this moment was the best he'd ever experienced, a moment of exquisite purity. But as the morning wore on, and they settled into easy conversation—Felicity still commanding most of the attention—he realized that this first moment was only a hint of all the joys to come.

Suddenly, the possibility overwhelmed him.

This was why he had delayed facing Dillie. He hadn't been ready to let down his guard, but it was happening anyway. His turtle shell was breaking apart, that hard outer layer he'd used to protect himself all of his life was beginning to splinter and crack. He no longer needed it now that he had Dillie and Felicity, yet his heart wasn't quite ready to accept all the changes taking place.

He wasn't yet prepared for happiness.

James never had his chance.

Quinn walked in and, with apologies for the interruption,

brought Ian's thoughts back to the present by handing him a letter. "This just arrived for you, Your Grace."

Grabbing at the opportunity, Ian was on his feet and muttering something about an important matter that required his urgent attention. A feeble excuse, and no doubt they all saw through it, but the memory of James struggling in the icy water, slowly sinking into his watery grave, was too painful to keep contained. He had to leave before his facade of calm and control fell apart.

Dillie, who had been on her knees on the carpet sacrificing her ears and nose to Felicity's curiosity, quickly handed the child back to her nanny and scrambled to her feet as best as she could on one good ankle. "Ian?"

"Don't follow me, Daffy. Not this time."

CHAPTER 16

DRAT! IAN HAD called her Daffy again. What had happened to suddenly overset him? Was it the letter? He hadn't even opened it before he'd shot to his feet. They'd all been having a lovely time. Felicity was an adorable mix of imp and angel, and Dillie had loved her on sight. Who wouldn't love those bright eyes and kissable, pudgy cheeks?

She turned to her father, who'd also come to his feet and was now standing beside her, one arm around her shoulder. "Give him a moment, sweetheart."

She nodded.

Miss Poole, a woman of infinite good sense and discretion as far as Dillie was concerned, quietly bundled Felicity in her arms. "Time for Her Highness to take a nap. Please excuse us." She scooped up the child's blanket and a couple of toys that were on the carpet, and then bustled from the room, leaving Dillie alone with her father.

Dillie wasn't certain how much time passed, perhaps only a few minutes, but it felt like eons. She strode to the tall windows that overlooked the back garden and peered out, hoping for a glimpse of Ian. When coming here, the road had wound parallel to a stream, and she realized the stream probably ran behind the lodge, just beyond the stone fence at the rear of the garden. "I don't see him. He must have hopped over the garden wall."

Her father joined her by the row of windows. "Give him a little more time. Sometimes a man just needs to be alone."

"I'll give him all the time he needs, Father. But he's been alone far too long. That's the problem, isn't it? He's been making his own way since he was a child of four. *Of four!* No one to help him. No one to comfort him. Worst of all, no one to forgive him for the accident that defines him."

She sighed and turned to him. "In truth, that tragedy still defines him, for he won't allow himself to get past it. I want to help him, but I'm not certain how to do it. I've never experienced anything but love from our family. He's never known anything but pain. Caring and affection are new sensations for him. He isn't quite ready for them. I suppose that's why he's suddenly clawing the air as though suffocating and needing to escape his tomb."

Her father nodded. "Are you afraid he'll look upon your marriage as that tomb and wish to escape from his confinement, wish to escape from you?"

"I don't know. He seems reconciled to marrying me. He *wants* to marry me. I think he's afraid he'll disappoint me as a husband." She paused a moment and swallowed hard. "He won't, of course. I love him, and won't ever love another man as I do him. I don't regret a moment of the time I've spent with him, and hope we share a lifetime together. I think he wants the same, only he believes he's undeserving. He's having a hard time accepting a partner. Me."

"Lily always thought you were the smarter twin," her father said, putting his arm around her once more as he kissed her on the forehead. "I'm sure he'll come around. He isn't a fool."

She relented and rested her head against her father's shoulder. "Thank you for being so patient and wonderful with me. Papa, I love you very much."

He let out a soft laugh. "What's this? You haven't called me Papa in years, not since you and Lily started considering yourselves all grown up." He gave her shoulder a squeeze. "Your mother and I feel much the same about the five of you. We're quite proud of all of you. Especially you, Dillie."

She gazed at him in confusion. "Me? Why?"

"There's a quiet, loving strength about you. I believe the duke recognized that strength when he first met you. Thinking back, it's no coincidence that he always seemed to be close at hand when you needed help."

"Not always, Father. He wasn't stalking me like prey."

He shook his head and sighed. "Of course not, he isn't the slimy sort. What I'm trying to say is that he noticed you, seemed to enjoy your company. Seemed to care about you and wished to protect you."

"Indeed, he did just that when Charles Ealing, the clunch, tried to seduce me." She rolled her eyes. "He got what he deserved. He and Lady Mary will keep each other unhappy for the rest of their arrogant lives."

Her father cleared his throat. "Yes, well. You properly put Ealing in his place. Be that as it may. I was wrong to worry that the duke was marrying you merely out of a sense of duty. I noticed the way he looked at you this morning. All morning long. As though he were drinking you in and it still wasn't enough to satisfy his thirst." His expression turned affectionately mawkish. "I look at your mother that way. Always have, from the first day I set eyes on her."

Dillie blushed. "He hasn't said he loves me."

"He's never encountered a force of nature such as you. I'm sure he doesn't know what to make of you. He just knows that he's been hit and doesn't stand a chance. I give him no more than a few months before he's on his knees before you, proclaiming his love."

Dillie rolled her eyes. "I doubt it."

He grinned. "Fathers are wise and all knowing. He will, mark my words. Now, stop wasting time talking to me and go find him. A man shouldn't have all that much time alone. He might find out he likes it."

Laughing, she threw her arms around him. "I do love you," she said in an emphatic whisper.

He returned her hug. "You can conquer worlds, Dillie. Your mother and I were so worried about you when you were a toddler, a twin to Lily, who could read and write by the age of three. She had mastered Newton by the age of eight. How could anyone compete with that? Much less her twin? But we saw something remarkable happen between you girls. Lily knew facts, but she relied on you for knowledge about life. She always turned to you, looked up to you, even though you were the youngest."

Dillie snorted. "By all of five minutes."

"Lily followed you around like a little puppy, marveling at your brilliance. You never failed her. We knew then that you would be just fine. Better than fine. That the man who captured your heart would be fortunate indeed. Now, run along. Remind him just how fortunate he is."

"UGH! IAN, I'M stuck!"

Ian was sitting under a sturdy oak, his back resting against the tree's hard trunk while he gazed into the rushing waters of the stream and thought of James, when he heard Dillie call out to him. He turned toward the stone wall that separated the Swineshead gardens from the stream and saw her impertinent head sticking up over it. Her fingers were gripping the smooth top stones while she tried to gain a foothold atop those stones, no easy task with a bruised ankle.

He quickly folded the letter he'd been reading and tucked it into his boot. Then, shaking his head, he rose and hurried toward her. "What in bloody hell do you think you're doing?" He easily hoisted himself onto the wall, and then reached down and carefully hauled her up beside him.

She let out a soft breath, her face pink and her hair a little disheveled from her exertion. "The obvious answer is that I was trying to scale the wall. It's much higher than I realized."

He jumped back down, and then took her by the waist and gently set her down so that she was standing on the soft grass beside him along the bank of the stream. They could no longer be seen from the house, and he meant to take full advantage. "The obvious answer? Is there more than one?"

She nodded. "I was worried about you."

A light breeze wafted through her dark curls, mussing them so that a few slipped out of their pins and whipped against her cheeks. Her eyes sparkled a soft, crystal blue, as they always did when looking at him. "So was I," he admitted.

She glanced toward the stream, staring a long moment at its sweeping current and the little caps of white foam formed by the wind and underwater rocks. "You were thinking of James."

"You don't pull your punches, do you?" He sounded angrier than intended. After all, he'd been the one to bull his way out of the lodge without a word and leave them all wondering what had just happened. "Sorry, I didn't mean to sound resentful. I was the one who acted rudely."

She slipped her hand in his. "Farthingales have thick skins. We rarely take offense."

He traced a finger along the line of her jaw, and then placed his hand to the back of her neck and drew her in for a long, lingering kiss. "No, your skin's quite soft. Delicate. I ought to know, for I've studied it thoroughly."

She smiled a soft, Dillie smile that warmed his soul. "Thoroughly? You've only just begun to know me. I believe you'll require a lot more study before you can make any assertions, Your Grace. A lot more study."

"I quite agree." He wrapped her in his arms and kissed her again, pressing his mouth against her sweet, welcoming lips, loving the way she accepted him, drew him in, responded to his touch. She eased his soul. A moment ago he'd been staring at the stream, thinking of the day James had died, thinking of the two of them sinking under that icy water and no longer able to breathe.

Those dark thoughts faded whenever he was with Dillie. The darkness that shrouded his heart was no match for the girl. Her smile alone could kick the hell out it.

As he continued to kiss her—Lord, she felt so good—he heard the *whoosh* of water flowing with the current. *It's just a stream meandering through the countryside, not a child's watery grave.*

He felt a light breeze dancing across his body and the warmth of the sun upon his shoulders. He caught the scent of grass and water and the peach scent of Dillie's skin. *I want this. I want Dillie. James, forgive me.*

But he no longer needed his brother's forgiveness if the words in the letter he'd just read were true. He didn't dare believe it, didn't know what to make of it.

"Oh, dear," Dillie whispered against his lips. "We're not even married yet and you've already lost interest in my kisses." She tried to keep her voice light and teasing, but he could see that she was concerned about him. Surely, she had no doubts about their impending marriage, even though he was an ass and unable as yet to express his feelings for her.

"That will never happen." He drew her up against him, taking her into his arms and holding her so that their bodies were practically molded into one. Then he kissed her again, his lips taking hers, plundering and conquering, hot and unrestrained, holding nothing back. He wanted her to feel the heat of his desire and know it would never fade. Not now. Not years from now when they were old and gray. Not ever, for it seemed as though Dillie had been made for him, as though someone had reached into his heart and created the perfect girl, the only one who could ever make him happy.

Had James done it? Had he purposely thrown him and Dillie together that night in Lady Eloise's lilac-scented garden?

He eased away to stare at her. "You sneeze when you eat sardines. You can face down an army of villains, yet you're easily rattled when out in society."

"I am not." She let out an adorable, breathy *eep* when he began to trace his finger along her throat.

"You *eep* whenever you're ruffled, usually when I'm near. You blush whenever I touch you, turning bright red from the tips of your ears to the tip of your nose. You're blushing right now."

He stopped her when she opened her mouth to protest. "Dillie, you crawl around on carpets with your cousins, and your hair is never perfect. There's always a stray curl dangling over your forehead or about your ears."

She frowned. "Is there a point to your inventory of my faults?"

He reached out to tuck back her hair, surprised she'd taken his words the wrong way. "They're not faults," he said in a throaty whisper. "They're all the reasons I wish to marry you. I don't want cold, society elegance. I've lived with cold my entire life. I want chaos and meddlesome warmth. I want someone who gives a fig whether I live or die. I want someone who will love me even though she thinks I'm an idiot."

"Oh, Ian. I haven't called you that in a long while. And you know I never really thought you were an idiot."

He nodded. "The point is, I don't want perfect. I want you."

She shook her head and laughed. "I think that was a compliment. If so, I'll take it. Although it isn't quite the down-on-your-knees-desperate-to-have-you speech I was hoping for, but it's a good start."

He was about to withdraw the letter he'd tucked into his boot when Dillie suddenly let out a soft cry. A butterfly had landed on her hand. "Ian, look! It's so beautiful," she said in an excited whisper, her eyes widening in delight. "Look at how the colors on its wings shimmer, the emerald green and purple amethyst. I'm afraid to move or even breathe. I want it to stay. I want to hold on to it and never let it fly away."

"You have to let it go."

She frowned lightly. "No. Why should I?"

"It has to move on in order to survive. You can't—" He suddenly felt as though an anvil had been dropped on his head. Dillie's desire to hold on to that butterfly was no different from his desire to hold on to James' death. All his life, he'd been trapped by his memory of that dreadful day. He hadn't moved on. He'd never been able to let James go.

Bloody hell.

He stared at Dillie, wondering just how she'd manipulated him into saying the words aloud. *Let it go. Move on.* She wasn't looking at him, but smiling at the butterfly. "How...?" He shook his head. "Never mind. You're scary, you know that?"

She cast him an innocent gaze, her gorgeous eyes wide as she took him in. "Because I like butterflies?"

"Yes."

She laughed and shook her head once more, tousling her curls. "I have no idea what you're talking about." The butterfly flitted away, and they watched it disappear over the stone fence. Dillie turned to him, her gaze soft as she nestled against his body, her curves fitting so perfectly against him. "All I know is that everything feels right when I'm with you. I don't understand why."

"Blame it on the Chipping Way curse," he said.

She looked up at him and smiled. "It isn't really a curse, thank goodness. I'm so happy when I'm with you. I love being with you. Even when facing down blackguards in a stable or a fashionable London street."

"You've always believed in me."

"It wasn't hard to do." Her eyes were sparkling as she continued to gaze at him. "I love you, Ian. My heart twists in knots every time I think of the pain your family has put you through. James' death was an accident. If the situation were reversed, you jumping in to rescue James, I know you would never have blamed him."

"Dillie," he said, his voice and every limb in his body shaking. He wanted to say more, but didn't know where to start. Instead, he reached into his boot and withdrew the letter he'd just finished reading when she came upon him. He led her back to the tree where he'd been sitting and handed her the letter. "I'd like you to read it. Hell, I don't know what to make of it."

She sat on the grass, propped her shoulder against the trunk of the old oak tree, and unfurled the letter. Ian felt too much on edge to sit beside her, and instead began to pace along the water's edge. "Tell me what you think, Dillie." He ran a hand roughly through his hair. "You're the only one I trust to tell me the truth."

DILLIE'S HEART WAS pounding through her ears as she began to read. Ian trusted her, valued her opinion, and she simply couldn't make a mistake. He'd handed over more than this mere letter, for along with that sheaf of paper, he'd handed her his heart. She knew this was the most important letter she might ever read in her life.

For that reason, she took her time going through it, not just once but several times before she dared to set it down. However, she still had questions. "Ian." He stopped pacing and cast her a grim smile. Indeed, grim was an apt description of how he must be feeling, his insides painfully knotted and thoughts confused. "Who is this Mr. Badger?" She was referring to the gentleman who'd written the letter.

"Celestia and my cousins had let a house in Belgravia. Badger was their head butler. He came with the house, as did the rest of the staff."

"What an odd name." In truth, Daffodil was little better. *Duchess Daffodil. Ugh! Almost as bad as Duchess Daffy.*

"I thought so, too. I only met him a couple of times, when I stopped by to visit Celestia." He ran hand through his hair again. "I never stayed long. You know how suffocating a mother's affection can be at times."

The sarcasm was evident in his voice, but so was his anguish. If only that horrid woman had ever held him, praised him, or kissed him goodnight. Just one hug, one kiss, or kind word would have been enough to sustain Ian. But it had never happened, not even once. "I'm sorry."

She dared say nothing more, for he'd take her words as pity. He wanted honesty, no matter how brutal those words might be.

"I didn't know what to make of Badger when I first met him. He looked so familiar, yet I couldn't place him. There was something about his eyes, and something in his manner... a paternal kindness about him. I don't know. I just sensed it. But what would I know of kindness?" He sighed and shook his head. "I shouldn't have told you anything about him. I want you to form your own opinion of the man. For all I know, he could be a bounder, paid to write that pack of lies at the behest of Celestia. This would be the sort of cruel hoax she'd devise."

"If it's any consolation, I also thought Mr. Badger was an honest man. I sensed a pain in his own soul, and I don't think that is something easily faked."

Ian strode from the water's edge and knelt beside her, arching one eyebrow. He looked handsome enough to melt her heart. "Go on, Dillie. Tell me more."

"The letter sounds more like a confession, as though he's wanted to relieve his burdened soul for several months now, but never quite found the courage. I'm glad he finally did, though I can't blame him for his hesitation. It could not have been easy for him to open these old wounds about your brother." Dillie felt her eyes misting and knew she'd likely be in tears before this conversation progressed much further. "We have to talk about that day, Ian. Do you trust me enough to tell me everything?"

He stroked his finger lightly across her cheek, his touch quite comforting and tender. "I have no secrets from you."

Dillie was surprised by his earnestness. In truth, he could have lightened his words by calling her a snoop, for she was an incorrigible one, always with her ear to the keyhole. But he'd just been open and heartfelt about it. He wanted her to know the workings of his heart. "I love you, Ian."

He grinned. "I know."

She felt herself melting again. *Crumpets!* How could any woman ever resist this man? She turned away to peer down at the letter now open on her lap and began to read it aloud. *"Your Grace. My sister, may she rest in peace, was in your father's employ, charged with the care of you and your brother."*

Ian immediately tensed beside her. "She was our nanny at the time of the accident," he explained, his voice tense and raspy. He seemed reluctant to continue, but Dillie encouraged him with a nod, for he needed to speak the words, the haunting thoughts he'd kept bottled inside for all these years. "She was with us that day. We called her Miss Nell. Never knew her full name. Just Miss Nell. James and I liked her. She was a cheerful, decent sort who rarely shouted at us, even though we often deserved it. We always got into mischief."

"All little boys do. It's in their nature." She returned her attention to the letter. *"My sister told me what happened shortly before she died. That was several years ago. Your Grace, please believe me when I say that she had no idea of the suffering your family has put you through. She would not have stayed quiet had she known."*

Dillie reached out to take Ian's hand.

He laughed softly and gave her hand a light squeeze. "Still trying to protect me?"

"I can't help it. I want to throw my arms around you and kiss away your pain. But I know that you're no longer a little boy." She now had her fingers entwined in Ian's hand. His touch felt good, but it always did. She hoped her touch felt as good to him. *"You and young James were playing by the frozen pond when your mother's carriage passed by. She'd just opened the door to issue instructions to my sister when her dog jumped off her lap and bounded after a squirrel."*

"Raggles, her little terrier," Ian murmured.

"The squirrel took off across the frozen pond and her dog chased after it." She paused a moment and swallowed hard. *"Your brother ran onto*

the pond, thinking to catch him and return him to your mother."

Dillie paused and gazed up at him. "James was the one who ran onto the ice."

"So Badger says, but I don't know if I believe him. Problem is, I don't remember most of what happened, only that James died and I was blamed for it."

"You and Nell were on the shore, calling out to James and begging him to come back, but he was determined to catch the dog. The blasted creature finally ran back to Nell. She had just carried him back to your mother and was hurrying back to the pond when your brother suddenly fell through the ice. You were closest and ran out to him, then fell in as well when the ice broke under your feet."

Dillie felt Ian shudder, couldn't begin to imagine the anguish he was feeling. He knelt beside her, unmoving and brittle. She felt his composure begin to slip away. She was beginning to unravel as well, her heart lodged in her throat as she imagined what four-year-old Ian must have been thinking and feeling. "You ran to save your brother. I believe it, Ian. This is exactly what you would have done."

He rubbed a hand across the back of his neck. "James would have done the same for me."

She nodded, for although she knew almost nothing of James, the brothers had been close. No doubt James was as valiant as Ian, and she felt a sincere tug of regret that she had never known him. More important, she deeply regretted that Ian had lost the only person who had ever loved him. What a horrid family! *"Both of you went under, Your Grace. Nell found you first and hauled you out, then jumped back in after your brother."*

Dillie let out a groan as she wiped at the tear rolling down her cheek. She must not have been very quiet, for the next thing she knew, Ian was putting his arms around her and drawing her onto his lap. "I'm trying to be strong, but I feel as though my heart is about to burst and all my feelings about to spill out. Oh, Ian! Nell said you had been holding onto James, but your hands were numb and James was so frightened he kept struggling against you. You were so little! Too little to hold on to him."

"I remember that part," Ian said softly, "much the way Badger described it in his letter. By the time Nell reached me, I'd lost hold of

James. I recall the struggling. I thought I had been the one frightened and pushing away. The water was deep where James and I had gone under. I blacked out, never remembered Nell hauling me to shore. Never remembered being tossed into my mother's carriage."

"Badger writes that your mother remained in her carriage, that she never ran down to the pond to help Nell or her coachman save you boys." Dillie perused the letter still held in her trembling hands. "And then she wouldn't give up her fur wrap to warm you and James. Her only concern was for Raggles." Another tear rolled down her cheek. "The driver and Nell had to give over their cloaks. How can any mother be so callous? I would have—"

"You would have been first in that water." He stroked his big, warm hand along her back, ran his fingers gently through her hair. "You would have given your life to save your children."

Still sniffling, she nodded against his chest. "Precious moments lost, you and James suffering from the icy shock, and no help for it until you'd reached the manor house."

Ian took the letter from her hand and began to read aloud, the rich depth of his voice tremulous as he spoke. *"I don't know if Nell could have saved James. She tried her best, but his body was blue by the time he was stripped and put into his warm bed. One of the footmen had started a fire in the hearth, tossing on enough wood to make a roaring flame. Another footman did the same for you as you lay in your room. Nell knew that you were in better shape and would survive, so she spent most of her time with James."*

He paused and let out a soft oath. "Celestia did nothing but fuss over her damn dog. James was her son and he lay dying. Her greatest worry was that Father would fly into a rage and order Raggles destroyed."

Ian let out a bitter laugh. *"She paid off the coachman and ordered him to leave Edgeware forever. She tried the same with my sister, but Nell would have none of it. When Nell heard your mother lie and blame you for your brother's death, she tried to tell your father."*

"But he wouldn't listen," Dillie said in disgust.

"Celestia had gotten to him first, and my father was an arrogant bastard anyway. He wasn't the sort to take the word of a lowly nanny, probably believed Nell was covering for her own mistakes."

He rubbed his hand along the back of his neck again. "I don't know if any of this tale is true, Dillie. I want to believe Badger. If it is true, then he did the right thing in telling me."

Dillie nodded. "I believe him, Ian. No liar could have crafted such a letter."

"Badger bears a resemblance to his sister, in the shape and color of his eyes. That's why I felt as though we'd met before, as though I'd known him for most of my life."

She pursed her lips. "In a way, you had."

"Badger thought it an odd coincidence that he should come into the service of the Markham family all these years after the incident that had gotten his sister sacked. He was reluctant to admit it to any of us, fearing we'd discharge him as well."

"Then he realized how awful your family was and did his best to set matters right," she said, her lips still pursed and her brow lightly furrowed.

He kissed her brow and drew her more firmly against his chest. "Well, I wanted to show you the letter. My mind's still reeling. I feel as though I've been gored by a bull."

She caressed Ian's cheek. "You've been given a lot to take in all at once. He ended the letter with *Bless you, Your Grace. Forgive me for opening horrific old wounds.* A blessing and a request for forgiveness. Those are the words of an honest man. And he isn't hiding from you. If we have more questions for him, we'll know where to find him."

"No wonder Celestia hated me so much. Every time she looked at me, she must have worried that one day I would remember exactly what happened. That *her* dog ran onto the ice, that it was *her* dog James was trying to catch when he fell in and drowned." He kept his arms tightly wrapped around her. "Bugger. Tell me something pleasant, Dillie. Anything to stop me from thinking about this. And what does it matter now? Nothing will change. My mother will still hate me. My father, the old bastard, is long dead."

She sat up and turned to face him. "Everything has changed, Ian. You've changed, finally accepted moving beyond the accident. In truth, I think you were already on the way to forgiving yourself before this letter arrived. You had already chosen to move forward, to marry me and embark on a new life."

She edged off his lap and rolled to her knees, still facing him. "I suppose I'm glad Mr. Badger wrote you this letter, but it doesn't really matter anymore. You were a child. You and James always loved each other. Whether he chased after you or you chased after him on the pond that day doesn't change how two brothers felt about each other. It doesn't change how I feel about you, how much I respect and admire you."

She let out a squeal when he suddenly rose and scooped her into his arms. "What are you doing?"

"You respect and admire me?" She could see that he was still struggling with his own feelings. He'd been suffering too long to merely snap his fingers and expect the memory of James or that awful day to flit away as lightly as the butterfly that landed on her hand a short while ago. "Say it, Dillie."

"What am I to say?" Her smile broadened as he gazed at her in expectation. "Oh, that." She kissed him softly on the lips. "I love you, Ian. Always have and always will love you. Now, will you take me back to the lodge?"

He nodded. "Through the gate this time. No more leaping over stone walls. We have a wedding to plan."

CHAPTER 17

DILLIE HAD LITTLE time to dwell on Ian's reluctance to utter those three little words, "I love you." Especially not today, almost three months after their quiet wedding, for their guests would soon arrive at their London townhouse to celebrate in style. All of her family, indeed most of London, had been invited to the Duke and Duchess of Edgeware's ball, and almost everyone had responded with an acceptance. Even the Prince Regent.

Even Lady Withnall.

Dillie stifled a groan as she imagined the *thuck, thuck, thuck* of the little harridan's cane resounding on the floor while she made her way up the receiving line toward her and Ian, her bat ears and hawk eyes ever at the ready.

Mercy! Dillie quickly dismissed all thought of London's most prolific gossip, for she had more important matters on her mind. Their ball promised to be a crush, quite the grandest party of the London season. That she happened to be the Duchess of Edgeware still astounded her.

She paused at the entrance of the ballroom. All furniture had been removed and the floors polished. Indeed, furniture had been removed from most of the rooms, save the dining hall. Nothing was left but chairs and a few tables scattered against the walls of the ballroom and ladies' salon. For those who didn't wish to dance, gaming tables had been set up in makeshift card rooms near the ballroom. Guests could play whist or the rowdier speculation that was more suited to the younger crowd.

Butlers, footmen, and maids were all scurrying about to put the final touches on each room. Dillie walked from one to the other, making certain the negus, lemonade, and champagne were in place in the refreshments room, that fresh biscuits were set out beside the punch bowls, and that Mrs. Mayhew—borrowed from her mother for the night—had supper under way for a crowd that might swell to five hundred at the height of the ball.

She gazed up as members of the orchestra began to tune their instruments. They were hidden in the ballroom's balcony, behind a row of potted ferns. A glance at the ormolu clock on the entry hall table showed it was approaching eight o'clock. She closed her eyes and took a deep breath. *I love you, Ian. I hope this party is a success.*

Candles in the chandeliers, candelabra, and wall sconces were now lit, their red-gold flames shimmering against the crystal and silver fixtures. All appeared to be in glittering order. Felicity was at Daisy's, happily spending the night in the care of Miss Poole and Ivy's nanny. Dillie already missed having the little imp underfoot. Their townhouse had been far too quiet all day, even with all the upheaval of preparing for the ball.

Ian came up behind her and enveloped her in his arms. "You look beautiful, Duchess Daffy." He planted a fat kiss on her neck.

"Ugh! You fiend, don't you dare call me that in front of our guests." However, she could never stay mad at Ian for very long, and certainly not now, for he looked devastatingly handsome in his formal garb, black jacket, waistcoat, and trousers contrasting with a crisp white shirt and tie. "Ashcroft did a nice job of dressing you."

He turned her in his arms and cast a boyishly appealing grin. "And I hope you'll do an even nicer job of undressing me after the ball. Promise you will, Duchess Daffy."

She burst into laughter. "Stop calling me that, you wicked man. And don't you dare call me that in front of Lady Withnall. I'll never shake off the name once the old gossip spreads it about."

"You're in no danger from Phoebe. She likes you. Always has."

Dillie shook her head and laughed again, surprised by his remark. Did he still consider Lady Withnall a friend? "That know-it-all is the reason you had to marry me. I'm sure she's the one who tattled on us, who told the world you'd spent a week in my bed."

His grin broadened. "I think it worked out rather well. Have I complained?"

"Well, no."

"Nor will I ever. I'm not going to kick you out of my bed, even though you snore like a foghorn and always fidget like a kitten trying to curl up in just the right spot." He leaned forward and planted another wet kiss on her neck. "I like having you beside me." His grin faded slightly. "Sleeping next to me can't be all that comfortable for you."

She nodded, understanding what he meant, even though he tried to make light of the nightmares he sometimes had about his brother's drowning—frightening dreams that left him in a cold sweat and gasping for breath. Those dreams had happened less often since their marriage, and only once this past month. But Dillie's heart gave a little tug recalling the first time she'd witnessed him in the violent throes. He'd looked at her so hopelessly afterward, expecting her to be horrified and demand to be moved into separate quarters. She'd disabused him of the notion at once. "I love waking in your arms. I always love being in your arms."

"I know," he said, his voice a husky whisper. "I adore the way you respond to me. *Ooh, Ian. Ooh, ooh, Ian, my powerful, irresistible stallion.*"

"You are a fiend!" She burst into laughter again. "I've never called you any such thing. See, that's why I'm still miffed at Lady Withnall. I'm stuck with you and have no way out."

"Fine, be that way. But she didn't start the rumor. As I said, she likes you. She'd never do anything to harm you."

Dillie pursed her lips and frowned. "You keep saying that, but she hardly knows me."

"She knows me. She befriended me when I was at one of the many low points in my life. She likes you because you had the presence of mind to fall in love with me. She likes you because I like you. I always have."

Having Ian *deeply in like* with her wasn't perfect. It would have to do for this evening. "If she didn't start the rumor, then who did? I think we ought to find out."

"No need. I already know."

She gasped. "You do? Who did it? How long have you known?

And why keep it from me?"

"I'll tell you later. After the ball. Wipe that pretty pout off your face. Our guests are about to arrive." He leaned forward and gave her a quick kiss on the lips. "By the way, you look beautiful. Far prettier than the diamonds at your throat." He kissed her again. "Or those dangling at your ears." And another kiss. "Or those in your hair." He sighed. "You're so damn beautiful, you steal my breath away."

She was surprised, didn't know how to respond.

She was glad that he was *deeply, deeply in like* with her.

"WELL, HOW LONG are you going to deny it?" Lady Phoebe Withnall said, approaching Ian as he stood on the receiving line. The ball was under way, most of the guests having been announced. He and Dillie would soon open it officially with a dance and then mingle among the throng of guests. The Prince Regent would arrive later, and Ian was glad of it. He had something important to do and didn't wish the royal appearance to distract him from his purpose.

He glanced at Dillie, who was practically leaping out of her skin with joy, for Lily and Ewan had just arrived and she'd spotted them making their way slowly up the long queue of guests. He turned back to Phoebe. "I don't know what you're talking about."

"Dear boy, I'd smack you in the shins with my cane if you weren't needed to open the ball. When are you going to tell her?"

"Stop glowering at me. I plan on telling her tonight."

"You had better. Lady Eloise and I will be watching you."

He raised Phoebe's gloved hand to his lips and planted a light kiss. "I have no doubt."

More guests came by—countless Farthingale relations, including all of Dillie's sisters and their husbands. He watched Dillie break into a beaming smile as Lily and Ewan now reached them. They had come down from the Highlands for this affair, and although Dillie and her twin exchanged letters almost daily, she couldn't contain her joy. She threw her arms around Lily and hugged her fiercely. Lily responded with affection and equal lack of restraint.

Ewan turned to him and laughingly shook his head. "The Chipping Way curse is powerful indeed. Och, I dinna think ye'd ever fall under its spell. Look at ye now. The duke who was never going to marry. You're as well tamed as the rest of us." He nodded toward Gabriel, Graelem, and Julian, who were standing beside their respective wives, Daisy, Laurel, and Rose, and seeming in no hurry to move away.

These rare creatures were known as happily married men. Never in his wildest imaginings had Ian thought to become one of them. But he was. He was also a monumental ass, taking all Dillie offered while holding back the one thing she yearned for most.

He waited until Dillie had greeted the last of the seemingly endless stream of Farthingales, and then took her hand and led her into the ballroom to officially start the ball.

Dillie blushed furiously as they stood in the center of the room, all eyes upon them. She was anything but cool and collected, and held his elbow in a death grip. "You can do this, sweetheart," he said in a whisper of encouragement.

She let out a little *eep*. "I don't think so. We ought to have practiced. Why didn't we think to practice the waltz? Oh, crumpets! Eloise and Lady Withnall are staring at us."

He took her into his arms, preparing for the dance. "Everyone's staring at us."

She *eeped* again as the first notes struck, now in obvious panic. "Don't tell me that!"

"Very well, what shall I tell you? I know." He guided her steps as the music started, but instead of whirling her in a circle around the ballroom, he whirled her across the floor toward the terrace.

Her eyes widened. "Ian, what are you doing?"

A murmur of confusion arose from the crowd as well, but he continued toward the open doors leading onto the terrace. Their guests began to follow.

"Ian?"

He grinned at her look of utter confusion, the delicate arch of her brow above her glorious, blue eyes, and the purse of her full, rosy lips. Dillie grew more beautiful by the day. She looked so beautiful even now in full, crimson blush. As for him, he knew exactly what he was doing. Indeed, this was the first time he was thinking clearly. Once out of the ballroom, he stopped waltzing and knelt before her, ignoring the music as the orchestra played on.

Dillie let out a soft gasp. "Everyone's watching. You have to get up."

He took her hand and gave it a light squeeze. "I'm a duke. I can do anything I please." He glanced at the crowd of onlookers and saw Eloise and Phoebe poking their way through the doors to the front. "I can *say* anything I please."

"Oh, no. Don't say anything idiotic that you'll regret."

He laughed lightly and shook his head. "And what pleases me is... you. I love you, Dillie."

She looked at him as though she might faint. The crimson blush on her cheeks had faded to chalky white, even against the torchlights. "I love you," he repeated, rising to take her into his arms before her legs gave way. Fortunately, the crowd mistook his gesture and thought the way he embraced his wife quite romantic. In truth, Dillie was about to swoon and he meant to catch her before she fell and did herself harm.

The music continued softly behind them, the melodic strains wafting from the ballroom onto the terrace. He kissed her on the lips, putting his heart and soul into that kiss, possessive and hungry and tender as his lips locked onto hers. He held the kiss longer than deemed proper, held it until he heard the titters and gasps of the onlookers, and held it because he wanted everyone to know how much he loved his wife. *His wife.* She wasn't an obligation arising from a scandal. She was his salvation.

As she regained her composure, he slowly resumed the waltz. "Thank you, Ian. You didn't have to do this."

"Yes, I did. *I love you, Dillie.*" Hell, he'd taken far too long to get around to saying it. He bent his head to hers and kissed her again in a way that left no doubt as to the truth of his words.

He kissed her and whirled her across the dance floor in time to the waltz. Their guests erupted in chortles, gasps, and gleefully horrified chatter, but Ian wasn't nearly ready to behave himself and refused to end the kiss until he was satisfied that he'd thoroughly scandalized the old biddies in attendance... and until the music stopped and he finally heard the *thuck, thuck, thuck* of Phoebe Withnall's cane behind him.

Reluctantly, he released Dillie and turned to grin at the old harridan.

"About time you finally let the gel up for air." Phoebe, in her usual forthright manner, pounded him on the back. She then turned to smile at Dillie. "Well done, lass. Well done indeed. What a scandalbroth your wicked duke has created. No one ever thought he'd marry, certainly never believed he'd fall in love, but I've never seen a more pathetic, love-bitten fool than Edgeware. That kiss will be all anyone talks about for the rest of the season."

"Good," Ian said, the grin still on his face. "Are you quite finished, Phoebe?"

Dillie's eyes glistened and her smile was as broad as a moonbeam. Ian loved her smile. He loved the sparkle in her eyes, meant just for him. *He loved her.*

"Almost. I haven't told Dillie who started the rumor that got you into so much trouble."

Dillie's eyes rounded in surprise. "Lady Withnall, do you know who did it? In truth, I thought it was you."

"No, my dear. Although I would have had—"

Bloody hell. Ian stepped forward. "My mother did it."

Dillie's gaze darted to his. She laughed, and then noticed that neither he nor Phoebe had joined in. "Ian, is this true? *She*? Why? She must have known what the outcome would be."

"No, she didn't think I'd ever marry you. And even if she were wrong and I did propose to you, she expected I'd be dead before a wedding could take place, killed in the stables at the Black Sail Inn, leaving you alone and ruined." He clenched his jaw, trying to stem his anger. He didn't wish to give Celestia another moment's thought, but Dillie appeared ready to ask more questions. Better to tell her quickly and be done with it. "This is the nature of my family. Celestia and my cousins wished to punish you because you'd saved my life, foiling their first attempt in November. For that, you had to be made to suffer."

She shook her head and simply stared at him. Confusion, surprise, disbelief were all mirrored in her eyes. "How did she know about us? About your stay in my bed?" Suddenly, she groaned. "Of course! Those men reported back to her. She knew exactly where you were."

"It's all behind us now." He dipped his head and kissed her again, the kiss deep and tender. "The irony of it is, she did me a great favor. I've always loved you," he said in a whisper. "I was just too stubborn to admit it. Then that clunch, Ealing, came along and I couldn't let him have you. I didn't want anyone to have you. Only me, but I didn't deserve you. I was almost ready to let you go."

The sparkle faded from her eyes. "Would you have done it?"

"No, sweetheart. I knew I couldn't ever do it, but I wasn't able to admit it to you. Then the scandal broke, giving me a safe excuse to marry you. I didn't have to put my heart at risk. Everyone would believe I'd married you out of a sense of duty."

Phoebe struck him lightly with her cane. "Not well done of you. How could you leave the sweet girl in doubt for so long?"

Dillie stepped closer and put a hand on his arm. "It doesn't matter anymore." She smiled up at Ian, stars once more glistening in her radiant eyes. "You love me," she said in a whisper.

"Forever, sweetheart." He caressed her cheek. *"Always."*

Phoebe let out a snort. "Enough, you two. Stop foolishly gazing into each other's eyes and pay attention to your guests." Her command given, Phoebe turned and walked away. *Thuck, thuck, thuck,* the sound of her cane diminished as she made her way across the ballroom.

Ian took Dillie's hand, but she held him back a moment. She looked happily bemused. "Thank you," she said again.

"For being a stubborn ass? For being an arrogant, idiot duke?"

She nestled against his chest. "For being you. For wanting me as much as I want you. I love you so much."

He kissed her again. "There's only one girl I could ever marry. Only one girl I could ever love. The girl I kissed beside the lilac tree. The girl who almost shot me with an elephant gun. You, Dillie. I love you. You're my forever girl."

EPILOGUE

Lake District, England
Christmas Eve 1819

Dillie was sitting in the nursery at Coniston Hall, her parents' large country home, fussing over Felicity. She had dressed Felicity in a gown of dark green velvet with a matching ribbon in her hair, but Felicity was having none of it, tugging at her little curls and wailing. "Oh, well," Dillie said finally. "I don't suppose anyone will notice the lack of a ribbon."

The house was filled to the rafters with Farthingales gathered for the traditional Christmas Eve supper. Rose, Laurel, Daisy, and Lily were downstairs with their husbands and the other adults, while their children were chasing each other up and down the hall outside the nursery. All save Ivy, of course, who was in the arms of her nanny, Miss Grenville, waiting to be brought downstairs. Ivy looked like a little princess in a gown of red velvet trimmed with white lace at the collar and sleeve cuffs.

Miss Poole, who had been helping Dillie with Felicity, rose from the chair beside her. "Time to get the children down to supper. I'll come back up as soon as the little hoydens are safely delivered to their parents."

Dillie laughed as Felicity began to bounce on her lap, no doubt eager to join the others. "You needn't bother. I'll be down in a moment with Her Highness."

All had been invited to Coniston for a week of Christmas celebrations, and Dillie was looking forward to a long, noisy evening with the sisters, parents, and assorted relatives. Ian hadn't arrived yet, but she knew he would be along soon.

She untied Felicity's ribbon, which really was no loss since the child had very little hair and what existed was adorably unkempt. Felicity abruptly stopped complaining.

With the military efficiency of a Roman general, Miss Poole quieted down the horde of little Farthingales, mustered them in a single column, and then marched them downstairs.

Now alone in the nursery with Felicity, Dillie took several deep breaths to steady herself. She was feeling a little dizzy, but didn't wish anyone to know. Not yet, anyway. Not until she spoke to Ian. Where was he?

It wasn't long before she heard his carriage draw up to the front of the house, and then a moment later she heard his footsteps on the stairs, taking the steps two at a time. He must have encountered Miss Poole in the entry hall and she must have said something to make him rush to her side.

Suddenly, he filled the nursery doorway. "Sorry I'm late, sweetheart." He strode to her side and kissed her on the lips, an achingly gentle kiss. "I was delayed at Swineshead. Mr. Dumbley had a mountain of papers delivered for me to sign. Took forever to make my way through the stack." He gave her another gentle kiss, then cast a boyishly tender smile that melted her heart. "Miss Poole said you looked a little pale. How are you feeling?"

Before she could answer, Felicity let out a squawk to gain his attention.

"I'm getting to you," he said with a laugh. "Do you think I'd ever forget you, Your Highness?" He bent to nuzzle Felicity, but her chubby little fingers went straight for his nose and tugged on it. He let out a pretend yelp that Felicity thought was hilarious. She let out a hearty laugh, all giggles and squeals.

Ian took Felicity into his arms. He looked quite at ease as he settled the playful child against his chest and lightly tickled her belly, but his gaze was trained on Dillie. "Sweetheart?"

Dillie felt a tug to her heart. Ian looked so comfortable and content holding Felicity. He was meant to be a father and would make a wonderful one at that. Crumpets, she loved him! She rose to stand beside him, but must have moved too fast. Her head began to spin and she sank back into her chair.

"Dillie!" He set Felicity in her crib and quickly returned to her side, taking her into his arms. "You're clutching your stomach. Does it ache? Bugger, do you have a fever? Have you eaten anything today?"

"No fever. I'm fine. I've been eating enough to feed an army," she said. "Haven't you noticed? I've put on a bit of weight."

"Well, your breasts look bigger. I'm not complaining. No, indeed." He tipped her head to his and kissed her gently on the lips. "We can forget this evening's celebration. I'll carry you straight to bed. I'll make our excuses to the family."

She sighed. "I want to have supper with my parents and sisters." She put her hands on his shoulders and drew him forward for another kiss. "There's something I was going to tell you later this evening after the party, but I think I had better tell you now."

"Oh, hell. You are ill. Is that it? Why didn't you tell me?"

"Nonsense, Ian," she said, the merriment bubbling inside her. She rose more carefully this time and took Felicity out of her crib. It felt right to have the child in her arms as she broke the news to her husband. "I really wanted to wait until we were in bed together, but you look as if your heart's about to burst from worry. I promise you, I'm fine. In fact, I'm happier than I've ever been."

She paused a moment as her lips began to quiver and tears filled her eyes. "Ian," she said, her voice barely above a whisper, for she suddenly felt overwhelmed, "we're going to have a baby."

"What?" He gaped at her, and then a slow grin crossed his face. He wrapped her and Felicity in his arms. "Say it again," he said with aching tenderness. "I don't think I heard you right."

She cast him a beaming smile. "Felicity's going to have a new cousin. I love you, Ian. And so will our baby. You're going to make a wonderful father. Happy Christmas... Papa."

DEAR READER

Thank you for reading *The Duke I'm Going To Marry*. On the surface, Ian is a handsome, wealthy duke, seemingly without a care in the world. However, having been raised in a cold and loveless family, he was just begging to find happiness. Love is the one thing all his money could never buy, and Ian had resigned himself to a lonely existence until Dillie came into his life. Their first kiss changed everything for him, but moving beyond his cruel upbringing and forgiving himself for his supposed past sins was not easy to do. It took Dillie's courage and her faith in him to bring them to their happy ending.

Book 3 in the Farthingale Series is *Rules For Reforming A Rake*, which is actually the prequel to *My Fair Lily* and *The Duke I'm Going To Marry*. It is Daisy Farthingale's story. Daisy is the middle daughter, who has taken on the role of conciliator among the boisterous family. To protect one of her sisters, Daisy took blame for an unfortunate incident involving a gentleman of dubious reputation. Although innocent, she enters her debut season with a slight tarnish. Her beloved Farthingale family no longer trusts her or respects her judgment. Daisy is determined to make the family proud of her again, and decides to do it by marrying the most respectable man she can find. Unfortunately, her heart refuses to cooperate and she falls in love with worst man possible—Gabriel Dayne, a dissolute rakehell who may be spying for the French! Read on for a sneak peek at Daisy's story, the third in the Farthingale Series.

-Meara

SNEAK PEEK OF THE NEXT BOOK:

RULES FOR REFORMING A RAKE

BY MEARA PLATT

CHAPTER 1

To attract a rake, one must first make an elegant impression.

London, England
Late February 1815

"GABRIEL, DON'T WALK down that street!"

Gabriel Dayne turned in time to see his friend, Ian Markham, Duke of Edgeware, jump down from an emerald green phaeton and dodge several passing carriages as he raced toward him, waving his arms and calling for him to stop. Quickly scanning his surroundings,

Gabriel reached for the pistol hidden in the breast pocket of his waistcoat and prepared to defend himself.

But from whom?

He saw nothing untoward on Chipping Way, one of Mayfair's prettiest streets. Indeed, the sun shone brightly, birds chirped merrily, and buds hinted of early spring blooms along the fashionable walk. Ladies and gentlemen strolled leisurely toward the park, and another elegant carriage led by a pair of matched grays with fanciful gold feathers on their heads clattered past.

Not a footpad or assassin could be seen.

"Put that weapon away," Ian said, reaching his side and pausing a moment to catch his breath. "I didn't mean to frighten you, just stop you from making one of the biggest mistakes of your life."

Gabriel frowned. "A simple 'good afternoon' would have caught my attention. How are you, Your Grace?"

"Me? I'm right as rain. But things have changed around here. I thought you should know." He withdrew a handkerchief from his breast pocket, removed his top hat, and proceeded to wipe his brow.

Gabriel gazed more closely at Ian's handkerchief... decidedly feminine... embroidered with pink hearts. He arched an eyebrow. "So it seems. You never mentioned that you'd acquired a wife."

Ian followed Gabriel's gaze. "The devil! Things haven't changed that much! I'm not married and hope never to be. No, this dainty piece of lace belongs to my new mistress. A shapely bit of fluff with cherry lips and hair to match."

"I see."

"Ah, but I don't think you do. I stopped by your townhouse shortly after your return from France to congratulate the wounded war hero, but you were in very bad shape—"

"Don't call me that," Gabriel warned, keeping his voice low, though they were quite alone for the moment. "As far as my family and London society are concerned, I'm the wastrel they believe I've become, shot by a jealous husband while hunting grouse in Scotland."

Ian shook his head. "I don't see the need to continue this pretense. The war's over. Why won't you and Prinny," he said, referring to the Prince Regent, "allow the truth to come out?"

"No," Gabriel said quietly. "It will come out in time, when Napoleon is no longer a threat."

"But he's in exile and under constant guard. What harm can he do now?"

"None, I hope. However, matters are still unsettled on the Continent. I may have to return." Though he was loath to do so. Having spent the last three years slipping from one hellish battlefield to another, and been close to death more times than he cared to remember, Gabriel was now eager to take advantage of this momentary lull to live life to the fullest.

Ian and he had saved each other from numerous scrapes with the enemy during the war and had become more than friends. One could say they were as close as brothers, though Ian did not care much for family. Indeed, he was an unrepentant rakehell with an excellent eye for the ladies, and just the person to guide him back into the carefree bachelor life. "Now tell me, does your delightful mistress have a friend?"

Ian laughed. "Veronique has several charming friends to suit your... er, needs. Come by White's tonight for a drink. We'll discuss your return to England and the joys of bachelorhood further."

"Look forward to it," Gabriel said with a nod. "Now, what is this nonsense about my making one of the biggest mistakes of my life?"

Ian tried to appear serious, but the corners of his mouth curled upward to form a grin. "The danger is real," he said, a glint of amusement in his eyes. "You must not take another step toward your grandmother's house."

Gabriel humored him by glancing around once more. For the life of him, there was nothing out of place on this street.

Ian took a deep breath. "Right, then. Your grandmother resides at Number 5 Chipping Way, and General Allworthy resides at Number 1 Chipping Way. He's no problem, of course, being the quiet, retiring sort. So is your grandmother the retiring sort, though I understand she was quite something in her younger day."

"Get to the point. I'm already late."

"Yes, well. The problem resides at Number 3 Chipping Way. The Farthingales moved in about three years ago, shortly after you went off to... well, you know. Ever since they took up residence here, this charming street has become a deathtrap for bachelors."

Gabriel frowned. "Ian—"

"Oh, I know it must sound absurd to you, but let me explain. The Farthingales have five beautiful daughters, and I don't mean just pretty. They're stunning and of marriageable age, which is a problem for us simple creatures."

"Simple creatures?"

"We bachelors, haven't you been listening? What chance do we have against a pair of vivid blue eyes? Soft, smiling lips? None, I tell you. Our brains shut off the moment our—"

"I understand your drift," Gabriel shot back, rolling his eyes. "But years of battle discipline have trained me well. I have an iron control over my body and therefore am in no danger from the Farthingale girls. They are mere females, after all."

Ian shook his head sadly and placed a hand on Gabriel's shoulder. "Julian Emory said similar words to me two years ago while on his way to visit your dear grandmother. He made it as far as the Farthingale gate, heard Rose Farthingale's kiln explode and then heard her cries for help. She was trapped inside, along with her shattered pottery."

"A riveting story," Gabriel said dryly.

"Julian heroically dug her out of the rubble, lifted her into his arms, and as he carried her from the destruction, disaster struck. She opened her eyes and smiled at him. They were married before he knew what hit him. I doubt the besotted fool will ever recover."

"I'm not Julian."

"Curiously, your cousin, Graelem Dayne, said those exact words to me last year. We stood right here as I tried to stop him from visiting your grandmother. I failed, of course. He made it to the Farthingale gate, only to be trampled by Laurel Farthingale's beast of a horse. The beast broke Graelem's leg, but did your cousin care? No, because Laurel had jumped down from that four-legged devil, thrown her arms around Graelem, and cradled him in her lap while some medical relative of hers set his busted leg. Laurel and Graelem married a short time after that."

"Thank you for the warning." Gabriel started for his grandmother's house.

"Daisy," Ian called after him.

"What?"

"Daisy's next. She's the next eldest of the Farthingale girls. You know, first Rose, then Laurel, then—"

"Of course, Daisy Farthingale." Her name sounded as foolish as his friend's warning.

GABRIEL STRODE PAST General Allworthy's townhouse at Number 1 Chipping Way, and then paused to look back at his companion because he had heard him mutter something about it being too painful to watch. Ian, along with his emerald green phaeton, was gone.

"Stuff and nonsense," Gabriel grumbled, dismissing his friend as an alarmist. Julian and Graelem had been ready to marry. It only took the right sort of girl to tame them. He, on the other hand, had every intention of remaining the unrepentant bachelor.

Indeed, marriage was the farthest thing from his mind. Bad women and good times were what he wanted.

He took a deep breath, squared his shoulders, and marched straight past Number 3... well, almost.

"You, sir! Please! Stop that baby!"

"Wha-at?" Gabriel turned in time to see a little boy toddle at full speed from the Farthingale drive onto Chipping Way. The infant was stark naked and headed directly toward a carriage that was traveling much too fast for this elegant neighborhood.

"There, sir! Please stop him!" a young woman cried, leaning precariously from one of the upper windows.

Gabriel tore after the little fellow, snatching him into his arms just as the little imp was about to fall under the hooves of the fast-moving team of horses. The boy squirmed in his arms, but Gabriel wouldn't let him go. "Let's get you back to your derelict governess, young man," he said, wrapping the unclad child in the folds of his cloak, for there was a chill to the air.

But the boy, having no enthusiasm for the idea, began to shriek. "No! No!"

Lord! Where was that governess?

Gabriel drew the inconsolable child against his chest, speaking to him quietly but sternly in an even tone until his shrieks subsided. As they did, Gabriel patted his small back and soothed his anguished sobs. "There, there," he said, quite at a loss. "No need to fuss."

His actions worked to some extent, for the boy did suddenly stop wailing. "Papa... Papa..." he repeated softly, resting his head against Gabriel's shirt as he emitted trembling gasps of air from his little lungs.

"I certainly hope not," Gabriel muttered, brushing the tightly coiled gold curls off the boy's moist brow. "Ah, there's a good lad. Feeling better now?"

The boy responded with a tiny nod.

Quite pleased with himself and the efficiency with which he'd restored order, Gabriel turned back to the Farthingale house as the young woman burst through the gate, followed by a small army of children in varying states of disarray. She paused but a moment to order her squealing troops, "Back inside!" and to Gabriel's surprise, they promptly complied.

The young woman then turned toward him, her black hair half done up in a bun and the rest of it falling in a shambles about her slender shoulders. "Thank you! Thank you! You saved Harry's life! We're so grateful."

He frowned down at the seemingly appreciative girl. She was young and slight, barely reaching his shoulders. She took no notice of his displeasure, and instead smiled up at him, her eyes glistening as if holding back unshed tears.

Still smiling, she turned to the boy. "You gave me a terrible scare, you little muffin. I'm so glad you're unharmed."

Gabriel thought to chide her, but the girl chose that moment to smile at him again, and the words simply refused to flow from his mouth. Well, she did have an incredible smile. The sort that touched one's heart—if one had a heart—which he didn't, having lost it sometime during the war.

Her eyes were bluer than the sky.

His frown faded.

She shook her head and let out the softest sigh. "You're so wonderful with him. Do you have children of your own?"

"You ought to be more careful with your young charge," Gabriel said, clearing his throat and speaking to her with purposeful severity. The girl's attributes, no matter how heavenly, did not excuse her lapse in duty.

"Oh, Harry's not my charge... well, he is in a way. You see, he's my cousin. And the nannies have all quit our household, so I'm left all alone with the seven children until my family returns." She wiped a stray lock off her brow and then put her arms forward to show him her rolled-up sleeves. "I was trying to bathe the littlest ones."

He noticed that her finely made gown was wet in several spots. "It seems they bathed you."

"What? Oh, yes. They did give me a thorough soaking." She laughed gently while shaking her head in obvious exasperation. "Harry was the last, but now I'll have to bathe him all over again."

"Don't let me delay you." He attempted to hand the squirming bundle back to her, but before he could manage it, Harry decided to leave him a remembrance.

What was the expression? No good deed ever goes unpunished? Gabriel watched in horror as an arc of liquid shot from the naked imp onto his shirt front, planting a disgustingly warm, yellow stain on the once immaculate white lawn fabric.

He didn't know whether to laugh or rage. He'd been undone. Brought to his knees by an infant and an incompetent guardian.

"Oh, dear," the girl said, closing her eyes and groaning. "I'm so sorry. So very, very sorry."

So was he. He ought to have listened to Ian, but not because the Farthingale women were dangerous. It seemed all Farthingales were dangerous. Young. Old. Male. Female.

The family and their servants were to be avoided at all costs.

"We'll pay for the damage, of course," she continued in obvious distress, her eyes remaining firmly closed, as if not seeing the damage would somehow make it go away. "We'll replace whatever needs... er, replacing. Please have your tailor send the bill to Miss Daisy Farthingale. I'll make certain it is paid at once."

Gabriel's heart stopped beating. Yes, it definitely stopped. And then it began to beat very fast.

"You're Daisy?" he mumbled, his tongue suddenly as numb as the rest of his body. Not that he cared who she was, or what Ian had warned. He wasn't afraid of any female, certainly not this incompetent slip of a girl.

She opened her eyes and graced him with a gentle, doe-eyed gaze. "I am."

Very well, Ian was right. She was a force to be reckoned with, but so would any woman be with glistening blue eyes, pink cheeks, and cream-silk skin.

"Sir, may I be so bold as to ask who you are?"

"I'm late, that's what I am." He plunked Harry in her arms and hastened to his grandmother's house.

Rules for Reforming a Rake
is available in paperback and e-book

ACKNOWLEDGMENTS

To Neal, Brigitte (my fair Gigi), and Adam, the best husband and kids ever. I'm so lucky to have you as my family. To my intrepid first readers, Barbara Hassid, Lauren Cox, Megan Westfall, Rebecca Heller, and Maria Barlea. To my large and supportive extended family, who have shown me just why I love you all so much. Sincere appreciation to longtime friends and terrific authors in their own right: Pamela Burford, Patricia Ryan, Jeannie Moon, and Stevi Mittman. To my wonderful web designer, Willa Cline. Heartfelt gratitude to the best support team that any author can have: Laurel Busch, Samantha Williams, Jennifer Gracen, and Greg Simanson. They are my dream team and I look forward to working with them on many more projects.

THE FARTHINGALE SERIES

London is never the same after the boisterous Farthingales move into their townhouse on Chipping Way, one of the loveliest streets in fashionable Mayfair. With five beautiful daughters in residence, the street soon becomes known as a deathtrap for bachelors.

Interested in learning more about the Farthingale sisters? Join me on Facebook at facebook.com/AuthorMearaPlatt Additionally, we'll be giving away lots of Farthingale swag and prizes during the launches. If you would like to join the fun, you can subscribe to my newsletter at bit.ly/mearasnewsletter and also connect with me on Twitter at twitter.com/mearaplatt. You can find links to do all of this at my website: mearaplatt.com

If you enjoyed this book, I would really appreciate it if you could post a review on the site where you purchased it or other sites where you subscribe. You can write one for Goodreads. Even a few sentences on what you thought about the book would be most helpful! If you do leave a review, send me a message on Facebook because I would love to thank you personally.

Please also consider telling your friends about the FARTHINGALE SERIES and recommending it to your book clubs.

About the Author

Meara Platt is happily married to her Russell Crowe look-alike husband, and they have two terrific children. She lives in one of the many great towns on Long Island, New York, and loves it, except for the traffic. She has traveled the world, occasionally lectures, and always finds time to write. Her favorite place in all the world is England's Lake District, which may not come as a surprise since many of her stories are set in that idyllic landscape, including her Romance Writers of America Golden Heart award winning story to be released as Book 3 in her paranormal romance Garden series, which is set to debut in 2016. Learn more about Meara Platt by visiting her website at mearaplatt.com.